All enquiries to: g8ulm@hotmail.co.uk

Printed by www.lulu.com

First Printing: February 2011
Second printing May 2011
ISBN 978-1-4466-4864-3

Introduction

When I first set out to open the can of worms filled to bursting by the early (and not so early) London casinos, I wanted to do it in a film. I trawled my address book in search of a film producer. Not one. I knew that an elderly unknown wannabe clutching a dog-eared pile of A4 paper would not make much of an impression on the film men of Wardour Street and Golden Square. So I decided to do it in a book, the first I have written during the last seventy-one years. A book that sounds like a film when you read it out loud. Handy if you've got a friend who's blind. Big on action. Low on philosophy and all that intellectual stuff.

Not to be left lying around where young impressionable people might pick it up.

Follow me through the gambling rooms and bars and alleyways where I happily mis-spent my youth. Meet colourful characters, some best met on paper, on health and safety grounds, some well worth meeting in the flesh if only we could turn the clock back.

I hope you get as much pleasure from the pictures in your head as I got from the real thing. Don't try most of it at home.

Best enjoyed with a face-curling, mind-freeing bottle of cheap red wine. Or two. Drink responsibly.

Contents

Not so Fast.

.

Robbing casinos was fun. And easy. You just had to be in the right
place at the right time and avoid joints whose owners would break both
your legs or cave your head in with a brick if they caught you with your
hand in the till. The right place was London, the right time was roughly
1962, when it all began, to about 1981, by which time an unholy alliance
of better and better closed circuit television and the accumulated wisdom
of managers (many of them once as crooked as the rest of us) made the
old ways out of date and turned a whole generation of skilled thieves into
dinosaurs.

Some historians beg to differ. One does anyway. On December 17
2004, almost exactly forty years after I started work in a London casino,
the Guardian newspaper published a plaintive speech by Lady Penny
Cobham, the head of the British Casino Association. The speech was a
protest against the Blair government's decision to severely reduce the
number of Las Vegas style super-casinos that British casino companies,
often in partnership with foreign companies whose owners you would not
want to move in next door and marry your daughters (unless you were
really strapped for cash) were raring to open up all over the British Isles.
One sentence leapt from the page: 'For forty years British (casino)
companies had a level of integrity and probity which has not been
questioned and now the government has taken the rug from under our
feet.'

Not so fast, Lady Penelope. You forgot the British, French and
American career criminals who owned and operated many (most) London
casinos, quite openly, during the nineteen sixties. Before you launch into
another speech praising the integrity and probity of my co-workers and
me (and our long-dead employers) google Knightsbridge and Esmeralda's
Barn and Peppermint Lounge. Put your best frock on and slip into a
world where celebrities and wealthy gay men enjoyed a mingle with
London's most famous twins. Then have a word with the Met and the
Home Office about the French owned River Club, on the Embankment
only a short way from the Houses of Parliament, which closed down in
the mid-sixties (the casino, not the Parliament) when its owner was
expelled from our green and pleasant land and declared persona non grata

for about twenty five years. Last, and definitely not least, check out the Colony Club on the South side of Berkeley Square, set up by the American Mafia's impressively competent gambling honcho Dino Cellini. There, in the most brilliant public relations move in the history of London casinos George Raft, veteran star of many a gangster film, wandered round in a cloud of whisky fumes and made the gamblers feel like they were starring in one of his old films. Plus endless smaller joints, some described later in the book, all owned by or protected by criminals who never did and never will make it into the headlines. Their chapter is as good as it will ever get for them, publicity wise. You also left out the supposedly respectable businessmen, bookmakers mostly apart from the American Playboy company (more into girls) who took over where the proper criminals left off after the 1968 Gaming Act introduced licences and rules and all that law-abiding stuff. They nearly all lost their casino licences in 1980 and 1981 when the courts established that an awful lot of law-breaking had still been going on at the top, quite separately from the largely undetected efforts of the skilled professionals further down the food chain. Leaving out one of the above groups could be looked on as carelessness, milady, but leaving out both looks to me suspiciously like an intention to deceive. Do your homework properly next time. You never know who might be listening. But thanks for the compliment, even if the intentions were commercial rather than courteous and the contents wholly fictitious. Every time I look into a mirror I half expect to see a halo shimmering above my head.

There were objections to the fervently hoped for super-casinos. A few Labour MPs spluttered from the back benches, still convinced that they were in some way connected to the government. No-one took a blind bit of notice. Holy men brought God into the fight. He didn't get very far either. Then the Daily Mail ran a spirited campaign against super-casinos, low on facts but high on moral indignation, which went down a storm with their middle-class readers and was probably the deciding factor in the drastic reduction of numbers that Lady P was going on about. Somebody had to shout. British voters didn't get a look-in as leading figures in the Blair government, lobbied to the tune of roughly a hundred million pounds, laboured hard to get their super-casino plan off the ground. No loose talk about a referendum. You may remember the most unfortunate political photo-opportunity in Labour party history: Tessa Jowell dressed up as a (female) croupier and smirking at us from behind a roulette table. You may also remember John Prescott, second only to Prince Charles in the list of British marksmen who aim exclusively at their own feet and never miss, explaining that he only came home with a present of some nifty cowboy boots, after a visit to the ranch of the wealthy American casino operator who wanted to turn the Millennium Dome into a super-casino, because riding the range with his new friend (on a particularly sturdy horse I hope) reminded him of playing cowboys when he was a little lad. Casino? What casino? No wonder they made him a Lord.

The official view was that there was no chance of us sensible Brits getting addicted in droves, like those backward colonials in Australia when their government did unto them what the Blair government was as keen as mustard to do unto us. Then Gordon Brown, whose dour features I rather miss, shut the plan down, just like that, shortly after he became our unelected prime minister.

You may feel that I have gone on a bit about the open-to-all super-casinos that hoped to pick the pockets of the man and woman in the street, but it's because I have a good side. I earned my living by latching on to the gambling addiction of my fellow men and women, but only in top casinos where arms dealers and arms manufacturers, foreign royals whose countries are better described as family firms (some of whose dreams Julian Assange has recently shared with us), property dealers, inheritors of great wealth, con-men and other criminals, drug dealers and other mass-murderers, casino owners and bookies threw their money away. I had, and have, no qualms about that. But I once, a long time ago, sat in a poor persons' casino and watched a working man slowly empty an old-fashioned brown paper cash pay-packet on to a low-stake roulette table. I've never forgotten the look on his face when he walked away skint, no doubt thinking deeply about what his addiction was doing to his family. I knew he had a family because we had a brief chat before he lost all the money he'd earned in a week and I lost all the rather larger amount of money I had acquired the night before, thanks to a bit of skilled sleight of hand. Casino gambling is for the rich and the crooked. Leave ordinary people alone.

End of sermon. But watch this space if I've made a convert. Get ready to oppose a new wave. Paint your banner and march on Downing Street if it all comes rolling back again. A stiff licence fee and a stiff tax on profits might well appeal to a government hell-bent on paying off the national debt in three weeks, and a second chance of a dip in the honey pot would be welcomed with open arms by the spenders of all that lobbying money. You saw it here first.

The world of nineteen sixties casinos (and well beyond in some cases) was a world of shadows. I want to shine a light into some very dark corners in what little time I have left. Bollocks to the libel lawyers. British libel lawyers have far too much power. Wealthy people are much too easily protected. All you need is cash. No legal aid in libel cases. One law for the rich and one for the poor, here and now in the 21st Century.

The problem is that in crooked casinos very little information was put on paper. Make that none, in the pre-Gaming Act joints owned by proper criminals. A nervous literary agent, interested in my book but understandably anxious not to upset the wielders of power and their guarantors of silence, asked me if I could produce any evidence, like receipts. My answer had to be no. We didn't do receipts. He backed off. I can't blame him. He has a living to earn at an economically difficult time for the publishing business. It's not his fault that the system is rotten. And not only are the receipts missing, nearly all the witnesses are dead. Or scared to talk and blemish their reputations as respectable pensioners. So think of my book as oral history written down. No footnotes. No references to "Protection Rackets in West London, 1960 to 1966" by Reginald Kray, paragraph 2, page 118. There is no bibliography. I made that title up.

It's a lot to ask, I know, but you have to trust me. I could have made up the heavyweight blackjack fight between Frank Sinatra and John Aspinall. I'm the only survivor of that game and I'm sure there are no clues anywhere, even in the Swiss bank that handled the money. No good sniffing around Zurich. But I didn't make it up. It happened, with my help. I could have invented Lily the Pimp, the Fat Man, the French Connection, the Cockney Frog, Bernie the Waistcoat, sweaty casino managers sneakily filming after-hours live sex on a dice table, the lovely Dutch girl who reduced a crowded bar to silence just by walking through the door, or the Molotov cocktail incident. But I didn't. I'm not big on imagination. All I offer is the truth, the whole truth, and nothing but the truth, as told by someone who was actually there and wants to share the story with you before he slips off to the Great Casino in the Sky.

Follow me through the shadows of a world that has long passed into history, but should not die unrecorded, or, in a curious way, unlamented. You won't need a gun. It's only a book. You can come too Lady Penelope, if you want to complete your education. But no speeches please.

A small claim for my own personal probity and integrity. Because I am incurably liberal you will find no discrimination in the pages that follow. The bad guys (and girls) are Christians, Muslims, Jews, Hindus, Bhuddists and atheists. Their skins are white, black, brown, yellow and red. They come from Europe, North and South America, the Far, Middle and Near East, Africa and Australasia. So would the good guys and girls too, if there were any.

4

The Curzon House Club.

The Curzon House Club was one of London's top casinos, right from day one. The name came from the grand house the business was located in. Turn into Curzon Street from the southbound side of Park Lane and you'll see the Curzon House on your right, standing proud between a small cul de sac and a short alley leading down to the narrow one-way street that circles round the Hilton hotel. The front entrance is very impressive, as you would expect of a house where earlier Lords Curzon entertained the rich and the powerful and plotted the course of the once mighty and rapacious British Empire, and where Oswald Mosely, England's answer to Adolf H once wooed one of the daughters of the house before settling down with one of another lord's little girls, a kindred spirit who shared his admiration of the late, unlamented Adolf.

When I started work there in 1964 the Curzon House Club was a den of thieves. It took me three days to work that out. I was very naïve then. The best pickings were at the top but those at the bottom got more than crumbs, as my more enterprising colleagues and I soon found out. The owners of the Curzon were two brothers, Bob and Alf Barnett, former night club owners in the prosperous West End, a couple of miles from the run-down East End where their family started life in a new country, like so many who came to England to escape the murderously violent Polish and Russian anti-semitism which, once it evolved into Nazism's final solution was quite enough, even without Richard Dawkins' persuasive rhetoric, to put anyone with any sense right off religion for life, in this world or the next.

The night-club may not have been the first business the ambitious newcomer set up. I once overheard Abe the American, of whom more later, say to an American gangster and gambler, a man who got off on breaking pretty girls' arms before having sex with them at a much higher fee than when no breakages were involved, that Bob once ran a cat-house (American for brothel) on the East Side (an obvious Americanism for the East End) and even spent a short time in stir (American for prison). Which may or may not have been true. Abe was a very good public relations man and knew that his fellow American was very partial to thoroughbred cats, so long as they didn't mind the odd bit of high-value GBH, and may well have invented an appropriate conversational gambit while he was giving him the oil. Anyway commercial sex was of absolutely no interest to me, with or without the sound of breaking bones. I was far too young to pay for what had suddenly become free, as the sixties turned into the late Mary Whitehouse's worst nightmare.

In those days a posh night-club was a well-disguised whorehouse with an elegant restaurant and a good chef, high prices that kept the riff-raff out and the profits in, and smartly dressed musicians who could bang out a mild form of jazz. Black man's music from New Orleans, long before it drowned. The white audience didn't want to be treated like blacks of course (the Empire was still alive and well, and well segregated) but they did like the throb of jungle music, however faint. It was all clever window-dressing, skilfully laid out to get the punters through the door. Let's drink champagne and dance with a tart to black man's music in a Jew's night club, came the cry. Let's live dangerously. No need to be nervous Bertie. We'll still be white and Christian when we get home.

Tart is the key word. The most important people in a successful night club were the hostesses. Their pretend job was to drink watered down champagne (or plain water when times were tight) and dance with the single men, or with the married men who had left their wives at home and come over feeling all single again. Their real job was to have sex with the men, off the premises. A very important part of their job description, those last three words. If the couples had been hard at it upstairs when the cops burst in the club would have qualified as a brothel, the joint would have stopped jumping (however sedately), the money would have dried up, and the people thoughtful enough to provide all the fun would have ended up in stir.

The wives and other female companions of men not looking for a hostess knew nothing about the ladies of the night. They enjoyed their Madame Bovary moments in a heady atmosphere of exciting music and fashionable clothes and good food and real champagne. Jolly good fun, eh girls? Events behind the scenes were of no interest to the respectable ladies. Actually I'm being too kind. Too patronising. Too old school. Way out of line with the modern, honest world which recognises that even women get randy sometimes and don't always reach out for their legally wedded husbands when the itch becomes too fierce to wipe away with a quick scratch. It wasn't only the men who got an expensive bit on the side. I'm lying. A small but enthusiastic minority of the upper-class ladies voted with their vaginas and got a leg over some of the more exciting and exotic musicians. The Beatles and the Rolling Stones didn't invent groupies, however enthusiastically they may or may not have upheld the old traditions. The most popular stud to strut his stuff, back in the good old days, was the musically gifted Hutch, aka Leslie Hutchinson, a very handsome black man with a prick like a tree trunk, according to the late Lord Mountbatten, an authority on the subject courtesy of the fact that

6

his wife Edwina shagged Hutch silly for the best part of thirty years. (What an unlucky man Lord Louis was. He had a fine war story but his wife was forever at it with somebody else, usually rather darker of skin than he was, and when he was an old man the IRA killed him with a hidden bomb, along with a very young relative, in one of their shittiest little murders. Winning the war must have seemed like the easy bit).

Bob quickly rose to the top of his new business. By the time the 1950s came round his night club near Leicester Square was so fashionable that Princess Margaret was a regular. I think it was called the Embassy, but this is a book about casinos, not night clubs, and once I stray off my chosen subject I get a bit hazy about the boring details. It could have been the 400. Or some other joint. If the night club had been a casino my description could be lifted verbatim and uploaded into Wikipaedia, but night clubs rather passed me by. A nice jazz club was more my bag, from the age of fifteen. Older readers with the odd memory cell still fizzing will know the name, and may even remember seeing the fun-loving princess slip into a private room with an elegant bunch of hooray Henries and their beautifully dressed Henriettas. Younger readers may only know her as an old lady in dark glasses who smoked too much and went round in a wheelchair on the TV news, but Princess Margaret once occupied the spot (revived and massively expanded thirty years later by Princess Diana) as the only Royal since Henry the Eighth to do anything interesting. She was even rumoured to have made carnal contact with the energetic Hutch. Not to mention the odd gangster.

Nothing good lasts for ever. The sixties came storming in. Rock and roll replaced crooners and diluted jazz. Hutch found himself singing to eight deaf pensioners at the end of a pier, for the price of a pint and a stale cheese roll on a good day, and had to sell his Hampstead house and his Rolls-Royce. Discotheques elbowed aside the night clubs where you dressed up old-fashioned and drank champagne with a tart. Suddenly it was all blue jeans and mini-skirts and high-heeled boots and cockney accents. The new pop stars had their own tables at the new spots and the new wannabe night-lifers danced next to pop stars, not princesses in dresses designed by a Parisian ponce. Sex was free until you got married. The old order was rapidly changing. Noel Coward crept out through the back door. Mick Jagger came swaggering in through the front.

Hutch didn't have a second act. Bob did. One door closed and another door opened. In 1962, just in time to rescue Bob Barnett from a ship that was sinking fast, British casinos got off to a legally shaky but very profitable start. Bob's Curzon House casino was soon the front runner, rivalled only by Crockfords when it was a stone's throw from the

Mall, and John Aspinall's Clermont, outsinging the nightingales in Berkeley Square.

When I met Bob Barnett in 1964 he looked like the gang-boss in one of those old American black and white films. Short and heavily built, with hooded eyes and an unmistakable air of menace. James Cagney all over again. But it wasn't acting. He was pushing seventy the night he threw a much younger man down the casino stairs, in an argument over money. When Mr. Bob, as he liked to be called, interviewed me in his office I left my joke book in my pocket and kept quiet about being brought up in Germany. I rather took to him, for reasons I find hard to explain. I don't know what he thought of me, but it can't have been all bad because he did give me a job. Not that I was all that bothered about jobs then. In my mind I was still going to university as a mature student of European literature, any day now. A job in a casino was just something that would pass the time and raise a bit of cash to spend in the varsity bar. Then I would turn into a student again and graduate and become a lecturer in modern languages and spend the rest of my life droning on about Lope de Vega.

Bob's brother Alf looked like a cartoon spiv: a shiny bald head above a shiny mohair suit and little bits of hair over his ears neatly combed and shining with oil. I never really took to Alf, nor him to me as far as I know.

Bob and his brother set up and ran some of the most successful casinos in London. Then they made the mistake of floating their urban goldmine on the Stock Exchange and were forced out of Lord Curzon's old house and several other prestigious London premises in the early seventies when the Coral book-making family firm launched a successful dawn raid on Curzon House shares. The Barnetts got a packet for their slice of the action, but lost control, and that hurt. They were active entrepreneurs, not passive investors.

Meet the Neighbours

When I first worked as a croupier I lived in a dark brown bed-sitting room opposite a side entrance of Harrods. The food hall was my corner shop. I often nipped in wearing slippers and dressing gown (if it wasn't raining) in gross defiance of the dress code introduced later by Mohamed al Fayed, to buy milk, breakfast cereal and red wine, my staple diet in what could loosely be called my home. As soon as I found out how much money I was going to earn at the Curzon House the brown bed-sit seemed unworthy of a man of my status. I moved to a two bedroom flat in Mayfair, in Half Moon Street, a short street that runs between Curzon Street and Piccadilly. The rent was surprisingly low and the flat was about three minutes walk from work. I liked that. I've always hated commuting.

I quickly found out why the rent was low. A harsh-toned pay phone on the living room wall rang throughout the day. The same voice grated down the line, again and again, speaking aggressively in a rough accent and warning me that great harm was coming my way. I began to feel like the car driver in Spielberg's Duel who never sees the driver of the lorry that keeps trying to kill him. I shouldn't have written the book, the voice repeated over and over again. I don't write books, I write cheques, I told the voice, trying to sound like someone who had always lived in Mayfair and wasn't in the habit of talking to lower-class people on the telephone.

He really pissed me off when he called very early one morning. Croupiers don't do early mornings. I was clapped out after a hard day's night and a hard night's drink after work. I asked him what fucking book he was fucking talking about. He laughed his sinister laugh and told me to stop pretending to be somebody else. He was talking about the book I'd written about the murder. And he didn't just know my phone number. He knew where I lived.

The bad language must have had some effect on the invisible man whose voice I was learning to hate. The next time the phone went the rasping voice told me who I was supposed to be (and who he still believed I was. He wasn't letting me off that easily). The flat belonged to a writer who had written about a brutal killing in a lover's lane. The man found guilty was hanged, but in many peoples' opinion the wrong man got it in the neck, and the perceived injustice was a big factor in the soon to come

9

abolition of the death penalty. The caller who kept me awake was the man the writer had named, very bravely (and possibly correctly) as the real murderer. Unfortunately the writer's bravery didn't extend to staying in his own flat and listening to death threats blasting down the phone. He left that to me. For a modest rent.

To give credit where it may be due, the aggressive caller may have had a point. Nearly forty years later the highly principled lawyer (they do exist) Michael Mansfield, who has righted more wrongs than Robin Hood, was hired by the hanged man's family and asked to clear the dead man's name. You can't win 'em all. The body was exhumed and DNA tests made. DNA from the corpse matched the hanged man's DNA found on a handkerchief that had been wrapped around the murder weapon. Or something forensic like that. Oops. But someone did say that after so many years the evidence may have been contaminated, or may have been set up at the time of the killing. Guilty or not guilty? Take your pick. I'm staying on the fence. I like it there.

Between my temporary home and the casino there were a couple of turnings into Shepherd Market, a charming warren of little lanes shared by prostitutes with lit up door bells that tell the customers who's who, a nice old-fashioned pub and, in those days, a tourist orientated restaurant called Tiddy Dol's, named after a local character from long ago. Probably a tart. The houses were small and quaint and very different from the grand mansions of Curzon Street and Charles Street and nearby Berkeley Square. In the old days there really was a market there, selling all sorts of things to the good people of Mayfair (including dead sheep). When I lived next door the sheep had long gone, but alcohol, over-priced meals (except in the Italian caff where I had breakfast every lunch-time), short term sexual relationships and gambling were on offer to all those with the cash to spare.

The Italian caff was a gem. I much preferred to munch my bacon and eggs there, in peace, rather than at home where the death threats rasping down the phone were guaranteed to ruin anyone's digestion. The peace was only threatened once, when I foolishly shook a tomato ketchup bottle without checking if the top was on properly and shot a flood of red sauce all over a tart sitting at the next table, heartily stuffing enough pasta into her face to provide the strength needed to deal with a new bunch of ghastly punters lurking on the pavements of nearby Curzon Street. She came at me like a snake poked in the eye with a sharp stick and demanded immediate cash money to pay for the cleaning of the dress, hissing out a sum that sounded more like the purchase price of a dress than the price of cleaning one. Not that I was in the habit of buying dresses, you understand. I was never that way inclined, sartorially or otherwise, but I

10

had often seen the prices of dresses in shop windows while dragging along behind former girl-friends and desperately hoping not to have to make a payment in kind.

Two colleagues, lunching with the lady now covered in tomato sauce, took her side, vehemently, but another, possibly the tart with a heart you'll meet later in this chapter, looked at me with a kindly eye, as if trying to tell me that she knew I wasn't the sort of person who throws sauce over strange women purely to liven up a dull day, but she was sure that I would fully understand if she kept this knowledge and the accompanying sympathy to herself, in the heat of the current moment. More worrying than the support team (or the victim) was the presence of a hard-eyed man a couple of tables away who had begun to take a keen interest. I guessed that he was in the same business as the ladies, but at managerial level, and almost certainly had a sharp knife or open razor somewhere about his person and the ability to cover the distance between our tables in a terrifyingly short time. That coiled spring look. I liked to think, probably wrongly, that if I'd been the right age to join in the fight against Fascism I would have sauntered forth with the same courage as all the other young men who fought and died between 1939 and 1945, but in the Italian caff craven cowardice won the day. I handed over half of my previous night's swag to the lady in red and stuttered out what was meant to sound like a sincere apology. Counting started, and went on far too long in my heavily biased opinion, hissing stopped, and I got back to my bacon and eggs with my face still intact.

An English croupier I knew at the time, a respectable young man from a middle class background who only stayed a short while in casinos before going back to something more middle class when his future wife kicked up about night work, not knowing at the time that she would find an infinite number of other things to kick up about over the next twenty odd years, always finding a quick replacement for issues that died a natural death, told me of the time he fell into temptation and pressed one of the lit-up door-bells that twinkled along the lanes of Shepherd Market. He said that it wasn't because he couldn't get it for free, or for the price of a dinner, or because he was lonely. It was pure curiosity. He was living the low life now, he said, rather insensitively I thought, but let it go with nothing more than a lightly raised eyebrow, not being one to start a fight with a friend just because his normally high standard of courtesy took a temporary dive. It seemed like a natural thing to do, he continued, in a matter-of-fact tone of voice that made no concessions to my slightly miffed expression. You know, finding out what it's like to go with a tart. Something he would never have dreamt of doing when he was properly middle-class. But (unspoken) no doubt something that casino people like me got up to all the time.

It didn't go well. He got to the top of the stairs, checking that the condoms were still in his pocket and trying to keep his mind off diseases that weren't always easily cured by penicillin, expected to meet a hot young whore from France (like the ones you see in the livelier French films) and was greeted by a woman old enough to be his mother. Much worse, she actually resembled the good woman who brought him into this world. The erection that had led him up the stairs evaporated into thin air. He feigned an attack of nerves, paid the asking price without a haggle and disappeared into the night, hoping that the middle-aged French woman wasn't too hurt, emotionally, by his sudden change of plan.

The vision of his mother, through a glass darkly, wouldn't go away. In an attempt to burn off his guilt he made a date with two pretty young prostitutes who, in a break from tradition, plied their trade in Curzon Street from the inside of an open sports car. You may remember the car if you were around at the time and in the habit of walking down Curzon Street at night, for whatever reason. It was a dark blue Sunbeam Alpine. You may even remember the girls, but we won't go into that here. At a flat near Knightsbridge, after a brief chat about the weather, a subject of great interest to two people who spent an important part of their working life in an open-topped car, he had the sort of experience (in duplicate and unaffected by erectile disfunction) that he had hoped for the first time round.

It worked a treat. The vision of his mother, through a glass darkly, grew darker by the minute as he hopped around a large bed with the two lively girls, themselves only too pleased to have a handsome, virile young stud to deal with rather than the usual sweaty middle-aged drunk with whisky breath and a much more limited range of hops, and had disappeared completely by the time his time, costing little more than the average working man's weekly wage, was up. My passing friend even claimed, perhaps with justification (he was very scientific) that one of the girls made all the right noises in the heat of one particularly complicated moment. He was convinced that it wasn't the well rehearsed orgasmic symphony she no doubt laid on for the usual middle-aged sweaties, at no extra charge, to create an illusion of greater value for money and drum up repeat business in the same hot breath, always remembering to vary the repertoire a bit when a satisfied customer did come back for more. Close attention to those finer details can make all the difference between moderate prosperity and the accumulation of real wedge at the upper end of the world's oldest profession, a level the girls hadn't yet reached but were hoping to get to before long. Men, especially middle-aged men at the start of their long decline, can be very sensitive at heart and are easily bruised, emotionally speaking (and liable to spend their money elsewhere) when they hear the same sequence of gasps and shouts twice in a row. Billie Piper could probably get us up to speed on the technical details. She must have looked into that sort of thing, purely on a need to know basis, when she made all those programmes that men watch when their wives aren't there (no, not Doctor Who).

When my long-lost friend slipped out of my world and into the well-ordered world of suburban homes and respectable jobs in the City (before the thieving there easily surpassed anything he might have encountered in casinos if he'd hung on a bit longer) I bet he sometimes missed the low life he once dissed so insensitively, right out loud, in my presence. Lap-dancers take more and give less, as a rule, than the girls whose car he once flagged down like a taxi and who were soon all over him like a rash. Serves you right, City boy.

I came to realise that Half Moon Street was as plain and dull as a short street of houses deserves to be. No caffs, no pub, no twinkling door bells, just house after house after house after house, right until you got into Piccadilly. My Mayfair snobbery wore off and I began to think of myself as a Shepherd Market man. A livelier sort of chap. The market had a centre, and a buzz that was lacking in Half Moon Street. In short, the market was more colourful. And the neighbours were more interesting.

The racing driver Stirling Moss had a small house at the Western end of the market, not far from the back wall of the Hilton hotel, the ugly skyscraper that looks like a giant mouth-organ standing on end. Once, pissed and listening to a Bob Dylan album at a volume loud enough to blot out the sound of the phone, I imagined a giant blow-up Bob Dylan doll floating horizontally across Park Lane, attaching its lips to the inverted mouth-organ, and blowing hard into the tenth floor. On another night, a night off, while slowly getting drunk in the posh Market pub that had a public telephone inside a genuine sedan chair, greatly admired by passing tourists, I thought of knocking on Stirling Moss's door (only round the corner) and, if invited in, telling him all about the Jaguar XK120 with special light-weight aluminium body that I bought for two hundred honestly acquired pounds a year before I started work in casinos and drove up the recently opened M1 motorway at 140 miles per hour, seriously reducing my chances of celebrating my forthcoming twenty third birthday. As the green and pleasant county of Hertfordshire flashed by in a blur I suddenly remembered that although the engine was in fine condition, the tires were bald, the steering was clapped out, and in an emergency the brakes would only bring about a gentle reduction in velocity. My nervous system blew a fuse. I drove home at the sort of speed I drive at today, whenever a kind young relative lends me a car.

I thought, courtesy of the beer, that the famous racer would be fascinated by my story because, according to the man who sold me the fast but lethal Jaguar, it was one of only six ever made, and that one of the other five had been driven by Stirling Moss himself in one of those endless road races, the Le Mans 24 Hours or the Mille Miglia, if that's how you spell it. It's not every day that a fellow hot Jag driver knocks on your door. But in the end I decided to stay in the pub and have another pint, rather than look for a new friend and a chat about cars gone by. It was probably the right decision. After my nerve went I sold the car for about what I paid, shocked by the quote for the repairs that were essential if I wanted to stay alive. If the car's pedigree was real, rather than sales hype (the vendor was an arms dealer; you know what they're like) it probably stands in an air-conditioned garage somewhere and goes out twice a year to win a vintage car competition, if it's not raining. Yours for half a million cash.

Bob Guccione's Penthouse Club, the poor man's Playboy Club, was making a small fortune at the Eastern end of the market. Instead of bunny girls they had Penthouse Pets, pretty girls who were supposed to be naughty but nice, one of them told me with a dirty grin some time after she reached middle age and had to make do with being nice because no-one wanted her to be naughty any more.

Early one morning, in the grey light of dawn, just before she lay down to sleep, one of my newly adopted neighbours, a tart with a heart, looked out of the window of her Shepherd Market flat and saw a man firmly tied to a nearby chimney, with a tape fixed across his mouth. No smoke was coming from the top of the chimney, but she knew that it belonged to commercial premises, probably a restaurant, and that it was due to start up soon and would smoke heavily all day. She also knew that the man tied to the chimney would die of suffocation soon after he began to breathe hot smoke instead of cool air. She was too kind-hearted to sleep soundly while he passed from this world to the next. She phoned the police, insisting on strict anonymity. A sensible precaution. Nice people don't tie men to chimneys with the express intention of choking them to death. If she was identified as a grass she might be the next person breathing smoke. She was none too keen to die herself, but she just couldn't let the unknown man die while she slept, and that compassion led her to take a chance that could have saved the unknown man's life but cost her her own. Being a tart doesn't necessarily make you a bad person.

The condemned man was duly rescued and almost certainly never met the girl who saved his life, out of pure human kindness. He probably never even knew her name. I might be able to tell you his. A reliable source claimed that the lucky man was David Litvinoff, a very close friend of super star gangster Ronnie Kray, and, among many other things, the man who introduced the director and cast of a film called Performance to the London gangsters he knew so well and caused the actor James Fox to create the best impersonation of a sadistic young murderer I have ever seen in a British film.

Litvinoff was one of the more personable gangster figures, a star-fucker who loved to mix with the many film actors and film makers and rock and rollers who lived in Chelsea in those days. Some of the celebrities returned the compliment, often in a pub in King's Road where many of the younger and less powerful gangsters used to hang out, looking ill at ease among the flower power folks. And vice versa.

Mick Jagger was very good in the film. He played a reclusive rock star, believed to be based on the late Brian Jones, the best looking of the original Rolling Stones and, according to some reliable sources, the best shag. You can buy the film on dvd. It's just been released for the first time. Catch it if you can. It's a very authentic work of art, but don't expect it to boost your faith in the essential goodness of human nature. It's very rude for its time. Maximum legal use is made of the physical beauty of a young Anita Pallenberg, who in real life went out with the real Brian Jones before settling down with Keith Richards, and of the natural charms of a French girl with modest chest measurements who never made another film, gravely disappointing the small but possibly growing number of men who have a thing about pretty French girls with little tits. When developing started, and the rudeness of the action was there for all to see, some of the film stock had to be destroyed (for legal reasons, not to avoid spontaneous combustion) but what's left is still very lively, even now. Be careful who you watch it with. That Mick Jagger was hot stuff circa 1970. Don't take your wife. She might get ideas above her station. My future wife once ran after a taxi Mick was in, in 1972, when all three of us lived in Chelsea. She never caught up, possibly to their mutual disadvantage.

Although the man (long deceased) who told me who was who was the most reliable informant I ever had where matters low-life were concerned, at first I found it hard to believe that the man on the chimney really was David Litvinoff. In those days nobody with any sense did things like that to a close friend of Ronnie Kray. Except Ronnie himself, of course. That might be the clue. No-one will ever convince me that Litvinoff (if it was he) climbed a chimney, taped up his own mouth and tied a rope around his own body with the sole intention of choking to death when the sun came up over Shepherd Market. But he was a very addicted gambler, often owed large sums of money to casinos, and Old Ron owned a casino or two before the 1968 Gaming Act tried to make the business respectable. RK may have been owed enough money by his old friend to make tying him to a chimney outside a tart's bedroom window seem like a good idea at the time. It might just have been a slap on the wrist. The victim might have been released with nothing worse than a sore throat. But he might not. The Krays weren't sentimental when debt came between them and their friends.

By chance, when the death threats and the lack of sleep finally drove me out of my noisy Mayfair flat, something interesting happened and I moved out to the country, a part of the scenery I'm still not very keen on, to live with an actress who once lived with a poet.

The Extras.

When I started at the Curzon there were four Englishmen already working there and, like me, being groomed for jobs on the French roulette. All had previously made a precarious living as film extras. Being a film extra was well paid when the work came along, but it was very on and off and not much use to a chap who wanted to get married and take out a mortgage and support children. So they took regular well-paid night work in the casino, leaving them free to moonlight on a film set during the day. They all had interesting stories to tell, from a shadowy world I was not yet familiar with.

The first was once rather more than a film extra. He'd been a successful child actor in a TV adaptation of Richmal Crompton's Just William stories. Later he worked with Noel Coward, from whom he picked up the habit of finishing or beginning every sentence with the phrase "dear boy." In every other way he was excellent company. Sadly, like so many child stars, he failed to jump the gap between childish dramas and adult acting. No more speaking roles came his way. He accepted work as a film extra and hoped that one day the good times would come rolling back. But they didn't. Perhaps because of his decline as an actor he became less fussy about the company he kept.

He told me of the day he welcomed the well-known con-man Dandy Kim back to England (well-known if you were around in the fifties and sixties). Dandy Kim, who got his name by dressing more stylishly than almost any other man in post-war England, was called Michael Caborn-Waterfield by his mother, but Dandy Michael sounds pretty silly, so he became Dandy Kim. (Kim is almost Mike spelt backwards, if you're not very good at spelling. Perhaps that was the origin). He got up to all sorts of minor moves at the beginning of his career, and then became more ambitious. The old fatal attraction. He made a plan to rob the French Riviera villa of Jack Warner, the fabulously wealthy head of Warner Brothers, the famous film company. Kim's main target was Jack's wife's very expensive jewellery. One night Jack was due to go to the casino in nearby Monte Carlo, to play in a very high stake card game. The villa was to be left empty, except for a French maid. Kim seduced the maid. She fell madly in love with him, as girls tended to. He was very handsome as well as very elegant. You know what girls are like. She agreed to let him into the house on the night of the big card game. The maid was to be left tied up and defenceless while Kim helped himself to the priceless jewels. Then, after the swag had been turned into hard cash and the police had lost interest in interrogating a stupid maid, the handsome prince would whisk his beautiful princess off to South America, where they would live happily ever after. For him it was the card so high and wild he would never have to deal another, in the immortal words of Leonard Cohen. For the maid it was the end of saying sir and madam to people she didn't like and never having any money to spend in the posh shops that catered to the Riviera set she cleaned up after.

It all went horribly wrong. Kim seduced another local girl, just to pass the time. News of Kim's second romance got back to the maid, who had rashly come to believe that she was the one and only love of his life. She took it badly, but didn't let Kim know that she knew. She contacted the police and told them all about the foreign criminal who had tried to talk her into betraying her employer.

The police congratulated the maid on her exemplary behaviour. They hid in the villa on the big night and caught Dandy Kim in a classic sting, with an awful lot of jewellery in his hands. He was found guilty and sent to jail. The maid was given a generous reward for her honesty. Probably rather more than she would have got from Kim if Plan A had gone ahead. Kim would not have left her in France to be arrested, and perhaps implicate him in the robbery, but he would surely have left her somewhere (with enough money to keep her quiet, but no more) rather than lumber himself with an uneducated servant girl who would spend her mornings stuffing his stolen money into her handbag in preparation for the day's shopping spree and her nights pestering him for sex. I felt his pain. There's only so much a chap can take.

The card game at Monte Carlo was fixed. Not by the casino owners, but by skilled staff working with skilled players. Their aim was to relieve Jack of as much money as possible, Jack being far and away the wealthiest gambler at the table. Unlike Kim's their plan was a great success.

As soon as he got out of prison Kim travelled by train across France and arrived, penniless, at Victoria Station. The only person in the world to welcome him back to England was my new friend. Both of them were broke. The actor's days as a child star were sadly over, film extra work was thin on the ground, and Dandy Kim was an ex-con with a cardboard suitcase. But never write off the truly ambitious. Kim suggested they spend the night at one of the seedy hotels clustered round the station, regally brushing aside all pleas of poverty. Not keen, but unwilling to upset an old pal, my new friend finally agreed to the plan and resigned himself to slipping out through a window in the pale hours of the early morning (if their room was not too high up) and running like hell.

Dawn broke. Kim calmly prised open the coin machine used to pay for the gas fire. The coins easily covered the bill, and left a bit to spare for a mid-morning drink somewhere far away. My friend was horrified. Surely no hotel owner could be stupid enough not to work out where the money had come from. Even in Victoria. But he had over-estimated the hotel owner's intelligence and under-estimated Kim's radiant charm, which had lost none of its lethal power in the French prison. In the morning, after a hearty breakfast, Kim gave the hotel owner a cock and bull story about the coins and soon had him eating out of his hand, visibly honoured that such a fine gentleman had spent the night in his modest establishment.

The two friends said goodbye to the friendly hotel man. They sauntered out, all smiles and waves, and walked slowly to the corner of the street. Once round the corner they ran full speed into a more prosperous future. My friend did well in London's new casinos. Kim charmed some wealthy backers, stepped out for a time with the fantastically gorgeous Samantha Eggar, owner of seven names no less, and became a legitimate and very rich businessman. And rather a bore compared to his old disreputable self. But never saw the inside of a prison again.

The second of the extras was the funniest man I have ever known. Funny ha-ha, not funny peculiar. He didn't stand in a pub telling jokes and drive all the other customers out. His was a natural wit that drew humour from the world around him. Effortlessly. I still haven't caught up forty odd years later. Like most film extras at the time, or at least the ones I met in casinos, he was on nodding terms with the criminal low-lifes who seemed in those days to mix easily with the bottom end of the film business. One night he left the Curzon at about four in the morning and drove his new sports car to an illegal drinking dive in Soho, run by one such low-life. It was a warm summer night. He kept the hood down, the better to show off his handsome features. As you do when you're young and driving a sports car. Even at night. I used to do it all the time.

He parked close to the entrance of the illegal dive. There weren't many other cars about. Sixties Soho was not the 24/7 paradise it is today.

Seconds after the engine stopped a muffled burst of automatic gunfire disturbed the air.

A dead man tumbled down a steep flight of stairs and flopped on to the pavement a few yards in front of my new friend's car. He recognised the leaking heap as the remains of a small time crook he had known slightly when he was still alive. Quick steps could be heard as the man who had killed him hurried down the stairs. Panic froze my friend into a nightmare paralysis. He could have been seconds away from dying. In the early sixties murder, especially murder by machine-gun, qualified you for the death penalty, a rapid descent through a trap-door inside a skilfully knotted rope that broke your neck when you jerked to a sudden halt. If you killed one person and an unwelcome witness turned up it was best to kill him too. Your chances of getting away with the first murder were probably better with a witness out of the way, and if everything still went wrong they couldn't hang you twice.

In a second or two the killer would be on the pavement. Frantic dreams of survival raced through my friend's mind. The bad man might run the other way when he left the scene of the crime. Good. Or he might have checked the street for parked cars. You can't be too careful when you kill people in a country where the death penalty waits for the incompetent. Bad. He might even have heard the car arrive, in the quiet small hours, as he stood at the top of the stairs waiting for the man whose life he was about to end. Any moment now the barrel of the small machine-gun could poke into the car and go tap tap tap as the bullets flew from the gun's metal snout and left my new friend as dead as the man on the pavement. He felt sick.

Only tiny fractions of a second left. Too late to put the hood up. Too late to drive away. The terrified croupier slid under the steering wheel and tried to curl into a ball. But you can't, not properly. His stomach churned. Talk of shitting yourself in times of fear has strong roots in reality. He realised how visible he was to a wary professional killer passing by on foot. Not normally religious, although his parentage gave him the choice of Presbyterian Christianity or Judaism, he found himself praying that as soon as the killer hit the street he would turn to the right and run away from where the car was parked. He decided not to look up if the killer's footsteps stopped outside the car. No point in watching yourself die.

His luck was in. Or one of his gods was listening. Footsteps clicked off in the opposite direction. Relief flooded his body, followed by a second wave of gut-churning fear. Had the killer looked over to the left before running off to the right? Would he have second thoughts? Was that car there when I climbed the stairs? Should he go and check it out?

The footsteps faded. He sat up, trembling violently, started the engine and drove off in reverse, without lights. Bollocks to a drink. He still felt sick, and close to soiling his pants. He didn't contact the police. The murder was obviously a private matter. He turned into Shaftesbury Avenue, switched on the lights, drove to Piccadilly Circus, went round Hyde Park Corner and into Knightsbridge, past Harrods and into Cromwell Road, past the big museums, and on to the Western suburb he called home, on the river, not far beyond Richmond. As he drove, with the hood still down, he gulped the air he would no longer have needed if the ugly little gun had gone tap tap tap. He felt happy and glad to be alive, but when he got home he couldn't sleep until the afternoon was well on its way. His wife had to wake him up at seven in the evening and tell him it was time to go to work.

He always was lucky. Some people are. A couple of years after I first met him he was beginning to establish himself as an art dealer. One bright summer's day he and I were running late for an auction at Christie's. Finding a parking space there was normally mission impossible, but as we drove into the square, in the car he nearly died in, another car drove out of a space right in front of us. Zipping in to take its place, he grinned and said:

'I'm always lucky. You can call me Golden Bollocks.'
The name stuck.

The third former film extra was Golden Bollock's younger brother. We never really took to one another. He had inherited none of his brother's sense of humour and dedicated his life to making money. Very successfully, it has to be said.

The last of the extras looked very like the singer Bryan Ferry when he was young, which he was at the time. Long dark hair and that lounge lizard look. Before the casinos opened he worked for the infamous slum landlord Peter Rachman, the man who brought the term Rachmanism into the English language. Peter Rachman bought houses occupied by what used to be called sitting tenants, who paid very low rents which by law couldn't be increased. He bought the houses for about a quarter of the normal market price, or less, and then sent his hired thugs to bully the often elderly tenants into moving out. Incentives included roof removal, particularly effective on a rainy winter night, staircase removal, handy if the tenant was at least partially disabled, operating loud machinery in the house next door, once you had cleared it of undesirables, i.e. other tenants, and letting adjacent properties to economically active prostitutes.

All the while physically and verbally abusing the tenants and keeping up a climate of fear. Spitting on them was one of the gentler torments. Very few of the ageing tenants were able to take the heat. Or the spit. Once the tenants were gone the new owner could sell the house at about four times the price he paid for it, or take advantage of the abolition of rent controls by the then Conservative government, and let it at a much higher rent. It was also perfectly legal then, and very common, for a landlord to put up a sign saying: "No Irish, No Blacks." Not to mention "No Dogs." (So much for the claim that race relations laws are an unnecessary intrusion into our private lives and that everything could safely be left to the innate decency of the British people). Peter Rachman let a lot of his newly liberated houses to black tenants, recently arrived from the Caribbean at the invitation of British government ministers, including Enoch "Rivers of Blood" Powell when he was Minister of Transport and needed people of any colour to keep the buses and railways going. And thousands of well trained black nurses, without whom the NHS would have collapsed long ago. Rachman hadn't found God. He took on the black tenants because the prevailing racist attitudes allowed him to get high rents from people who had no-one else to turn to. He saw a lively market and went for it. There was no downside. If the first black tenants didn't like the high rents, and/or the low standards, Rachman's thugs kicked them out and found other black tenants who were a bit less fussy.

My new friend was not one of the spitting thugs, I'm happy to say. He provided girls for Peter Rachman. Rachman was unlikely to get by on natural charm, but as keen as any man to get a leg over the gorgeous mini-skirted girls who had appeared as if from nowhere to light up the streets of Swinging London. I'm not sure how my friend was paid, by Rachman or by the girls, or by both, but he claimed to have done very well. Much better than working for a living, at least until casinos came along.

But not for long. Disillusionment came quickly. He soon found that he wasn't all that keen on working as a croupier, rather than pimping for a crook. He liked to lord it over the girls, with minimum hassle from the boss. He could have gone a long way in casinos, with his smooth charm, and he would have made a lot of money as a manager, but he hated sucking up to the players and complained about having to be a buffoon. There is a long-held theory among casino owners that if you can make the mugs laugh they won't notice that you're robbing them. Or at least they won't mind so much. My last film friend had a high regard for his own dignity and felt that it was greatly diminished by that sort of fooling around. Not to mention taking orders from smarmy Frenchmen.

He left a short time after I met him, but not before telling me several times about the bright summer morning he finished work at the

22

Curzon and was walking home to his flat in Chelsea. It was about five o'clock. Somewhere near Harrods a beautiful girl in a coloured plastic mac waved a cigarette in his face and asked him for a light. Next thing he knew they were in one of those picturesque old red phone boxes that young people used to vandalise and piss in before they all got mobiles. He quickly discovered that the plastic mac was all the girl was wearing, apart from high-heeled shoes and a friendly smile. They had sex standing up in the phone box, in broad daylight, and never met again. Most people at work didn't believe him, but I did. These things do happen, to certain people. He had the right sort of face. I can't really explain that. You have to be there.

Another young croupier from one of the other classy casinos had a similar experience which backs up my theory about faces, but with a strong commercial element that was absent in my smooth friend's surprise morning. The other croupier lived close to King's Road too, like we all did then. He met two very good-looking girls in a pub, a blonde and a brunette, and bought them a drink, with vague hopes of sex to follow. Slightly to his surprise the girls finished their drinks quickly and invited him to a nearby flat, at the beginning of a bright summer's afternoon. Once inside they led him into a wide room where a double bed stood next to a very big mirror that took up almost the whole of a wall. Sunlight flooded in through a tall window and reflected off the polished brass ends of the big bouncy bed. Without a word spoken the two girls took off all their clothes and lay down close to the mirror, their heads pointing in opposite directions. Each girl pressed her face into the other girl's neat pubic bush--no shaving in those days--and each girl's hands firmly gripped the cheeks of the other girl's perfect arse. The upper, left hand of the girl furthest from the mirror occasionally strayed into the shadowy valley in between. Each girl's tongue danced lightly across the myriad nerve endings of the other girl's clitoris. Fingers did what fingers do. Low murmurings and the occasional sharp intake of breath rose sharply in volume and turned into the shouts and screams of two full blast female orgasms that even Meg Ryan could not have simulated, however much you paid her.

The young croupier was more aroused now than he had ever been in his life, even on the day he first discovered sex. He wondered if it was possible to die of too much pleasure when his own thrustings reached their natural conclusion, but decided to risk it anyway. At least he would die happy, a trick not everybody manages. He thought briefly about his girl-friend who lived in South Kensington, a pretty girl who collected nice things to put on shelves in the rose-covered cottage she was sure they would share one day in wedded bliss. He decided that what she didn't know about wouldn't hurt and mentally placed her in a parallel universe, to be returned to when he and the two girls became strangers again. He ignored the two bottles of wine the girls had provided, and occasionally drank straight from the neck, fearful that the alcohol might diminish the amazing hardness of the maniac he was tethered to.

When his turn came, with the blonde girl on all fours in front of him and the brunette kneeling at his side, her skilled right hand ready to create what pornographers call the money shot, the suspicion that had been growing in his mind that the big mirror on the wall was a one way mirror became a racing certainty. He just knew that there was someone on the other side, watching or filming the events of that hot afternoon. Possibly sleaze-bag Dennis Hamilton, the man behind the career of his partner Diana Dors, the pneumatic bottle blonde he worked hard to turn into England's answer to Marilyn Monroe, Jayne Mansfield and Brigitte Bardot, all at once. A man who didn't do things by halves. My old friend was sure that the girls were being paid for the parts they played so well. And that he wasn't being paid anything, but would have happily handed over a week's handsome salary to be where he was now (make that a month's salary). And that when it was all over and their quota of couplings had been met, the girls would have floated away on a tide of red and white wine and would have less use for him than they had for yesterday's newspaper. And wouldn't even remember his name. And that it wasn't their flat. And that they probably lived in the suburbs, with their parents. And that he didn't resent the impersonal handshakes and perfunctory goodbyes that were all he got when they put their clothes back on. And that he would never have such a good day again.

My smooth lounge-lizard friend from the Curzon House wasn't normally so repetitive when he told stories about his life. I'm sure the reason he kept telling the phone box story again and again was that on cold and rainy winter days he didn't really believe it himself, and only repetition kept the fond memory alive. I don't want to bore you with the resemblance between my friend and the singer, but whenever I see Bryan Ferry on television (with his always excellent backing musicians) I have to work hard to suppress an image of him doing rude things in an old red phone box with a girl wearing a plastic mac and a smile. When he was a bit younger. The resemblance is so striking that I sometimes get confused, especially when I'm pissed.

I saw my old co-worker one more time, about a year after he put casinos behind him, driving down King's Road in an elderly but impressive Mercedes convertible, with the hood down in spite of a light rain. He pulled up to say hello, without much enthusiasm. I asked what he was doing for a living, fighting back the urge to ask if he'd seen any nice

24

phone boxes lately. He told me he was supplying girls to dance in Beirut night clubs. Horizontal dancing. Then he drove off with a leer on his face. I suppose you could say he'd gone back to his old job.

The mention of Beirut reminded me of the two summers I lived there, in 1958 and 1959. Standing in King's Road, watching the ageing Mercedes disappear in the direction of Sloane Square, I thought of the days I'd spent swimming at the Sporting Club private beach club, close by Pigeon Rock and the suicide cliff with the expensive fish restaurant at the top. Some of the dancing girls from the Beirut night clubs came there too, to freshen up after a hard night's work. Sadly (or perhaps not, on health grounds) they showed no interest in a gawky English student and preferred to swim in peace, never once dipping their carefully combed hair under the water, or eye up the rich middle aged businessmen sunning their pot bellies and trying to forget that they had a wife at home. A long suppressed urge to go back to the Mediterranean flared briefly in my mind, and died in the English rain.

The part of London where Peter Rachman operated was Notting Hill, at that time a run down area with not a Hugh Grant or a Julia Roberts or a young Tory politician in sight. Another landlord in the same place at the same time, and with the same kind of business plan was Mr Nicholas van Hoogstraten, the man we all love to hate. A rather wizened figure now, not visibly improved by his recent short spell in prison, but in those days a very dashing and handsome young man, nattily dressed in Carnaby Street clothes.

Julian and Abe.

The extras and I were at the (very well-paid) bottom of the Curzon House food chain. A man called Julian was at the top. Julian fixed everything, for the owners, for the staff and, most enthusiastically of all, for himself. When the top London casinos first opened their doors to the super-rich their profits were way out of proportion to the capital and effort invested. But the security systems were rudimentary. We were all on to a good thing; even callow trainees like me were able to help themselves to a generous share. Greed was good, long before the eighties.

Julian the general manager was a very bold robber. His share of the swag far exceeded everybody else's put together. But don't panic; bankruptcy for the casino was never an option. Although the amount stolen in all the London casinos exceeded even the high salaries paid, there was plenty left for the owners to put in the bank (in Switzerland if possible). In the absence of staggering incompetence the ownership of a gambling joint in the middle of a big city is as near as you can get to printing your own money; better even than planting a fiver's worth of poppy seeds in a Third World field and selling the heroin for five grand on a First World street corner. And, usually, a lot less likely to get you killed. A casino table should have paid for itself by the end of the first night's play. After that the only limiting factor is the number of mugs you can pull through the door. And wages are free, in civilised countries where the staff are allowed to accept tips.

When I started work at the Curzon Julian was tall dark and handsome, very expensively dressed, and bursting with the professional friendliness of a successful salesman. But a certain individuality came through. A lot of people genuinely liked him, and the force of his personality kept the casino full. He was, in my expert opinion, far and away the best casino manager in London, ever; the benchmark against which all the others could measure themselves and be found wanting. He's dead now, but if he could miraculously re-appear at the age of fifty or so he could take over any top London casino and double its profits. That doesn't make him a good person, I have to agree, but it did make him a very good casino manager.

Julian spoke the new classless English, easily adapted to suit any audience. He could slide into a Yiddish-tinted London accent when he was talking to an East-End-made-good Jewish businessman, or go up-market and make the English aristocracy feel at home. He could even produce a mid-Atlantic twang (reserved for American gamblers), like somedisc-jockeys and pop-singers were beginning to adopt. Sadly, it was his least convincing performance: sad because more than he loved anything else (even money) he loved to get close to female American movie stars, and was convinced that they would get their pants off even faster if he talked to them in American.

I always rather liked him, except when it was him or me. If you were a threat to his money-making activities, or if your own efforts were suspected by the owners, you were instantly dispensable. I accepted that. Casinos were rough places.

Julian had a mousy little wife, a hangover from his days of comparative poverty (driving a taxi in Brighton according to one malicious gossip, self-employed in light engineering according to the man himself), before casino gambling catapulted him into the ranks of the nouveau-riches. The wife hovered in Julian's shadow, on the rare occasions he brought her into the casino, looking uncomfortable in the flashy surroundings that were her husband's adopted home. As far as I know they had no children, but I'm sure she would have made an excellent mother. She had that kind of face, soft and kind like a mother's face should be. But rarely seen. We saw much more of Julian's glamorous blonde girl-friend. She looked like a modern footballer's wife and spent a lot of time in the casino boosting Julian's macho image.

Julian's very public friend was Roger Moore. Julian liked to tell anyone who would listen that he and Roger had grown up together, and often repeated the same story to the same person as if constant repetition added to his own reflected glory. Roger seemed quite happy about the schmoozing, probably because Julian treated him like a VIP customer although he was actually quite a small player compared to the anonymous businessmen whose annual losses were many times higher than his. At that time, before 007 made him even richer than Julian, Roger Moore played "The Saint" on television. He made good money from wearing a halo and dishing the wicked plans of the ungodly, but nothing like the earnings of the property developers sitting next to him and playing for much higher stakes. Star-fucking, that coarse but eloquent expression that so vividly describes excess devotion to celebrity, was Julian's only weakness.

On TV The Saint drove a glamorous Volvo sports car. In real life Julian drove an identical Volvo sports car, registration JP 30, to tell the world that anything The Saint could do Julian could do too, and that he was thirty years old (which he was about ten years before he bought the car).

It's possible that playing French roulette led Roger Moore to the acting technique that took him into a multi-million dollar career as 007. That's my theory anyway. In those days it was customary to tip the croupier when you won. Nearly all the gamblers knew that the casino owners regarded the tips as part of the takings, and stole them from us at the end of the night, but most players continued to tip. It was the polite thing to do and they didn't want to look stingy in front of the other players. Some pretended to believe that we actually got the money, and even made helpful suggestions about how to spend it. We did our bit to keep up the pretence. Even though we were the victims of the daylight robbery of our tips, we were better paid than we would have been in the cold world outside.

A French roulette payout is made with a long stick with a flat bit at the end, used by the croupier to push the chips over to the lucky winner. When the winnings arrive in front of the player the croupier pulls the stick back a few inches (to let the player get his hands round his winnings) and then keeps it stationary for a while, ready to collect the almost compulsory tip. Like holding out a hand, but more elegant, as befits the servile but sophisticated atmosphere of a top casino. But sometimes a payment was made to a player who wasn't willing to tip the owners of the casino who, in his opinion, already took quite enough of his money. On those occasions the brief moment stretched out rather. But not forever. Life goes on. After a carefully measured interval one of the senior Frenchmen would raise his left eyebrow in an expressive Gallic gesture that spoke volumes to the surrounding silence, and signal to the croupier (with his other eyebrow) that it was time to give up. I haven't obsessively studied Roger Moore's acting techniques before and after he took up casino gambling (and most probably never will) but I think a careful biographer might find some clues there. Or maybe the Frenchman was copying Roger Moore. I hadn't thought of that. He was our most prominent celebrity. Perhaps I'm keeping up the habit of a lifetime and backing the wrong horse.

As time went by (and money poured in) Julian became ever more star-struck, constantly raising his sights in his search for reflected glory. It was the only commercial failing of a man who seemed to be made out of bank-notes. On a normal night he would make a beeline for the biggest gambler, tongue at the ready, because that is what a casino manager does. But it all went out of the window when a film star appeared, especially a good looking American female one. A Hollywood star called Linda Christian came in one night, with the usual crowd of hangers-on. She was exquisitely beautiful, but even her most loyal fans couldn't accuse her of acting, and neither she nor any of her hangers-on put any money down. But neither mattered, to her or to Julian. Her talent for marrying rich men soon took over from an acting career that never really was, and Julian couldn't have cared less whether she gambled or not. She was an American movie star he hoped to get a leg over. Not realising, yet, that he was way out of his depth, Julian homed in like a guided missile. She stared at him coldly for about thirty seconds, then turned to one of her minders and said, in a flat, expressionless voice "get this asshole away from me." It took him several minutes to recover.

Even away from the casino Julian never dropped his guard. At the races his car shone like a showroom; his clothes were immaculate; every hair was in place; and every conversation dropped a name, along with the amount of money the name could put his hands on. Same in a restaurant or a night club. Immaculate clothes again, the beginnings of a bald spot concealed with millimetric precision, like one of those delicate fans popular with tourists in Spain; a Rolex watch glowing in the dark, a beautiful female companion, champagne frosting in a silver bucket, the most expensive dish on the menu, smiles and waves for anyone rich sitting nearby.

Once, only once, I thought I saw a chink in his armour. At the end of a winning night he talked to me about a popular musical that filled theatres in the sixties. It was particularly popular with middle-aged men because at one crucial point all the girls in the cast appeared naked. I agreed how colourful it was (all the different shades of pubic hair) and how lively, and how inspiring to see all those young people enjoying themselves with nothing on. I didn't mention that I hadn't actually seen it. Not that it mattered. Julian didn't expect a reply when he was talking. You just kept on nodding. He ran out of breath and lit a cigarette. I grabbed my chance. I told him how great it was to sit in a jazz club like Ronnie Scott's, half pissed, in clothes lifted from a heap on your bedroom floor, and let the sound of a saxophone carry you off to places you never even knew were there. For a brief moment an expression I'd never seen before came into his eyes. I thought he was going to buy a pair of blue jeans and meet me at Ronnie's. But I was wrong. Or guilty of wishful thinking. Like so many rich people, especially ones who get rich suddenly, Julian lived his life behind a transparent wall of exceptional thickness. You could look but you couldn't touch. He asked if they served champagne in jazz clubs. I silently awarded him first prize for wilfully missing the point and gave up.

When Julian was about sixty years old he married a girl in her twenties. His young wife produced a daughter, who brought real spontaneous joy into his life, probably for the first time since he was a boy. But the marriage didn't last. His young wife moved out and took the little girl with her. He died, in 2004 I think, alone in his house in Spain; the mousy wife gone, the footballer's wife gone, the young wife and the daughter gone, the expensive house in England gone. I have to admit that a tear came to my eye when I heard that he was dead. Not so much for the man I worked with for six years, who would have dumped me out on the street without a thought if I had got in his way, but for the man I was sure was hiding behind the mask, for reasons only he could tell you if he wasn't dead.

The other senior person at the Curzon House, outside the Barnett family, was a short, slightly built American who looked to be at least seventy years old. His name was Abe Aronson. I never really got to know what Abe was for, or exactly where he came from, or what he did before he worked at the Curzon. Several stories floated around. One said that he once played the saxophone in a night club belonging to Al Capone, but didn't explain how that led to a senior job in a London casino, a long way from a 1920s Chicago dance floor. Another hinted at a Las Vegas connection: Abe was in London to make the high rollers from the desert feel at home. There was some evidence that this might be true. On the night the very large, very scary-looking American who spent a lot of money on young prostitutes who agreed to having an arm broken (for an extra fee of course) on top of the usual activities that whores are paid for, came in clutching the hand of a gorgeous girl whose other arm was in a sling, Abe spoke to him for a long time, very respectfully. I marvelled that a pretty young girl allowed her arm to be broken for money. She could have got a job in a casino and stolen some instead. The most sensational story was that Abe had been a professional killer in Al Capone's gang, carrying a tommy-gun in a violin case and blasting Al's business rivals to death, Chicago style. When necessary. I thought it unlikely. He didn't look big enough.

My own theory, based on hints and whispers at the time and the deferential but familiar way he spoke to the gangster who got off on breaking girls' arms, was that a connection between Abe and American organised crime did exist, and that his presence was a visible deterrent to London protection gangsters like the Krays; if you messed with the Curzon House Club you came up against the Yanks and wished you hadn't. Like our deal with NATO during the Cold War. But these arrangements are rarely put into writing and as almost everyone in the know is dead it's unlikely that the truth will ever come out to play.

Abe kept the same routine every night: dinner in the restaurant, followed by several hours leaning against a wall and staring at the main French roulette table. His eyes were always narrowed down to slits, like a man just this side of asleep. Abe's eyes opened properly when a gambler known as the cigarette man lost the largest amount of money I had seen, so far. I was spinning the wheel for most of the game. When it was all over Abe came over to congratulate me on my good spinning. (Many otherwise intelligent people believe that croupiers can actually choose the numbers the little white ball drops in to. If only). I looked hard into his eyes, searching for a clue that a killer once lived there and snuffed out peoples' lives with a small machine-gun, like the man at the top of the stairs in Soho. But all I saw was the joyous greed of a happy businessman.

Abe's eyes opened wide another time when a small middle-aged French croupier with a droopy moustache walked away from the roulette table without noticing a trail of emerald green five pound chips slipping soundlessly from the bottom of his left trouser leg. He smiled obsequiously at Abe as he walked towards the arched doorway that led to the stairs down to our scruffy rest-room in the cellar. Abe moved away from the wall, eyes wide open, at some speed for a skinny old man who had just woken up, and confronted the small Frenchman. He pointed down at the chips, pointed up at the Frenchman, and repeated "you, you, you," several times, as if too shocked to get a whole sentence out in one go. The Frenchman had obviously not noticed the chips sliding past his belt from their hiding place under his shirt. He looked behind him, saw the chips, looked at Abe, said "non, non, non" and jumped away from the evidence. Unfortunately the supply was not yet exhausted. He'd had a busy night. A lively player was winning five pound chips on the second roulette table and losing them on the table the little Frenchman was working on; he'd seen an opportunity and gone in strong, not realising that the combination of his heavier than usual load and the law of gravity would give the game away.

The little skippy jumps made the chips flow even faster. Abe and the Frenchman shuffled out of the room. Their duet of "you, you, you," and "non, non, non," echoed faintly up the back stairs. The Frenchman was fired but not prosecuted and got a job in a casino down the road, after a couple of days on the Pernod. The long arm of the law was not invited to intervene. There was a reluctance to call the police, partly because of the dubious legality of the gambling business at that time, partly because of the dubious nature of the West End police, at that and most subsequent times.

I had often watched the little Frenchman fiddling nervously with his bow tie. I thought he was a timid man who found his job stressful and relied on a bit of fiddling to get him through the night. Like some men play what we called pocket billiards when I was a boy. I didn't realise that each fiddle meant another fiver down his shirt. I knew it was a common route for carefully folded banknotes (meant to go, unfolded, into a locked tin at the top of the table and be counted at the end of the night and paid into the Barnett bank accounts, less the twenty or thirty percent that Julian nicked), but I hadn't realised that a skilled man could do the same thing with a big solid chip. I was very young then.

That sort of activity was not casual theft. It had to be carefully rehearsed, like a conjuring trick, before you were good enough to do it in front of several people watching you like a hawk, including Muriel, Bob's loyal wife, only a few feet away, playing roulette with house money and keeping a sharp eye on the shop. It's the close attention to the little details that separates the men from the boys when they embark on a life of crime. I put in many hours of hard practice before I gave bow tie fiddling a go. And tightened my belt till my stomach hurt.

Profit Sharing.

A French roulette table closes at the end of a night's play. Julian, as general manager, is trusted to supervise the closing, count the cash, and not help himself to any of it. He sits at the bottom of the table, opposite the wheel. His favourite cashier sits next to him. Two croupiers, one either side of the table, empty on to the green baize the heavy metal boxes kept beside the wheel during business hours to store the cash the mugs hand over during the night's play (less any notes skilfully slipped down shirt fronts and carefully stored downstairs). The croupiers sort the notes into denominations and hand them to Julian. Mostly tenners, the largest note available at the time. Julian squashes the notes into a thick U shape, gripped tightly in his left hand, and flicks ten of them off with his right thumb, the method used by on-course bookies at the race track to stop the punters' winnings blowing away. Very sensible at the track where the winds blow fiercely across the wide open spaces, but strange inside a house in Mayfair with the windows closed.

The penny dropped. Early casino arithmetic was very flexible. Two plus two easily made five, or a lot more in the right hands. When Julian had flicked off a nominal ten notes he passed the bundle to the cashier. The cashier walked very quickly—almost ran—to the cash-desk at the top of the sweeping staircase that rose majestically from the ground floor, placed ten notes in a neat pile on his desk and put a rubber band around them. Bob Barnett got those. The remaining three or four notes went over to the left. Then the cashier ran back for the next bunch of notes. The flexible arithmetic gave Julian and the energetic cashier three or four hundred pounds a night to share between them, except on Fridays (Julian took Friday nights off, probably without much enthusiasm), at a time when the average wage in London was about twenty five pounds a week. Nice work if you can get it. The arrangement lasted for at least a year, on several tables. Then, one sad day, Bob Barnett found out what was going on. From then on the banknotes were counted the way they still are today, laid flat on the table, one by carefully separated one, stepped in fives and picked up and rubber banded in tens. (Real tens now, the number between nine and eleven). Everything is agreed by everyone present, out loud. The number of notes of different denominations is recorded on paper, and on a computer in recent years. The bundles are taken to the cash desk. From start to finish a CCTV camera takes pictures and a microphone listens for whispers from anyone with a plan. The cashier stays in his cash desk. The old sense of fun is long gone.

No action was taken against Julian. Au contraire. He was given a substantial pay rise to compensate for his loss and to discourage any selling of his undoubted flair for public relations to another casino. Julian was very good at persuading people with money to throw away to throw it in his direction. He could have sold sand to a man in a desert. Bob Barnett knew that. A righteous feeling of justice being done was poor compensation for an empty casino. He needed Julian more than Julian needed him.

I often wondered whether old Bob worked it out for himself, or if a member of staff turned informer, envious of rich pickings he wasn't getting a share of. We all knew what was going on, but we always thought live and let live and don't kill the golden goose. We might get a chance to grab an egg one day. In with the in crowd. Perhaps a colleague took a different view. Envy is one of the least attractive characteristics of the human race.

In 1964 and 1965 chemin-de-fer, usually shortened to chemmy, was the main game at the smart casinos in London. In the very beginning, a couple of years earlier, it was the only game. A smart lawyer saw that chemmy, a card game in which the players bet against each other rather than against the house, seemed to comply with a sentence in the gambling laws that said everything was OK if all the players had the same chance. In a chemmy game each player took the bank in turn. The odds were against all the players betting against the temporary banker, but as they all had a go at being banker it all balanced out in the end, said the smart lawyer, in a private game on a private table that the private players paid rent to sit at, in a club where they had to be members. The riff-raff couldn't wander in off the street, the general public would not be corrupted and dragged into debt, and there was no sharp-eyed banker with a green visor pulling in the losers' money. You could hardly call it a casino really. Let there be casinos, said the Lord, but let's call them gambling clubs. And so it came to pass.

Imagine yourself standing next to a sixties chemmy table. Watch the croupier's neatly manicured hands shuffle the cards (half of them pink, half of them baby blue, at the Curzon) pick them up, pat them into a neat rectangle, and offer them to the player whose turn it is to cut. And then put them in the shoe. Not a shoe like you wear on your feet. A wooden box with a see-through lid at the top and a round wooden handle at the back that allows the players and the croupier to manhandle the box around the table. The shuffled cards go in at the top. At the front of the box a metal lip guides the cards as the croupier deals them out one by one. See an early 007 film for details.

The shoe goes to the player whose turn it is to hold the bank. All the players throw in their shoe money. This is the rent the players pay to play the next shoe, as each session is called. Which will last about twenty three minutes if the croupier is good at his job. (If he isn't good he'll last about an hour before he's back on the street. It wasn't all peace and love in the sixties). The rent, or shoe money, is roughly a third of the minimum opening bank. When the opening bank is twenty five pounds, about three hundred in today's money, the rent per person per shoe is eight pounds, or about one hundred today.

In the early casinos the rent (shoe money) was the sole source of profit, before the owners were bold enough to bring in the bank games where the players bet against the house. But what a profit. Think of a large table in your house today. Nine people chuck in a hundred quid each every half hour, and keep it up for about six hours. (We're talking modern money now). And when they win they tip the croupier, so you don't have to pay him any wages. You have to give some of the players a free dinner and the odd drink and a tree-trunk cigar, but that's not too hard with eighteen hundred pounds coming in every hour. Then imagine three or four such tables in your house. Now you have a sixties casino. Don't spend it all at once.

Chemmy is a very simple game. The opening player puts in the opening bank and one of the other players bets an equal sum to try and win it. The challenger wins the bet and gets the shoe and becomes the new banker, or loses the bet and sees his chips added to the bank in the middle of the table. If he loses he has to bet twice as much next time to get his first bet back and win the opening bank. If he loses again he has to double again, to win the quite small opening bank and get back the disproportionate amount of money he has already spent. It really is one of the silliest games in the world, like betting on the toss of a coin and doubling up every time, but with the odds stacked slightly against you, and rent to pay. To make it even worse the player hoovering up your money can take it all out any time he likes, and pass the shoe to the next player. But it looks great. Something very addictive comes to life among the brightly coloured chips and the expensive cards and the gently curling cigar smoke and the highly skilled croupier with his sophisticated French patter.

The croupier collects all the eight pounds payments on his palette, the long wooden thing you see the croupier waving around in the casino scenes in those early James Bond films, and arranges his collection of small chips so that they form a visible sixty or seventy pounds or so. With an elegant flick of the palette he sends them over to a man standing in the shadows behind the seated players. The changeur (French for changer, which exactly describes the work he does, ignoring all sidelines) scoops up the small chips and replaces them with a chip or chips of larger denominations, taken from an antique bureau just visible in the darkness behind him. The croupier flicks the bigger chips from the changeur into his free hand and drops them through a slit into a locked metal box. The box the shoe money goes into isn't very big and would soon overflow if the small denomination chips weren't replaced by a smaller number of chips of larger denomination. A small clipboard hangs on a hook under the table, by the croupier's right knee, containing a sheaf of identical pieces of paper. On each sheet there is a small box for the shoe number (starting at one, when the evening's fun gets started), a diagram of the table layout's nine numbered seats, a box where each player's shoe money is recorded, and a box for the total amount collected.

All the players leave the table when a shoe ends. To stay at the table when the croupier is shuffling and the waiter is cleaning up (in more ways than one) was social death. The casino's owners strongly supported this custom when the newer games came in. In fact they probably invented it. They hated to see people sitting around and not losing any money. They liked to see a few bets on another game, and no-one coming back to the chemmy table until Julian strode through the roulette and blackjack rooms, chest out, head back, declaring loudly that "La partie continue au chemin-de-fer" in a not very convincing French accent. Another "rule" encouraged players to leave some of their chips on the table, to reserve the seat, allow the croupier to collect shoe money for the next shoe while the players are away, and flaunt a big pile of chips if they were big players, or small players on a rare winning streak.

While the players are away the croupier collects the shoe money from the piles of chips at each numbered seat and flicks them across to the changeur, as described above. Usually the bigger chips come back, but every now and then the croupier flicks the small chips over and nothing comes back. Something no-one would notice unless they were looking very closely. A private fund builds up inside the elegant cabinet. Close to a thousand pounds each time on the high stake table and about three hundred on the small stake table, in today's money. No small piece of paper is filled in. The shoe never happened. The books still balance at the end of the night. The private fund is split later, in very unequal portions, between the changeur, the croupier, and the smooth Frenchman in charge of the room.

I don't think Julian ever got in on this act, though I wouldn't want to be dogmatic about that. He didn't miss much and his lust for money only took a break when there was a glamorous woman in the room. But I did once see him hurriedly conceal a five hundred pound chip (at least five thousand today) in the tight waistband at the back of his expensive trousers when Bob Barnett walked into the chemmy room one night and rudely interrupted a whispered conversation between his general manager and the Frenchman in charge of the chemmy. Bob was supposed to be in Cannes, on business, but he flew back early and came very close to catching Julian with his trousers down, or, more accurately, with a lot of Bob's money going down his trousers. I think it was a transaction unrelated to the normal flow of business between the chemmy croupiers and the changeur, and none of my business. But an opening for me. With a ghost of a smile and a raising of an eyebrow, I made sure that Julian knew that I had seen the big chip. (Roger couldn't have done it better). It kind of levelled the playing field if something went wrong with a transaction of my own and Julian caught me stuffing something valuable down my much cheaper trousers.

As far as I know the nice little earner remained undetected for as long as the chemmy game survived. But I can't be sure because I moved on to French roulette and got a pay rise which, for a while at least, left me a lot worse off.

Up to now the player's money is still intact, apart from the deduction of the shoe money. But other predators are on the prowl. While the players are in the other rooms, the waiter (called a valet, to make the joint sound posher) tidies the tables, takes away the empty glasses, and cleans the ash trays. The ash trays are big and thick, to hold the fat cigars rich men love to suck on, and made of dark green glass, a colour the head valet has chosen on account of its elegant appearance. The waiter holds one dark green ash tray in his left hand and and pours into it the fag-ends and wet cigar butts and ash from all the other trays on the table. He holds it in a way that seems wrong, with his thumb on one side and a couple of fingers on the other side; not cupped from underneath as you would expect. A wad of freshly chewed chewing gum clings to the bottom of the ash tray, invisible through the elegant dark glass. The gum (any flavour will do) brushes briefly against one or two of the chips the players have left on the table. Small value chips become part of the tips shared out among all the valets. Bigger chips are treated as individual booty and cashed in with the changeur, for a cut. In half an hour another shoe starts.

In the early days the waiters were mostly Spanish, Italian or Portugese. The system of recruitment was feudal. The head valet sold jobs to the highest bidder. In a place like the Curzon the sum involved was enough for a deposit on a small house. There was never a shortage of takers. Stories of how much money you could make in a London casino had soon spread around the sunnier (and poorer) parts of Europe.

One night at the Curzon the feudal system went badly wrong. The head valet sold a job to a young man of his acquaintance, quite possibly a poor relation. The young man arrived in London and reported for duty at Lord Curzon's house, clutching a brand new English phrase book and an unopened packet of Wrigley's spearmint gum. The previous owner of the job had made enough money to go back home and buy his native village. Villas sprang up where once olives had grown and he made a fortune, thanks to a nice smile and a few packets of gum. The newcomer was at the other end of the scale. He couldn't pay in one go but had scraped up just enough cash from close relations back home to make a down payment. And he'd come a long way. It was agreed that he could hand over what he'd got and pay the rest of the money after a few weeks of hard ash tray cleaning.

The fight broke out on the night the head valet asked for the rest of his money. The request was declined. The new recruit had spent his never before seen wealth on loose women and betting on horses, the two luxuries he had dreamt of every night in his long years of poverty. There was no money left. He asked for more time to pay. His polite request was impolitely refused. At about one in the morning, at the height of a very big game, the unmistakeable sound of breaking glass spilled out from the drinks room in the darkness behind the chemmy table. The head valet who had sold the job and the new boy who had not quite bought it came barreling out of the little doorway, punching and kicking and shouting very bad words in Spanish. Or Portugese. Or Italian. It's hard to tell the difference unless you know the rude words. The chemmy game stopped. All eyes were on the fight.

One of the chemmy players was a bookmaker in his day job. He tried to take bets on the outcome, but it was too dark to see who was thumping who and no punters put their money down. I felt sorry for him and put a fiver on the head waiter, figuring that with right on his side he would fight harder. Sportingly, and rather surprisingly, when the fight was stopped the bookie called it a draw and gave me my fiver back, the first and last time I ever saw a bookie give a refund to anyone who wasn't holding a gun. It was Julian who spoilt the fun. He bundled the small fighters back into their room and threatened them both with the sack. Poverty loomed, reality returned, the fight stopped, the card game started up again, addiction got its grip back, and soon it was as if nothing unusual had happened.

I once won a small bet during a break between chemmy shoes. Long before the mid-seventies leap in the price of oil brought dozens of Saudi princes into London casinos, a young and dissolute Saudi prince called Abdullah was already a player at the Curzon. I never once saw him when he wasn't stoned or pissed. Or both. Or without Freddy, his big scary English bodyguard, an ex-regular soldier turned mercenary who once fought in one of the most vicious wars in Africa but now spent his working hours helping Prince Abdullah find his way from one casino table to another without falling over and damaging the royal frame. His Royal Highness had seen a game played with matches, in an interminable but beautifully photographed pseudo-intellectual French film called Last Year at Marienbad. He challenged me to play against him, for twenty pounds. Quite a lot of money at the time. I took him on. I could just about remember the rules. In the cinema I woke up half way through the game that appeared half way through the film, and went back to sleep before the game was over, but I figured that a drug-addicted piss-artist wouldn't be too hard to beat. I was as sober as a judge and I hadn't smoked a joint for six months. He was in his usual state. It looked like easy money. It was. I won the game. The prince gave me a black look and refused to pay. I appealed to Freddy, as one Englishman to another. He told me to fuck off. Maybe he was Welsh. Then the chemmy players began to drift back and I had to get back to work and the occasional bit of fraudulent conversion. Whenever I mentioned the debt on other nights I got a blank look from the prince, who never remembered anything that happened more than five minutes ago, and a very threatening black look from Freddy, who never forgot anything that might cost him money. I wrote off the debt. Soon afterwards the prince stopped coming in to casinos. I heard he died at a young age, a common fate among those of us who live on a mixture of narcotics, alcohol, and the odd mouthful of caviar. Or perhaps they hid him away somewhere.

One last chemmy scam: players who wanted more money to play with, after a succession of losing hands, didn't have to leave the table and sign a cheque at the cash desk. Julian or the smooth Frenchman in charge whizzed across with a cheque book, really a book of IOUs because payment wasn't expected on the spot in those heady days, scooted off to the cash desk, and came back with the requested wedge in the form of casino chips. Minimum interruption of the game was the underlying theme. One night Julian wasn't there, and the smooth Frenchie, Monsieur Chiron by name, if you're a stickler for detail, and Bob Barnett had fallen out. A middle class sort of chap, one of the trainees chosen for his French skills, like me, was the changeur. Bob told him to take over the cheque book, much to M. Chiron's annoyance, for the rest of the night. Bob Barnett got his chips the same way, though of course his chips were on the house as he owned the joint. The middle class chappie's luck was in, big time. Bob couldn't win a hand and kept on calling for more money. Knowing that it wasn't real punter's money that was being signed for, my smarter than me colleague rapidly taught himself to forge Bob's signature, slipped in a couple of cheques of his own, trousered the resulting chips and, through the usual channels, turned it into a slightly smaller but still significantly large amount of cash. It was his ticket out. A week or two later, anxious not to hang around in case things were looked into deeply, and keenly aware that where you aren't is often more important than where you are, he handed in his notice and left the casino business a lot richer than he was when he first came in.

The chemmy room was not the only place in the casino where private enterprise flourished. In early casinos it was everywhere. Anything that could be bent was bent, until the owners evolved ways to fight back. It was surprisingly easy. Anyone who read Lady Penelope's speech or, even more painfully, had to sit and listen to it, probably doesn't realise that almost all the early casino owners were criminals, or ex-criminals, or soon-to-be criminals. People like that were often so pleased with their own talent for stealing money that they didn't believe that riff-raff like me and my new colleagues had the sense to do the same.

If you walked from the big chemmy room, through the brightly lit ante-room where the cashier sat smugly behind his desk, in one case thinking of the money he would pocket later that night, you arrived at the French roulette room. At about midnight the room was full of gamblers firmly convinced that they could beat the odds and go home rich. In a procedure copied from the poshest casino in Cannes each player was

40

asked to hand over a one pound session fee. Even big players had to pay for the privilege of being allowed to lose their money at the roulette tables. The tax was levied by a changeur, taking a night off from the chemmy games but still looking for a bit of cream on the cake. The changeur carried a roll of tickets and gave one to each player in exchange for the reluctant payment of a pound. Some players paid the money but contemptuously refused the ticket, to show their disapproval of this night time version of daylight robbery. They didn't mind risking hundreds or thousands of pounds if there was a chance of a win, but asking them to pay that one measly quid was seen as taking the piss. Which it was. But we still pressed them for the money because, as usual, there was something in it for us.

You soon got to know the refuseniks. When they paid up you didn't give them a ticket, and you put the pound into a different pocket. If a ticket wasn't ripped off the roll you didn't have to hand over a corresponding pound at the end of the night. In a couple of hours you could easily make about half a working man's weekly pay, and not feel so bad about missing the action in the chemmy room. You hit the refuseniks first, in the hope that the more timid players would copy their macho stance and add another pound to the stash in your left hand pocket. The casino got the lion's share, respectably folded in your right hand pocket.

If you were lucky you would also find money on the floor. But you had to be very quick to beat the valets. They felt a deep sense of failure if a dropped chip made it all the way down to the carpet. One night I spotted a ten pound chip on the floor, bright red and glowing in the semi darkness. A sharp eyed valet sliced across the room, skilfully cutting a way through the packed crowd. I was determined not to let him win. A tenner in those days paid for a very good night out. My foot pressed the chip into the carpet a fraction of a second before the valet came in for the tackle. I stood swaying like tall grass in a high wind as roulette players surged past me, rushing from table to table in search of a winning number. The valet tried to dislodge my foot with a sharp kick. I kicked back with my spare foot and nearly did a princely dive, a bad idea without Freddy on hand to catch me. Not that he would have bothered. A player summoned the valet at just the right time, with a contemptuous click of his fingers. He had to go and serve the customer. I sneered at his back and dipped down to collect my night out.

At the bottom of the crowded French roulette table Bob's wife gives up her seat to a paying customer. One pair of eyes you didn't have to worry about any more. A regular player stands very close to one of the croupiers, beckoned by a sign only he and the croupiers know. He puts some chips down on the table and murmurs a bet in French. It should be

41

repeated clearly and audibly by the croupier, but it isn't. The bet is made as late as possible, just before the little white ball drops into the wheel. When the ball drops the croupier calls out a winning bet in French and flicks one of the chips onto the number. If things are looking really good he places all the chips on and around the number and creates a bigger payout.

The French croupiers called the special players barons. I never found out why. The baron deducted thirty or forty percent for himself and gave the rest to all the croupiers present at the time of the transaction. Distributing the money on the premises was a bad idea. A favourite place to do business was the all night restaurant in the Cavendish hotel, a smart place in elegant Jermyn Street, just South of Piccadilly, a little way past Turnbull and Asser, shirtmakers to Prince Charles and to dodgy croupiers in low-slung sports cars who saw the nice shirts in the window as they went to collect their stolen money at the Cavendish hotel in the early hours of the morning. Sadly, one of the best of the barons when actually nicking the money at the table, an Italian restaurant owner who had already lost five of his six restaurants by playing roulette with too much enthusiasm, rarely made it to the Cavendish. He was so addicted to roulette that the money burned a hole in his pocket while he was waiting for the boys to finish work and meet him over a cup of red wine, and disappeared into the black hole otherwise known as the French roulette table at the Italian owned White Elephant, an electrifying joint we'll visit shortly. He always claimed that he was hoping to double the money before he got to Jermyn Street, but that was just a lie. Perhaps self deception would be a kinder and possibly more accurate term. He simply couldn't get past the White Elephant with money in his pocket, even money that didn't belong to him (or, strictly speaking, to the people who had recently given it to him). Although determined to hang on to his last restaurant, and quite happy to turn to crime in pursuit of that happy ending, the truth is that as soon as he went racketing round the West End with money in his pocket he was like a man playing snakes and ladders on a board from which an unkind hand had removed all the ladders. Unsurprisingly his career as a baron was brilliant, eventful and short.

In those innocent days you could only get an alcoholic drink in London in the small hours at a couple of specially licensed places, and sadly the Cavendish hotel was not one of them. But where there's a will there's a way. The manager of the all night restaurant solved the problem by buying in his own bottles of dark red wine which (once you were accepted as one of the good guys) was served to you in a coffee cup, where it looked exactly like a cup of black coffee. It was crap wine, but in the wee small hours of the morning one couldn't be too fussy. That explains the cryptic reference to cups of red wine in the preceding paragraph. The price of the wine was high, but not high enough to deter a clientele who brought with them a fair share of the takings of the roulette tables of London. The profits went straight to the night manager, less a small percentage the waiters got to keep them quiet. The hotel owners got the money from the real coffee, without ever knowing how much happiness their establishment brought to a growing number of its nocturnal customers. If the manager had been found out he would certainly have been fired, and probably prosecuted for a serious breach of the licensing laws. But he wasn't. Crime usually pays if you don't get greedy, commit it in a posh place, and keep your mouth shut.

Another refuge for the late night boozer was the all night restaurant (now known as the Connoisseur casino) in the Royal Garden Hotel, at the Western end of Kensington Gardens, next to the now famous palace where Princess Diana reigned, along with her loyal paparazzi and her ambitious butler. Once again the alcohol was served without the knowledge of the hotel's owners. Although much appreciated by its lawless customers as a place to go for a last piss-up before the sun rose too high in the sky, the Royal Garden all-night restaurant never caught on as a money exchange centre, apart from the odd minor transaction when someone desperate hit one of the small casinos in Kensington. Too far from the West End where all the big action was. But it was very popular with the better class of prostitute and with the ordinary class of croupier, both looking for a quiet drink after a hard night's work. Or sometimes, for the tart, an extra customer slipped in on her way to bed. Perhaps a lonely croupier with a pocketful of somebody else's cash, emboldened by the illegal wine and killing the pain of his loneliness by bouncing off a pretty girl trying hard not to fall asleep.

For a few years more money changed hands in the luxuriously appointed gents' lavatory of the Cavendish all-night restaurant than over the counter of many a bank in many a small country town. The legitimate hotel guests must have wondered just who the small bands of shifty looking men huddling close together in the gent's, smelling strongly of red wine and passing round thick bundles of currency, could have been. Now they know. Everything comes out in the end.

The French Doctor.

His name doesn't matter any more. Anyway it might not have been his real name. He's probably dead. He smoked a lot and drank a lot and took no exercise and hung round a casino most nights and he'd be in his nineties now if he was still breathing. There was a rumour that he died of cancer in the early 1980s, but it could have been a cover. The good times were over, except for a very small and privileged few, and he might have gone back to France to retire and didn't want to be pestered by the people he had to mix with when he lived in London.

The Doc rented a comfortably furnished flat in Hampstead, set back from the main road, down the hill from the tube station, a short walk from the old European café where intellectual Jewish refugees played endless games of chess and set the world to rights, surprised to be alive still after the horrors of the nineteen forties. He looked like a middle-aged medical man in a sleepy old town in the middle of France, where centuries go by without anyone really noticing. The sort of place that drove Madame Bovary mad.

The reality was very different. His medical work divided into two categories. He patched up injuries suffered by French organised crime

44

foot-soldiers in the course of their duties, injuries which would raise embarrassing questions in the casualty department of a hospital in Paris or Marseilles, where gunshot wounds are not part of every day life. He did this work in London, on wounded men fit enough to be brought here, because it wasn't safe to set up a "private" doctor in France. Too easy a target. The French police could pick up a wounded criminal much more easily than at a gang's headquarters, and make use of wounds and bloodstains and resident bullets as forensic evidence. Or word could get out to a rival gang that there was a doctor in the house, and qualified men could be sent round to kill a wounded rival at a very vulnerable time. There's nothing like an anaesthetic to kill the will to fight back. The doctor's life would also be in danger. Nobody likes a witness.

His other job was to carry out abortions for the girl-friends of French criminals. The girls themselves might be reluctant mothers, or their violent boy-friends might be reluctant fathers who wanted nice slim young women to keep them warm at night, not ballooning matrons surrounded by hordes of screeching kids. Legal abortions were much more easily arranged in England than in France in the 1960s, probably because the Catholic Church had much less influence here than there. It's quite possible that the doctor, a fully qualified and very skilful practitioner, was registered and licensed for that part of his work.

I've always taken a lively interest in what other people do for a living, and how much it pays, but I never asked the doctor if he was paid individually for each operation, whether it was prising out bullets or removing unwanted foetuses, or if he was a regularly paid member of the gang. You don't ask questions when you're mixing with professional criminals, or even with their physicians. Call me a coward if you like, but these are people who sometimes kill nosey people. Or hurt them really badly. It's a major part of their job description.

The doctor didn't get up at the crack of dawn, unless there was an injured French villain banging on his door or an expanding waistline to deal with. Most days he did nothing. Most evenings he went to a casino. His favourite had recently opened in what had been the ballroom of a hotel in Mayfair. The interior was modelled on a French Riviera casino, with bright lights in big chandeliers and all the tables arranged in groups in one huge room.

There were two busy French roulette tables. Most of the croupiers were French nationals, not yet displaced by French speaking English upstarts like me. The doctor knew many of them from the South of France, where in the old days most casinos were owned and controlled by French criminals. Friendships were re-established. False bets were taken.

Illegal payouts were made. Incomes rose. But in casinos, like everywhere else, nothing good lasts for ever. The staff were adept at cooking the books, to hide winners with whom they were on particularly good terms. The inspector, the man who sits at the top of the table and keeps track of how much money each player has invested, and how much he is holding in chips paid out from the table, transfers funds on his piece of paper from legitimate mugs to the baron, in this case the doctor, and makes it look as though he is losing when he is winning, or winning a bit when he is winning a lot. He does this on a sheet of paper on a clipboard he holds in his hand. But fancy paperwork can only go so far. After a while the managers noticed that the doctor still had a lot of winning nights, aka not enough losing badly nights. The easy days were coming to an end.

CCTV cameras had not yet appeared (oh happy days!). Surveillance had to be done with the naked eye. Every time the doctor came in a senior manager or a member of the family that owned the casino hovered near by, discreetly at first, keen to catch the doctor cheating and throw him out, along with a croupier or two (pour encourager les autres). Neither the croupiers nor the doctor were surprised when the surveillance started. For a while they were able to continue, but very carefully. When there was only one snooper it was easy. The inspector on the next door table manufactured an incident and called for help. If the snooper was a manager he had to go over and sort things out. That's what managers do. While he was away the croupiers on the other table could make a couple of dodgy payouts and get the accounts back in the black. But, like leaks in the plumbing, things only ever get worse. Soon, confident that the doctor was definitely at it, the whole heavy mob congregated around him: general manager, managing director, a member of the owner's family, sometimes even a junior manager trying to suck up. All watching the doc's every move and making no effort to hide the fact. The doctor greeted them all warmly and carried on playing, winning or losing according to the rules of the game.

He couldn't afford to do that for long. Playing roulette is expensive, even for low stakes, and even for a professional man with no tax demands to weigh him down. The doctor was in a dilemma. To stop playing was an admission of guilt. To continue meant going skint. He had to find a new strategy. He liked to go out in the evening, unless he had a bullet wound or a stabbing or an abortion to take care of, and a casino was his natural habitat. The bright lights and the coloured chips and the dressed-up women and the thrill of the game were what he liked best, not to mention the extra income from his illegal wins. And the French atmosphere made him feel at home. He didn't like the cinema unless there was a French film showing, preferably about gangsters, he wasn't a theatre-going man, he hated English pubs (and most of the people in them) and he wasn't much of a dancer. In fact he didn't like living in a foreign country. It was casino or bust.

Everybody knows that it takes about eight years of hard studying to become a proper doctor. So a doctor is, by definition, a man in possession of a good brain. By contrast you could become a reasonable casino manager in less than a year, given the chance. I've seen it done. The main qualifications are a rat-like cunning and a thick skin. Two qualities that always got me through the night when I became a manager. Seeing the big picture and planning long-term wasn't expected.

The fight was on. The doctor won hands down. The eight years of brain exercise plus his own fair share of rat-like cunning tipped the scales heavily in his favour. He called a meeting at his Hampstead flat and had a long talk with his favoured croupiers, some of whom also worked with other barons for smaller stakes, small fry who didn't show up on the radar. A plan was formed.

The doctor came in and played at his favourite table, for lower stakes now that he was subject to the cruel laws of chance. The usual swarm of snoopers crowded round. Another baron played at the other table, for higher stakes than before. No-one took the slightest interest. All eyes were on the doc. The newly recruited assistant baron had to share his easy win with the good doctor, but as he was now playing for higher stakes the actual cash the new baron received was at least equal to his former earnings, and the risks were less because everyone was concentrating on the medical man. It was a good deal for the new boys. All barons had a shelf life and got chucked out one day, or banned from playing certain games. The new arrangement extended their working lives, especially as the intellectual doctor insisted that his new partners rotated their appearances at the table. That brain again. There was still a small risk of prosecution, but in practice only a tiny number of operators were ever convicted, and then only when stakes were very high. The other barons were also well aware of who the French doctor worked for, he made sure of that, and they knew that if they were caught they were on their own. If they involved the doc they involved the French crime gang and the gang leader's punishments were much harsher than anything handed down by a British judge.

The new system worked well, and worked even better when the American roulette tables came forth and multiplied. A bond was formed between the Frenchmen on the French roulette tables and the mostly British and Italian staff who worked on the American tables. The doctor's team of barons, now nicknamed the Crazy Gang, spread across the new tables like a rash. They never spoke to the doctor, or to one another. The doctor carried on playing in his usual spot, still attracting his swarm of snoopers, still greeting them cordially, still playing strictly ballroom. On one occasion he threw back a genuinely accidental over-payment and chastised the unfortunate croupier for his bad arithmetic. In good English, for the benefit of the snoopers, whose linguistic skills were no match for his. Over time the number of watchers diminished, and sometimes disappeared altogether as the Brits congratulated themselves on their sorting out of the dodgy Frog. Once in a while, when nobody was watching, the doc even had a false bet or two, just to keep his hand in.

A happy ending for the doctor. But in those early days things were never quite what they seemed. Even with his new disciples working for him the French doc was only a pin-prick in the side of the hugely profitable casino. The real, gaping wound was to come from within. A very senior member of the management, always the first to appear beside the doctor, was preparing a master plan that would allow him to steal three million pounds. That's three million then, about thirty million now, to be removed very skilfully from the casino group he was valiantly defending against the wily Frenchman. He would soon make as much in a good week as the whole Crazy Gang made in a year. He got away with it for a long time, starting in the late sixties and carrying on into the early seventies. His massive swag makes him a contender for the title of the most successful thief in English history. Next to him the Great Train Robbers were a bunch of tossers who threw a brick through a shop window, once you calculate how much each of the train spotters actually got after the cash was shared out among a big crowd. And some of them got caught. Yet at least three films were made of their big day. The master criminal of Mayfair never got his due recognition. The next chapter will put that right.

The Vicar.

Julian of the Curzon House, the first casino manager I ever knew, had the knack of seeing a chance and grabbing it with both hands. Seize the day and shake it till all the fruit drops off the branches. He would have been a fine junior army officer. Up front and up and at 'em as soon as he saw the whites of their eyes. No dithering while he worked it out on paper. But he didn't do long-term. He wouldn't have made it into Ocean's Eleven.

A man with what George Orwell once described as a bunny face, the smooth, smug look of a well-fed vicar from the upper-middle class, rose rapidly through the casino ranks of croupier, inspector, etc, and formed a plan. He waited for a couple of years, to avoid being dismissed as an upstart, and then offered the owner of the casino he worked for (who also owned three other casinos) the names of all the French croupiers who were making a dent in the profits. Allegedly. The owner was overwhelmed. Pound signs flashed before his eyes, blinding him to the fact that anything that seems too good to be true nearly always is. At last a chance to stop the rot, to plug the leaks, to clean out the stables. No-one had made this kind of offer before. The vicar was strolling through an open door. The saviour had appeared. The casino owner jumped in feet first.

What the vicar didn't tell the casino owner was that the names would come out a hat. The good the bad and the stupid would all be denounced together. No discrimination. No time wasted on facts. They were cannon fodder to be thrown into the first battle, which he hoped would decide the outcome of the whole war. It was all smoke and mirrors. When the saviour was accepted and given the promotion he was sure would follow he would turn into a Trojan Horse. Immunised against suspicion, hailed as the chief, he could steal much more money than the Frenchmen and their British friends (or even Julian) had ever dreamt of. Nobody had done anything like this before. He was new. He was the Martin Luther of the casino business.

At one time he approached me and asked for help. He told me to give him names of colleagues who were stealing from the casino, particularly Frenchmen. It was simpler than it seemed, he explained, with a sinister smile. There was no need for anyone to have actually stolen anything. Names were all he needed, not the truth, the whole truth and nothing but the truth. Information would be especially valuable coming from such a reliable source he said, trying to make me feel really, really important. Promotions and pay rises would come tumbling my way. I declined. His face darkened. He made it clear that I would not be among the favoured few when he arrived at the top of the ladder. I might even find myself among the denounced. I'll take my chances, I replied, with commendable courage and some nervousness. He did get to the top, just before I left the business, temporarily, in 1970, and trousered about three million pounds. I heard all about it a year or two later when I was studying the mating habits of the future King of Saudi Arabia at the Casanova casino.

Once he was accepted as the man who would clean up the West End, with his own bare hands if necessary, he instituted a psychological reign of terror in the three casinos he now controlled. Stroppy staff were fired (it was much easier and cheaper then). Survivors were intimidated. Strict rules were strictly enforced. All of no real value, but very impressive to the casino owners. The vicar and his closest cohorts strutted around like men in jackboots, making it clear to ordinary mortals that they were not to be pestered with silly complaints. Failure to maintain respect would end in the sack. A kind of Fascism filled the air. Tough-talking croupiers went quiet, faced down by someone even stroppier than themselves. It was the perfect environment for a man who wanted to do what he wanted when he wanted, with no one asking silly questions.

He operated mainly by shrewd corruption of the everyday paperwork used in every London casino. The big money spinner was the improper use of fill slips. When a table runs short of chips after a losing run, the inspector calls for a fill. A fill is exactly what it says on the tin. It fills a gap in the number of chips kept on the table. Let's say a table starts with two hundred chips valued at one hundred pounds each. A hundred or so of the chips are paid out to a lucky gambler. He takes them to the cash desk and swops them for cash or a cheque. The table is now short of hundred pound chips. Another hundred chips are brought from the cash desk to fill up the float (the name given to the chips put on the table at the beginning of a day's business). The hundred new chips are accompanied by a piece of paper known as a fill slip. The slip is signed at the cash desk by a manager and a cashier, and at the table by a croupier and an inspector. The game goes on and the accountants are happy. But the process was easily corrupted. You sneakily got four signatures on to the fill slip while nobody honest was looking and slipped the now very valuable piece of paper into the sealed box on the table where proper fill slips go. The crucial difference between a regular fill slip and a bent one was that at no time did the chips mentioned on the bent fill slip actually move from the cash desk to the table. The now spoken for chips (in the dull world of accountant-speak) remained at the cash desk to be changed into paper money by a corrupt cashier and given to the man trusted by the casino owners to beat the bad guys and protect their enormous earnings. (So enormous that they didn't actually notice the absence of the odd three million pounds. About thirty million today, as I mentioned before).

The vicar was not able to do this entirely on his own. He had to have a friendly cashier in each of the three casinos. He also needed friends throughout the casinos. Co-operation from underlings was a necessary evil that had to be paid for. He struck a brilliant deal. Instead of sharing the loot in fair measure with the other rogues, like all previous casino robbers had done, willingly or otherwise, he provided them with a second wage, in cash, in a brown paper envelope, with no annoying tax or national insurance deductions. The money was roughly equivalent to their legitimate wages (after deductions).

The arrangement was happily accepted by the second-liners. They didn't have the nerves of steel the main man was lucky enough to be born with. They liked the money but they liked to stay in the shadows. More chance of ducking when the shit hit the fan. And not so expensive for the vicar. The sleeping partners were pit-bosses, the men (no women then in senior positions) assigned to oversee the day to day running of the pits, as each collection of tables is called (all the American roulette tables together form a pit, all the blackjack tables etc). And junior managers, slightly senior to the pit-bosses. Both groups were almost certainly safe from prosecution if things went wrong. They had taken no direct part in the skulduggery and their blindness could be disguised as incompetence if they found themselves in court. You can't be sent to prison for being stupid. Yet. The people who signed the fraudulent paperwork got more than the wise monkeys who saw no evil. They might have survived too by claiming to be stupid, but their risks were higher. The helpful cashier, whose identity was never revealed, obviously got a much more generous share. He was the cornerstone of the house of cards and most certainly would have had his collar felt if everything had gone wrong. We'll never know the details of his part in the drama unless he makes a death-bed confession, the moment for which may well have passed.

Well-meaning believers in the probity and integrity of the British gambling business, with or without titles, are no doubt assuming that the bad guy's downfall came about through smart detective work by a person or persons of upstanding character, determined to root out the corruption blighting their otherwise spotless industry. Sorry to disappoint. It unravelled when a very nasty viral infection kept our hero at home. A less senior figure, not in on the action, took it upon himself to ensure that everything went smoothly during his absence. He shuffled through the papers in God's office and at one point came across a thousand pound cash packet in a drawer, but thought nothing of it. A thousand pounds in a casino desk is like a pound in a trouser pocket. Next day he couldn't resist opening the drawer again, if only to get a thrill from holding so much cash in his hot little hand. A thousand was nothing to a casino (I just said that), but to an individual it was a lot of money. Five of them bought a two bed-roomed terrace house in a half way decent suburb. There were two packets where one had been. Unwilling to harbour any suspicion of God he assumed (correctly) that something was going on that he didn't know about and assumed (incorrectly) that it was something he didn't need to know about. A few days later the cash pile in the drawer had grown to several thousand pounds. He knew then that he was out of his depth. He spoke to one of the owners. He was still unwilling to believe that his casino God had done wrong, but he knew that the cash wasn't put there every night by elves. And that if it was crooked and someone else found it his failure to mention the magic drawer where money grew in the night would get him into trouble. (It might have occurred to him to remove the cash to the safety of his own pocket. He would have got away with it. It was obviously hot money. The people who put the money in the drawer would never dare to ask where it had gone. But he didn't. Like most of his kind he lacked the necessary moral fibre).

It was the beginning of the end. The owners smelt a rat. They went through the paperwork much more thoroughly, found hard evidence of a discrepancy involving a few thousand pounds, and called in the police.

All of a sudden the Emperor had no clothes.

The owners never got to the bottom of the mystery of the multiplying cash packets, the spark that lit the fire of suspicion. You're the first to know. They were part of a routine arrangement between the criminal genius and the dodgy cashier. The cashier had found a way of siphoning off a round thousand on each and every day of the year, and a way of making the transaction invisible. I sometimes wondered why he hadn't cancelled the arrangement while God was away; I suppose it might have been difficult to balance the books. The money filled the slush fund that filled the brown envelopes that were handed to the partially sighted helpers. It was a rough and ready calculation, but always enough. When it exceeded the amount required the master criminal and the cashier split whatever was left over. Better to have too much than go short. Better safe than sorry. Underpaid underlings might turn against you, in that beastly way people sometimes do.

Word got back to the vicar that the police would be knocking on his door. Any minute now. He left London immediately. A very close Continental friend arranged for him to stay in a basement flat in the family castle, away from the public eye and surrounded by hundreds of acres of foreign land. Hidden in a castle like Martin Luther when Frederick the Wise saved him from a holy barbecue after Luther pissed off the Pope in 1521. On the run? Men in uniform looking for you? Step into my castle. Works every time. The two friends took with them all the stolen money that was stashed in their London flat. You couldn't stick three million in the Chelsea Building Society in those days, like a modern Russian businessman looking for somewhere to keep the small change. Not without getting your collar felt. Nobody had cash like that.

Things looked good. London's finest were unlikely to make a foreign stately home their first port of call, very few coppers were experts on Martin Luther, and the English thief and his very close foreign friend had kept their relationship as secret and undocumented as possible. And the drive from the front gate to the castle was about a mile long.

Fate intervened. Martin Luther left Frederick's castle a free man, four centuries earlier and not that far away, and got on with persecuting Jews and letting Henry the Eighth off the hook. The champion robber wasn't so lucky. His foreign friend couldn't keep his mouth shut. Like the London celebrities in the Krays' casino in Knightsbridge who got a thrill from rubbing shoulders (very carefully) with real life murderers, he liked to mix with the local low-lifes. In dodgy bars he talked about the bold casino robber who lived in his castle. He hadn't thought this through. The local villains were more interested in the robber's gold than in their posh friend's status symbol. They turned up and demanded a share. That's where things get difficult. You can kill one of the cheeky blighters. Or two or three if you really want to make a point. That usually works. Death sends a strong message. But you have to lack squeamishness and have an idiot proof way of disposing of a body or two without embarrassing a friend whose family owns a castle. Tricky. Or you can give away a little of the cash and hope the baddies have low horizons and leave you alone. The vicar tried the second, more peaceful approach. It didn't work. Every day the boys walked away with more of his money. Finally the three million pound man (less quite a bit) headed for Brazil. Not so smart. He should have gone to Marbella like all the other villains. Word got around Rio that the smoothy-chops Englishman who looked like a vicar was on the run with a load of cash. The much more murderous Brazilian criminals rapidly relieved him of the lot. Lucky to be alive, sadder, wiser and skint, he came back to London and gave himself up.

His former employers concentrated on the minor discrepancy (involving a Rolls Royce too many, given to the very close foreign friend) and ignored the missing millions. They knew their money was gone for ever and they didn't want the evidence produced in court to be used as a tutorial for the next generation of casino robbers. Bad enough being robbed once, even if you could easily afford it. No need to make it worse by telling a whole lot of other fuckers how to do it again. And they didn't want everyone to see how easily they fell victim to a smart operator who would probably never have been caught if it hadn't been for that damned virus. Self-esteem ruled. In their own eyes they were tough, shrewd casino owners and much smarter than the mugs who came through the door to gamble, or the dopes who worked for them. To allow the world to see that one of the dopes had taken them for three million was too much to swallow.

The vicar got a lenient sentence. But he was possibly the most successful criminal in British history, for a while at least, and I don't like to see a genius go unrecognised. If you're still alive reverend, I hope you're swelling with pride, praised at last for your outstanding achievements. Have a drink on me, but keep your hands to yourself. If you're still dead, I'm sorry I took so long. And if this book makes me any money, don't even think about suing me.

I didn't like the multi-million pound man personally, and I don't share his sexual preferences, but I admired the coolness he maintained in a very lonely position. If he had been rumbled the little people whose pockets he lined would have betrayed him without a moment's hesitation. There was almost always honour among the casino thieves who stuck their necks out and shared the risks and the cash in equal measure, but never among the lily-livered ones who looked the other way only for as long as the brown envelopes kept coming. That type always head for the door when the shit hits the fan. No moral fibre. No probity. No integrity. No nothing.

Down by the Riverside.

Most of the early casinos were owned and run by men of ill repute. Pay no attention to Lady Penelope's ravings. At least three were owned and run by organised crime gangs. Our own British Kray twins got in early, the American Mafia came a little later, under the direction of the highly efficient Dino Cellini (more about him in the next chapter) and a rarely identified French godfather was the man behind a very sophisticated gambling club on the Embankment, not far from the Houses of Parliament. In 1970 I took a break from casinos and spent a lively summer by the Mediterranean. Eighteen months later lack of money well spent drove me back into a new casino job in London, where I met a man I came to know as the French Connection. He told me the following story.

The Frenchman's casino was very well run, as you would expect from a man who had already had plenty of experience in his own country, and soon notched up a handsome profit. But it was hard to keep a secret. The big bucks he was pulling in came to the attention of one of the native London gangs. Probably the Krays, always on the look out for new names to add to the list of people they protected from danger.

They called round and introduced themselves. Senior staff escorted them in to the boss's office. The Frenchmen they spoke to guessed what business their visitors were in, and treated them with due respect. Even when the offer of protection was made and the outrageously large share of the profits to be handed over was spelt out in numbers, the Frenchmen kept smiling. But there would be a short delay. They explained, politely, that the boss was in France that day. It was a lie. He was in the next room, listening carefully. They would contact the owner and he would come straight over from Paris tomorrow to speak with his new friends, the gentlemen from London.

Next evening the London gangsters came back, confident that the smarmy Frogs wouldn't give them any trouble and that another nice little earner was in the bag. They were ushered, very respectfully, into the same back room. They saw a Frenchman they hadn't seen before sitting at his desk, a hand raised in greeting and a welcoming smile on his face. As the door closed behind them they saw two more men standing a few feet away, unsmiling, each one pointing a small machine-gun at their chests.

The way a professional killer holds his gun hits you in the face like a fist. No nerves, no awkwardness, no anger. It's not like the gun is a part of the man, it's more like the man is a part of the gun. Military training does that. The pulling of the trigger that explodes the bullets that take your life away becomes a reflex action, no more subject to conscious thought than turning into your driveway at the end of a journey back from work. He won't miss. Excellent aim is part of his training. Especially from four feet. The certainty of death chills the soul, even if you're a professional criminal yourself with a gun under your jacket. In less poetic language, you shit yourself. France had fought two doomed colonial wars, in Vietnam before they sold it on to the Americans and in Algeria before they gave up and went home. Many foot-soldiers of French organised crime came to the gangs with a long history of killing people, legally, in uniform, with weapons financed by the taxpayer. The Londoners knew that if a decision had been taken to kill them, pour encourager les autres, they were as good as dead. It was just a matter of how many minutes they had left. They were armed, but they knew there was no chance of getting their weapons out. So did the men with the machine guns. The Frenchman's smile faded.

He announced that he was no longer inclined to enter into a financial agreement.

The English gangsters were still not off the hook. Their own experience told them that some people like a chat before they kill you. They enjoy the fear in your eyes, the sweat on your skin, the urine stains that spread across your trousers, the uncontrollable shaking when you finally lose control. Murder can be much more than just a job.

It probably occurred to at least one of the Englishmen to go for his gun. There was no hope of firing it but it fitted every man's natural preference to die in action rather than wait for another man, not unlike himself, to squeeze his trigger. But nothing had been said. The Frenchman might have decided that a stand-off was acceptable. A stand-off that would allow him to carry on his very profitable business without extra expense. He might be confident that the Londoners would not come back after seeing the fire-power they were up against and the skill with which it was deployed. Going for a gun was suicide. Not so attractive when there was still a possibility, however small, that you might have survived if you had waited. Anyway there were other fish in the sea. If only you knew for sure. Minutes later it was the Englishmens' lucky day. They were ushered out, still carrying their guns. No-one shook hands. At that point the French Connection's narrative ended.

It looked pretty much like one nil for France. But in the sixties we all heard on the grapevine that a French owned gambling club had been shut down and that the boss had been expelled from the country. I wondered then why this drastic step had been taken, not knowing at the time anything of the events in the back office, as narrated by the French Connection. I was working then for an ex-criminal who seemed to be immune from the law, the Krays had casinos, the criminal Harry Meadows had the Twenty One Club in Chesterfield Gardens (where the casino scenes of the spoof James Bond film Casino Royale starring David Niven were filmed), and lots of other criminals had casinos. In fact being a major criminal and not owning a casino was social death. So why pick on this hitherto unknown Frenchman? Here's my theory, arrived at independently, with no help from the French Connection: the London gangsters left the French casino glad to be alive, but very angry at being humiliated on their own turf by a foreigner. They wanted revenge but they didn't want to spend any more time standing in front of the men with machine guns. They contacted a corrupt policeman (not hard to find in the notoriously crooked Metropolitan Police of the nineteen sixties) and used him as a conduit to people in high places. The bent copper was told the relevant parts of the story, with a strong emphasis on the automatic weapons. Such heavyweight weaponry was not common currency at the time. He was instructed to inform the higher ranks. The top men were generally clean and would pass the details on to the Home Secretary, the man with the authority to order the closure of the club. The expulsion of the Frenchman was probably an unexpected bonus, ordered by one of the clean top cops, or possibly the Home Secretary himself, alarmed by the escalation of the arms race and nervous about foreign gangs settling into London at a time when there was so much corruption in the police.

All speculation I freely admit, but it fits in well with the known facts. The French Connection's story about the boys in the back room is not something I can check on, or would want to, but everything verifiable that he ever told me was true. He only lied when he was telling his wife where he had been last night, or when he was talking to the owners of casinos he was robbing. In private, among friends, he was a very honest man.

Another story concerning the mystery Frenchman, also related by the French Connection would, I think, be too difficult to invent. Frenchy told me that his countryman fought with the French partisans against the Nazis during World War Two and didn't fancy a nice quiet job at the Post Office when the war ended. He and a few former comrades in arms bought a truck load of cigarettes cheaply in Switzerland and crashed it through a frontier crossing into France, where cigarettes were much more expensive. At the crossing they didn't worry about any damage done to the French guards, men they saw as as gutless collaborators who kept their heads down during the Nazi occupation, in contrast to their own roles as suicidally brave fighters for France. Assuming, as I do, that the story is true, they had a good point. From then on it was all up hill. The profits from the sale of the cigarettes financed the formation of a very successful organised crime syndicate, still rumoured to be in business today, in spite of the occasional challenge. And you thought cigarettes were bad for you.

Dino.

Before the 1968 Gaming Act brought licences and a veneer of respectability to the London casino business, the American Mafia opened a casino at the bottom end of Berkeley Square, just beyond the trees where nightingales once sang. It was called the Colony and is now a car park and should not be confused with the current Colony casino in Hertford Street, next to the Park Lane Hilton, which opened in 1971 as the Park Lane casino and now belongs to the Genting Corporation, a Malaysian conglomerate that started life running cruise ships with built-in casinos across the seas of Asia and then came to England in the early two thousands with high hopes of making a packet in the Blair government supported super-casinos that dour Gordon sent tumbling down once he got the top job.

The American Mafia's Colony Club was set up by Dino Cellini, the massively competent Italian-American who was already in charge of the Mafia's very profitable casinos in Las Vegas and the Bahamas. In a public relations exercise that rivalled Hugh Hefner's brilliant idea of dressing Playboy Club bunnies in low-cut swimsuits with a powder puff on their bottoms, Dino Cellini hired an elderly American actor called George Raft, famous for portraying gangsters in a long series of mostly forgettable films, and in one brilliant film, Billy Wilder's Some Like it Hot, in which he played the unlucky Spats. All George had to do, for a decent wage and an endless supply of free booze, was to wander round on a cloud of expensive whiskey, look like a gangster, only smile the most sinister of smiles, and make the punters feel like extras in one of his old films. It was a massive success. Then, just as the money was really rolling in, the government expelled the Frenchman mentioned in the last chapter, along with all the representatives of the American Mafia, and closed their casinos down, nervous about London turning into a British Chicago run by well-funded and very professional career criminals.

I once almost met Dino Cellini, in the Park Lane Hilton. In the sixties the big American casinos in the Bahamas made a fortune from a tidal wave of American tourists, on what were officially British islands. The Duke of Windsor was appointed governor there during World War Two, to keep the width of the Atlantic between him and Adolf Hitler, but by the time the sixties came round the almighty dollar had taken over the economy, American tourists filled the hotels, and the American Mafia controlled the casinos. British staff were welcomed as croupiers, especially London Italians. The American branches of the Mafia were still very conscious of their Italian roots. The managers and pit bosses were American, usually veterans of Las Vegas. Pay was even better than in London. Thieving was rare. Very few croupiers tried on the tricks they had learned in London. If you were caught stealing even small amounts of money your hands were stretched out on a table and the fingers broken by hitting them hard with the butt of a revolver, for as long as necessary. And you thought only old-fashioned Muslims did things like that. Then you got off the island quickly before something nasty happened to you.

Bahamas jobs were popular with the boys from London. As well as the good money there was sunshine and swimming and an endless supply of American girls on holiday, frantically looking for a good time. Your British accent is so cute (shame about the teeth). And cheap cocaine from the Northern countries of South America, a bargain before prices doubled on the way across the Atlantic. For the ambitious there was a faint

60

possibility of a job and promotion in Las Vegas, the Mafia's other branch. It wasn't easy to get a green card, but a few lucky ones did make it to Vegas. A light-skinned Indian whom I once knew, a British subject who spoke English with an impeccable Oxford accent, courtesy of his expensive public school education, passed himself off as an English aristocrat with an American suntan and did very well in the desert. By the way, on the subject of Nevada towns, if you want to cut a dash with those who know, always say Vegas. Las Vegas is strictly for the birds. Los Vegas, heard in pub conversations between people anxious to impress but with a poor grasp of Spanish, is plain wrong.

Dice dealers were paid the most, followed by blackjack and roulette staff. Roulette was for wives and girl friends. On the Western side of the Atlantic real men don't play roulette. The segregation fitted in well with the Mafia's old-fashioned patriarchal views. Like the Taliban the Mafia sees women as wives and mothers who stay at home and look after the children and the cooking, or (in the Mafia's case) as useful people to employ when you're setting up a whorehouse. There's nothing in between. A feminist would have a hard time in the Mafia, unless she managed to kill a lot of men in a short time and take over while the survivors were still in shock. Which has happened, but not very often.

My very good friend Golden Bollocks went for a Bahamas job interview at the Park Lane Hilton in 1966, purely out of curiosity. He had no intention of leaving London and his pretty wife and their young children, but he was always keen to meet someone new. I went along for the ride, hoping to meet the legendary Dino. Not because I was an admirer, but because I had never met a Mafioso before. There was no chance of my getting a job even if I had wanted one. In those early days I only knew French roulette, a game that never caught on in the Americas. Too goddam slow. To our disappointment we didn't get to see the main man. A bossy fat American man interviewed us, sitting behind a desk specially brought into his hotel room, and turned us down flat in less than a minute. As we were leaving the room GB asked our interviewer if he needed a permit to work in the Bahamas. You know, as you're an American citizen working on British territory. The Mafia man said something very rude about our mothers and told us to shut the fucking door on the way out.

We went for a drink in the bar on the top floor, the one with a view over the gardens of Buckingham Palace. On a clear day you can see the Queen hanging out her washing. No, not really, but you could see the place where she would if times got hard. I think the old top floor bar is a restaurant now, but I haven't been back to check. I don't like going there any more. A friend of mine was killed in the lobby of the Park Lane

Hilton, in the seventies, by a bomb belonging to the IRA. He had already passed the spot where the murderer left his deadly package and was moving towards safety and a normal life span. Then he turned back, to buy a newspaper, and walked straight into the blast.

A man GB and I worked with went to meet the American Mafia in the Hilton at about the same time as we did. He really was looking for a job. He was a Londoner with unrealised ambitions in the film business, and decided that moving closer to America might change his luck. He couldn't act his way out of a paper bag, but he had a flashy charm which could have got him a job in a television series if he'd had a little bit more luck and his hair hadn't fallen out so early. For several years he made enormous efforts to make it in the movies, even dying the top of his head dark brown in an attempt to make the sparse hairs look like a thick mop. Without success in either field. It really was a shame. He worked very hard. The hair effort reminded me of one of Ronnie Scott's regular jokes, the one about the beautiful red-head he met the night before: no hair, but oh what a beautiful red head. Applause and laughter and a tear for poor old Ronnie.

Unlike us, the man with the dark brown head got an interview with Dino Cellini himself, which raised his hopes of getting to Las Vegas via the Bahamas and then, in a Vegas casino, bumping into Frank Sinatra and Dean Martin and moving to Hollywood as soon as he had bowled them over with his charm. He was big on long-term planning. And why not? When you're at the bottom the only way out is up. Sometimes. The aspiring movie star met Dino Cellini in an upper lobby of the Hilton, on chairs laid out near the doors to the lifts. The man with the brown head was taken aback. He had expected a leading light of the Mafia to meet him in a private suite, surrounded by looming bodyguards and an atmosphere of sinister opulence, not in a public lobby where any old Tom Dick or Harry might stroll by. The penny dropped. As they talked, Dino Cellini kept his chair pushed hard back against the wall, giving him a good view of everybody passing through the lobby and making it impossible for anyone to sneak up behind him. His eyes darted continually from side to side. He checked out every man who came and went, but took no notice of women and children. Or of two heavily built men sitting at a table not far away. He looked nervous, even frightened. Suddenly it all made sense to the man with a brown head and high ambitions. Cellini was a long way from the armed back up he could have taken for granted in Las Vegas or New York or the Bahamas. Hence the nervous, darting eyes and the visible fear of death, and the indifference to the big men at the nearby table, heavily armed and pledged to die in defence of their boss if the shit suddenly looked like hitting the fan. And the choice of a public place with plenty of witnesses rather than a closed room where enemies could storm in and commit murder with silenced guns wrapped in tape that didn't hold fingerprints and could be left at the scene, along with the bodies, in the days of innocence before those goddam Limies invented DNA. Throwing the weapons down wasn't bravado or carelessness. It took away the need to carry or hide guns with terminally incriminating ballistic details that linked the owners with the murders.

I realised back then that members of an organised crime gang live tribal lives. On their own patch they are safer than the average citizen, thanks to their small arms skills and instant back-up when things turn nasty, but once inside the boundaries of another tribe they are thin-skinned, vulnerable, outnumbered and easily put to death. Not the job for a chap who has trouble reading a map. But don't think that the Americans have a monopoly on gut-wrenching violence, just because the Godfather films made a few billion bucks. We Europeans can still put on a show. Not that long ago, in a European capital you can travel to by train, a Jewish upstart decided to oust the established Catholic godfather of the capital city and put himself in the top spot. The top man's brother was strolling home after an expensive lunch in a part of town popular with well-heeled tourists. A police car screeched to a halt and two men in uniform jumped out. They fired several bullets, well beyond the usual ration of two slugs in the head (deux balles dans la tete in French underworld argot) into the brother's brain. He fell down and his blood pumped out on to the pavement. Passers-by were surprised, but assumed that a film was being made in a well-known tourist spot and that the blood was the usual tomato sauce that stands in for the real stuff that runs through our veins. The killers jumped back in their car, put a magnetised blue light on the roof and roared off, their journey made easier by the law-abiding drivers who pulled off the road to let the officers of the law pass by. In the suburbs, later in the day, real policemen found a stolen car full of fake police uniforms. The main man was supposed to die next, but reacted much faster than the wannabe crime lord had budgeted for. The upstart and his family, including a two year old child and an eighty year old grandfather were quickly despatched. The turf war was over before it really got going.

No wonder Cellini looked nervous.

Long Tall Alice.

      I haven't told you much about the gamblers at the Curzon House, apart from brief descriptions of a dissolute Saudi prince who rarely knew what year it was, a bookie who gave me back a five pound bet and shook my faith in human nature, and Roger Moore, who would one day save the world as James Bond, 007. Several times. I'm not counting the barons. The barons were not, strictly speaking, gamblers. They were men (almost exclusively men; Lily the Pimp, whom you are yet to meet, was one of the few women with the necessary skills) who were trying to make a living, albeit illegally and with a good chance of getting their collars felt or their balls kicked in, depending on the quality of the establishment in which they plied their trade. For obvious reasons I was biased in favour of the barons (so long as they paid up) but even discounting my natural bias I have always had more time for likeable rogues than for straight punters. You may come to share this view, but I want to give you a full picture of the casino business, warts and all, and must therefore include the occasional honest man. I won't go on too long. Just a few chapters here and there. With a health warning: even people who are incredibly fascinating in their private lives become boring (or much worse) when they are playing roulette, blackjack etc. It comes free with the addiction and is not confined to casino gamblers. Try getting a lively conversation going in an opium den, or among hippies passing round a joint. Everyone is having a great time inside his own head, but to someone who doesn't share their addiction they might as well be dead.

I'll start with a man I really liked.

Leonard Tobin was at the opposite end of the social scale to the French doctor and his Crazy Gang of barons, or Dino Cellini, or the Frenchman with a casino down by the river. Or me, if you want to get really personal. He was the biggest regular French roulette player at the Curzon House, my place of work from 1964 to 1970. Bigger or more famous players came and went in short bursts, and may have lost more money on the rare occasions when they did show up, but Leonard Tobin was in the same chair at the same table nearly every night of the week. That's what made him a star. He was a supreme example of the successful outsider who becomes part of the Establishment. The only aspect of his life he might regret from beyond the grave would surely be the endless hours wasted at the roulette table.

He was brought up, by his formidable mother, in a poor part of East London. She ran a small clothing business that kept her and her son fed and housed during his formative years, and made sure that he worked hard at school and beyond. He walked through all his exams, like hard-working people do, and qualified as a lawyer. At school he was almost certainly picked on and bullied for being short and fat and Jewish, not necessarily in that order, but he survived, his determination to succeed strengthened by the ordeal. He set up a business specialising in commercial law, and turned to property dealing at a time when the value of commercial property in London was soaring. Everything he touched turned to gold. He became a Justice of the Peace, which enhanced his standing in society and allowed him to put something back into the society that had rewarded him so handsomely for his hard work. There was no mention of a father. I assumed he had died, possibly a victim of anti-Semitic violence in Eastern Europe. Or maybe he just couldn't keep up.

One night I listened to Leonard Tobin talking to Bob and Alf Barnett. When they were boys the future casino owners roamed the streets that Leonard could see from the window of his mother's modest flat, in what was then a Jewish ghetto in the East End. No schoolbooks for them. He said that he sometimes watched them through the window and dreamt of escaping from his studies and joining them in the street. It might have been true, but I very much doubt it. I think he was just being polite. Bob Barnett grunted a neutral response, something he was very good at, but Alf never picked up on his brother's diplomatic skills. He gave a gruff laugh and said: 'Good thing you didn't. We'd have killed you.' The short sentence had a ring of truth about it, and visibly discomfited Leonard Tobin. He was trying to be friendly to the Barnetts, but deep down he must have hated the addiction to roulette that put him so firmly in their hands.

Leonard Tobin always brought Alice, his wife, into the casino. She was as tall and as skinny as he was short and chubby. It was impossible not to see them as a comical couple, a shorter, chubbier Popeye and a bossier version of Olive Oil. Alice thought roulette was silly. She mocked Leonard when he lost, told him him what a waste of money it was, and nagged him to go home. She was very rich in her own right and well able to hold her own if Leonard got stroppy. I liked Leonard Tobin, even if he wouldn't have been my first choice of companion for a lively night at the pub, but I found it very difficult to warm to Alice.

He offered her money and suggested that she played too, in an attempt to shut her up. She declined his offer and worked hard at being ever more irritating. Then one night she gave it a try. She put a look of contempt on her face, as if the chips in her hand were something the cat had brought in, and a pound on number twenty, a number she had convinced herself came up more often than the others. It may have been her birthday, a number many roulette players think is favoured by whichever God they hope is looking down on them. Her chosen number didn't come up very often. They don't. There are thirty seven roulette numbers and only one roulette ball. Any idea of favoured numbers is all in the head. But sometimes numbers close to twenty were the winners. Alice began to play twenty and the neighbours, a five piece bet that sophisticated gamblers among you will recognise as twenty and the two numbers on the wheel on either side of twenty. 1, 14, 31 and 33 if you want to get technical.

Soon Alice noticed that numbers just outside the magic five kept coming up. Her bet spread until it covered twenty five of the thirty seven numbers waiting to take her money. You may have thought there were thirty six numbers in a roulette game, the last number down at the bottom of the table being thirty six. As you've seen at the cinema. But don't forget zero. We pay you thirty five to one, which would be true odds if there really were only thirty six numbers. Sneaking in the zero is how we get you. That's all it takes. One number that stands for nothing and a mighty business is born.

In no time at all Alice was a goner. The addiction got a tighter and tighter grip on her brain. She never nagged Leonard to go home again (the good news, from his point of view). But there was a payback. Sometimes Leonard was winning and cashed in and wanted to go home as early as two o'clock in the morning. Now it was Alice who wanted to stay. Leonard always played big on one number and made a packet if he had a win or three before he'd invested too heavily in his dreams (the way to go if you ignore my well-intentioned advice and insist on playing roulette without a personal relationship with the croupier), but Alice played odds-on, the best way to make sure you lose. They became like two old bar-flies in a pub, always there at chucking out time. Affording it was never a problem. I didn't worry about their ability to pay for the groceries. Or my wages. But their moral degradation depressed me. All that money and all they wanted to do was stare at a roulette wheel as if the next number was the only important thing in the world. Which it is of course, to an addicted gambler.

Alice degraded in other ways. Leonard Tobin was as bossy as the next billionaire. Shrinking violets don't even make millions, never mind billions, and as a super star gambler he knew that he could take liberties in a casino that he wouldn't get away with anywhere else. But Leonard drew the line at being personally offensive to the croupiers. Alice jumped right over the line. One of the croupiers had a face which could be described as a little bit fish-like, if you really couldn't fight back the urge to be personally offensive. Something about the lips and the eyes. The sort of boy who gets teased at school and hopes it will stop when he enters adult society. Not to be. Alice called him Fish-Face, right out loud, and kicked him under the table every time the ball dropped into one of the few numbers she didn't bet on. He put up with it because he was earning three or four times the English national average wage and planning an early retirement in a pleasantly rustic part of his native Belgium; tolerating insults and minor physical pain was part of the deal. To soften the blows he took to wearing football socks under his suit.

There was a price to pay for all of Leonard's hard work and success in business. Like a lot of very rich men he couldn't ever admit to being wrong. One night he came in and showed off his new solid gold cigarette lighter. He flicked it to light one of his endless chain of cigarettes and reared back in fright when a flame several inches long shot up in the air. But he didn't adjust the lighter, like a lesser man might have done. He bent his head back and carefully brushed the cigarette against the outer millimetre of the raging inferno, only just managing not to singe his eyebrows. Every cigarette brought a repeat performance. I was dying to say why don't you adjust the flame, you silly bugger. There's a little wheel just next to your thumb. Made of gold. But I kept quiet. Success can be very lonely.

I saw him again in the mid seventies, at Ladbroke's Hill Street casino. By his standards he was skint. I had always assumed that his gambling money came from his law firm and from raising the odd office block in his spare time, but apparently the bulk of his fortune was invested in a massive private company belonging to William Stern, in his day the biggest slum landlord in England. Stern wasn't a thug who intimidated his tenants, like Peter Rachman and Nicholas van Hoogstraten used to in Notting Hill (a business plan the latter once described, with some pride and in impressive detail, to one of those frightening female journalists who are so good at interviewing bad people). As far as I understood, which may not be very far, given my deplorable lack of business sense, Stern bought vast numbers of tenanted houses for a song, their low rents fixed by law in those days of molly-coddling the poor. The low rents severely depressed the value of the horrible little houses and William relied on death by natural causes to relieve him of the tenants and make possible a sale at a large profit, as soon as the funeral was over. Or something like that. Although the rents were piddly, with so many houses in one man's hands there was a lot of piddle. I may be quite wrong, I happily admit. It was a private company and Mr Stern was under no obligation to tell the world how he made a living. But whatever the business plan was it capsized under a sharp rise in interest rates during 1973, when a very British boom turned into a very British bust. Stern went bankrupt (but managed to spend the rest of his days in a mansion that turned out to belong to somebody else), and most of Leonard's money went down with him. Leonard Tobin's days as the king of the Curzon House were over.

We greeted each other with genuine warmth when Leonard came over to the French roulette table in Ladbroke's Hill Street casino, my place of work from 1974 to 1978. It was the first time I'd seen him for about five years. I knew nothing of his decline. I expected a big bet, a heap of high value chips around his favourite number twenty nine. But things had changed. He slipped a ten pound chip on a low odds bet paying five to one—including twenty nine, for old time's sake—and avoided eye contact. Another croupier came to give me a break. I stood up and grabbed the opportunity to talk to Leonard Tobin. We covered everything except the change in his betting habits, surrounded by the new oil fuelled gamblers from the Middle East and Nigeria, all playing the way he used to play when he was king. And then some. I felt genuinely sorry for him. He looked like a schoolboy dropped from the football team. I had an urge to put an arm round his shoulder and say something sympathetic. But I didn't. We would both have been deeply embarrassed. You don't hug billionaires, even when they're skint.

He brightened up when I told him I was married, with a very young daughter. No longer the carefree bachelor he had known at the Curzon. He seemed really pleased. Perhaps it reminded him of life as a little boy, and the debt he owed to his dedicated mother.

He had probably stopped going to the Curzon House, unable to bear the shame of being a small player in a place where he had been a star. Gamblers do that. It really hurts to be ignored while the manager makes a fuss of the big players who have taken your place. Or, even worse, to be doled out a carefully rationed burst of the old sycophancy, just in case you get back in the money one day.

One of the Hill Street managers was glaring at me from behind Leonard's back, indicating that I should stop talking and go away (shut the fuck up and fuck off, in casino language). Most casino managers don't like croupiers talking to customers, especially when you do it better than they do. I went on my break. When I came back Leonard had gone. It had been his first visit to Hill Street, no doubt looking for a new top-end casino where he could play small and not be recognised as a man who had gone down in the world. But he knew that I would be asked for all the details of our chat. Casino managers in the old crooked casinos were very paranoid about conversations between staff and customers (not without reason). I would have to tell the management who he was, and the full story of his slide from superstar to small fry. Leonard didn't know that I didn't know. He probably assumed that old friends of mine at the Curzon House would have kept me up to date. So Hill Street was out. Playing small among whispers about his downfall would be nearly as intolerable as staying at the Curzon and accepting second class status.

I never saw him again, but I never stopped liking him. I admired his achievements and I admired the sense of fair play he tried to hide behind his gruff exterior. I just wished that he and his wife could have found something better to do with their time. Money comes and money goes, but time only goes. Alice was nowhere to be seen that night. She may have managed to turn her back on number twenty and all the other numbers that let her down. Or maybe she stayed on at the Curzon, indifferent to her husband's loss of status and unable to drag herself away from kicking poor old Fish Face in the leg. I suppose they are both dead now. Rest in peace, Leonard and Alice. Let somebody else worry about the numbers.

The Cigarette Man.

During the sixties and probably well into the seventies (long after I'd left) Patrick O'Neill Dunne was one of the biggest gamblers at the Curzon House. When he came in for the night he almost always lost more than Leonard Tobin, and stole the little man's thunder. He was the overseas boss of one of the major tobacco companies, hugely well-paid and a long way from the grasping hands of the British tax collector. We didn't see him very often. In those stricter times he was only allowed to stay in England for a few weeks every year, or pay tax like the rest of us. Poor Patrick. If he'd hung on for a while he could have commuted from Monte Carlo, like any old tosser can now, stay in London for as long as he liked, and still not pay any taxes. He was a man before his time.

Patrick covered every number on the roulette table, with a little extra on the numbers in the centre column, 5, 8,11,14,17 etc. Regular gamblers often have a touching faith in the middle numbers, believing (against all available evidence) that they come up more often than the inferior numbers on the outside. Or that they bloody well should and if they don't there's something wrong with the croupier. That attitude is as mad as it sounds, but we're talking about addicts, remember, who are all mad. If they weren't they wouldn't stand in a casino every night and throw their money away, however easily they came by it, or however much they managed to keep from the taxman.

Patrick was a casino owner's dream. Many of the numbers he played lost him money. He got a payout, but it was less than the chips we raked in. Casinos really like that. When the ball fell into the centre numbers he got a bit more than we pulled in, a win, but only a modest one and soon wiped out when the ball strayed away from the magic centre and dropped into a few of the numbers on the outside. Unless he hit a tremendous run on the centre numbers, which does happen, but not often enough to turn roulette into a steady living, the casino was in for a good night.

His wife often came in with him and played blackjack in an adjoining room. When one of Patrick's big numbers came up he ordered us not to clear the table in the normal way, but to wait until he had proudly shown Mummy what a clever boy he'd been. He always addressed his wife as Mummy, rather confusingly. It took me a while to catch on. Mummy came in, feigned interest in Patrick's clever win, and hurried back to her blackjack table in the next room. If another player had to wait while Mummy was away an apology for holding up the game fluttered from her lips. And then she did it again, and again, every time the call came from roulette. When Mummy went back to her card game we were permitted to clear the losing chips off the table and pay Patrick his winnings.

Although he was a complete fool when he was playing roulette, Patrick was a shrewd and competent businessman, very adept at shifting cigarettes in huge numbers. And technical with it. He invented a new way of making menthol cigarettes, the ones that make you throw up for a few years before the lung cancer gets you. The smelly fags used to be difficult and expensive to manufacture, but Patrick hit on the simple plan of putting the menthol in with ordinary cigarettes before the foil was wrapped round them. By the time the cigarettes flew off the tobacconist's shelf the menthol had soaked into the tobacco and given them that special sickly favour.

By coincidence his wife went to the same hairdresser in Bond Street as my then girl friend. She remembered Mummy coming in on a windy day and asking someone to comb her hair quickly, regally ignoring all the other ladies waiting for a snip. She didn't want to look scruffy as she walked down Bond Street buying jewellery and other essentials.

Patrick often came in with a small man we wrongly called Dr. H. Wrongly because he was just plain Mister H. He never corrected our mistake. Maybe he enjoyed the promotion. Mr H was born in the Middle East, but moved to the Sudan and bought a chunk of land the size of Wales to grow tobacco on. He sold the deadly crop to the company Patrick worked for and created a lot of work for people who really were doctors. At some stage he became a British subject, perhaps because Sudan was once part of the British Empire. Gordon of Khartoum and all that. Mr H began to play roulette for small stakes, very much in Patrick's shadow. In the eighties, his own man now, he became a very big gambler on his own account at a different casino. He played heavily on number twenty nine, and then ruined his chances of ever winning anything worthwhile by covering the rest of the table with losing bets, just like his friend Patrick had done some twenty years before. Predictably he became one of the casino's biggest losers, and in rare bad years single-handedly kept the accounts in the black.

People who take an interest in the odder forms of human behaviour might like to study my theory of military defence, as modified by roulette players, and adopted to an extreme degree by the two players in this short chapter. If you're researching a Ph.D in the psychiatry of gamblers you can use anything you read here free of charge.

The military player usually starts with one favourite number. It doesn't come up very often. The arithmetic decides that. It's thirty six to one against. The player becomes convinced that the nearby numbers are coming up more often than they should. Like Alice, in the last chapter. He (or, but not very often, she) starts to put extra chips on the table to protect the investment in the magic number. In the end, when the madness has really got a grip, every single number has at least one chip on it.

Picture a fort, on high ground, in the desert, in the old days. Like in ancient black and white films. The serious ones, not the Marx Brothers piss-take. A man with a rifle peers out from every gap in the battlements,

72

waiting for the enemy soldiers to rush across the desert, stick their ladders against the walls and storm into the fort, shouting and shooting and slashing with bayonets. As soon as he sees the whites of their eyes he fires at the bastards, fervently hoping there aren't too many more of them crouching behind the sand dunes. If the commander of the fort knows his job there will be soldiers looking in every direction. No nasty surprises if a sneaky enemy creeps up from behind. In military terms the all-round coverage makes perfect sense, and would be handy to remember if you ever find yourself in command of a fort in the middle of a desert. On a roulette table it's about as stupid as it gets. The more numbers you cover the less you get paid when one of them comes up. I don't mean the odds change. I mean that you get paid thirty five chips, but you lose perhaps thirty two other chips which are not on the winning number. That's a very silly thing to do. By playing that way you are actively assisting the enemy. You might as well hold the ladders for them.

You'll make one friend. The casino owner will love you, at least until all your money has gone. At that point you rapidly become invisible. I mean all your money full stop, not the amount you brought in on the day. If there's a chance of your coming back next day (or next year) with more money the casino owner's love will linger longer.

Many gamblers still play that way, and shout loudly in protest if the croupier moves his (or her) hand towards the wheel as if about to spin the little white ball before every soldier is firmly in place. Military players who read this (some chance) will brush my compassionate advice to one side and carry on regardless. Like the diamond man (you know who you are). And good casino staff will actively encourage gamblers to play soldiers, in the interests of the casino's profits and their own promotion prospects.

If you disregard my sensible advice and take up roulette in these days of high-tech cameras, make sure you concentrate on one number. If your luck is in and that number comes up—which it has to occasionally— you get the whole payout. It doesn't mean you can give up your day job, and it's not a patch on what we got up to in the old days before television cameras started poking out everywhere. But if you go home when you're winning you will sometimes even have a winning year, if you don't play too often. Try it at home with chips of no value. You'll feel just like James Bond when it goes well. Don't try it for real in a real casino. You might get addicted. Or fall into the military trap.

I saw Patrick, the first man I ever saw playing the military system, one more time, in the eighties. And then never again. He was sitting down. No more standing up and dominating the table and barking out orders. He looked old and tired. He played roulette absent-mindedly, for very small stakes, and handed out an unending stream of unsolicited advice to the player sitting next to him, who was obviously wishing that the old boy would shut up but was too polite to say so, unlike many gamblers I've known. Mummy was nowhere to be seen.

When he retired from the cigarette business Patrick wrote a slim book called "How to Win at Roulette." He must have forgotten the rules on the last night I saw him play. He lost his small stake and went home. Perhaps he was hoping for a place in the world's most misleading title competition. Perhaps he won. Or maybe he was just taking the piss. If you see a copy on a dusty shelf in an Oxfam book shop, don't buy it. It could cost you money if your brain slips a gear. It isn't even funny. Make a small donation to Oxfam and go home with your fortune intact. Read my book instead. I never take the piss.

Brian and the Boys.

Brian Epstein was the man who turned the Beatles into the biggest rock stars of the nineteen sixties. He was also one of the keenest chemin-de-fer players at the Curzon House, the only one who still played aggressively in the dying days of the game that had once been the only game you could play. The few remaining enthusiasts only played when Epstein came in. He was raw meat to vultures who saw a chance to squeeze a bit of someone else's money back out of the table that had taken so much of their own.

In the beginning everyone played aggressively. By that I mean that whenever a bank was running there was always someone willing to risk a lot of money to get a small amount of money back. Chemin-de-fer is a very sophisticated game to look at, but very silly when you think about it in the cold light of day. Over the years, as gambling losses drained their bank accounts (or the money from under the mattress), most players stopped betting recklessly against the bank and tried to make money from the very few dickheads still stupid enough to keep on doubling up against them when they got their hands on the bank. That's what I call defensive playing.

It's not hard to spot the fly in the ointment. Everybody wanted to run a bank and make lots of cash when someone else bet against it. But nobody wanted to bet against the bank when somebody else was running it. Catch 22 or what? The old reckless spirit was gone. The game began to die, except when Brian Epstein sat down and played the old way. Everyone loved Brian. He banged his money down when the other players ran their banks and didn't seem to notice, or care, when the croupier had to struggle to get any of the players to bet even small amounts against an Epstein bank. He was a born loser when he sat down at a chemmy table, however good he was at making money in his day job.

I didn't actually see the man with the little round specs, he came in on my night off, but I was told that Brian Epstein brought John Lennon in one night and tried to turn him into a gambler. Just as once, reputedly, he tried to turn him into a gay man. Addicts often try to get others to share their fun. He failed, twice. I did once see Paul McCartney playing French roulette. I was having one of my first goes at working the wheel and dreaming of spending my pay rise on a new sports car, my own incurable addiction at that time. The man destined to become the wealthiest Beatle put his hand in his pocket and played roulette for small stakes. I guessed that it was the first time he had gambled in a casino. It may have been the last. I never saw him at the Curzon again. He looked very nervous about the whole thing, like a young teenager sucking too hard on his first cigarette. The radiantly beautiful Jane Asher stood back from the roulette table, stared at (discreetly) by Tony, a big, bald but very handsome Frenchman who looked just like a Roman emperor, and always had at his side a tiny married woman who was even more obsessed with him than she was with roulette. A middle-aged Frenchman who looked like a cad from an old English film, only French, and still had a very keen eye for the girls, stared too, through the dark glasses he wore all day and all night and which gave him his nick-name. Jane Asher looked bored and disapproving. At the time she was famous for being a Beatles' girl-friend. Later she was famous for being a Beatles' ex girl-friend when she dumped Paul, for reasons only she and Paul McCartney and perhaps one other person could tell you. Then, after a few very reasonable stabs at acting, the still dazzlingly beautiful Jane Asher became even more famous for baking really tasty cakes.

I was enormously pleased to see Paul McCartney and Jane Asher in the Curzon House. Not because I was a Beatles fan. Bob Dylan was more my cup of tea. Nor was I a lover of fine cakes. Not that cakes loomed large in the life of young Jane. In public anyway. I was pleased to see them because they were young and good looking. They cheered me up no end just by being there and being better-looking than the old, weary, addicted gamblers who shared my nights and were beginning to bring me down. I was very ageist when I was in my twenties. Very unfair, but when I look in the mirror now I understand why.

Some of My Best Friends are Jews.

During the early nineteen sixties Jewish Londoners were a lot more clannish than they are today. It was an understandable reaction to centuries of discrimination, and slow to disappear even after the armies of Britain, the USA, the USSR, and many other countries defeated Nazism and put and end to the most meticulously organised and most ruthlessly prosecuted programme of murder that Jews had ever suffered.

Many London Jews disapproved of marrying out, aka marrying a partner from another religion. Of more importance to a casino like the Curzon House, whose first generation of customers were predominantly Jewish, most of the regular Jewish punters clung to the old tradition of staying at home with the family on Friday night. It may have been coincidence, it was the start of the weekend I suppose, but there was a definite increase in Gentile and aristocratic attendance on the night the Jews stayed at home. A big change came over the Curzon. Yiddish was out. Braying was in. I heard at least one sotto voce comment (my hearing was much better then) that it was nice to see so many English people in what was after all Lord Curzon's house, not some Eastern European ghetto. I didn't always agree, but I was too conscientious a club servant to point out to a paying customer that very few of the absent Jewish gamblers had foreign passports. No-one ever spoke out loud that cutting phrase 'some of my best friends are Jews' though the words always seemed to be hanging in the air, right next to Hilaire Beloc's nasty little rhyme.

I missed them because I started working at the Curzon in late 1964, after the scandal broke and the main man died, but co-workers with glazed eyes and a look of unfulfilled yearning told me that Doctor Stephen Ward and his two finest assets Miss Christine Keeler and Miss Mandy Rice-Davies were regulars at the Curzon House, often on Christian Friday, on the lookout for rich and/or aristocratic customers for the girls and aristocratic friends for the doc. Ward desperately wanted to be part of the aristocracy and quickly realised that the best way in was to provide hot totty for wealthy male aristocrats. It worked first time. Being a posh pimp (a word he hated) brought him a nice house in the grounds of an aristocrat's mansion, at a very cheap rent, and just enough cash to live like a lord.

You may have seen the film Scandal. People who claim intimate knowledge of the ins and outs of the Profumo affair say that the film sticks very closely to the truth. I don't know if they're right. I never got to swim in Lord Astor's pool with a crowd of happy naked girls, worse luck, and I've never seen the film. But I did see one of the girls in real life, or at least I saw a girl who a friend claimed was Mandy Rice-Davies (he may have been lying to make himself look good), in a pub near Belgrave Square, run by an Irishman with a big mouth and a fiery temper. The girl certainly looked a lot like the newspaper photographs we all drooled over.

The pub had once been a quiet local for Belgravia nobs, but morphed into a loud social centre for pretty girls who shagged wealthy married men for cash. Between drinks they discussed their trade in detail, with liberal use of the appropriate four letter words. They even laughed about the size (or not) of the organs that provided them with a living. The hussies. The only printable comment, in a book you might leave around where your servants could pick it up, came from a pretty girl talking confidentially to a friend in an actressy whisper that carried all round the pub. It concerned a relatively young and handsome man whose money she was seeing a lot of lately. He had, she said, the sort of cock that just melts in your mouth. Laugh, they never stopped, her co-workers, perhaps in envy as they thought about some of the old crocks they had to swing a leg over in order to pay the rent and buy a few rounds in the popular pub. The men in the bar looked uncomfortable. Some dared to intervene. That's how us chaps talk. You can't talk like that. You're girls. What is the world coming to? Stop it now. But the girls spent far more money than the men ever did (they would, wouldn't they?) and the Irishman always took their side when complaints rose above a whisper.

There was a Russian involved. He worked as a spy at the Soviet embassy in London when he wasn't hammering away at one of Stephen's girls, or two of them on a good day. Or night. The Russian connection was the big push behind the downfall of John Profumo, Dr Ward's most high-profile client. Profumo was Defence Secretary, our first line of defence against the Russian Bear, and there he was sharing a girl friend with a Russian 007. He had to go. Vital military secrets might cross the Iron Curtain between orgasms, fake or otherwise. The orgasms I mean. Or perhaps the secrets too. I hadn't thought of that. Maybe the Russian was being fed false information. Cunning or what? Now there's a plot for a book, if you're good at conspiracy theories. The resignation was quite honourable, I suppose, from a patriotic point of view, but I don't believe a word of the story behind it. Not even the one I've just invented. I think the Russian was having the time of his life, well out of sight of the Kremlin puritans who, like puritans everywhere, lived in constant fear that someone, somewhere might be enjoying himself. I'm convinced that he had long ago lost any interest in the Cold War and sent home just enough reports (based on military stuff he could find in any serious British newspaper) to cling on to his job in Swinging London. Hot totty, hot music, nice restaurants, casinos even. Why should Sean Connery have all the fun?

Right. No more respectable gamblers. Enough already. Avoid Boring People. Great book title and excellent advice to all writers. In the next few chapters I'll take you on a trip round some other casinos. Some high, some low. All expensive. In the company of bad people.

The White Elephant.

The White Elephant casino was a few doors down from the Curzon House Club, on the same (Southern) side of Curzon Street. Late at night, as the regular crowd began to thin out, a select group of croupiers finished work at other West End casinos after an evening spent augmenting their wages in a variety of ingenious ways, put on their proper clothes, and headed for the White Elephant. The late shift, who should have known better, brought a second wave of prosperity to the Elephant's owner, a colourful London Italian called Tony Mancini. To the best of my knowledge nobody ever stole anything from the White Elephant, but several people, including a particularly skilled Curzon House changeur and the Italian restaurant owner who doubled as a Curzon House baron felt compelled to spend their ill-gotten gains at a place where there was no possibility of negotiating a refund. No, I don't understand it either.

In its heyday the White Elephant ran a poker game where players could take on the boss in unarmed but very skilled combat. In most other West End casinos chemmy was where the players took personal aim at the geezer who owned the joint, but Tony Mancini loved poker and never much cared for the simplicities of chemin-de-fer. If you wanted to get your money back from the man whose staff had relieved you of it on the roulette or blackjack tables you had to become a red hot poker player. Or lose even more.

The White Elephant poker table seemed to float, untouchable by mortal hands, in an invisible bubble of intense concentration. Distraction was highly unwelcome. Black looks and hisses were hurled at anyone standing idly by and chatting. Quite rightly. Poker demands of its players a fanatical focus on every aspect of the game, a faultless grasp of the odds, and a perfect memory if you're going to play the game strictly in accordance with the underlying arithmetic. And if you're not, find something else to do with your time. Bad poker players are eaten alive.

Mancini played poker very well. A lot of Italian men do. But when you're hot you're hot and when you're not you're not, however skilfully you follow the odds. One night he lost his Maserati to another very good player, after waving good-bye to all the cash he could lay his hands on. Apart from the cash in the safe, which was treated with the same reverence as the reserves in the Bank of England. The lucky winner was a true sportsman who might have given Mancini a chance to win the car back if he hadn't wrapped it round a lamp-post a couple of nights after winning it, more accustomed to handling a sedate Rolls-Royce than a hot Italian sports car, after a drink. On another night, during a big game where hands were so evenly matched and so hard to play right that you could have sliced the air with a knife, Mancini lost the casino. The deeds were thrown on top of a very big pile of chips and pulled in by the winner. Steve McQueen couldn't have done it better. Or Paul Newman on a train. What the winner didn't get was the cash mountain in the safe. But he did get a licence to print his own.

The winning player was another true sportsman. He bet again. The stake this time was his new casino against the sacred contents of the safe. If he won again he walked out (or stayed in) with the business and the cash, and Tony Mancini walked out with the clothes he was wearing and a look of deep despair. Sporty lost, much to Mancini's relief.

The electricity that crackled round the table when these crazy bets went down made the White Elephant the most exciting casino in town, and guaranteed that Mancini's poker game would never be short of players. Or silent watchers like me, too unskilled to join in, but unable to tear my eyes away. The Elephant was a wonderful place for a man in his twenties with money in his pocket and a sports car in the street outside, and a head full of dreams. I never played, but I loved to watch, silently, and dream of the day (which never came) when I would be the skilled poker player who scooped the pot. It surely couldn't be long, my feverish brain told me, before the most beautiful girl in the world stood naked in the middle of the table, waiting to jump into the arms of the man with the best cards. Feminists will be relieved to know that this never happened, but it could have done, easily, in those wild times. If the Good Lord had decreed, late on the sixth day, just before he put His feet up, that there should be but one casino in the capital of every country on the planet that He'd knocked up from a few bits of space junk left floating round the Solar System that He'd knocked up the day before, He would surely have decreed that London got the White Elephant, rather than any of its pale competitors. Some casinos made more money, some attracted more aristocrats, or more film stars, or more Saudi-Arabians when the oil price shot up like a rocket after the 1973 Arab-Israeli war, or more hot totty (Erik Steiner's Pair of Shoes the clear winner in that category), and my personal all-time favourite casino, for quite different reasons, was the Apron Strings, in Fulham Road, Chelsea, which you can read all about in the penultimate chapter, but none of the above ever generated more excitement than Antonio Mancini's all electric White Elephant. The man who came second, but not that close a second, first in his Clermont casino and later, often with my illegal help, in his Hans Street casino, of which more later, was the too often written about John Aspinall. JVA had his good points, and was certainly more interesting than the faceless bookies who dominated the rest of the field, but Mr Tony Mancini goes down in my history book as the man with the golden touch. RIP Tone, if you're a goner. Enjoy your blackjack if you're still here. You don't play BJ as well as you play poker, but you're not bad.

Many of the staff at the White Elephant were Italians who came from Italy in the late fifties and early sixties to work in London's Italian restaurants and coffee bars, and then slipped effortlessly into much better paid jobs in casinos. Others were London Italians, like Mancini himself, whose English roots went deeper. One such Italian Londoner was a doorman who upset a London gangster called Ronnie Knight (not a difficult task) on his way in for a punt. Shortly after the incident the doorman was stabbed to death. The London Italian community always blamed the killing on Ronnie Knight, a well-known hard man, and a much envied ladeez man too, in between handing out the grievous bodily harm and raking in the money. His name was often linked with a young actress who was making a name for herself and her chest measurements in comedy films, and still graces our TV screens today, in a rather different role. Or not.

There were no witnesses suicidal enough to testify against Knight, but a lot of bad feelings swirled around. No-one likes a bully, even if they keep quiet when he's actually in the room. Some London Italians talked of a whip round to raise enough money to have him killed. But nothing came of it. As far as I know he died in bed. Most of them do.

The White Elephant was in the second rank of West End casinos, just a notch or two below the top joints. Except at the poker table it didn't attract many of the really big players, who went to the Curzon House, or Crockfords when it was down by the Mall, or to the Clermont. But it got plenty of medium to large punters and Mancini made a handsome living.

The most flamboyant of the late shift dodgy croupiers came from Les Ambassadeurs, then owned by a Polish ex-soldier with the very English name of John Mills (borrowed from a film poster seen through an office window after an immigration bureaucrat's third attempt to spell the captain's Polish name had failed). Like many Jews who found refuge in England from the Nazis, and in Mills' case fought in the British Army, John Mills was probably one of the very few survivors of a large family, like the late Captain Robert Maxwell M.C. who also fought bravely in the British Army only to discover after the war was over and the death camps were closed down that his only surviving relative in Czechoslovakia was a female cousin. As a result Mills would have had no family to keep an eye on the shop when he was away on holiday, unlike Bob Barnett of the Curzon House, a much earlier immigrant. Bob had his wife, his brother, his brother's wife, and their two sons who could look out for thieves without filling their own boots, something no hired vigilante could ever be relied on to do.

Because of his weaker position, an unspoken agreement evolved between John Mills and the livelier members of his staff. Wages were about twenty percent lower than in the other top clubs, but the casino always lost in August (or made a lot less than expected) when John Mills was enjoying the sunshine at his villa in the South of France. The arrangement probably kept the annual balance about right. I must point out that the figure quoted doesn't include the usual twenty or thirty percent of the profits that leaked away during the rest of the year, and gave the livelier croupiers some money to spend in the White Elephant. John Mills didn't know about that.

The man from Les A (the cool way to speak of Les Ambassadeurs; only hicks from the sticks spell out the whole name) played big, and regularly threatened to turn the roulette table over when something displeased him. Which seemed to happen much more often to him than it does to most of us. He played the role of arrogant rich man with a talent no-one had recognised only a short time before when he waited on tables in a restaurant. His threats were taken seriously. He contributed a fair share of what should have been Les Ambassadeur's roulette profits, in Lady Penelope 's dream world, to the roulette profits of the never stolen from White Elephant. Especially in August when John Mills was on his expensive holiday. He was treated like a VIP, and quite often given some money back or had his bet moved to a more profitable pay-out, in what was looked on as a necessary expense. The trick was to strike the right balance between paying a bit extra often enough to keep his ego intact and his stolen cash rattling across the White Elephant French roulette table, or seeing him take his money elsewhere. Every casino has players like that. The afore-mentioned Captain Robert Maxwell M.C was a master of the art.

It always upset me to see a casino man handing over his takings to another casino. Why not keep it, I used to think? I knew our way of life couldn't last forever. The bad guys always win in the end. He must have known it too. He wasn't stupid. But I was beginning to understand that it's easier to shake the heroin monkey off your back than it is to escape from roulette.

I never saw the Italian restaurant owner throw my money away at the White Elephant, hoping to double his money on the way to the Cavendish and give us all a treat. I was always at the Curzon when he was playing, looking forward to my red wine in a coffee cup and dreaming of my share of the money. In the early days I didn't even know that it was being squandered at the White Elephant, and that few of my dreams were destined to have a happy ending.

The casino was on the first floor. The restaurant on the ground floor of the White Elephant casino was also known as the White Elephant, confusingly, and was where the film people went to set up deals, or to celebrate done deals, the dull money men mixing with the more colourful film stars. Or sometimes the other way round. The White Elephant survived the rigours of the 1968 Gaming Act (Mancini was clean, prison record wise, unlike so many of his contemporaries), and only shut down in the seventies because he sold it to a company called London Clubs. Perhaps he got bored with all the probity and integrity. London Clubs transferred the licence to print money to the Ritz Hotel, and opened the new Ritz Casino in the basement of that august Piccadilly landmark. The White Elephant restaurant stayed open as the film stars' eating place, but went slowly downhill, and became a casino again in the nineties when John Aspinall (you'll meet him later, in spirit at least) sold his Aspinall-Curzon casino for a fortune, bought the old Elephant for a song and turned it into the most fashionable gambling club in the world.

I had a friend who was an inspector at the White Elephant in the early seventies, before the sale. Basic pay wasn't bad, and every inspector got an illegal percentage of his table's winnings at the end of the night. It was a good incentive to run the table well and probably increased the profit in the long run, although even a casino owner can't beat Lady Luck every night. (The percentage was illegal because it was paid in cash, away from the grasping hand of the taxman). Payment was made on the understanding that everyone kept quiet. Mancini would have lost his casino licence and he and his croupiers would have been nicked if some bigmouth had blabbed. I can talk freely now because I'm a historian, and anyway the joint has been shut for ages and nobody gives a toss any more. My friend did well and was very sad when the casino shut down and he faced the prospect of working somewhere dull. But the sadness didn't last. He found a job in a casino in Amsterdam, some years before casinos in Holland were legalised, and regularly came home with a briefcase full of cash that wasn't really his. The illegal Dutch casino owner was no match for a fast-fingered Italian who had learnt the tricks of his trade in London, England.

Beware of Greeks Bearing Gifts.

We've done the Italian. Let's go for a Greek. The Greek came to London from his home in Cyprus, with a small amount of money and a bag full of ambitions. In the casino Big Bang of the early sixties he raised enough cash to open a joint in just to the North of Hyde Park, and prospered. From day one. But the shoestring starting capital still left him defenceless against the local protection gang. He couldn't afford to fight back. Killing people cost a lot of money, and could qualify for the death penalty; serious injuries were almost as expensive and might fail to have the desired effect on professional criminals for whom violence was an every day occurrence. He bit the bullet and paid up, for a while.

The Greek was a patient man. When he had enough money, after a couple of years of high profits and low tax (he didn't flaunt his new wealth in front of the tax-man), he hired an American gangster to frighten off the local pests. A big man called Buggy flew over from New York, first-class. Buggy pointed his very big gun at the London hoods and told them that their contract with the Greek was terminated, with immediate effect.

The Londoners took him seriously. Buggy's accent was hard to follow, but his gun and his killer's eyes were easy to understand. In fact it was all bluff, apart from the gun. The Londoners could have got together and killed the American, or had him killed by someone else, except for one small problem: they didn't know that Buggy was the Lone Ranger. He and the Greek gave the impression that Buggy was the point man for the New York Mafia. A man with connections like that you do not shoot.

Everything was looking good. The American got his payment and was already fingering the return half of his ticket to New York. The London protection gangsters got the message. Casino profits were set to rise by at least fifty percent. Everybody dance! But there's always one. Somebody told Buggy that he was a fool to do so much for so little. He should ask for double what he had been paid, or, better than that, take over the whole protection racket and get a regular income. He was a big-time New York gangster, not some punk from Hicksville. And his English adviser would be happy to join in, for a decent share of the loot.

Buggy was no intellectual, but he had a lot of confidence in his gun. Nobody he had shot with it ever stood up again. It sounded good. Not running the protection racket. Too much hassle. And it might involve staying in London. He would miss the Bronx, and the limies were beginning to get on his nerves. But double the money would come in handy. Life in New York wasn't getting any cheaper.

He went back into the casino office, pulled out his very big gun for the second time and explained that his fee had doubled. The Greek was in the office with two or three of his top men. He feigned instant surrender and told Buggy that one of his men would go to the safe in another room and come back with more cash. Lots more cash. He gave instructions in Greek, a language the American had never mastered. Buggy thought it was all in the bag, but kept his finger on the trigger just in case.

The messenger left the room by one door, slipped silently through a door behind the American and shot him in the back several times. Buggy fell down dead. The Greeks wrapped him in the rug he had been standing on, quickly, before the blood seeped through and stained the floorboards, took him out of the back door of the casino, manhandled him with difficulty in to the back of a van and drove to a secluded spot on the Essex coast where the remains of redundant criminals were often disposed of. Buggy was transferred from the van to a motor boat, weighed down with something heavy, and buried at sea. If there is anyone still alive who was there on the day, even if you were only a witness, please don't get in touch. It's over now. Let bygones be bygones.

There was something in a daily paper a while later about a body that washed up on the Essex coast, identified by dental records as an American from New York. Foul play was not suspected. If it was Buggy the time he spent underwater had removed any evidence that he had been shot. I was drinking whisky in an illegal late night drinking den when I was told this story. I really didn't want to know, but the story-teller wouldn't shut up. Someone else had told it to him and he was trying to unload some of his fear on to me. People do that. I wished he'd picked someone else. The alleged murder had only recently happened and alleged murderers can do unpleasant things to people who know too much. It was one damned thing after another. A week or so before we were talking, or rather my friend was talking and I was trying not to listen, a man was arrested and charged with a murder that took place very close to the dive we were drinking in. There was no connection, but knowing about it made me uneasy. And we were very close to the Greek casino. Just to shred my nerves a little more, the mad Irishman we were drinking with did a very silly thing.

The dive wasn't run like your average English pub. No beer, no cissy wine, and definitely no orange juice. Real men only drank spirits, from a bottle marked by a pencil line (very) roughly at the level where the last drinker left off. When you finished drinking you took the bottle back to the bar and a new pencil mark was made. The barman measured the difference and payment was made by the inch (rounded up to favour the house), at an extortionate rate. Given the company we were keeping and the price of the booze it was probably safer and cheaper to drink whisky in Dodge City. The mad Irishman (not a term of racial abuse, or a lazy stereotype, he really was as crazy as a loon) noticed that we had drunk an awful lot of inches of whisky and would have to part with an awful lot of cash. He moved the bottle under the table. I heard a sound like running water and realised with genuine horror, not to mention intense fear, that he was peeing in the bottle, to raise the level and lower the price. He must have been going through an uncharacteristically stingy phase; he was only saving a fraction of the money he had in his trouser pocket, most of which didn't belong to him anyway, strictly speaking. Or he was having a particularly mad day, even by his already high standards. Given the chance, which had now gone, I would rather have paid double and walked out in one piece. How could you piss in a shared bottle in a room full of some of the most dangerous characters you could ever hope never to meet, you fucking nutter, I found myself asking, very nearly out loud.

We were as far as it was possible to be from the steps that led up from the basement room to the front door and the comparative safety of the street. Out there it was the sixties. Peace and love and flowers in your hair. I remember it well. But none of that hippy stuff cut any ice in the cellar where whisky was sold by the expensive inch, with or without an optional side serving of piss. The mad Irishman went to pay. I held my breath and prayed that none of the hard men had seen the Irishman's knob balancing delicately on the top of the whisky bottle and decided to shoot us all. Serious criminals take respect very seriously. Pissing in a whisky bottle that they might well have drunk from themselves, as the dawn light came closer to peeping through the curtains, would have been considered very disrespectful by the vast majority of our fellow drinkers. We didn't even do that at boarding school. If we had escaped the attention of the hard men, by a miracle, I fervently hoped that the barman wouldn't notice a difference in the colour of the whisky, or a lingering aroma of piss. Our luck was in. The hard men stayed in their seats. The barman measured the distance between the pencil marks and came up with a quote. The Irishman handed over the cash as if nothing had happened. And a generous tip. Maybe he drank so much whisky that he peed pure alcohol with exactly the right colour and smell. A real genuine miracle if ever I saw one. Anyone can turn water into wine, with a bit of sleight of hand, but turning whisky into piss and getting away with it is much harder, especially in a room full of men with guns.

The door was still miles away. But we made it into the night air, unharmed by human gun. I ran to my car and drove off fast, not giving a damn where the hell anybody else was. One friend had burdened me with the story of a recent murder, and another came close to turning me into a murder victim. I should form a circle and hold their hands?

Those dodgy bars only opened when the pubs and the proper bars shut. During legal opening times no-one with any sense sense paid five times the price for whisky an Irishman might have pissed in.

A few years after the whisky incident, when he had made a fortune from his now independent London casino, the Greek set up a casino at the top of a Greek mountain, not too far from Athens. Greeks are probably the most enthusiastic and addicted gamblers in Europe, although I can't prove that scientifically. He made a second fortune, even bigger than the first. Then things went badly wrong. A gang of Greek colonels staged a military coup and installed a Fascist government. The new regime, similar to the Fascist government of General Franco in Spain, was supported by many wealthy Greeks, including John Latsis, a Greek ship owner who was alleged to have collaborated with the Nazis during their occupation of his country during World War Two and, much later, occasionally lent his yacht to our own Prince Charles and his two wives, probably not at the same time. Obviously not friendly enough with John Latsis and his like, the Greek casino man became an enemy of the colonels. Maybe the soldiers who stole the country lost too much money gambling in his casino, and took it personally. Late one evening the Greek's limousine was climbing up the steep winding road that led to the top of his mountain. On a piece of ground by an exceptionally sharp bend, with a very long drop from the edge, an unlit military vehicle lay in wait. As the big car passed by, very slowly because of the bend and the very long drop, bullets from a heavy machine gun flicked through the steel and glass and into the bodies of the men inside. The big gun moved from side to side and up and down, following the procedure for which I believe the correct military term is sweeping the target area. Then the military vehicle pushed the car over the cliff at what was obviously a carefully chosen spot, thanks to its long drop to the unforgiving rocks below, and put an end to anyone who had miraculously survived the long burst of machine gun fire. A spokesman for the army that had stolen the country sincerely regretted the accident, officially, but made no mention of the many bullets in the car and in its occupants, an unusual feature even in a country where road rage is a way of life.

After the Greek died his son took over the London casino. Sadly he lacked his father's business acumen. One story tells it all. He noticed that the dice table at the Greek casino was losing heavily. Being the only person in the casino who hadn't twigged that the table was losing money because it was being robbed very enthusiastically by the staff, anxious to fill their boots in case the casino didn't survive the change of ownership, a strong probability, he came to the eccentric conclusion that the game was luckier for the players than it was for the house, casually ignoring the well established rules of arithmetic and the long and profitable history of the game. To cash in on his new theory he played dice for high stakes at another casino, where the relationship between staff and punters was all above board, and lost even more money than his skilled staff were nicking from the dice table back home. Original thinking isn't always a good idea.

On a lighter note than murders and politics and all that heavy stuff, a very funny thing once happened at the Greek casino. Shortly after day shifts were brought in—in the early years all gambling took place after dark—some of the American roulette staff prepared a hit. A couple of barons came in, with half a dozen hangers-on who were brought along to form a human shield that would keep undesirables away from the table. Television was still something you watched in your living-room, but it paid to be wary of people standing close behind you when you were robbing a joint. The pit-boss arranged for a carefully chosen dealer and inspector to be on the table, along with another carefully chosen dealer to pick up the chips.

The pit-boss had told the crooked players not to start playing big until the dealer adjusted his bow-tie with both hands. With a flourish. Ostentatiously even. Then, whatever the winning number, a lot more money would leave the table than was put down on it and be shared out at the Cavendish early next morning. It would all happen as soon after the two o'clock opening time as possible, before anyone not required to help had properly woken up.

A problem arose. The manager had hired a new croupier and he was starting work that very day. Unfortunately he hadn't told the pit-boss. He brought the new recruit over to the table and instructed the pit-boss to put him on first, to give him a chance to get used to the new place during a quiet afternoon game. The pit-boss couldn't refuse. But it was just a hiccup. He was a pro. He could leave the new boy on the table for half an hour and then put the proper croupier on and get back to plan A. There was no need for a Plan B. As a bonus, as soon as the trial run was over, the pit-boss could take the new boy away from the table and over to the manager, and waffle on about how good his performance had been. (Or not). The task of robbing the casino would be left in the capable hands of the chosen inspector and dealer, with plenty of time to make a decent job of it. The bent players would just have to play small for a while.

There was a fly in the ointment. There was no way to tell the players about the change of plan. To make things worse, the manager hung around the table to see how his new dealer got on. Normally he would have been on the other side of the room, fiddling with his paper-work and drinking coffee in an effort to wake up at this ungodly hour, perhaps strolling across when he noticed that the table was exceptionally busy for an afternoon, by which time the dastardly deed would have been done.

The new croupier glanced at the players. Not a pretty sight. They looked like a gang of bloodthirsty pirates ready to jump his ship and hack him to pieces. Working in London suddenly seemed very different. You didn't get this shit in Brighton. He felt very nervous. In an attempt to calm himself down he pulled hard at both ends of the shiny new bow-tie he had bought to celebrate his new job. Hot to trot now that the signal had been given, like horses at the start of a race, the bent players scooped wads of cash out of their pockets and changed it for chips. The pit-boss experienced a sinking feeling in his stomach. He couldn't say put your cash away, the fucking manager's standing beside me. The thieves probably recognised the manager, but thought he was part of the team, standing there to keep a close eye on his money. A bent manager wasn't a rare breed, back in the good old days. The croupier spun the ball. An avalanche of chips crashed on to the table. The number that came up was one of the few with not many chips on it. The croupier paid out the small winnings, which were much less than the total stake. He noticed an ugly mood among the players, nervously adjusted his bow-tie again, and sent the little white ball spinning round for the second time. Once again came the avalanche of chips. Once again came a number with a small number of chips on it. Once again a correct but small pay-out was made. The mood of the players grew uglier. The pit-boss tried to communicate with them by means of facial expressions, and failed. Mime isn't everyone's bag. After a few more lucky spins for the house the bent gamblers had lost all their money. They left, muttering threats of violence in the general direction of the pit-boss, whose face had run out of expressions.

When they had gone the manager publicly congratulated the new boy and silently congratulated himself on shrewdly picking such an obviously lucky croupier. What judgement. Must tell the boss. Not many managers could have hired a croupier straight from the sticks with such an uncanny ability to find so many nearly empty numbers on a table covered with so many chips. The new croupier was pleased to get his London job, much better paid than his job in the sticks. His nervousness wore off and was replaced with pride as he listened to the manager saying all those nice things about him. But after he settled in to the new place he noted sadly that some of the other roulette staff never really took to him. In the last place he'd got on well with everybody.

90

The pit-boss was careful to avoid dark alleys. He always left the casino with a crowd, especially late at night. He stayed with a girl-friend for a couple of weeks, in a dreary suburb miles from the casino, without explaining why she had suddenly become so irresistible. He kept well away from his own flat, uncomfortably close to the casino, and escaped without injury, I'm glad to say. The boys had probably cleaned up somewhere else and were too busy spending their money to waste time kicking the shit out of a plonker. It wasn't his fault anyway. Just a twist of fate. The worst ones always came out of a clear blue sky. Or out of a dark night, high up on a mountain.

In the next chapter we'll stay international and take a close look at the ups and downs of an American in London. I think you'll like him. I did, some of the time.

Skip.

As chemin-de-fer began its long slide into oblivion the new London casino owners and their smart lawyers became ever bolder in their search for more games. The American dice game known as craps, or crap dice (or just plain dice) followed in the footsteps of roulette and blackjack. You may remember seeing Marlon Brando playing the game with the inelegant name in the film version of Guys and Dolls, and singing "Luck Be a Lady Tonight" at the same time. Not easy, even for someone who can sing. The Playboy Club, a natural magnet for American visitors, many of whom thought the Bunny Club was the only casino in London (an error never corrected by the senior staff) made the most of its American connections and quickly built up the best dice game in town.

The managers of one well-known casino found a novel use of the space where dice are thrown and money is lost. Late one night, just after closing time, a female employee in her middle thirties (still a good-looking woman, but feeling the chill winds of forty blowing colder by the day), was easily talked into climbing on to the dice table and having sex with a handsome young croupier, in full view of the newly installed closed circuit television camera. The naked lady, acutely aware that the boys in the back room held her much needed pay-rise in their hands, put everything she'd got into her performance. The young man, very happy to be where he was but blissfully unaware that he had an audience, put everything he'd got into her. Their joint efforts brought great joy to the men huddled round a screen in a small sweaty office many floors above the empty streets of early morning Mayfair. I don't know if the lady got her pay rise, but according to one of the eye-witnesses it would be a travesty of justice if she didn't.

Next day's dice players never once suspected that a quite different game had taken centre stage among the numbers they were addicted to. The two actors cleaned up carefully after the show, rightly confident that the regular cleaners would not take kindly to scraping dried semen off the green baize. If a smudgy black and white tape still exists it must be worth a packet to a collector of casino memorabilia. Sure beats furry dice dangling in the back of your car.

Every game has to have a boss. A familiar face for the mugs to become accustomed to and someone for the casino owner to shout at when things go wrong. There were a few Brits good enough to deal the game, mostly young Londoners who had learned dice while working in the Bahamas, carefully, but none with sufficient experience as leaders of men. One top casino seduced a pit-boss called Skip (no, of course it's not his real name) from a well paid job in Las Vegas and flew him over to an even better paid job in London, England.

I expected someone like Dean Martin to come bustling in, all teeth and big hair, to set up the loud and vulgar and very profitable new game on virgin English soil; but Skip looked like Dave Brubeck without a piano. It didn't matter. He ran the game very well, as was to be expected from an experienced Nevada professional.

Skip worked closely with a middle-aged Londoner known as a shil, a Yiddish word that describes a man paid by a casino to act like a gambler when no real gamblers are around. The shil's presence ensures that the mugs don't come to a cold and lonely table and lose their nerve and walk away with their money still in their pockets. Casinos don't like that. We're not there for fun you know. So in the early days every top London casino hired a shil to lean on the dice table, look as much like Marlon Brando as nature permitted, throw a few dice, play with a few chips, and help the first mug to overcome his shyness, pull out some cash and get a real game going. Once real money changed hands the shil stopped pretending to play dice and became a public relations man, with the help of a greasy smile and an endless string of clichés. Being a shil wasn't the most exciting job in a sixties casino, but it was easy and it was well paid and you didn't get flak from the losers. Even the dimmest of the mugs knew that the shil was the little sprat dangling in the water to catch the much bigger mackerel, but they willingly accepted him as one of their own. People leave their brains at home when they go out to gamble. In return the shil pretended to sympathise when the paying customers lost (and paid his wages) and sometimes even pretended that his own losses were real.

Employing a shil became illegal after 1968. Not that it stopped us from having one at Aspinall's when we opened in 1978, ten years later, well into the era of Lady Penelope's respectable casino owners devoted ever more fervently to probity and integrity. Our shil was an affable old piss artist with an aristocratic manner, a superb wine connoisseur who selected the club's fabulous wines when he wasn't pretending to be a roulette or punto-banco player. (We didn't have dice at Aspinall's). His name was Ian Maxwell-Scott. Ian, or possibly Iain, I suppose he must have been Scottish with a name like that, played with chips I advanced him for free. Or somebody else did if I wasn't there. It was blatant law-breaking, but in a small private casino in Hans Street nobody sees you cheat. Ian Maxwell-Scott was very good at playing roulette or punto banco with somebody else's money, and making real players feel less lonely. I think he had been a gambler once, until his money ran out. In the outside world he was rumoured to be the last person to see Lord (Lucky?) Lucan alive, apart from the gangsters who killed him. Allegedly.

The dice game took off, big time. Skip earned good money and settled down happily in London, England. Then he discovered that

93

anyone with a bit of cash could open a casino in London. You didn't even need a licence. He couldn't believe his luck. He checked out the new information with several people, in case the piss was being taken out of a gullible foreigner. In old Las Vegas you had to have a licence, and good friends in the Mafia, and abide by all sorts of irritating regulations. And hope you didn't upset someone with serious small-arms skills. Or an electric drill (don't ask). In London you just got some tables, hired some dealers, opened the door, and watched the waves of cash come pouring in. Then you retired to Florida and lived high off the interest. How could a go-getting American resist? Skip gave in his notice, rented a basement room just off Oxford Street, in the area sometimes described as North Soho, bought some second hand tables, hired some dealers, and prepared to live the American dream in London, England.

In the beginning all his dreams came true. Money poured in, not from dangerous big players who could occasionally kill you (financially) but from lots of small players. Small players very rarely have a winning streak. But nothing lasts for ever. Or, in this case, for very long. One evening, around midnight, Skip's joint was jumping. Waves of money were flowing across the tables and into Skip's early retirement fund. Then the nightmare began. Four men with girls' stockings pulled over their faces swaggered into the little casino, waving shotguns.

Skip kept his cash locked away in his tiny office, with no plans to burden the taxman with the job of working out the government's share. He gave it all to one of the men with guns and didn't waste time discussing the rights and the wrongs. The hard men had the rights and Skip was at the wrong end of a shotgun. When the safe was empty he opened the cash boxes on the tables and handed over all the money he had hoped to win that night. One of the other gang members ordered the women in the room to line up along a wall, pull their knickers down, and leave them resting round their ankles. Try that at home (with your wife's knickers if you're a man) and see how fast you can run. The men, including the dealers, were lined up against the opposite wall with their trousers down and their hands in the air. No-one should be stupid enough to wave a pop-gun at four widely separated men with sawn-off shotguns, but the robbers were professional men who took no chances. To everyone's relief the men were allowed to keep their underpants on.

Trying not to sneer at the knobbly knees and the sagging thighs, the gang members collected all the watches, jewellery, wallets, cash in pockets, contents of handbags, and even the wallets and the handbags themselves if they looked more than averagely expensive. And two small hand-guns the owners were sensible enough to leave in their pockets. One of the younger robbers noticed that a young woman's legs were bare. He flicked

94

up her short skirt with the business end of his gun. The cheeky action brought a blush to the poor girl's face, and a murmur of appreciation from some of the men when her small triangle of dark curly hairs flashed into the room. It was impossible to approve of such a reaction at such an inappropriate moment. It wasn't funny. Fear of rape must have flashed through the poor girl's head. She was the best looking woman in the place. By a mile. If anyone was going to get raped it had to be her. But when you've lost most of your money gambling and you've given the rest to a man with a shotgun and you're skint and you're scared and you're standing against a wall with your trousers round your ankles and you're wondering what would be left of you if one of the shotguns went off, you need all the entertainment you can get.

The men with the guns and the money walked off into the night and locked the door behind them. Knickers and trousers were pulled up, someone forced the door open, everybody went home, and Skip's first casino bit the dust.

A lesser man would have given up, admitted the limeys weren't the jerks he'd taken them for, and gone back into paid employment. Or bought a ticket home. But Skip was made of sterner stuff. Now that he knew that London had criminals too, just like Vegas, he set up shop again. He found premises in Stoke Newington, in those days a low class area where many gangsters came from. And, not by coincidence, the site of the most corrupt police station in the capital. He arranged a protection contract that said goodbye to a considerable percentage of his anticipated profits but promised immunity from men with guns, and waited confidently for the second flood of cash to come pouring in. Sunny Florida floated back into view.

Skip hired a small hard core of permanent staff, and arranged for a few dealers from his old casino to work for him on their nights off. Cash in hand and all the tea you could drink. Everybody else was invited along to have a punt and contribute to Skip's early retirement fund.

Golden Bollocks had made friends with Skip. He suggested popping into Skip's new place after we finished work. Always ready to do something stupid, I jumped at the chance. The casino filled the combined living and dining room of a grey and ugly terraced house in a grey and ugly street. In the hall a scary looking hulk glared at potential customers from behind a small table. A badly concealed double-barrelled sawn off shotgun lay across his feet. He held a big glass of clear liquid in his hand. The hulk's job was to point his gun at anyone he thought might be thinking of holding up the joint, based on his encyclopaedic knowledge of London's criminal classes. Rumour had it that in his day job he was a constable at the local police station. I began to feel nervous. GB and I had arrived at about four in the morning. We got lost on the way. We only knew the posh parts of town, apart from Soho, and in those days Stoke Newington definitely wasn't posh. The joint was busy. We walked up to Skip and talked to him in a very we're good friends of the boss sort of way, to show the other players that we weren't any old riff-raff strolling in off the street. The new place had been open for about a week. The money was piling up, Skip assured us, and he was as safe as houses under the protection of the hulk in the hallway.

I recognised a friend from the Curzon, dealing at the only blackjack table. It was Pat, the mad Irishman and whiskey diluter in the illegal drinker in Bayswater, on what used to be known as the wrong side of the Park. A man who had come closer than anyone I knew to getting my brains blasted out of my head. But not maliciously. It was just a knack he had. As a person I really liked him. I began to feel uneasy. Last time Pat and Golden Bollocks and I were together in the same room (in similar company) things very nearly went seriously wrong. Against my better judgement I headed for the blackjack table. Directly in front of Pat a very big man with a look of intense concentration on his ugly face was playing blackjack. He looked like his shoulders would burst out of his jacket at the slightest provocation and he would rampage round the room killing anyone he didn't like the look of with his bare hands. Or teeth. Men like that are truly terrifying to share a room with, never mind a gambling table. I changed my mind about playing blackjack. Some people don't like the way other players draw cards. I could handle snide remarks but I didn't fancy getting my head ripped off.

The big man was just settling into a winning streak when another very tough looking man came up behind him, wrapped both arms around his huge barrel chest, and shouted out some very rude words. We found out later that the man playing blackjack and the man holding him tight had once robbed a bank together, as good friends sometimes do. Then the man playing cards shopped his accomplice to the police and grabbed all the loot. When his old friend was behind bars the gambling man lived the life of Riley, with twice as much money as he should have had by rights. He obviously didn't know that his fellow bank robber had paid his debt to society (or found a ladder) and come looking for his old pal.

The gambling man wrenched one of his arms free and pulled a very big automatic pistol from under his jacket. The angry man grabbed the gun in his own shovel-like hands. The barrel waved about as the two men struggled, but was always in a perfect position to convert Pat's chest into a bloody, bubbling crater. The Irishman froze in fear. His right hand stayed in the air, still holding the bank-robber's next card. It seemed best

96

not to make any sudden moves. He rediscovered God and silently muttered some prayers. The man behind the man in front kept trying to pull the trigger of the big automatic. A sensible move from his point of view. The gun would no longer be a threat if all its bullets were in Pat's chest. Or half in Pat and half in the wall. I wished I'd gone home.

The blackjack player managed to twist round and dislodge his ex-partner's grip on the gun. The other man jumped backwards and drew his own gun, with impressive speed. I still wished I'd gone home, but I couldn't help admiring the skill and bravery of the two thugs playing out their deadly game in front of us. Men like that earned medals in wars, in circumstances where I would have stayed hidden behind a rock.

Both men were on their feet, about two yards apart, each with a gun pointed at the other's chest. A classic stand-off. Fucking Hell thought Pat, I'm still in the line of fire, and dropped down under the table. He knew he should have done it before but, he told me afterwards, you don't always think at the time. He was better off on the floor, though not by very much. He was still close to the gun pointed roughly in his direction, but crawling across the floor seemed like a bad idea. There's something about a moving target. The two hoods could have snapped off a couple of shots before freezing back into their stand-off. At least he had a solidly built blackjack table between some of his body and the guns. It was better than standing up straight like a man in front of a firing squad. He was very careful to avoid eye contact. You do that. A very foolish part of your brain tells you that if a man with a gun hasn't looked you in the eye he won't shoot you. It's absolute bollocks of course, but it does make you feel better.

GB and I were to the side of the stand-off, near the roulette table. We dived under the table, along with most of the other people in the room. A man I'd never met before said that if the man with the automatic switched it on, a technical term I hadn't heard before, we were all dead. I wished he'd shut up.

They say that your whole life flashes past you when it seems likely to come to a sudden end. On the few occasions when I stared death in the face, very unwillingly, I always focused on one incident. My mind jerked back to when I was three or four years old and the Second World War was still raging. I was standing in a shop doorway in Barnet, not all that far from Stoke Newington, clutching my mother's hand and watching a V1 rocket, the first guided missile to be used in anger, come flying in from the East. The V1 was small and ugly and looked to a little boy like a model he could have made in his bedroom, with a bit of help from his dad. The engine switched off. Even at that age I knew that now the flying bomb would crash to the ground and blow up. You grow up quickly in a war. I was sure it would head straight for the shop doorway and kill my mother and me in a huge flash of flame. I buried my face in my mother's coat and waited for the end. But our luck was in. The rocket crashed into a nearby field and the only casualty was an unlucky cow, munching gently on its last meal.

I'll never know how long the stand-off lasted. The flashback helped to pass a few minutes. Or quite possibly a few seconds. I tried not to think of what would happen if a stray bullet hit my head, or any even softer part of my twenty five year old body. I thought useless thoughts about what I should have done instead of coming to Stoke bloody Newington. A glance at my watch told me that if I'd gone straight home I would be tucked up in bed now, instead of hiding under a second-hand roulette table listening to some bloody fool talking about switching on pistols.

All of a sudden it was over. The hulk from the hall had talked to the combatants, quietly, all through the stand-off, trying to negotiate a peace treaty. I noticed that he left his sawn off shotgun under the table in the hall, in flagrant breach of his contract. By nature I'm a fierce opponent of capital punishment, but if the hulk had killed both the men with guns with a barrel each from his sawn-off shotgun I have to admit that I would have been the first to applaud. Pull those triggers, you fat bent copper. Aim for the face. Wipe out all identity. Bang, bang, you're dead and nobody can tell who you were. Hooray.

The hulk's talking paid off. I started breathing again. The two ex-friends put away their guns and left the building, perhaps to murder each other somewhere else. Not that I gave a shit if they did, now that my own life seemed set to go on a bit longer. The man at the door waved his gun around and told the punters to sod off, quite unnecessarily. Most of them were already heading for the street. The big glass of neat gin, or vodka, that looked just like water but tasted much nicer, was nearly empty.

I ran to my car and drove off, not caring where I was going so long as it was out of Stoke Newington. Somewhere in East London I recognised a road I knew and drove home through the more expensive parts of town. Residents of upper class areas might invest in companies making money from bombs and missiles that can say goodbye to a medium-sized town, or get secretly excited when they watch TV and see hi-tech bombs and missiles raining down on a bunch of foreigners, but they almost never rush into the streets and wave guns at you. Class discrimination does have its good points.

Back in the empty casino the big man jabbed his shotgun hard into Skip's chest, informed him that the protection contract had expired, and relieved him of all his money. Skip noticed for the first time that his ex-business partner had really bad teeth. It was too much for Skip. Too many sawn-off shotguns pushed into vulnerable parts of his body. Too many sweaty drunken fingers curled round too many triggers. Good luck couldn't last for ever. No more comebacks. He spent his last few dollars on the cheapest ticket he could find and flew home to the peace and quiet of Las Vegas.

Some Real Dumps.

The money that their most valued customers took out of their pockets and flung into the air put the Greek (Cypriot) and the (London) Italian in the top casino class, compared to some of the joints that sprang up during the Wild West days of the early sixties. I only ever worked in posh casinos in London, but in my private hours I spent a lot of time (and money) feeding my addiction in some right old dumps. I'll give the word dump a proper, dictionary-style definition: a dump is a casino where mugs play for low stakes, lose what little they have fairly quickly, and bugger off home wondering why God is so unkind. The social backgrounds of the players vary widely but none have regular access to large amounts of money, and if ever they do wave large sums about you can be confident that they nicked it and that they won't have anything like as much to wave about tomorrow.

Nearly all of the dumps belonged to crooks and nearly all of them shut up shop when the 1968 Gaming Act threw a spanner in the works. You can't go and check them out for yourself, unless you have access to a time machine. But don't worry. I'll fill you in. Trust me, I'm a croupier.

Most casinos and most whorehouses have one virtue in common: all mugs are equal, whatever the colour of their skin, as long as they have money in their pockets and aren't too bothered about keeping it there. One early casino in the Earl's Court area was the exception that proved the rule. Like a government with no confidence in its policies the joint bowed to the wishes of its customers and put in place a floating colour bar. Wednesday night was blacks only. Thursday was Paki night. The rules were vigorously applied. Even the keenest gambler from the Indian subcontinent arriving on a Wednesday night was greeted with 'fuck off Paki, you know it's niggers' night. And if you didn't know you fucking do now.' Threatening look replaced by greasy smile. 'Come back tomorrow'. They weren't big on public relations in that part of Earl's Court. Or geography. Or politics. There was no formal recognition of the difference between Indians and Pakistanis. A Paki was a Paki was a Paki, whether he came from Karachi or Calcutta. Even when India and Pakistan were having one of their wars. And a nigger was a nigger, whether he came from the USA, the Caribbean, Africa or one of Peter Rachman's slum houses in Notting Hill. The verbal message was backed up with violence, when necessary.

I must stress that I'm using these offensive racist terms because I promised to give you an accurate description of London's less salubrious gambling joints. The rude words were used by the proprietor and his staff. I don't talk like that, even in private or in exclusively white company. I might be a (retired) thief but I'm also a bleeding-heart liberal, and very polite. Whites were welcome at any time, theoretically, but in practice

100

most of them only came in when the casino wasn't full of black or brown faces. After a while an extra night was dedicated to the Indian subcontinent, in recognition of the growing strength of the Indian and Pakistani business communities. Chinese were treated as whites, partly because Chinese Britons have always enjoyed a kind of invisibility in their adopted country, partly because they almost never got into fights, unlike the whites and blacks, and, to a lesser degree, the browns. (But on the rare occasions when a Chinese fight did take off some very scary kitchen knives flashed in the night).

Needless to say the casino did not survive the 1968 Gaming Act. The owner would have had trouble getting a driving licence, never mind a casino licence. He left casino gambling behind him, invested heavily in the expanding drug trade, and disappeared. There were strong rumours that he fell out with someone who had been in the drug business rather longer and that he was embedded in one of the concrete columns holding up the Hammersmith fly-over. Drive carefully if ever your sat-nav guides you over that busy raised road. Especially during rush-hour. If all the dead gangsters who are supposed to be curled up in those columns really are there it's a miracle the whole damn thing didn't fall down years ago.

There was a seriously low-life casino called the Golden Spinner, in a dirty, grey street close to Euston station, rarely walked along by middle class commuters. A friend of mine took six months off from respectability and became a mini-cab driver, rattling around in an old but trusty Mercedes. One of his first regulars was a gambler at the Golden Spinner. He asked to be picked up at midnight, on the dot, three nights a week. Watches were synchronised. The Mercedes screeched up to the entrance, engine running, passenger door kicked open, two hands firmly gripping the steering wheel. The gambler ran from the well lit entrance of the casino and dived into the front of the car. The Mercedes took off with a screech of tires and a smell of burning rubber. Not for show, or for fun, or because the gambler needed the exercise, or because he'd seen someone drive that way in a movie. If you were a big player, by the very low standards of the Golden Spinner, your chances of walking any distance down the street without being mugged were zero, particularly if you had won some money and (much more difficult) succeeded in getting the cashier to hand it over. The default option in crap casinos was to tell winners that their money would be kept on deposit and given to them to play with next time they dropped in. Only very determined regulars were given their winnings, grudgingly. It was obvious that there was co-operation between the thieves inside the casino and the thieves outside on the street. The street guys always hit the winners first. The gambler explained all this in detail to my friend, well in advance of the first pick-up, continually stressing the need for speed. My friend asked him why he didn't gamble somewhere safer. The man said that all his friends went to the Golden Spinner and that he would be lonely without them.

Somewhere near Kensington High Street there was a small casino called the Up All Night, not to be confused with a bar of the same name still trading to a specific clientele, as far as I know, in Fulham Road. I can't remember where it was exactly. I only went there once, in a taxi, drunk, with an alcoholic friend whose name was also Dave. Half way through a bad blackjack shoe I ran out of money and gave up my seat. You're not allowed to sit there and cry. A shifty looking man took my place, stuck a knife into my friend Dave's well-covered ribs, and demanded the equivalent of about fifty pounds in today's money. Dave told him to fuck off, quietly but rather bravely, possibly more bravely than he would have done on one of his rare sober days, and sat with the knife pressed against the left side of his rib-cage until he had lost all the cash the knife man had hoped to lose for him. I never went back. I don't suppose Dave did either.

Throughout the mid sixties little casinos sprang up everywhere in central London, and in the suburbs too. I rarely went out of the centre. West End criminals seemed more professional and less given to indiscriminate violence than their suburban cousins. And I was rich and spoilt and still clinging to a certain snootiness, not long after leaving an English public school, a German equivalent, and a private American university. The night I nearly got killed (nothing personal, wrong place at wrong time, still dead if it had all gone wrong) during my ill-advised trip to Skip's place in Stoke Newington strengthened my natural distrust of the criminal underclass, gave me a feeling that things fell apart in direct proportion to the distance from Piccadilly Circus, and reinforced my belief in the virtues of snootiness. Snooty people might have all sorts of other bad habits, but they very rarely kill or maim anyone they're not married to.

I did go out into the wilds one other time, to a casino in Clapham or Streatham (I always get them mixed up) that belonged to the Kray twins. Allegedly. The inside was all done out Wild West style. Saloon type swing doors and girl croupiers dressed in cowgirl outfits with lots of cleavage. And probably plenty of guns too, if you knew where to look. I lost all my money and didn't try to cheat in an attempt to get it back, bearing in mind the robust nature of the casino's owners. But on the way out I saw something glinting, deep down in a crack between the floor-boards. I prised it out with the Swiss Army knife someone gave me for a birthday present (I always knew I'd find a use for it one day) and trousered a gold coin that was worth a lot more than the contribution I'd just made to the Kray family firm's finances. Beat that for good luck in hard times.

Early in the sixties a policeman called Ted Box, allegedly, saved enough money from his wages to open the Connoisseur casino, in a basement below a pizza restaurant in Fulham Road. It was sometimes affectionately referred to as the Sewer, which rhymes if you don't speak French very well. The Sewer was popular with the younger Chelsea set. On some nights it was like a poor man's Apron Strings, a casino described in detail in the penultimate chapter of this very comprehensive book. The main difference between the two casinos was that in the Sewer cheques weren't welcome and riff-raff were, in limited numbers.

The staff were paid in cash, until the 1968 Gaming Act cleaned things up a bit. I had a Portugese friend who once worked at the Sewer. Saturday night was pay night. After the customers had gone home skint policeman Ted emptied the cash boxes on to the tables and handed out the wages in used notes. It was less than you earned in smart West End casinos, but with no tax taken off the difference soon disappeared. No good for a mortgage, but good pay for spending your evening in the company of young fun-loving people instead of the old gamblers who made life so dull in the posh joints, unless there was something illegal going on.

In the eighties Ted the cop sold the Sewer to a respectable company, for about a million quid, and died before he could make a real impact on the biggest lump sum he had ever seen. The respectable company was after the licence, not the premises, and moved the Sewer to what had been an all-night restaurant on the right hand side of the very expensive Royal Garden Hotel, next door to Princess Diana's old palace. The place I mentioned a few chapters ago where croupiers and better class tarts could get a sneaky after work coffee cup of red wine and sometimes exchange a bit of money. Last time I looked in it belonged to the Rank group. The staff all pay tax, in these hard times, and earn about a quarter (in modern money) of what their predecessors did when Ted the copper was in charge.

The gold medal for longevity among dumps goes to a casino called Charlie Chester's, once Soho's finest, which flourished for nearly forty years among book-shops and cinemas where the story of Adam and Eve is repeated over and over again, with variations (and accessories) that could not have been put on by the limited cast of the Garden of Eden. The serpent is dead. Long live the magic one-eyed trouser snake. Not far away, close to the old Windmill theatre where female nudity made its first legal stand, a primary school has bolted high extensions to its gates and walls in an attempt to limit the extra-curricular education the pupils of many nations might absorb from the surrounding streets, and hide them from the eyes of passers-by dreaming of partners even younger than the ones on sale outside. Something nasty haunts the pavements where men put away their childish things and visit parts of every big town in search of new, grown-up games.

The early owners of Chester's managed to get a licence in the clean up that followed the 1968 Gaming Act, and survived the 1980/1981 blitz during which the majority of the more salubrious West End casinos were shut down for breaking the new gambling laws in an attempt to hang on to their big players and, if possible, pull high rollers away from their rivals (an episode that I don't remember being referred to in Lady Penelope's plaintive speech). Charlie Chester's didn't have big players and had no need to run in that race. CC's customers were miscellaneous Soho low-lifes, and Chinese and other local ethnic restaurant owners and their staff. And me. I went in once, without enthusiasm because I had no arrangements with the boys and if I really have to play straight I like to get paid when I win. Sure enough I put a fiver on red and a red number came up and a tart nicked the fiver I won, along with my original stake. I protested, lightly, knowing that the lady wouldn't give in easily and that the croupier (who I knew, but not well enough) would back a regular player rather than a one-time wanker who played the even chances. On top of that the ho's pimp might tickle my ribs with a knife as a punishment for upsetting his valuable employee. Not worth it for a fiver.

Gambling has been called the Jewish disease, by a Jewish writer I believe, so that's all right, but it could just as easily be called the Chinese disease. Most casinos in boring provincial towns would be lost without the money brought in by local Chinese businessmen, often the owners of your local take-away. A more accurate description of the London gamblers' addiction would be to call it the disease of the self-employed, or of the ethnic groups most likely to contain a high proportion of self-employed businessmen. And businesswomen. Sorry. In sixties London this included Jews, Chinese, Indians, Greeks and Greek Cypriots, and Italians. Many an ethnic restaurant passed most of its profits to the nearest casino owner.

My friend the mad Irishman worked at Chester's in the late sixties, when things got too hot for him in the posh joints. He started on the day a blackjack table was installed in the reception area, opposite where the customers hung their coats. The idea was to catch a player, possibly a winner, shock horror, before he got his coat on, and get him gambling again. The new table was very unpopular with the staff. Most of the time there was no game, no inspector to talk to, and only three walls (you weren't supposed to turn around) and some coats to look at. Boring. Newcomers were dumped there until they screwed up the courage to complain. On Pat's first night a tough looking man came out of the main gambling room and pulled a long heavy raincoat over his shoulders, but didn't put his arms into the sleeves. He had his back to Pat and spent some time shuffling about under the coat. Pat wondered idly if the dirty devil was playing with himself, but quickly dismissed the idea. He didn't look the type and the soft clicks and mechanical noises didn't have a sexual tone. Then the man half turned towards Pat, on his way to the door, and gave Pat a glimpse of the sub machine gun he had been busy loading. Pat looked at a different wall, anxious not to make eye contact with a man carrying a lethal weapon. Once bitten twice shy, after the events at Skip's place.

Machine-gun Kelly left, and came back half an hour later. Pat was still standing at the same table. There was a dull clunk as the man hung up his coat. A big bundle of cash was thrown at Pat, and a gruff order to get shuffling. Why do men with guns always pick my fucking table, Pat asked himself, assuming that the cash was the haul from a quick and efficient hold-up of a nearby business. As the late Al Capone is supposed to have said: 'You can go a long way with a nice smile, but you can go a lot further with a nice smile and a gun.' Pat vaguely hoped that no-one had been killed in the raincoat man's search for a stake.

Writing about Soho has reminded me of another now-you-see-it-now-you-don't dump that I forgot to put on my dump-to-do list. A casino existed, briefly, in a cellar below the Windmill theatre, the up-market strip club that entertained a mostly male audience a few hundred yards from Charlie Chester's, and half that distance from the high-walled primary school that provided a liberal education for the children of Soho. I dropped in one night and found myself standing at the first dice table I had ever seen that was staffed entirely by girls. Very good-looking girls. The only other players were four boisterous Americans, talking (shouting) the kind of bollocks that only American dice players can get away with in public. The dice were clear and transparent. The American whose turn it was to throw the dice picked up the colourless cubes, wrapped them tightly in his big hands, shouted out some of the old dice-players' prayers--baby needs a new pair of shoes etc, etc--and threw a shiny pair of orange dice down the table. Loaded orange dice, of course. Please, I thought, if you're going to switch the dice, a popular move down the ages in casinos where there's a reasonable chance that you won't be killed if you're caught, at least make sure that the loaded ones are the same colour as the ones thoughtfully provided by the house. Size doesn't matter that much, but colour really does.

The girls either didn't notice the sudden change--they were obviously new to the game--or they were in on the act. Unfortunately I had no way of knowing which. I thought briefly of joining in, with bets that were guaranteed to win, but I left the casino and never went back. I assumed that the owners were not from the officer and gentleman class and I didn't want to suffer physical harm if the shit hit the fan and the casino's non-gaming staff hit the Americans and then hit me when they decided, reasonably enough, that I was their British ally. Or too smart for my own good. Which was just as bad. It was probably a lost opportunity, but you never know. A year earlier I would have dived in regardless, but the goings-on at Skip's two joints had played havoc with my faith in the essential goodness of human nature. Going home skint and waking up in bed was a better bet than waking up in a Soho alley with a broken leg, empty pockets where my winnings had been, and severe damage to my youthful good looks.

There was a small casino called the Village Club, in Lower Sloane Street, just South of Sloane Square. I hesitate to describe the Village as a dump. I always try to be fair. I learnt that at public school. On the one hand (as economists say when they back into a corner under attack from a real-world question) the Village was a dump because it attracted mostly small players. On the other hand (the economist springs back out of his corner) it wasn't a dump because some of its modest players were really rather posh. I'll include it anyway, with both hands.

The Village was opened in the early sixties by an Englishman, a Frenchman and a Spaniard (I'm sorry if that sounds like the opening line of a bad joke), but not as a casino. It was a typical sixties bistro serving quite reasonable food and drink at quite reasonable prices, the sort of place where a chap could impress a female companion with his Chelsea sophistication. The interior was vaguely piney, and in a basement. In those days basements were all the rage for entrepreneurs with limited resources. Rents fell sharply if you conducted your business underground. A pretty girl with long blonde hair played several chords on a guitar and sang folk songs at the same time. Not everyone can do that. She didn't sing like Joni Mitchell and she didn't play guitar like Jimi Hendrix, but she had a very nice chest and a very nice smile and that was more than enough for the likes of me. If I wanted famous musicians I could go home and switch on the gramophone. She actually looked very like a girl I saw recently (late July 2009) in the car programme on telly. The one who navigated for James May in a Majorca car rally and got lost, but made up for it by painting pretty flowers on his helmet. Not everyone can do that either. She didn't burst into song but the facial resemblance was striking. The car wasn't moving while the helmet painting was going down, I hasten to add.

106

No health and safety issues there. James and his artistic navigator obviously didn't win the rally. You tend not to if you get lost and then waste valuable driving time on helmet decoration. But if such frivolities were included in serious petrol-head competitions he would definitely have copped first prize in the best helmet category.

The bistro hadn't been open very long when an anonymous looking young man who would never have been picked out in a line-up even if he was covered in blood, came in carrying something that looked like an ironing-board. He explained that the mystery object was a kind of blackjack table. Just like they had in the new casinos in Curzon Street, only smaller and easily folded up if someone you really didn't want to talk to came clomping down the stairs. He was willing to pay a modest rent if he could erect it for a couple of hours a night, opposite the bar. Stakes were low so there wouldn't be any suicides. The Englishman and the Frenchman and the Spaniard all agreed that the ironing-board was a good idea. The rent would be handy, and their better-off customers could show their girl-friends what sophisticated devils they were and increase their chances of getting a leg over that night. Or early next morning. All the girls love a bad boy. Especially when he wins. Nobody would get too involved, or lose too much money. And the bistro would get the rent in cash, tax-free, with no liability to pay out on losing nights, the faceless man told them reassuringly, not bothering to mention that it was very unlikely that there ever would be a losing night.

After a while the Frenchman noticed that the ironing-board was making a bigger profit than the bistro that it was erected in for two hours a night. He didn't ask the board's owner how much money he was making (he would have been lied to anyway) and he didn't stand at the end of the table and count the takings. Too crude. But from the bar he was able to estimate the big difference between what went in and what went out. He was highly impressed. A few nights later the Englishman and the Frenchman and the Spaniard gave the man with the ironing-board the elbow and put in a full-sized blackjack table of their own, with rather higher stakes and no limits on how long the good times could roll. The Village bistro was now the Village casino.

When it was still a bistro with or without a casino on an ironing-board under the stairs the Village attracted a young, middle class clientele who worked in boring but financially promising jobs in the City, shared Habitat-furnished flats in Chelsea and Kensington, and bought their clothes at Mary Quant (the girls, mostly), before moving out to the suburbs or (even worse) to the country to marry and reproduce, usually in that order in those more innocent times. But when the gambling started in earnest the class profile moved simultaneously upwards and downwards.

At the top end of the social scale, genuinely wealthy young men (and women) began to come in. One of them was the son of a highly respectable and very rich chairman of a public company who dedicated his early adult life to seeing how quickly he could transfer his father's fortune to the casino owners of London. He started at the Village, probably because he lived close by, but soon moved to the late John Aspinall's Clermont casino, a much more appropriate venue for a fully paid-up member of the upper classes. Once there he continued his disposal of the family fortune, right up to and including the day his old man refused to come up with any more cash and he was forced to break the habit of a lifetime and get a proper job (as a casino manager, if you're kind enough to count that as a proper job). I first met him as a customer at Aspinall's next casino, in the late seventies, by which time he had become a serious gambler again, probably on inherited money. I may be wrong there, but his lively conversation never included references to anything as boring as work. Not that anybody held that against him in a club where I once heard a languid young man say (quite energetically for him) "DO? I don't DO anything," in response to the question "and what do you do?" that came at the end of a long and boring description of his interrogator's own business career.

The chairman's son became a celebrity, in his own small way, famous for being the man who won the most money in one night at the Village blackjack table. It was about four hundred pounds. Not exactly breaking the bank at Monte Carlo, you're right to bring that up, and I'm fully aware that nowadays one could easily spend that much without going anywhere near a blackjack table, especially if one likes to stuff one's face in restaurants owned by chefs who swear a lot on television. But in the sixties it was a tidy sum for a small casino to lose or for one man to win. Stick on another hundred and you could have bought a nearly new sports car (my white MGB with wire wheels for example, if I was a bit short at the time) and cruised along King's Road with the hood down, leering at mini-skirted girls from out of town and proving yet again that the best part of living in Chelsea is sneering at people who don't.

The prodigal son was inordinately proud of his achievement at the long-departed Village casino club. I remember him still talking about it in 1980 or 1981, at Aspinall's casino. I never told him because you don't upstage casino customers when you're a casino manager in case they get the hump and throw their money away somewhere else, but I actually beat his record in 1973, just after I got married. Sadly, unlike him, I had to give most of the money back. I was in the club with my wife and one of her many sisters and the sister's then fairly skint husband. I was the only one playing. Showing off, really. In fact I was the only one present who knew how to play, and the only one with any money to play with. A claim I can no longer make, being an undischarged bankrupt at the time of writing. I hit a winning streak of the quality you hit once every five years, if you're very lucky, and found myself up about six hundred pounds, well ahead of the previous record, of which I knew nothing at the time.

The Frenchman wasn't pleased. Casino owners don't like winners at the best of times, and new record holders are especially unwelcome. Unfortunately, although I always signed in under a false name, he knew my real name and he knew that I worked at the Playboy casino and he knew that my employers didn't allow me to go to other casinos, on pain of instant dismissal, and he knew that the Gaming Board regulations didn't allow croupiers to gamble in other British casinos, on pain of instant loss of their croupier's licences. And he probably had an idea that the money I was playing with wasn't strictly mine, not that that ever seemed to worry him on my losing nights. He stood at the end of the blackjack table and gazed at me with what I can only describe as a wintry smile. The dealers had just changed over. The departing dealer would have told the Frenchman that some snooty little bastard with a stunning girl-friend was breaking the bank. Snooty because my accent always went up a notch when I was winning, as if the classy Cambridge college that I didn't go to after all was calling me back home, and girl-friend because real men don't take their wives along when they play blackjack, for a very good reason. The odds change. If you lose you get a bollocking for wasting valuable family money, if you win she nicks the cash and goes shopping. That's not chauvinism, by the way, it's social studies.

No words were needed. The wintry smile told me that if I cashed out at the height of my winning streak, as my wife and my in-laws were very sensibly urging me to, the Playboy management would read all about it before my Chelsea boots hit the top of the Village stairs. My wife and I were beginning to suspect, rightly as it turned out, that there might soon be three of us, so getting fired and being black-listed was a really bad idea at the time. There was only one way out. I had to lose most of my winnings back to the casino. But I refused to lose it all. I had some pride, once. I stopped playing when I was still up about a hundred, confident that this would be acceptable to the Frenchman whose smile was becoming less wintry with every pound I returned to his casino. My wife and my in-laws watched with a mixture of compassion for a loser and contempt for an addict. I made no attempt to tell them the truth.

At the same time as the nobs appeared, so did the taxi-drivers (some of whom were mobile drug dealers as well as chaps who took you from A to B), and other working-class entrepreneurs, not all of them in strictly honest businesses, who were becoming part of the new, classless,

109

rock'n'roll sixties scene. The Village became a dump on some nights and a posh place on other nights, or more often than not a mixture of both. Money talked at the blackjack table, no change there, but away from the table the old British class system crept back in. The nobs and their ladies sat on one side of the room and the geezers and their girls sat on the other. Like oil and water separating in a test tube. I never quite knew where to sit. Life wasn't easy for a man with a foot in both camps. The nobs and I talked the same (like the Queen, but not so high pitched) and had been to the same sort of schools. The geezers were very similar to the people I robbed casinos with. In fact in some cases they were the people I robbed casinos with. But this wasn't something we discussed out loud, even in a casino we didn't rob. In the end I avoided eye contact with both sides and sat nervously in the middle, staring diffidently at the girl with the guitar.

When regulation and legality loomed in 1968 all three casino owners assumed that they would have to shut the casino part of the business and go back to food and wine and folk-songs. Possibly minus the folk-songs. In the brave new world of legal casinos they couldn't even erect their own ironing-board under the stairs. At the last minute the Frenchman and the Spaniard decided to fill in the forms anyway. Just for a laugh really, along with a tiny glimmer of hope that someone in a distant office would screw up and they might scrape through. Just like someone has to win the lottery, but at slightly less than fourteen million to one. The Englishman took a more realistic view, kept the money that would have gone on legal fees in his pocket and sold his share of the business to his partners, for a song. A rumour went round that he committed suicide when the licence came through.

The two survivors shifted the furniture around to comply with the new rules, slipped in an extra blackjack table, and made a small fortune every week. Much more than they made when they opened a charming little Chelsea bistro to avoid spending their lives working in an office or a hotel kitchen. And then in the eighties they really cashed in (just like Ted the copper) when they flogged the Village to one of the respectable and boring new companies that burst into the casino business during that dreary decade. The price wasn't published in the press, but I heard that it was well North of a million. The proud new owners used the licence to establish a low stake casino in the Gloucester hotel, just around the corner from Gloucester Road tube station. Pop in if you're passing. I'm sure they'll be glad to see you. The casino now belongs to the Rank organisation (unless they've sold it since I retired and lost contact with the real world). Be polite if you do drop in. Jokes linking the meaning of a J Arthur with the quality of their customers are not welcomed.

110

What happened to the musical girl with the nice chest, did I hear you say? Don't know. Maybe she got famous and made lots of money and went to orgies and died of a drugs overdose when she was still young and pretty. Or maybe she got married and faded away, just like the rest of us.

There were many other dumps in sixties London, before the 1968 Gaming Act made us respectable. You missed one every time you blinked. Most of them lasted only as long as Skip's two casinos, which I described at some length in an earlier chapter. They popped up and they popped down again, often for the same reasons that Skip came to regret. I couldn't have afforded to visit all of them, even if I had managed to squeeze through the door before they disappeared into the night. I have only included the ones I knew from personal and often expensive experience (apart from the Golden Spinner, described to me by the most reliable witness in this book), in order to maintain a high quality of reportage and burn off second-hand stories from unreliable low-lifes who'll tell you anything for a pint. I am a camera.

The Art Gallery.

Golden Bollocks had a natural eye for good paintings. To cash in on his talent he opened an art gallery in Chelsea, once the artist's quarter of London but in the sixties already becoming a place for rich and boring business people to set up expensive homes where once Augustus John used to pat the head of every passing child in case it was one of his, after a quick glimpse at the mother to see if there was a spark of recognition. It was the summer of 1968. GB invited a friend called Barry and me to share the new venture. We each put up part of the small amount required for the lease, helped pay the rent of about a fiver a week and spent a few hours, in shifts, dealing with the flood of customers we confidently expected to come rushing through the door. Barry was a croupier too, but really really hated the job and was desperate to find a way out of casinos that would still allow him to pay the rent on his flat at Chelsea Cloisters. A hammered stockbroker, who worked briefly as a Curzon House trainee after his hammering left him temporarily short of cash, often popped in between bouts of making and losing fortunes speculating in Australian mining shares. But I don't think he ever bought in to our art gallery. Too small-fry for a serious investor. His was more of a social connection. He lived nearby and sometimes dropped in for a chat and a pint when we shut the door after yet another day of not selling any paintings.

What we called an art gallery, to impress the art-loving public, was actually a little lock up shop in Smith Street, which runs South from King's Road to Smith Square. The shop was on the left as you walked from King's Road, just past a pub. There was a room at ground level and a decent sized basement. Barry covered the walls in brown hessian, to create a classy background for the pictures we hoped would hang there for the briefest of times before being snapped up by our appreciative clients.

I soon hated the afternoons when it was my turn to sit in the shop/gallery and think of all the much more interesting things I could be doing. One day I arrived early, by mistake. I parked in the little cul de sac between the shop and the pub and sat in my car with the hood down, enjoying the warmth of the sun's rays on my face. I'm really good at that. Anything to delay the dreaded moment when I had to go and sit in the bloody shop. While I was trying to think of a polite way to let Golden

Bollocks down and get my arse out of the art business, a lively group of young Americans, all jeans and tee shirts and glowing suntans, came out of the pub. They piled into an open Landrover, scrabbled round for somewhere to sit among the snorkels and flippers and brightly coloured bags, and talked excitedly about the trip they were making to a Greek island. Starting right now. The girls looked like the California Girls the Beach Boys used to sing about. The boys looked like the Beach Boys. I had a sudden urge to ask if I could follow along behind. I didn't, of course. They drove off to their island. I got out of the car and walked into the shop, my heart as heavy as lead.

My ability to sell anything is zero. It must be in the genes. My father was like that. As a journalist he wormed tiny fractions of the truth out of lying politicians more skilfully than anyone I knew, but he couldn't sell a pint of water to a man dying of thirst in the middle of the Sahara desert, some distance from the nearest oasis. I'm just as bad. If I like the person who wants to buy something from me I want to hand it over for free. That's what friends are for. If I don't like the person I don't want his grubby fingers on my stuff. As business plans go those two really suck. No chance of a job with Lord Sugar.

We didn't sell very many paintings. A rich middle aged woman living in a Smith Square mansion took a shine to our leader and bought a few small paintings. She even invited him round to the house to advise on where best to hang them. Yeah, right. We'd all heard that one before. He behaved himself, probably calculating that if he got romantically involved the lady would soon trade him in for a new model and we would all lose a customer. Our only customer at the time. Whereas if he could keep her dangling she might keep on buying paintings. Now there was a man who knew how to sell stuff.

One or two runners dropped in occasionally. In the art world a runner is a free lance wheeler dealer who goes around all the no-hope little shops, like ours, and looks for the rare bits of quality art he can sell on to the Bond Street dealers, the only operators in art who can persuade the wealthier members of the public to part with their cash. (In the real world the confidence they inspire is often misplaced. Plenty of unrecognised fakes slip through the net). The buyers are reassured by the luxurious premises and the well-dressed owners. It's like when you step into a richly appointed estate agent's office, or the agent comes round to your house in an expensive car. If he's doing that well he must be good.

My favourite runner was a very likeable Jewish man from the East End of London. He rarely bought anything. Golden Bollocks was very skilled at buying paintings, and didn't put a five pound ticket on a fifty pound painting. But the runner always stayed for a chat if I was on my own. Maybe he was as lonely as I was. His only real fault was to keep repeating the old shopkeeper's mantra: 'there's only three things that count when you open a shop: position, position and position.' Wise words of course, but they do lose their edge when you get into double figures. Once in a while, in between mantras, he would shake his head sadly at our folly, opening up a shop down a side street and right next to a pub. He was dead right. We closed down after a couple of months, to my great relief. We did make money overall, but not from the shop, and only thanks to Golden Bollocks' fabulous eye for hidden quality. At Bonham's auction room he spotted a hint of an elbow, the only faintly visible feature in a big painting that looked like a view down a mine shaft, painted late at night. Two of the best known West End gallery owners were looking round at the same time as us and both failed to spot the tiny clue that a major work of art was hiding behind the dirt. Needless to say, so did I. GB bought it for almost nothing, had it very carefully cleaned around the elbow and put it back into the next auction. The auctioneer recognised it as a sketch by one of the Italian Old Masters, what the experts call a cartoon, which later became part of a large and famous painting that still hangs somewhere in a public gallery. One of the Bond Street dealers who had looked at it when we did, and failed to appreciate what he was looking at, bought it for at least fifty times the price we paid.

The shop shut. GB realised we weren't going to sell much in Smith Street. We split the money and wriggled out of the lease. GB went free lance. He took to working from home and prospered, or so I heard. I spent more time in pubs, dreaming about sharing a Greek island with a bunch of California girls. Without the Beach Boys. I realised that I was lucky to get my share of the elbow. I hadn't done anything to deserve it, but as we were still partners at the time I was paid in full. Golden Bollocks was a very honourable man.

An odd bod we often saw at auctions sometimes dropped in to the shop. He had a way of standing in doorways as if he expected to be thrown out. Perhaps he often was. Rather to his surprise we always invited him in. He was from the East End of Europe, probably Poland, and was always known as the Count, which he may well have been before Stalin took over and did for the odd few members of his family that Hitler missed. The Count dressed shabbily, like a down and out, and lived in squalor in a rented flat at what was then the rough end of Kensington, not far from where Peter Rachman ran his slum business. He shared the flat with a collection of paintings worth at least a million pounds in today's money (probably much more), all of which he'd bought at auctions or in junk shops. Most were canvasses without frames, piled casually against the walls of his dirty old flat, behind a flimsy door with a simple lock. If he had seen the Bonhams elbow before Golden Bollocks did he would have grabbed it first, and then kept it for ever. Like GB the count had a master's eye, but he refused to even think of selling any of his paintings, much as he loved to show them to other connoisseurs. I often wondered what he lived on. He didn't seem to have a job, and obviously spent nothing on clothes, but he must have had to pay the rent and eat, and pay for his treasures. Perhaps a fellow countryman or a rare surviving relative recognised his talent and had the decency to keep him off the street.

Another regular visitor to the gallery (all right, shop) was a very handsome blond man in his early thirties, often to be seen striding along Kings Road looking hot and sexy. He was a sailor once but he got sick of the sea, many sailors do, and had recently started a new career as a gigolo. He made a precarious living, but much less than a close study of his classical features in the bathroom mirror had convinced him would come pouring in, tax-free. Midnight Cowboy with Big Ben rather than the Statue of Liberty. Minus the hat. Business failed to boom and never got any better, leaving him forever on the look out for the fiver that no-one in his right mind would lend him. His street name was TFB. I thought it was an obscure naval rank that only experts could decipher. I was wrong. It stood for Tongue First Bill and referred to a procedure that played an important part in his second career, but sadly not often enough to earn the sort of money the mirror had promised. I really liked old Bill, in spite of his dodgy finances and his dodgy name, and the dodgy way he earned what little money he could ever call his own. I've always had a soft spot for life's more colourful characters. I didn't even mind buying him the odd pint, even though I knew that his round would never come. But I always kept my fivers in my pocket.

Another man I sometimes saw in Chelsea had no connection with casinos, or with the refined world of classical paintings. He was a friend of a friend of someone I knew in the Hertfordshire village where I once lived. He never set foot in the shop where we didn't sell paintings, but he had an interesting though short life story which I would like to share with you. I knew him as More Pace MacSomething. I'm sorry, I can't remember the second part of his surname. More Pace, which wasn't on his birth certificate, or, not that much later, on his death certificate, was named after the catch phrase he used daily in an effort to speed up what he saw as an otherwise dull life. He was a young army officer in a smart regiment and when anything was moving which he felt should be moving a bit faster, a military vehicle, a sports car, a motorbike, skis, sledges, or a girl he felt was falling behind in the race to orgasm, he yelled out 'more pace, more pace' so often that the catch phrase became his highly appropriate nick-name.

On a ski-ing holiday in Austria, some of it spent at no pace at all when his skis stuck in a wall of hard snow at the side of a mountain road he had tried to jump across, leaving him standing in mid air still strapped to his skis, to the great amusement of the passers-by who helped him to his feet when he fell on to the tarmac, no doubt still yelling out his famous catch phrase, he met a young Pole and went on the piss. The Pole was as crazy as More Pace, a lot of them are, and challenged him to a drinking race. The Pole had to drink a bottle of vodka, by the neck, as fast as he could. More Pace had to down a bottle of brandy in the same crude fashion. How could he resist? Whoever finished first would even win a small amount of cash. More than enough to pay for the rapidly inhaled alcohol. The competition was timed and adjudicated by a nearly sober person acceptable to both parties, a type of person not easy to find in an après-ski boozer, late at night. More Pace won the race by a fraction of a second and fell down dead, his big heart overwhelmed by the sudden rush of alcohol. If only he had had the sense to take the bottle out of his mouth at half time and give the audience a few yells of 'more pace, more pace' and himself a quick shot of oxygen he might still be around today, making the world a slightly better place. I wish he was. You don't meet enough people like More Pace. I'm sure he would have got over losing the drinking race, and the money was too modest to mention. Don't try it at home.

Shortly before the shop shut down forever a Saville Row tailor with artistic pretensions asked to exhibit his pride and joy, a half dozen expensively framed rectangles of high quality suit material, neatly arranged in different coloured stripes. He was strangely convinced that they would sell like hot cakes, at ten times the combined cost of the cloth and the elegant frames. We invited as many people round as we could, and even bought a few bottles of undistinguished sparkling wine in the hope of loosening their grip on their wallets. About half of the people we invited turned up. Nobody bought anything. I thought the exhibits looked like very nice suit material unaccountably trapped in frames that would have looked much more at home around the outside of oil paintings. All of our very small number of regular customers obviously agreed.

That was the beginning, the middle and the end of my short career as a dealer in fine art. My own failed career change. I can't say I missed it when it was over. Not half as much as I missed More Pace. But those young Americans falling out of a pub and into a Landrover gave me the best idea I ever had in my life.

Career Change.

In spite of the high wages, and the sports cars, and the chance to strut your stuff along King's Road, and the ability to pay for as much alcohol as the young male human body can absorb on this side of the after-life, a large minority of the new British croupiers were keen to get out of the fledgling casino business. The money financed the kind of private life that most of us had only dreamed of, but the working conditions were humiliating. The sort of job that only foreigners put up with (in those dying days of the British Empire, and of poverty in Southern Europe). You were bossed around in a way that no longer happened in most places of work, and the rudeness of the gamblers (especially the losing ones) went far beyond anything normally encountered outside a casino. The money was better, and so were the hours, but you felt like a servant in an 18th Century aristocrat's house.

The silent majority put up with the abuse and counted their money. They were realists. They knew that if they stood up for themselves they would feel better as they looked into the shaving mirror, but the casino would fire them rather than back them up, much happier to lose a good croupier who could be replaced than lose a good customer who might not. The misfits, the square pegs in round holes, the dreamers who knew (or at least hoped) that there was more to life than childhood, school, work, suburbia, marriage, old age, illness and death, wanted out. In the words of the old jazz song Oh Didn't he Ramble, we wanted to ramble in and out of the town before the butcher cut us down. If you can listen to the words of that song and not feel a sense of romance stirring in wherever you keep your soul, you might be at one with the silent majority who did their sums and worked out their mortgages and married dull partners (with just the odd bit on the side) and, if they lived long enough, turned into the sort of boring old farts you trip over in golf club bar-rooms. But I hope not. Minor promotions came to most of the squares, as the Frenchmen faded out and the new American games moved in. A small minority of the silent majority brown-nosed their way further up the ladder of success, actively elbowed the Frenchmen aside, and got their hands round the real money. There were benefits beyond the extra cash. Promotion cured many psychological problems. No need to kick the dog when they got home. Or the wife, for the suicidally brave. They could take it out on the croupiers when the gamblers took it out on them and go home with their mental equilibrium in perfect balance. And if they weren't quite as dull as they had seemed at first sight, they could steal more money once they were in charge of the till. But sadly, most of the dreamers died disappointed. Not many got off their arses and put their money where their mouths were. And most who did failed to prosper.

There were exceptions. As recorded in an earlier chapter, the man who once found girls willing to shag the sweaty slum landlord Peter Rachman (for a stiff fee, much of it spent on memory suppressing illegal drugs) left the Curzon House behind him and set up an agency that provided dancing girls for night clubs in Beirut. With great success. From his point of view. Some of the girls may have taken a different view. It looked good on paper. Dancing in sophisticated night clubs in the town once known as the Paris of the Middle East seemed like a natural stepping stone on the road to international stardom if you were a wannabe exotic dancer. But in real life the dancing was mostly of the horizontal kind. Hollywood talent scouts were thin on the ground and the club owners only opened their wallets for girls who opened their legs. Some came home in high dudgeon, some took it lying down. My old friend didn't care. He got paid anyway.

Golden Bollocks did well as an art dealer (under a different name. Would you buy a used Rembrandt from a man called Golden Bollocks?). His brother opened a casino in a London suburb, and then bought the Pair of Shoes, a small casino that once belonged to the happily sex addicted Erik Steiner, an American with Scandinavian roots. Sadly the cops shut down the re-opened Pair of Shoes in 1971, just as I was about to start work there (as related in a chapter still to come). Not a man who gave up easily, GB's brother opened a big casino in oil rich Iran and had a couple of excellent years, until business was rudely interrupted by the departure of the Shah and the arrival of Ayatollah Khomeini, not the most fun-loving leader in the history of the world. The hammered stockbroker made a pile speculating in Australian mining shares, lost it all, made it back again, opened a restaurant and lived happily ever after. A man with a girl friend who sniffed invested the money he made from forging Bob Barnett's signature on the bottom of some good-sized cheques, and did well. He didn't start a business but he had a good career in something middle class, and lived in a much bigger house than he would have had without his lucky night at the Curzon House. Many others tried their hands at running their own businesses and failed, often with indecent haste. One young croupier was fired on suspicion of being too generous to an American roulette player, in the early days of the game when not many people knew what was going on. But one smart one was enough. Out of work, with a bit of cash still under the mattress, he went to Portugal and tried to open a second disco in a small fishing village with one pub and one disco, just before the village exploded in size and brought huge profits to those with the happy knack of burying beautiful coast-lines under millions of tons of concrete. Unlike the property men, my friend and one-time flat-mate made no profits at all. He failed to open his money spinning disco and failed to cash in on the enormous increase in tourists looking for somewhere to meet new friends of the opposite sex. There was a problem with sense and money. He didn't have enough money, and he didn't have the sense to bribe the right people. Not that he could afford it anyway. Before the disco plan evaporated like water in the desert, another friend and I nipped over on a cheap flight to see how our man was getting on. We rented a cheap room in his house, vastly increasing his cash flow for two weeks. Unable to find a girl each in the one disco that was up and running, we established a joint relationship with one beautiful Swedish girl who just couldn't decide which one of us she liked most. Or least. I wish I could remember her name.

Two co-workers tried to make it big in the drug trade, traditionally a fast route to a fortune or an early death. Or a jail sentence if you're stingy with the bribes. One of them, a Londoner, had briefly owned a share in a casino that was shut down. The short blast of big bucks left him with a taste for the high life. To get back in the money he flew to Beirut and bought a heavy load of Lebanese Gold, the pot smoker's equivalent of a Monte Cristo cigar. Quite brave of him considering that he was Jewish. Not that the Lebanese wholesalers were too worried about religion in those early days. It went badly wrong. You meet some awful people in the drug business. They sell you the stuff, for cash of course, and then hand over all the details of the transaction to the local police. The police arrest you and take your stash and sell it back to the dealers at a heavy discount, increasing their meagre wages no end. The good news is that you're not usually charged with a crime. Some evidence would have to be produced in court, and in these shady deals the evidence is valuable merchandise designed to be burned in joints rolled by paying customers, not on a bonfire in a yard behind a police station. So you either walk free but skint, or die resisting arrest, or get shot dead, sneakily, while walking along a hot pavement minding your own business and wishing you could still afford taxis. Or the dealers inform the cops and a prosecution does take place, but only involves a small part of the merchandise. Which can mean that you only serve a small part of what could have been a very long sentence in a hell-hole third world jail. The good news. The bad news is that killing new, weedy inmates is often the only entertainment available to the regular inmates and officers of prisons of that quality. Drug dealing is very complicated, and best left well alone by those of us who look forward to dying peacefully in bed. Leave it to the professionals.

These devious dealings are not confined to third world countries populated by sinister foreigners. I feel obliged to mention that in case you're feeling smug and British. In the late sixties and early seventies there was a disco (night club if you're under forty) not far from Regent Street, owned and frequented exclusively by people of Afro-Caribbean descent, in a refreshing reversal of the racial discrimination that still lingered on in the capital of the fast disappearing British Empire. The music was good, but wholesale drug dealing was the main source of the company's income. On one occasion a naïve white boy bought a decent quantity of drugs from the owners, intending to vastly multiply his money by selling the stuff on the street in much smaller and heavily diluted portions, an idea he got from a film he saw on television. The club owner took his cash and immediately informed the overwhelmingly white local police (before one of the many clean-ups) who arrested the fledgling dealer for owning about a quarter of his stash and sold the rest back to the original owners. The white boy was disappointed that his new business lasted such a short time and was so unsuccessful, but kept quiet about the shrinkage because if he had been charged with owning the whole stash he would have got a longer sentence. So almost everyone was happy. And yes, since you ask, he was once a croupier.

I never did hear what my friend got up to when he got back to London, skint, after the failure of his business in my old home town (I lived in Beirut in 1958 and 1959). We weren't all that friendly, even before he became a drug dealer. But I'm sure I would have heard about it if he'd done any good in whatever he did next. I liked him, sort of, and I was very pleased to hear that he had at least clung on to his life. He bought a very expensive sports car while he was still working as a croupier, justifying the expense (not that I asked him to) by saying that he didn't drink and he didn't smoke so he had to spend the money on something. No pockets in a shroud and all that. Sad bastard. No-one with any style drives a sports car without a cigarette jammed between his lips at a jaunty angle and an open bottle of wine in a holder next to the gear stick. I wasn't surprised when he failed in his life of crime.

Another doomed drug dealer was a former Spanish dice dealer, known to his many friends as Spanish *****. A slender and good-looking, but prematurely balding man, he decided that there was more to life than robbing dice tables. I won't tell you his real name in case he's still got a

120

knife and finds out where I live. Only a joke. I hope. Spanish ***** grew what was left of his hair very long, wound a bandana round his head, like Peter Fonda in Easy Rider, bought an old camper van, and drove it to Morocco, like all good hippies did in the early seventies. The van had a secret compartment under the floor. In Morocco Spanish ***** jam-packed the secret space with hashish, or marijuana, or cannabis, or whatever you like to call it, that he bought from a friendly man he met in Marrakesh. What's in a name? I'm talking about the stuff you roll in with the legal cancer weed and voila! you have what is known as a spliff, or a joint, or a reefer if you're as old as I am. When it's all smoked out and your chemically enhanced imagination is taking you on flights round the known universe the stub left burning holes in your hand is known as a roach. That's more modern. Well it was in 1968. You knew you'd got value for money when you started to talk a load of bollocks and sincerely believed that you sounded just like Bob Dylan.

Spanish ***** put his old camper on the ferry and brought it back into Spain, dreaming of all the things he was going to do when he sold the shit and the money came rolling in. Unfortunately the Spanish customs men had a machine that weighed the van, the sneaky bastards, and decided that Spanish *****'s vehicle was a bit overweight. Unlike its owner. The hashish / marijuana / cannabis was soon discovered, filling every cubic centimetre of the secret compartment. Hauled before a Spanish judge, Spanish***** suggested that a criminal drug smuggler, one of those dodgy foreigners who live in Morocco, had broken into the van while Spanish*****'s back was turned and stashed the drugs into the secret compartment he didn't even know was there. He had often wondered what the extra key on the key ring was for. He asked for police protection, in case the criminal came looking for his merchandise and didn't believe Spanish*****'s outlandish story that the customs officers had nicked the lot. His life could be in danger. Now there was a man with style.

Sadly for Spanish ***** the judge didn't buy any of it. Perhaps he'd never heard of Bob Dylan. Spanish ***** went to prison and the judge went home. Another one bit the dust.

Looking For a Greek Island.

In early 1970 my relationship with the very talented actress whose house I lived in hit rock bottom. The age difference took hold and didn't let go. The bad times had started towards the end of the previous year. One sunny day in the autumn of 1969 she and I drove to Berkhamsted Common, a massive acreage of woodland and open spaces where I went long distance running when I was a schoolboy (and on hopeful walks with girl-friends after I left school), and where Graham Greene once played Russian roulette with a loaded revolver, luckily missing the live round that would have cancelled the career of the finest English writer of the twentieth century. We walked in silence and lay down on warm dry earth under a tree on the edge of a clearing. A carpet of fallen leaves spread all around us. The actress broke the silence with a line from a poem. She spoke of us being buried under the leaves and vanishing from life, peaceful for ever. I knew it was only a quote from a rather beautiful poem, not a suggestion that we commit joint suicide. I never met a person less inclined to kill herself. Or drag anyone down with her. But the mention of death depressed me. The actress who had seemed ageless suddenly seemed old. I was young and selfish and I wanted to travel to the Mediterranean, not be buried in a line of poetry. I stayed silent. The actress sensed that something was wrong and suggested that we go home. Soon afterwards a rock-solid friendship based on an uncanny similarity of character turned to dust, crushed by the weight of a double digit difference in years spent alive. It was awful and I behaved awfully. Then I was gone.

I quit work in May 1970, grew my hair long, bought a pair of tinted glasses to match the cool shades worn by Peter Fonda in Easy Rider, and planned a trip to a Greek island. Just like those sun-tanned young Americans I saw in Chelsea a year or two before. Move over Leonard Cohen, Dave the Rave is coming to town. The actress's son asked if he and his girl-friend could come along. I jumped at the chance. He and I had lived in the same house for five years and always got on well, and his girl-friend was a gentle soul who didn't do hissy fits when

122

things went wrong. And they would keep alive a link with what was about to become the past.

We drove out of the village on a lovely sunny day, in a dark blue Sunbeam Alpine with a soft top and a slightly tweaked engine that made it sound livelier but didn't make it go any faster. It wasn't the most masculine of sports cars, but it was comfortable and I liked it. Because it was a bit girlie I always kept it dirty to make it look more like a real man's car. Jeremy Clarkson would understand. Somewhere in France we lost our way and drove to Spain instead of Greece. Red wine and maps don't mix. Maybe Christopher Columbus was on the piss when he missed India and hit New York. But it all turned out well. Probably better than the original master-plan. We spent the best part of five months in Cadaques, the then hippified and cheap (but now smart and expensive) village where the painter Salvador Dali spent most of his enviably lecherous life and left behind the only museum in the world featuring a swimming pool shaped like a human penis. When Dali was alive and well and conversation was flagging he encouraged his glamorous female guests to dive in naked at the bollock end and come whooshing out at the business end, to a round of applause from the beautiful people gathered around his garden. Especially the chaps. I'm keeping the naked swimmers' names to myself. I know who some of them are, but I haven't got the sort of evidence that stands up in court. They might be wrinkly old grannies now, tempus fugit just as fast as it always did, but they're wrinkly old grannies with attitude and enough cash left over from the glory days to pay a lawyer to make mincemeat out of me.

One of the first friends we made in Cadaques was the (late) eleventh Earl of Kingston, a look-alike cousin of Lord Lichfield, the fashion photographer famous for snapping the photographs of naked girls that brightened the pages of the annual Pirelli calendar. Kingston, known as B to his friends, after the first letter of one of his many forenames, left a fashionable regiment after six years in the Army and went to Cadaques to open a discotheque in what had once been a garage (and still looked like one in the unforgiving light of dawn). He and I got on like a house on fire. He was looking for good times after six hard years in the military, I was looking for good times after six soft years in a casino. The only real difference between us, apart from a title and the odd million quid, was that he was married and I wasn't.

B generously allowed me to sleep, rent-free, on a scruffy camp-bed behind a room-divider made of empty beer crates in the storage area of his lively disco, and rescued me from the boredom that creeps in when the living gets too easy. More for the excitement than for the money he smuggled plain white T-shirts from (then) cheap Spain into much more expensive France, where a smooth Frenchman from Perpignan printed on a Saint Tropez logo and sold the low quality shirts for God knows how many times the original price to middle-class tourists hoping, usually in vain, for a quick glimpse of Brigitte Bardot's bare bum on Pamplemousse beach. B did most of the smuggling trips himself, but I took over when his car was out of order, or he had to go back to England, or he was busy with his real business, or busily bouncing off his French girl-friend. Some of the old feeling of danger came back when the car was stopped at the frontier. A bit like the feeling in a casino when a few loyal friends and I got our hands on one tenth of one percent of the owner's ill-gotten gains. You only miss it when it's gone.

The eleventh earl and I weren't the only ones bending the law in hippy Cadaques. One night he and I were eating fish and talking about girls in the only restaurant that Dali ever seemed to go in. We hadn't been chatting long when the great man himself sat down at the next table, with his elegant English secretary, who looked just like the actor David Niven, a beautiful Russian girl (probably Veruschka, who somehow escaped sixties Soviet greyness and made it big as a model in the decadent West), and a young Spanish man who kept handing over pieces of paper for Dali to sign. And an ocelot on a chain sitting close to my feet and fixing what I hoped wasn't a hungry stare on my right leg. Naively I whispered to B how nice it was that Dali wasn't above signing autographs, in spite of his massive fame. B laughed and told me, quietly, that the papers weren't autographs, they were sheets of drawing paper that now carried an authentic Salvador Dali signature. Next morning, in the bright airy studio just past the models' changing room with the private peep-hole through which Dali used to stare at his naked workers, with one hand curled tightly round the original of his swimming pool, the young man, a talented but derivative artist, would create what were possibly the most genuine fakes in the world, in Dali's own studio, with Dali's own pencils and paper and Dali's genuine signature on the bottom. Not for nothing was Salvador Dali sometimes known as Avid for Dollars. He was a ground-breaking artist, no doubt about that, in the beginning at least, but he wasn't into starving in garrets. Once again I felt like I was still in a casino. The feeling came on even stronger a few years later when Dali's elegant secretary snuffed it and the news broke that he had been creaming off a large share of the dollars that his boss had been so avid for. Is there anyone honest in this world, I sometimes ask myself? If you bought a Dali drawing from that era, rush over to Bond Street and ask for your money back, or sell it immediately to someone who doesn't read books about casinos. And if you bought a Saint Tropez T-shirt back then I'm truly sorry that it fell apart so quickly. But what do you expect from something a North African sweat-shop owner sold for a penny? I can only hope that you kept a photo to bore your friends with. And that you caught the long dreamed of glimpse of the illustrious bum. That's one thing you can't fake.

About a month after I arrived in Cadaques the most beautiful girl I had ever seen came into a bar where I was playing a losing game of dice with the owner (he knew the rules, I didn't). The girl's out of this world beauty silenced the room. I had never seen that happen before, and I've never seen anything like it since. To my amazement we became lovers, very quickly, starting in the womb-like back room of the long shut Bar Beatles, which you might remember if you were lucky enough to be around Cadaques in the late sixties or early seventies, before the music died. She came from Holland where she was paid to appear on the covers of expensive magazines, draped in expensive clothes. All the usual cliches followed her into the room. Love at first sight and all that stuff. Scientists tell us that what we call falling in love unleashes the same brain activities as a well-stuffed joint. They're right, as usual. An early morning close encounter of the rude kind, in a hidden bay at the daylight end of a night in a magical farm-house in the foothills of the Pyrenees, left me brain-damaged for years.

Dream Time.

In England I couldn't forget the unearthly beauty of the Dutch girl who walked into my life in a little Spanish bar and blew my mind clean away. I didn't have the faintest idea what to do next. I had had the best summer of my life, then it ended in a rush and I knew that things would never be the same again. I thought of getting into adventure travel, driving young travellers on camping trips to Africa and India, through countries you could still get to by road before all the wars started. But it was winter. Nothing would happen until next spring. For a while I stayed at my parents' house and depressed them with my sudden change from gainfully employed son to layabout, or surfed friends' sofas until I knew I was unwelcome and it was time to move on. Then came a stroke of luck, just at the right time. The actress's son had a friend from his school days whose mother worked for PEN, an organisation set up to defend the freedom of writers from all over the world.

The office of PEN was in Glebe House, 63, Glebe Place, London SW3, an elegant, quiet street that escapes southwards from the commercial clamour of King's Road. The main house is on four floors, with a second slightly lower part on the right hand side. PEN occupied the whole of the right side and the two lower floors of the main house. The two top floors had been sub-let, but were now empty. My friend's friend was offered the top floors for twelve pounds a week, obviously worth more in 1970 than today, but still only about a quarter of what we should have paid. He took it on and asked me if I would like to share. It was too big for him alone and he had only just finished studying and was setting himself up as self-employed, so even such a low rent was hard to pay. I went to live in Chelsea for six pounds a week, in a house probably worth twenty million today. When I lived there the house belonged to the Church of England, whose senior figures would no doubt have been horrified to know that one of their tenants, once removed, was a casino crook. There was another holy connection. Glebe House was originally a Huguenot church, built by Huguenot (Protestant) Frenchmen who were regularly persecuted and or murdered by the Catholic ruling classes in

126

their home country. To escape from being hunted on horseback by bored aristocrats, like animals (but more fun when it's fellow humans you're killing, so they say), many Huguenots fled to England.

Our two floors had four proper rooms, a kitchen and a bathroom, a walk through attic room, and a small roof garden. There was no separate front door. The stairs came up to our landing, and where the stairs ended our home began. We prowled the local streets at night, found a handsome old door in a skip, built a frame, painted everything to match the rest of the house, and revelled in our new privacy. The total building costs were about five pounds. The front room looked down on to the street and needed no decoration. There was a small fireplace at one end and a blank wall at the other, which we covered with dark green bookbinding paper. Not because it was needed but because it looked good, and the paper was a free gift from one of the artists at the Chelsea Arts Club. It was all becoming very turn of the century. Bring in Mrs Hudson, a violin, some cocaine and the odd needle and we could have been in lodgings in Baker Street. I felt at home the minute I walked in. To the left, off what was now the entrance hall, there was an old bathroom with a huge ancient gas boiler that exploded into life when you turned on the hot water. Very scary. Few visitors stayed long enough to qualify for a second bath. Further left was an odd shaped room with a small open fireplace in a short wall set at an angle to a narrow door that led into a tiny kitchen. The kitchen faced East, through a small window, and was always the coldest room in the house. In winter it was so cold that when I opened the door of the very small fridge I swear that the temperature in the room rose by a couple of degrees. The odd shaped room was painted a very shrill shade of red. (Try saying that with false teeth). On the wall above the mantelpiece you could see where an upside down cross had been screwed to the wall. Rumour had it that the flat had been shared by two gay devil-worshippers and that the odd shaped room was where they communicated with Lucifer, and perhaps with each other at the same time. Not being religious, or gay, or keen on garish red paint, my friend's friend and I painted the room a tasteful shade of cream. I half expected to see the red colour creep back through the new paint and the sign of the upside down cross reappear over the fireplace, just like in the horror films that go straight to video. But neither phenomenon disturbed our nights. The devil must have moved out with the boys.

A picturesque and very narrow staircase curved up to the top floor. Straight ahead was a small and pretty little room that became my bedroom. A tiny window lit up like a fire when there was a dramatic sunset over West London. I put a row of empty wine bottles on a ledge outside the window. When the afternoon sunlight shone through them the bottles painted their colours on to the white bedroom wall and reminded me of the Mediterranean. Lying alone and lonely in the small bedroom I spent many sleepless nights thinking about the Dutch girl. With heroic self-delusion I imagined her lying awake in Holland, across the cold North Sea, thinking about me with the same yearning. Perhaps, like me, reliving over and over again the early morning when, after a night in an old candle lit farmhouse in the foothills of the Pyrenees, we walked in sunshine to a hidden bay, for the obvious reason, and when it was all over clung to each other in a sports car at the top of the cliff, in what seemed like a rehearsal for the rest of our lives. She appeared in dreams, real night time dreams, not the day dreams I slipped into so easily. Some nights I was sure I could hear her footsteps coming up the little curved staircase. Once I heard her voice calling me in the night. I got out of bed and opened the bedroom door, half asleep, convinced that she was searching for me in the purple darkness, invisible but present, like God in a medieval church. The delusion seemed to last for hours, but probably took less than a minute. She wasn't there, of course. Nobody was there. It was a dream that lingered on for a while after I got out of my warm winter bed.

During the day, if the weather was friendly, I walked the streets of Chelsea and imagined the Dutch girl at my side. I showed her the sights, and told her the history of my new village. Like the black bollards on the pavement in the little road that led from Glebe Place to Cheney Row, supposedly made from cannons taken from a ship commanded by Lord Nelson. And other terribly interesting things. On sunny days we walked to Hyde Park, past the Albert Hall, and sat on a bench near the Round Pond. Or I hailed a taxi if her long legs were tired, opening the door like a gentleman as she got in and out. In the sunshine we held hands and watched the old men and the children tiptoe through duck shit and sail their model boats on the calm water. The old men would have looked at her other worldly beauty and remembered their own better days, if she had really been there. The children would just have looked, like you do at any age when Nature puts perfection in front of your eyes. I suppose I was as near to being certifiably insane as I have ever been, before or since. But it was an intensely happy and harmless form of craziness. Like a drug addict who doesn't need drugs, or a drunk who only drinks water.

Most evenings I went to the Chelsea Arts Club in Old Church Street with my flatmate, whose father was a founder member, to drink cut price beer and talk to real people. The Arts Club sounds very high culture and was originally opened as a place where only artists were welcome, but the motivation was to create a place where artists could drink alcohol more cheaply than in a pub, and on credit (you never know when you're going to sell the next painting), not drink healthy fruit juices and discuss the latest trends in French art. Augustus John, one of the other founders, was particularly fond of a drink or three, between fathering lots of children and, after a decent interval, having it off with some of the females among them. It could well have been named the Chelsea Piss Artists Club. That's not a criticism, I hasten to add. At the club the artists I talked to knew nothing of my dream life, although as artists they would probably have understood, sympathised even, before they called for the men in the white coats. But I never talked about my dreams. I thought that if I talked the dreams would fade away and I would have nothing left to lean on.

The dream time lasted until early the next summer. I went for a short holiday in Cadaques, with a friend I didn't really like. One hot bright afternoon I saw the Dutch girl again, in the bar where we first met, sitting very close to a good-looking man with a beard. I tried to act like it was still last summer, but I knew I was wasting my breath. After she said goodbye outside the bar, in July 1970, before her long night drive back to Holland with her husband I had made no attempt to contact her, except in the dreams that never left my head. Now it was June 1971. I must have looked a lot like a cold-hearted opportunist hoping for a leg-over after nearly a year of no effort, and nothing like the romantic fool who still loved her. She spoke angrily and buried my dreams forever. I didn't put up a fight. She was right and I was wrong. Now I had to pay the price. For a moment the events in a little bay and the happiness in a car at the top of a cliff faded from the part of my brain that keeps memories alive, as if the night full of sunshine had never happened. Then it all came back, and really hurt because I knew that such a bright early morning would never happen again. But at least the memory was back where it belonged. Like the jilted lover in the Jazz Age song sings so plaintively, and proves how right Noel Coward was about the power of cheap music, they couldn't take that away from me. But they took everything else.

I walked off sadly and got drunk on my own, in a dull little bar at the other end of the village, run by the sort of people who shouldn't be allowed anywhere near a bar, even as customers. It was the last time I ever saw the Dutch girl. Someone told me later that she went to live in Formentera with a German writer, the handsome man who was with her in the bar where it all started. There was no point in finding out if it was true. My time was up. All I could do was cling on to the memory. But what a memory. She once was a very good friend of mine, in real time as well as in dreams. For a few weeks, in the summer of 1970, she shared with me one small splinter of her life. If I'd had just a little more sense I could have had the whole damned tree.

Wired.

Back in Chelsea, after the failed encounter with the Dutch girl, in the bar where it all began, it sank in to my brain that I had spent the last ten months talking to an invisible friend and drinking beer and failing to notice that my money was almost all gone. Time to find a job again, but not where I had worked before. There's something disturbing about going back. It blacks out the good parts of your life. An old friend told me all about something that happened while I was away with the fairies. When he had finished I knew what I had to do.

Very few casino robberies involving players and croupiers working closely together resulted in prosecutions. This was one of the rare exceptions. I recognised the name of the player who went to prison. He was one of the biggest players on the then new American roulette that was replacing the old French roulette in my former place of work. He was a successful businessman who became totally addicted to gambling for high stakes. When he was running his company it wasn't a problem. His income was high and he didn't have much spare time to gamble in. He played straight and never tried any funny business on the table, or made overtures to the staff. Then he sold the business, retired on a pension about half the size of his previous income, and had all day to play roulette. It was still very good money, beyond the wildest dreams of ordinary people, but not enough to sustain a serious roulette habit that had expanded and filled up all the extra time.

The problem with gambling is that it's impossible to get the same thrill when you play for lower stakes. There's a strong resemblance to this in other addictions. I once worked with a man from the North who began buying pornography shortly after he came to London. What started as a young man behaving badly on daring trips to Soho became a mental illness. He went back again and again, always asking to see what was called the real stuff, kept under the counter in those innocent days and reserved for regular members of the dirty raincoat brigade. His addiction was heterosexual, in that all the photographs he bought were of men and their temporary girl friends, or of girls and their temporary girl friends (which is sort of heterosexual if you're a chap), but the things they got up to went on a steep rise from conventional sex, like you or I might have enjoyed during our youth if only we could have talked a few close friends into joining in, to scatological material that would have made Mozart blush. Then he married a very religious girl. He converted to her religion and became a born again puritan. His new addiction to God rescued him from his addiction to pornography, saved him a lot of money, and dealt a minor blow to the economy of Soho. I suppose the devout would blame his escape on God. I can't remember which God it was, but he obviously picked a winner.

The resemblance to gambling lies in the lowering of the stakes. If my friend from the North came home with pornographic material that was less extreme than the last purchase, his trousers hardly twitched and the money was wasted. It's the same when a roulette player who normally scatters ten pound chips all over a roulette table scatters one pound chips instead. Boring. The real excitement comes not from the intellectual (?) achievement of picking the right numbers, but in finding ways to do yourself the most harm. As any self-respecting masochist could have told you.

Our man had no success in curing his addiction, if indeed he ever tried. He carried on playing roulette for the usual stakes. His reduced income meant that he was soon playing beyond his means and had to dip into the money from the sale of his business, money which he now had no means of replacing. You might be tempted to sneer, to think that the rich bastard was lucky to have all that money in the first place and if he decided to gamble it all away it was his own silly fault. A lot of people would take the same view, but I think it's quite wrong. He wasn't born rich. He got up early every day and worked hard and created an honest business which harmed nobody and benefited many. He didn't run a sleazy night club cum brothel or an addiction-sucking casino, and he didn't deal in drugs or weapons of mass destruction. He didn't even sell cigarettes. He supported a wife and raised children, gave money to charitable causes, and during his working life he cost the taxpayer nothing in welfare payments or police time. But it all changed when he became mentally ill, the proper way to describe somebody irretrievably addicted to playing roulette. He took the plunge and talked to one of the senior table staff, ambiguously at first, so that he could pull back and pretend it was all a joke if the first small seeds of conspiracy fell on barren ground. In fact they fell on fertile ground, as he had every right to expect in a London casino during the early seventies.

The procedure was the same as the one I described on the French roulette. Late bets were placed on whatever number came up, still the only tried and tested way of winning at roulette. (If you know a better way you should write a book). And if nobody was looking the bet was overpaid to add a little extra to the pot. Over-payments are much easier on American roulette than on the French game. American payments are made by totalling all the chips belonging to each player on the winning number and paying it all out in one go. French bets are paid one by one, from the lowest odds to the highest. That method makes it easier for a passing manager or an inquisitive player to spot a bent payout on the French game. An American roulette payout for the same stakes contains a far larger number of chips and is much more difficult to follow, even for someone sitting at the table trying hard to keep up. (Just for the fun of it the more dashing among us used to do this sort of thing right under the nose of a manager we considered too dim to follow what was going on. Dangerous and silly perhaps, but great fun when it worked. Good training too. You concentrate better when there's no safety net).

At the trial there was many a mention of a mystery man, a man identified only by a capital letter. I got to know the mystery man well when I was a manager at Aspinall's a few years later. We became friends during quiet afternoon shifts, when neither of us had anything better to do. If he had money he sat down and played roulette and I left him in peace. But his income fluctuated violently between a lot and nothing at all. Some days he just came in for a free cup of coffee in a place which felt like home, in fact where he probably spent more time than he did at home. If none of his friends were about he and I got to talking, often quite seriously, about everything under the sun. He was an Israeli with a keen and very balanced interest in politics, which I liked to think I share. I think he was partly Arab, and so could be described as a native Israeli, unlike the majority of Israelis of the first generation, more accurately described as Jewish European colonial settlers who used their guns to create a colony where they could be free from the anti-Semitism that scarred Europe for centuries, and in the nineteen forties turned into the Holocaust. The only fly in the ointment being that somebody else already lived there. The old problem that always dogged the colonial powers.

Whatever his national or religious origins, Mr Capital Letter spoke fluent Arabic. After a while, if he came in with no money and the joint was empty I fixed him up with a car and he went out to find me some players in another casino. He often went to a place called Maxim's in Kensington, then owned by a wealthy Gulf Arab who was once big in the gold trade across the Gulf, with or without the approval of the local authorities. When he first offered to bring customers in I felt obliged to explain that I was unable to pay for this service, as was commonly done in the old London casinos, before they were nearly all shut down around 1980. He knew all about those arrangement. In fact there was very little he didn't know about the running of a London casino, legal or otherwise, as you might expect of a man who came to be involved in a trial of someone convicted of robbing a casino. He brushed aside my apology and reassured me that no payment was expected. He was just doing a favour for a friend. I found this rather touching. He always delivered the goods, including more than once a very pleasant Arab man with a beautiful Australian wife who was a croupier before she got married. Her sparkling presence brightened many a dull afternoon and her old man's money turned many a quiet shift into a modest winner.

The mystery man's own wife was a stunning beauty, a dark-haired French girl who would have won any glamour competition she chose to enter. I was told that when she had just started out as a (very) high-class call girl in Paris my mysterious new friend was her first client. They fell in love, in a real life version of Pretty Woman, and got married. She packed in her day job without a backward glance, but remained on friendly terms with some of her former co-workers. To guarantee the loyalty of the bent casino staff the addicted player, now more than ever determined to get his money back and avoid going bankrupt and throwing away his whole life's work, arranged for the mystery man's wife to bring some of her economically active French friends over to London. An expensive hotel room was booked, and filled with girls more beautiful and more willing than the boys were ever likely to meet again. At the trial the judge stressed that the mystery man was in no way connected with the alleged casino fraud which was the subject of the proceedings, and that he stood to gain nothing for himself. He was not on trial, nor accused of any wrongdoing. Hence his anonymity. I'm sure the judge was right. In fact I never found out why the man was mentioned at all. Most likely he was just providing a character reference, doing a favour for a friend similar—well, not that similar, I didn't get the girls—to the favour he would do for me a few years later. Unfortunately for the player (and for most of his accomplices) one of the young croupiers was beginning to lose his nerve. In a rare outburst of probity and integrity, one up for Lady Penelope, he told the management the whole story. They decided to turn this very rare betrayal into a classic sting. The police were brought in. The honest young man was shown how to strap a hidden tape recorder to his body and told to keep it running whenever he was in contact with his shady colleagues, except of course when he was naked in a hotel room full of of beautiful naked girls. The sting worked. The player and the croupiers were found guilty. Judas Iscariot got his silver. The rest got jail sentences. I'm glad I never had a friend like that. But at least the girls got their money. It wasn't a total victory for the bad guys.

I think the player should have been able to claim that he was of unsound mind at the time of the crime. That's a fair description of a totally addicted gambler who doesn't know how to stop. He'd been playing for years at the casino he finally decided to rob, a casino that was more than happy to relieve him of his money during all that time, and use every trick in the book to keep him at the table. Not that they had to work very hard. When you're that addicted you bring your own chains.

In the dying days of the 20th Century I heard that the mystery man went bust and his wife went off with somebody who didn't. I never followed this up. I preferred to believe that my old friend was still OK. But my informant was very reliable. Why is it only the bastards who get happy endings? Maybe he won the lottery, met another beautiful girl, and lived happily ever after. I hope so. He was one of the good guys.

Ghosts.

I had a qualified offer of a job at a small casino owned by a man I once worked with at the Curzon House. The Pair of Shoes in Hertford Street, next to the mouth-organ Hilton, was opened in the early sixties, the Wild West era, by a very handsome Swedish American called Erik Steiner. He ran the casino for two reasons: to make an easy profit in unregulated London, England, and to lure the lower ranks (and on a good day the upper ranks) of gorgeous Hollywood women away from the gambling tables and into his big round water-bed in the penthouse flat above the casino floors. In ones and twos, or threes even on a really good night. His most talked about encounter was with a very pretty girl in a sixties mini-skirt. She was introduced to Erik in the middle of the casino floor. After names were properly exchanged (Erik was a very polite man) he slipped his right hand under the tiny skirt, cupped the only body part that was of any real interest to him and kept his hand in place all through a lively conversation, in full view of everyone in the room. When the moisture spreading across his hand told him it was time, he left the profit-making to his staff and led his new friend to the bouncy bed on the top floor. Today's newspapers would call him a sex addict. I wouldn't. He was a man who liked to have a good time, arranged his life accordingly and, unlike most of us, got away with it. If that's being a sex addict, bring it on. But please don't tell me he was suffering from some kind of medical condition and that I should feel sympathy for the poor chap. What next? Free treatment courtesy of the National Health Service? Please.

Running a legal post-1968 Gaming Act casino fell a long way short of Erik's definition of a good time. He sold up, or stopped paying the rent and the wages and quietly walked away. It's possible that he had sinister Las Vegas connections and knew better than to waste time and money applying for a licence. My former co-worker bought the joint for a song. I made an appointment to see Monty, a mild-mannered chap I once worked with at the Curzon. Monty was now the manager of the Pair of Shoes, but sadly not for much longer. I went to sign up, in my best suit, and found Monty locking the front door. He looked grey and worried and in a hurry to be somewhere a long way away that needed a passport to get there. Before he rushed off he explained that the joint had been shut down and I was fired. Or, rather, not hired. Sorry Dave. And don't talk to those men getting out of the car with a blue light on the top.

Those with a keen interest in the spiritual world might be interested in some odd goings on in the Pair of Shoes, and in a house a short distance away.

When a casino closes down in the small hours of the morning most of the staff go home or, in better days long gone, to the Cavendish all-nighter to collect their ill-gotten gains. A small number stay on late to shut the tables and balance the books. Then they go home too. The manager stays on a little longer, to re-balance the books. Once the books are cooked he locks most of the cash in the safe and goes home with the cash that didn't qualify for safe-keeping. That was the way it was done when men were men and closed circuit television was science fiction. After the manager has gone a night security man is the only living being in the house. For the first few hours of his lonely shift he is on his own. He goes from room to room and makes sure that all the windows have been properly shut and that all the lights have been switched off. It's a spooky job, prowling around an old house in the dark with only the sound of his footsteps for company. When he's satisfied that all is well he sits alone at the reception desk and waits for the cleaners. That was when things happened that made it difficult for the Pair of Shoes to keep their night security men in long-term employment. One terrified man ran out of the front door and left it wide open behind him, running from something which literally drove him out of his mind. He never came back to the Pair of Shoes again, even to collect the modest sum owed to him in back pay. There were rumours that his body was found a few days later, nudging against a small boat in one of the quieter reaches of the Thames.

All the bizarre events happened on a first floor landing. Doors opening and closing. Muffled footsteps. Low voices. Presences hovering in the air. Some of the gambling staff experienced strange things even during normal working hours when lots of people were in the building. Of course that may have been a form of auto-suggestion. Everybody had heard the rumours of early morning supernatural goings on. It was easy to feel uneasy every time you walked across the scary landing, or looked up or down on it from the stairs. Only Erik was oblivious to the visitors from the other side. He saw no spooks, he saw gorgeous naked girls

136

trampolining on his hydraulic bed. He didn't hear things that go bump in the night, he heard gorgeous naked girls who went 'oh oh oh' in the night. How he suffered.

Being a firm believer that there is no afterlife, and therefore by logical deduction no spirits, ghosts or ectoplasmic apparitions, I listened to the stories with polite attention, murmured platitudes about strange things we really don't understand, mysteries of the universe etc, and tried to talk about something interesting instead. Privately I thought about old wooden floors sagging back to normal after hours of people coming and going, or old door frames and even door locks affected by a change of temperature in an empty house when the heating is turned off. All sound scientific stuff. But it's different when you're sitting there on your own and the darkness comes closer every time you look up.

The Pair of Shoes was one of a fine old terrace of elegant houses built on the graveyard of an old church, which still stands behind the long dead casino. When the graveyard was sold the gravestones were shifted to one end and the newly vacated land went for a high price, being right at the dead centre of town, ha, ha. Maybe those aggrieved dead souls made a grown man run out into the street in mortal dread, and made dozens of others see things that weren't there. Maybe I'll find out when I'm gone. A couple of doors down, a friend of mine lived in a house built on the same land as the haunted casino. A man of great charm and strong macho presence, he was a waiter in a smart casino, and then, very briefly, a croupier. When the chemmy games died the chewing gum lost its flavour and it was better to be behind a gaming table and making friends with the livelier class of gambler. Unfortunately he finished his training just as the new croupiers' licences came into force, based on a police investigation into one's past. His application was declined. Something about climbing up expensive drain-pipes empty-handed and coming back down with a pocket full of diamonds but on the last occasion leaving by the front door, firmly attached to a policeman. He and his beautiful French girl-friend lived in a bright airy flat with a bright airy bathroom in which a shelf, robustly screwed on, regularly detached itself from the wall and dumped broken bottles of brightly coloured girlie stuff onto the bottom of the bath. After one crash too many they moved to a very nice and much quieter flat in Chelsea, near where the film director Joseph Losey lived at the time. Maybe you shouldn't build houses on top of dead people.

I walked away from the closed casino, down but not out. As I passed the side entrance of the Londonderry hotel a slight, neat figure in a trilby hat and an expensive raincoat looked up and said hello. It was Victor, the elderly Belgian who ran the French roulette at the Curzon

House when I first worked there. I always liked Victor, a kindly, educated man who drifted in to the casino business when he was young and never quite drifted back out again. He told me that the door behind him was the entrance to the new Park Lane Casino, shortly opening for business on the first floor. He was the director. Would I like a job as a French roulette croupier? One door shut and another door opened, fifty yards down the road. I had about four pounds left in the bank, no overdraft arrangement, and credit cards hadn't been invented. Now I was back in the money. I wouldn't have to leave the flat I really liked, and may well have been the best bargain in Chelsea. I was that lucky once. I walked home, determined to enjoy my last few days as a non-employed layabout. You read that right. Not unemployed, like a common person who signs on to the dole. I'm privately educated you know. Like David Cameron. We have our pride. At the beginning of the dream time I decided to live on my own cash until it ran out. Someone who does that rather than choose to live off the state is classed as non-employed. Or stupid.

In the early seventies the Shoes was re-opened by Ladbrokes, and given a new name: The Hertford. As in Hertford Street. Ladbrokes always were dull in their choice of casino names and casino managers. The only interesting thing they ever did was break lots of laws and lose their casino licences in 1980 and prove that everybody has some good in them.

Working for the Captain.

I phoned Victor next day and went to sign on. The casino wasn't open to the public. Licence not ready. We got full pay for sticking stamps on invitations to the opening party. I like jobs like that. No real work and plenty of wedge. As always happens when a new community forms, the boys eyed up the girls and the girls eyed up the boys. I picked a girl who reminded me of my first ever girl friend, the daughter of an art teacher at my English school. She'd had a tourist job in the Mediterranean, a break from life in a London casino, but missed the casino pay and came back. Like me, sort of. We went out one evening. I can't remember where. I managed to lure her back to my Chelsea flat. The hot beginning quickly cooled. I was too nerdy and artistic for her liking. All right for an actress, or a beautiful Dutch girl floating on the edge of a dream, but no good to a down to earth girl who liked her men to be men. She probably watches East Enders. She dumped me, found a macho man and lived happily ever after, as far as I know.

While we were still talking she told me about a brief marriage she endured as a teenager. She was a typical art student at the time, talented, keen and skint, living on egg and chips and the odd glass of cider, on a good day. He was about thirty, a man about town with plenty of cash to chuck around. He swept her off her feet. Things changed after they signed up. He didn't want to go out so often. And he had plenty of money. No need for the missus to work, or hang around some college with a bunch of randy students. In the evenings he sat on the sofa and watched football. She did the cleaning and cooking. Followed by a bit of hanky panky and a solid night's sleep, for him. Off to work in the morning and a pretty girl alone in a flat, wondering how she could have been so stupid. One evening he was sitting on the sofa watching football. The young wife was about to wash up, after a silent dinner. The little men on the screen ran up and down the pitch. Every now and again her man rose to his feet and roared, a sure sign that one of the livelier players had nearly kicked the ball into one of the nets. In between roars she could see his head leaning against the back of the sofa. A happy man, doing what he liked best. For the first time in her life a murderous rage took over her brain. She looked lovingly at the full milk bottle in her hand, walked up to the back of the sofa, and brought the glass bottle down hard on the top of his head. The bottle broke and he slumped on to the sofa. Milk and blood sloshed all over. Mixed together they looked like brains, to someone with no experience of grievous bodily harm. She screamed, convinced that her old man was dead. Somebody scored a goal. She phoned her mother and told her to come round. Now. The husband regained consciousness. The women cleaned up the mess. The marriage ended.

The casino opened to the public. Well nearly. A crowd of people turned up on opening night, clutching their invitations and eager to get stuck into the free food and drink. But there was something wrong with the paperwork. The party guests crowded together on the wide stairs, held back by a rope and forbidden by law to step on to the gaming floor. The mood turned ugly. A smarmy public relations man marched around, smiling hard and trying to look confident. He reminds me now of the public relations man, Lord something or other, who did sterling work for Prime Minister Thatcher and was once seen jacking off in the window of a Hampstead house. His own presumably. Like the monkeys at London zoo when you walk by with young children. Some guests left. But not many. Most people who come to casino opening parties are never seen again and don't mind being kept waiting, but they complain loudly if anything goes wrong, hoping to disguise the fact that they are shameless free-loaders. The odd few who left were probably real gamblers who wanted to get on with a real game in a real casino that was open, not hang around waiting for Godot. And then, just like that, it was all sorted out. The free-loaders poured in, huffing and puffing and stretching out their hands.

The casino belonged to an elderly night club owner called Captain Ponti. He was born in Tunisia, fought with the British Army in North Africa during WW2 and, quite rightly, was allowed to settle in Britain when the fighting stopped. Like formerly Polish Captain John Mills, the owner of Les A, and formerly Czechoslovakian Captain Robert Maxwell M.C, war hero, publisher, newspaper proprietor, yacht owner and, briefly, the world's wealthiest pensioner. Captain Ponti quickly settled into his new role as casino owner. He walked the walk and talked the talk as if he'd been at it all his life, and fooled many of us into believing that he was the real boss. But in real life the Captain was nobody's fool. Shortly after the Park Lane opened the first croupiers' licences were handed out by a Gaming Board inspector. He came round with a brief case full of the things, glared at his miserable victims as he goose-stepped across the casino floor, and installed himself in the manager's office. I recognised him as soon as he came in. He was a British French roulette croupier who worked with me in my last days at the Curzon. An odd bod, once married, he spent his afternoons at tea-dances in the Café Royal, dancing with a variety of what he called young ladies who, he assured us, were real lookers and just gagging to set up house with a courteous old-fashioned gent like himself. We, his fellow croupiers and I, were seriously underwhelmed. We had no idea that tea-dances survived the nineteen fifties, or forties even, and were still going strong in the age of rock'n'roll. And would rather have been seen dead than seen asking nice young ladies at the Café Royal if they would do us the honour of sharing the next waltz. We were (mostly) of an age when we would have done almost anything to get a leg over any half-way decent crumpet that happened by, but one had to draw the line somewhere.

When the odd bod and I worked together at the Curzon the French roulette was still bent, but only just. A kind of lethargic thieving. No more than a reflex action. A twitch that wouldn't quite go away. A shadow of its former self. Even red wine sales at the Cavendish were in the doldrums, now that nearly all the Frenchmen had gone home. But the Untouchable was recruited from the Victoria Sporting Club in Edgware Road on the understanding that he was bursting with probity and integrity and had the technical skills to root out the few stragglers bent on keeping the old traditions alive. On completion of this noble task it was understood (by himself at least) that he would be promoted to high office and earn huge amounts of money. I got the sad impression that the promotion to high office meant more to him than the money. A friend came with him, a level-headed fellow without the slightest interest in all the probity nonsense. He just fancied a cushy job in a posher place than the Vic. The friend told me not to bother about the caped crusader. Just humour the idiot and everything would be fine.

The great investigator went to work. He shifted a couple of the remaining Frenchmen, diffident souls who probably never nicked a penny in their lives. His reward was a minor promotion and an extra fiver a week, rather less than he had in mind when he set out to clean up the West End. To make it much, much worse an irascible old Belgian called Maurice, a man with a one-strand comb-over, a man who could see the dark side of things long before the things themselves actually happened, was brought in over his head and put in charge of the newly cleansed French roulette. You can't do that to a man on a mission. Especially one who goes to tea dances. Mr Clean went bent. He tried to recruit me into his (as yet non-existent) gang, to help him get his own back on the casino that had so sorely wronged him. But he picked the wrong time. I had made it clear to anyone who was interested (not a large crowd) that I was now as pure as the driven snow and would soon be leaving the business and shagging myself silly on a Greek island. An ex-casino robber, not to be tempted by sordid dreams of money. He went ahead without me and muddled through as best he could. Quite well actually, when Maurice wasn't around. But robbing the joint that had robbed him was not revenge enough. He got a job as a Gaming Board inspector, the first croupier to be recruited by that august body. The motivation behind his career change was to hurt Julian, the Curzon manager whom he blamed, quite correctly, for the humiliations heaped upon him. Julian needed an honest man at the Curzon like he needed a hole in his head. From the moment they met he did everything possible to burn him off. As soon as his training was over the new government inspector came to the Curzon as often as possible, with one thought in mind: to make Julian's life hell.

At the Park Lane the newly licensed croupiers returned to their tables looking grim-faced and angry. Bastard, fucking arsehole, cunt, treats you like a dog, who the fuck does he think he is? All very negative. Then came my turn to go in. My former colleague smiled broadly, leant across the table, shook my hand, told me how nice it was to see me again, what a pleasure to work with me when he was (only) a croupier, gush, gush, gush. The licence was handed over politely, carefully even, in case I dropped it. Another handshake, a fond goodbye, a sincere 'look forward to seeing you again'. I knew that all the other croupiers' licences had been thrown across the table. If they missed their catch and the licence landed on the floor it was tough luck. You pick it up. You're the dog. I'm Gaming Board. The Captain stared at me. I sat down at the empty French table, but I wasn't alone for long. A couple of minutes later the Captain sat next to me and asked for the exact details of what I had on the Gaming Board man. My lies went in one ear and out the other. Great friends my arse. I persisted. The Captain got bored and walked off. He didn't sack me, but he never forgot. Six months after I left the Park Lane the Frenchman who took over as manager rang me and asked me if I would like to come back to a more senior job. Yes, yes and yes. It was a welcome chance to escape from a position that was uncomfortably close to being too hot to handle. But I knew the Captain wouldn't let me back in. The Frenchman phoned a couple of days later and said how sorry he was, he hadn't mentioned my name to the Captain when he first offered me the job, but now that he had the job was off. The Captain said something about not having that thieving bastard in his casino, over his dead body, etc, etc. So unfair. I never touched a penny of his money. He was too well connected for my liking. If only the fool had thrown my licence on the floor, like he did with everybody else, everything would have been fine. I would have crawled back to my table muttering obscenities, just like everybody else. You have to play the game. I wouldn't have sneaked on him. I don't do that. I'm public school.

Dark Water.

The Park Lane casino prepared for business. The staff who answered ads in the Standard, or heard on the grapevine that jobs were going in a new casino, or in my case bumped into Victor in the street while escaping arrest as sex-addict Erik's old Pair of Shoes turned into a black hole, all assumed that the new joint really did belong to Captain Ponti, the larger than life night-club owner who dominated the room where we sat around licking stamps and sending off invitations and generally getting ready for opening day. But in those days things were rarely quite as they seemed. The atmosphere soon blurred. We shared the room with croupiers who had worked for the boss in an earlier life. They all had Damon Runyon type names, Nick the Greek, the French Connection, Spanish Henry et al, and all hinted at a connection with a big time crime lord.

Some of the new staff had had their moments too. On an empty French roulette table, at the beginning of a long dull afternoon, shortly after opening day, I found myself sitting opposite a Frenchman known as the Cockney Frog. Above us, in the inspector's chair, sat a Frenchman with a more ordinary name. I'll call him Hashish. His name sounds like that if you say it quickly. He had no connection with drugs, I hasten to add, apart from the liquid one that pubs sell by the pint. My flat-mate in Chelsea, a man not always too keen on foreigners or on my tendency to congregate among them, once took a call from the Frenchman but didn't

143

quite catch his name. He told me with a grin that there was a foreigner on the phone and that his name was Hashish.

We got to talking, in French. The Frenchmen had a lot in common. Both had fought in Algeria as privates in the French army (the official term for cannon fodder). The Cockney Frog's career was fairly normal. Boring when not much was going on and very dangerous when shooting and being shot at interrupted the long dry spells of sitting round waiting for something to happen. His most vivid memory away from the battlefield was of a visit by one of the generals who planned to invade France from Algeria, where most of the French army was stationed, kill President Charles de Gaulle, and replace him with a bunch of Fascist generals. You've probably seen the film. Luckily for Charles, and for the rest of France, they made a hash of it.

The general came to review the troops at a base where the Frog was nervously waiting to go into battle. He had heard that a new type of machine gun had been invented, operated by electricity, and that one was avilable right there and then. Orders were passed down through the ranks. The brand new gun was set up. An Algerian prisoner of war was brought out of captivity and told to stand still a few yards in front of the gun, the worst case I ever heard of being in the wrong place at the wrong time. The gun and its operator were on the ground, aiming upwards at the unlucky Algerian's chest. Its modern mechanism fired so hard and so fast that the impact of its bullets lifted the Algerian clean off his feet and up into the air, before he fell back to the ground, stone dead. Always keen to embrace the latest technology the reviewing general gave the new gun the thumbs up and got back into his car amid a flurry of salutes, still dreaming of a French victory in Algeria and a military take-over in France. The soldiers dumped the Algerian in a shallow sandy grave and got on with preparations for the next day's attack, which ended the lives of several young Frenchmen and about five times as many young Algerians, but was seen as a victory because the Algerians went back into the mountains and urban Algeria stayed French for another day. Some of the dead lay a long way apart, on national lines, some lay close together after a final deadly embrace.

Hashish started his military career badly. He reacted to severe bullying from his sergeant by bashing him in the face and breaking his jaw. You're not allowed to do that. He was sentenced to a long stretch in a military prison. Just as his comrades were about to drag him off to the nick a big battle flared up in the mountains. Every available fighting man was urgently needed at the front. Hashish was offered a long spell of active service as a machine-gunner with the French Foreign Legion, a thinly disguised death sentence, or a much longer spell in a hell-hole

144

military nick. He decided to die in the open air, not long after he had left school, rather than in a hot and claustrophobic prison cell.

To his amazement he was still alive when it was all over. He took a short break to get used to the silence after what seemed like years attached to a machine gun, learnt to live without the company of the dead and the dying, and got used to a slight deafness in the ear nearest to the thousands of bullets he fired during his long spell of kill or be killed. Back in France he became a trainee croupier at a casino on the Atlantic coast, mastered the skills faster than most, and was among the first wave of Frenchmen who came to London when our own casinos opened in the early sixties.

When the military stories were exhausted the two Frenchmen turned to their early careers in the Britis casino business. I'd kept quiet so far, apart from the odd merde alors! or sacre bleu!, whichever seemed best to fit the mood. My own undistinguished military career began and ended as a not particularly skilled cadet at Berkhamsted School for Boys, 1954 to 1958. I can probably still fire a .303 rifle, and even change the gas setting on a Bren gun on a good day, my time in uniform wasn't entirely wasted, but I didn't think such mundane details would electrify my audience and kept them to myself. Then the casino talk began and they left me behind again.

The Cockney Frog didn't work for anybody else when he first came to London at the beginning of the sixties. The job we both started in 1971 was his first paid employment. His first business enterprise was a French roulette table in a country club on the outskirts of London. He spoke no English so he took on a Cockney partner who quickly taught the Frog all the English he would ever need to know. The Frog soon spoke his new language with that special French accent that makes English girls go all wobbly at the knees, but wrapped round a vocabulary made up entirely of Cockney rhyming slang. Don't go down ze frog and ze toad. Come wiz me up ze apples and ze pears. Let's 'ave a butcher's ' ook at ze breestol ceeties. Oh stop it.

The business was a roaring success. The boys paid rent, in cash, to the country club's owner. The rent was a tiny proportion of their profit but they didn't burden the owner with that information, any more than the owner burdened the taxman with details of his new source of income. A year or so later the owner got smart, perhaps impressed by the Frog's brand new Austin Healey 3000 sports car, and jacked up the rent by a multiple of five. It was still a bargain, but the Frog was getting restless. He said goodbye to his business partner, took out his share of the money, and opened a small gambling club in a Midlands town.

When he heard the name of the town, Hashish raised his left eyebrow high in surprise, making him look just like Roger Moore. He said that he'd had a gambling club in the same town, in a rented room over a bookie's shop. Business was very good. He'd hoped to keep the police off his back for a couple of years and then bollocks to ever working for a living again. He was keen to enjoy the rest of the life he had expected to lose in Algeria.

One hot summer night the joint was jumping. Really jumping. Waves of cash came roaring across the tables. Far more than he had expected in a provincial town, a long way from the bright lights of London's West End. Hashish felt the warmth of the Mediterranean sun as he slipped into early retirement, drink in one hand, crumpet in the other, his cash safely stashed under the mattress. The casino window was wide open to keep the room cool and discourage the punters from going home before they had lost all their money. A flaming object sailed through the window and landed on the carpet. Hashish immediately recognised it as a Molotov cocktail, a weapon popular with urban guerillas, quite capable of destroying a light tank and its terrified crew, not bad for a simple device easily made with ingredients from your local garage and the milkman. Hashish prepared to die, not for the first time. In Algeria it had been a daily routine. The other people in the room panicked and screamed and tried to escape through the one small door, all at once and with little success. Nobody had the sense to jump out of the window, perhaps worried about incoming fire.

A Molotov cocktail is a bottle half-filled with petrol (any grade will do) with a scrunched up rag in the top. Some people slip in a bit of sand. I've never found out why. Perhaps it reminds them of the seaside. The rag is the fuse. It's very important to get the design and the lighting of the fuse just right. That way the bomb explodes a few seconds after you throw it, like a hand grenade. Do it wrong and you're a suicide bomber. Don't practise at home unless you really hate the rest of your family. Luckily for Hashish (and his customers) the Molotov cocktail wasn't properly made, for reasons we are about to discover, and failed to explode.

There was a long silence. I began to wonder if I was mixing with the right set. I'm privately educated you know. We didn't do Molotov cocktails in the Lower Sixth. Even in chemistry. The Cockney Frog broke the spell. He looked embarrassed as he said, in a voice just loud enough to break the silence, I threw ze bomb. A deeper, longer silence followed, of the sort often described as pregnant by cliche-ridden authors of an earlier generation. Hashish raised both eyebrows very sharply, easily breaking his earlier record. I got ready to run.

146

The Frog went into more detail in his attempt to illuminate the thought processes that had inspired him to throw a fully switched on petrol bomb into a room full of people. His explanation was helped along by a gift of the gab that left most aspiring Irishmen in the shade. It went like this: his own casino in the same town had no rivals when he first opened the door to the local gamblers. He started to make serious money, even more than in the country club close to London, and all destined to land in one pocket. No more fifty-fifty. A few months later Hashish set up shop. Instead of dividing evenly between the two joints and giving both owners a fair crack of the whip--British fair play and all that--the fickle gamblers transferred en masse to the new place. That happens more often than you might think. Gamblers, who leave their brains at home when they head for a casino (but never forget to take their money) quickly convince themselves that the losses at the old place didn't really happen and that anyway they will win big at the new joint and get back all the money they didn't lose at the first place. If you see what I mean. Don't laugh. You might become an addict yourself one day and be amazed by the variety of things that go seriously wrong inside your normally level head.

Hashish was on the map. The Frog wasn't even in the margin. On the night of the bomb he was sitting in his empty casino, drinking champagne straight from the bottle (three bottles actually, at the final count) and feeling sorry for himself. He stared at the gambling tables where no-one was playing, and at the neatly laid tables in the pretty but tiny restaurant. The new place didn't even have a restaurant, for Christ's sake. How could the fools prefer that dump to his elegant joint? An idea crept past the champagne and into his brain. He made a Molotov cocktail, using a milk bottle filled with petrol from a can in the back of his sports car and a bit of old rag he found lying about in the kitchen. To avoid being identified by his own car he hired a Rolls Royce, just the job for a bit of inconspicuous bomb-throwing, and drove the short distance to the rival casino. He staggered drunkenly out of the big car, threw his bomb through the open window and drove off at speed, hoping that he wouldn't be breathalised on the way home.

By being drunk and sodding up the making of his bomb he narrowly missed becoming one of the most prolific killers in post-war England, rivalling the old IRA and the newer religious fanatics who took over where Paddy left off. It was the closest of close shaves. Hashish was sure the flaming rag was still in the neck of the bottle as it flew through the air, and he was an experienced observer of things that were likely to explode before he made it through the door. As was the man who threw the bomb, with commendable accuracy for someone with more champagne than blood in his veins. Luckily the standard of craftmanship was fractionally low, unlike the aim. When he got used to being alive again Hashish reckoned that the rag must have fallen out when the bottle hit the carpet, but would still have been burning only inches from the petrol that spilt on to the carpet. Guardian angels were out in force that night.

There was another silence, longer and deeper than the ones before. Pregnant even. The Frog got his breath back and continued extenuating the circumstances. I thought there must be more. The gift of the gad had never left him, but I felt he'd been a bit sparing with the details, and it's the details that count when you're doing contrition. He said, in a very sincere tone of voice, that he was very glad the bomb had not gone off. He wasn't quite himself that night. The champagne had sent his mind racing back to Algeria. The owner of the rival casino wasn't an unarmed man who had once been a soldier in the same French army in the same French war. He was an enemy holed up behind rocks high in the Atlas mountains. The thirty or so gamblers weren't foolish people hoping to make something for nothing in one of the new casinos that had suddenly sprung up all over England, they were armed and dangerous and trained to kill. Like a good soldier, which he had once been, he decided to get his shots in first. When he woke up next morning a cold sweat splashed out all over his body. He said again how sorry he was, really looking like he meant it. The story might even have been true.

Hashish said, quite politely, that he had been very pleased too. After surviving years of muck and bullets in Algeria he hadn't looked forward to dying in what might well have been the most boring town in England once Lady Godiva pulled her pants back on. He missed the money of course. They both did. After news of the bomb that didn't go bang in the night flashed round town faster than Godiva's horse the local gamblers decided there was a turf war going on between rival gangs, perhaps from London, swallowed their addiction and stayed at home, emptying both casinos. Hashish admitted that he would have preferred to have made his pile and gone off to bask in the Mediterranean sun. But money wasn't everything. And he understood completely how the past can rush up from out of nowhere and do funny things to a man's brain. When he was a boy in rural France, he said, entering in to the spirit of the thing with real enthusiasm, his grandfather, who lived in the same house, as country people often did then, still had flashbacks from the war in the trenches he had fought in all those years ago. Grandad had once gone looking for his bayonet so he could stab to death the grey grim German soldier coming at him from the East, but luckily he didn't find the bayonet in time to murder the neighbour who came round to help him mend the hen-house. These things happen he said, shaking his head sadly. The story might even have been true.

It felt strange to be sitting a few feet away from a man who could have killed a room full of people, admittedly while he was pissed, and the same distance from one of the people who could well have been turned into ash long before he arrived at the crematorium for what would surely have been a low wattage affair. The mood passed. I told myself to stop being soppy and make due allowances for men who spent their teenage years killing people no older than they were because their government gave them a gun and a uniform and a bit of training and told them to get on with it. We all shook hands across the empty roulette table, something you're not supposed to do in case you pass over chips that don't belong to you, and became firm friends, all in spite of my never having owned a single casino or spent even a minute rampaging around in a uniform and killing foreigners before they killed me. The three musketeers, some people called us. I'm sure Alexandre Dumas wouldn't have minded our hijacking his title, or objected to an Englishman horning in. My French was very good then and we're all Europeans now. And all for one and one for all was our rock of ages as we ducked and dived in harmony through the shadow-land of the old casinos. Your old phrase lived on Al. Two of us became blood brothers, a bond that still commands deep respect on Napoleon's first island. Sadly we drifted apart as marriage and divorce and job changes broke up the old gang. Someone told me not too long ago that I was the only one still drawing breath, but admitted that he could have been wrong. I hope he was. I get more lonely every day. RIP old friend and old blood brother if he was right, and you're in the ultimate shadow-land that waits for us all. Or come up and see me some time if he was wrong. I think it's my round.

An image of a pile of burning bodies on the floor of a makeshift casino in a dull town has never quite left a rarely visited corner of my mind.

After the bomb put paid to Hashish's brief stab at self-employment he slipped into well-paid jobs and a decent share of the loot in a variety of London casinos. The Cockney Frog opened a small casino in a popular South Coast resort and did well again, until the building fell down very late one night. Dodgy building work this time, not somebody else who'd been at the champagne. Luckily it fell down just before breakfast when there was nobody about. He hadn't wasted money on a night security man. He discovered, too late, that his insurance cover didn't rescue him from the unexpected disaster, went out of business, and started on his first paid job since the army at the same casino I stumbled into by accident when I stopped to talk to quiet Victor on the pavement

149

outside. Under his influence I became fluent in Cockney rhyming slang, sadly without ever getting to grips with the French accent that made the girls go all wobbly at the knees.

Rumours of a Mr Big in France went from a whisper to a shout. Half the managers were robbing the joint because the boss wasn't there, said the whispers from one side; the other half, loyal to the absent boss, were trying to protect his stash. Civil war. With no real casino experience behind, said the voices, the Captain was lost in the middle. Allegedly. Things could turn nasty. Guns could go off. I got nervous.

In the time of confusion one of the managers went to work at another casino and set up a complicated big money scam that involved rather more staff than is considered wise. He wasn't in quite such a wrong place at the wrong time as the unlucky Algerian, but it was close. He didn't know that the casino he picked was at the heart of the three million pound man's empire, probably well into his second million by then and not about to welcome competition from an upstart or the close scrutiny that would accompany a prosecution brought on by anyone other than himself. He was also very hard to fool, being the most skilled robber in the history of London casinos (the French doctor fooled him once, but the doc was a man whose c.v included seven years of hard medical study and thirty years of working for France's most eminent professional criminal) and quickly spotted what his new competitor was up to. After a brief word with his employers, impressed yet again by his devotion to their cause, he called in the plod. My former senior colleague and his new accomplices were caught in the act by policemen who hid in a false ceiling, focused their state of the art cameras, tuned in their listening devices, and never once fell through the plaster on to the green baize crime scene some fifteen feet below. The upstart went to prison, unlike the majority of casino robbers in the good old days. I was sad to hear about his sentence, but relieved to find that someone I took as a complete company man was actually one of us, skilfully hidden behind a very effective disguise. Shame he wasn't quite as smart as he thought he was.

His departure raised two questions, in those suspicious times. If he was one of the crooked managers (assuming that there really were any) why did he leave and take big risks somewhere else? If he was a loyal soldier, why desert his post? Nerve gone? Hardly, when you look at what happened next. A personal affront? Possible. He was rather touchy at times. But I never found the answer and I didn't ask any questions. Not with a possible crime lord lurking round the corner. After an eventful year the speculation and the rumours were getting to me. Word was spreading around that funny things were going on at the new casino. I got nervous about being tarred with the same brush and finding it hard to get work in

150

the future, and decided to leave while my probity and integrity were still intact.

Just before I went three croupiers on the French roulette table were told that the mystery boss was fed up with being robbed. He was sending a member of his gang over from France to play high stake roulette. Could they make sure that he won about thirty thousand pounds (about a quarter of a million now). It was the boss's way of getting his money back, the three croupiers were told.

Well maybe. The three croupiers were offered a thousand each, in cash. Here's where you have to check the arithmetic. If thirty thousand was paid to a big operator like the Fat Man, whom you'll meet later, the croupiers would have got six thousand each. That makes eighteen, and leaves the Fat Man to trouser the remaining twelve (or the whole lot more likely, but that's another story). In a normal risky hit six thousand was quite enough to tempt the nervous, but they wouldn't take the same risks for a measly grand. But a thousand with no risk, because you're under orders from the boss, was a handsome day's pay. Game on.

A real cool operator turned up, dead on time on the appointed day. He looked like Alain Delon, the very handsome French actor who glamourised gangsters in fifties and sixties French crime films and made such a good job of it that real-life French gangsters took to dressing and acting just like him. They copied the cool way he sucked on a cigarette and the sneer on his face when he gunned down a rival, using real bullets in their case. So perhaps the story was true. The visiting Frenchman certainly looked the part. But if you worked in a casino in those days, especially on the dark side, it always paid to assume that everybody was out to get you. Paranoia rules, OK? Remember the sneak with the tape-recorder under his shirt? Exactly. If the Alain Delon look-alike was posing as a gang member he would obviously have been chosen for his realistic appearance, to back up the cover story that he was working for the mystery boss. A four-eyed geek with a pen behind his ear wouldn't have fooled anybody. Perhaps someone smart did pay the croupiers well below the going rate and trouser the difference. I'll never know now. I don't think I'll ask the boss. He's a busy man. But even a thousand pounds was welcome, in early 1972, to the lucky three who got it.

The uncertainties were frazzling my sensitive nerves. I felt like a man swimming in dark water. I climbed out and started what turned out to be an all too brief job at the newly re-opened Casanova casino in Grosvenor Street, not far from the American Embassy in Grosvenor Square.

Casanova and the Prince.

As far as I know the Casanova Club was the only West End casino owned by a woman. Her first name was Pauline. I can't remember her surname. I was given a chance of a job there in the mid-sixties, thanks to the man with dark glasses, France's answer to Terry Thomas. He went there to escape the old trouts at the Curzon and to eye up the micro-skirted waitresses whose dainty way of bending down to pick empty glasses off small, low tables made the Casanova a roaring success. Before bureaucracy made it illegal a croupier applied for a job by working for an hour or so on the appropriate table, in a real game. If he made a good impression he got the job. I did my hour and thought it went well, but I didn't notice that a regular player was winning heavily when I was spinning the ball. Another croupier took my place. I walked up to Joe, Pauline's Irish manager, a shit-faced little man whose shirt collar was always two sizes too big for his scrawny little neck, and waited to be told when to start. Joe and Pauline were talking. I smiled at Pauline. I was hot stuff once with ladies of a certain age. She smiled back, hesitantly. Joe ignored me and said to Pauline he's effing unlucky, did you not see how much effing money he gave away? You need him here like you need a hole in the head. Pauline looked embarrassed and gently shook her head. I went back to the old trouts. The man with dark glasses waved goodbye. One day, possibly the day the 1968 Gaming Act made casino ownership

152

such a bore, Pauline married an American even richer than she was and left the London casino business behind her. The door was locked and the lights were switched off, and stayed off until 1972. In that year I got a job offer at the new Casanova, based on a recommendation from a Frenchman called Jean Roux (no, not the cook) who once worked with me at the Curzon. With Jean's help I became French roulette pit boss at the Casanova when it was reopened by a provincial casino company called Pleasurama, a company which no longer exists. It originated in Wales, founded by a man who was once thrown out of the Clermont when he was caught on camera trying to steal another player's chips, in what may of course have been a rare lapse in the usual high standards of probity and integrity of a man whose ownership of several casinos had already made him a multi-millionaire.

The general manager of the Casanova was usually described as Indian, but as I was told that he once served with the Ghurkas, the super fit soldiers from Nepal, I always assumed that he was of Nepalese origin. Perhaps he moved to India when he'd finished jumping out of aeroplanes without a parachute. He was without doubt the handsomest man I've ever seen. His parents found a loophole in the law that was supposed not to allow them to transfer money to England and sent him to the London Film School. The loophole suddenly closed. He had to abandon his studies and take a job as a waiter in an Italian coffee bar close to South Kensington tube station. The coffee bar, already popular with Swedish au-pairs, suddenly became even more popular. Serving coffee to (mostly) gorgeous Swedish girls wouldn't have been his first choice of career, but it kept him in England and kept alive a slim chance of getting back into studying film. The career change took place just as casinos were first opening in London. Most of the other waiters were young Italians. One of them left the coffee bar to train as a croupier at the Penthouse Club, in Shepherd Market, just off Curzon Street, close to my old death threat flat.

The Penthouse was the alternative Playboy, with Penthouse Pets instead of Playboy Bunnies. Tits and bums and bare legs still, but a different swimming costume and no powder puff with a deplorable tendency to get stuck in the lavatory. The Italian ex-waiter came back to see the ex-film student. He told him to stop serving coffee and start dealing in a casino. The money was much better, the work was easier on the legs, and there were hints of even more money if your nerves were up to it. There was plenty of crumpet and they didn't all rabbit away in Swedish. A few days later the Penthouse got a new dealer who rapidly became the manager, thanks to his good looks and his elegant dress sense and his easy way with the punters.

Pleasurama's Casanova didn't stay wholly Pleasurama for long. It opened to the public just before the hostile take-over bid for the company that owned the Curzon House Club. The cash-rich but casino-less Barnett family descended on the Casanova, with Julian in tow. They made a generous offer, grabbed with both hands by Pleasurama, and became owners of three quarters of the Casanova. Pleasurama kept a quarter share of the business (and of the soon to be massive profits), but were only sleeping partners. Julian and the Barnetts did the running of the casino. Actually word went round that Bob Barnett's official job was catering consultant, a position that didn't require a licence of any sort. But no-one ever saw him stirring the soup. Maybe Abe the American did know something the rest of us didn't about cat-houses on the East side. I stopped being French roulette pit-boss before I'd even started, and became assistant French roulette pit-boss. The pay was the same so it was OK by me. I've never been impressed by titles. Just show me the money. The top French roulette job was taken by a man I knew well, who had stayed at the Curzon after I left. He was one of the good guys, after a shaky start. Everything seemed fine, for a while.

The best known face at the Casanova belonged to Crown Prince Fahd of Saudi-Arabia, who became King Fahd when the old king died and the family business passed on to the next generation. The worst period of extravagance in his country's sad history was about to begin (or the best, if you were part of the royal family) and really took off in the mid seventies after the times five hike in the price of oil. One prince built a palace, another prince built one next door, visibly larger, the first prince built another one on the other side, visibly larger again, and so on ad infinitum. Luckily there was plenty of desert to build on. Saudi Arabia should have been the wealthiest country in the world but fell into debt, a remarkable achievement that deserves a place in the Guinness Book of Records. The incomes of ordinary people halved. Unemployment soared. The late Osama bin Laden built up a following, supported by the financially disadvantaged, the unemployed, and the (sometimes very wealthy) devout, the latter genuinely shocked by the extravagance and the gambling and the whoring of leaders who were supposed to live by the rules of the puritanical Wahabi branch of Islam. All still to come, in 1972, but the sharp-eyed could see the writing on the wall. The rest of us took no notice, or sold them arms via middle-men whose massive bribes, along with the various princes' share of the family loot were soon to make the smarter London casino owners rich far beyond their wildest dreams.

Crown Prince Fahd liked baccarat, the elegant French card game sometimes seen in old films, especially ones made in France. His second choice was punto banco, a simplified and vulgar version of baccarat, which originated in South America before quickly moving on to Las Vegas and Europe and the rest of the world. The Casanova had both games. Baccarat was played once a week. Fahd was always there, always next to the banker, the elegantly dressed man on whose skill, or lack of it, the profitability of the game depends. The banker has to work out the ever changing odds. It's a difficult job and very well paid, and can be even better paid, for a short time at least, if he makes a mess of it on purpose and a friendly player wins big. Which didn't happen at the Casanova, I hasten to report. Sometimes you just can't get the staff. A pretty young English girl was always at Crown Prince Fahd's side, looking rather like the film actress Patsy Kensit. It wasn't her, of course, the girl in question would be about sixty now, which Patsy Kensit visibly is not. But when I saw Patsy Kensit in a recent film I got the feeling that I'd seen her somewhere before. Then it all came flooding back.

Many years later, when Prince Fahd became King Fahd, he banned the other princes from throwing the country's oil money away in London casinos, like he used to, and a new profession sprang up overnight. When a prince went to a London casino he took a front man with him. The new employee became a member of the casino and signed His Royal Highness in as a guest. The naughty prince sometimes had a rich Saudi in tow who signed cheques payable to the casino and handed the chips to the prince, for settlement later, or the prince brought in a massive wad of unsigned traveller's cheques. In that case the front man signed the cheques in both places at the cash desk. A flagrant breach of normal security, but it kept the prince's signature out of sight. Another alternative was a massive wad of cash. All done to avoid a paper trail that could link a Saudi prince to a London casino and damage his promotion prospects in the family firm.

One hot night around the turn of the Twentieth century, when Fahd was still (allegedly) alive, but no longer in charge of Saudi Arabia, or of himself, and no new king had yet been put in place, relatives of the man everyone expected to be the next king came to play punto banco in one of London's top casinos. The visit was carefully arranged in advance by a non-royal but very highly placed Saudi. There was a delay before they came in. Armed British intelligence officers checked the street before the Saudis were allowed to step out of their limousines. When the all clear sounded the Saudis were rushed to the dark staff entrance a discreet distance away from the casino's front door and ushered through a normally locked door into a private room. Nobody in the casino saw them come in. Two employees would stay in your memory if, like me, you had been there. One was a built like a brick shit-house Saudi security man, with a bulge under his jacket and a military style radio that kept him in contact with the intelligence officers in the street, watching out for terrorists tempted by the juicy profusion of targets. He had a nice smile and a friendly manner, and even flirted with the very pretty waitress. I had expected a soldier in civvies with the I'm not really dead, you can tell because the rest of my body is still moving facial expressions of Steven Seagal, rather than such a natural charmer. But I was still glad I wasn't someone he didn't like. The other employee you wouldn't forget was a skinny little man who spent the whole night standing next to the obviously senior Saudi, with an ash-tray in his hand. He was there to spare the boss the effort of stretching his own hand out when the ash on his cigarette got a bit long. The tray was always just under the cigarette when the ash fell off, sometimes with the help of a discreet flick from the ash-tray holder's finger. And you thought your job was boring. About a million pounds changed hands, in favour of the casino. Then the carefully orchestrated entry was reversed and the Saudis and the brick shit-house and the human ash-tray melted into the night.

Back to the Cass. We've spent long enough in Saudi. I'm getting nervous. They might take it personally. The French roulette at the Casanova was much like any other French game in town. The main money came from big players in straight games. The biggest was an extremely wealthy Gulf Arab, a very big player even before the oil price went through the roof. We lost him as a customer when his son died in a car crash, in a Ferrari that his father bought him, unwisely, as a very young birthday present. The grief-stricken father decided that his son's tragic death was God's way of punishing him for his gambling, not the result of his giving an inexperienced young driver the nearest thing to a racing car that he could take out on the street, and gave up gambling immediately, much to the disgust of the owners and senior managers of the casino.

The more commercially minded croupiers made their money from medium stake players who knew the real rules of the game. The best, in terms of confidence and the ability to fool the owners and managers, was a man with a North African background, married to a very sexy Frenchwoman and living in North London. Sadly he had the same problem as the Italian restaurant owner, the most unreliable baron at the Curzon. He was very skilled at the black arts but the illegally acquired money burnt a hole in his pocket long before the time came to share it out with the boys. They always got some, but a good proportion was lost in a casino where he didn't have a special relationship with the staff. It was a shame. He was the best operator I ever saw, and never came under suspicion. To be fair he did once win somewhere else, in a straight game, and added his winnings to the pot, something the Italian restaurant owner never did (or owned up to).

156

One of the biggest straight players was an Englishman with a very aristocratic manner whose name I've forgotten. He was old fashioned and square almost to the point of caricature, and always asked for the awful pop music (his words) to be turned off while he was playing. (Most casinos have pop music playing quietly in the background, to fill in the awkward silences when someone loses a packet). The Edwardian relic was a very senior civil servant. Something to do with buying expensive things for government departments. Probably office blocks. I think the word procurement came into his job title. Millions of tax payers' pounds were involved. He played roulette with fifty pound chips, very big money for the early seventies. I always assumed that he was from a wealthy family. No civil service job could have financed that sort of gambling. But it emerged that the procurement officer was procuring a small percentage of the government funds for himself and spending it on his roulette habit. The evidence was overwhelming, but just before he was prosecuted he committed suicide rather than go to prison. He had an accomplice on the outside, a solicitor or an accountant, if you know how to tell them apart, who must have been very relieved when the main man did himself in and stopped his own part in the theft from being exposed in court, as might well have happened if the main man had tried to share the blame in search of a shorter sentence.

After eight months I gave in my notice and left the Casanova, for what could loosely be called personal reasons. The timing wasn't actually bad. Things were getting a bit out of hand on the French table. Most of the crew were sensible and self-disciplined, but one croupier, a small Italian, had picked up the bad habit of grabbing a handful of chips from the table float and flicking them on to the winning number. You don't do that. I always admired courage under fire, but not suicidal recklessness. Nobody was able to restrain him. I think he took drugs. Not very long after I left, and probably because of the actions of the crazy flicker, the French table was thrown out, along with some of the staff, one of whom could have been me.

I didn't have a job to go to. It was a time of confusion. (I'm being polite). My future wife and I had moved from Chelsea to a slummy part of North London, where rivalry between Turkish Cypriot drug importers occasionally erupted in gunfire. Freed from the need to go to work, we drove down to Cadaques and took another look at the place where we first met. The money ran out shortly after we got home. I found a straight job at lousy pay, a terrible combination, at the Knightsbridge Sporting Club, which shut down without a fight in 1980 or 1981. Luckily a job very soon came up at the Playboy Club and I was able to go back to doing what I did best. I'm sure I had a guardian angel in those long-gone days. Whenever things went wrong something good came out of the blue and things went right again. I wish it still happened. Where do guardian angels go when they die? If it's the same place we go to I've got some sharp questions for the bitch who left me in the lurch. But not yet. There were still good times to come.

The Playboy.

What sort of job did you do when you were young, mama? I dressed up like a bunny-rabbit and got paid lots of money. Ooh, can I do that when I grow up, mama? No darling. The police took our licence away and we had to give our costumes back. Anyway you're a boy.

A good friend, anxious to rescue me from a dismal future at the Knightsbridge, got me a job at the Playboy Club. If I'd been female the move would probably have been in the opposite direction. The Knightsbridge had a mole at the Playboy, an exceptionally beautiful girl, whose (untaxed) moonlight job involved poaching the prettiest trainees as soon as they were good enough to unleash on the public and sending them over to the Knightsbridge. It was an excellent arrangement. The Knightsbridge got the Playboy-financed training for free, paid the girls who took the bait a bit more money than the Playboy (not difficult) and got the pick of the crop at minimum expense and with minimum hassle. Private enterprise at its best. The girls were picked for their good looks and their nicely shaped bottoms--the hot pants once worn at the Knightsbridge were very unforgiving, and left a legacy of slim bottom mania long after the Gaming Board had ruled them out as a uniform-- rather than for their ability as croupiers. You could help a real cracker stolen from the Playboy to brush up on her dealing skills, but you couldn't turn a Plain Jane into a stunning beauty, even with the finest make-up, and you could wait forever for the casino lard-arse to stop stuffing her face with chocolate and shrink back to a size eight.

My move had nothing to do with my looks or, you'll be pleased to hear, I hope, with my bottom. Surprisingly, in a casino with an ultra-modern image, the Playboy had a French roulette table. Even more surprisingly it was a French roulette table, entirely devoid of Frenchmen, that stuck like glue to the old traditions. Exactly enough of the staff had the skills to make the few extra pounds that were the norm in the closed world of London casinos. But a crisis loomed. The sun was about to set on the afore-mentioned traditions, possibly forever. One of the good guys had decided to spend a lot of time near the edge of the warm Mediterranean sea, where his nights would be filled with music rather than with the nerve-jangling sound of roulette balls rattling around roulette wheels, booze was cheaper than cornflakes, and bookies gave odds-on that that a beach ball lobbed in any direction would land on an evenly tanned busty blonde bimbo in a bikini. Or, once he got the low-down on the local layout and found the places where nothing was allowed to come between a sun-worshipper and the sun-god, a busty blonde bimbo not in a bikini. His colleagues begged him to delay his departure, but their pleas fell on deaf ears. What he didn't tell them, in case they sneaked behind his back in a desperate attempt to keep him in town, was that his urge to be where he wasn't was in more than equal measure an urge not to be where he was. A girl-friend he was rapidly tiring of was talking more and more often about marriage. On bad days the hints crept into double figures. Enthusiasm was turning into obsession. He managed to choke back a hollow laugh when she quoted her parents' view that as they were now living together they should get engaged, not realising how many times we'd all heard that one before. But he knew he couldn't last forever in a battle that better men than he had fought and lost. He sometimes saw them in the pub, on the rare occasions they managed to escape. Shadows of their former selves, gloomily looking for the past in a pot of beer. He had to get away. A bust-out was not only a one-way ticket to an earthly paradise, if he played his cards right, it was an escape from impending doom. His ears became as deaf to his colleagues' pleas as they were to his soon to be ex young lady's plans for his future. His spine stiffened. He left the roulette table and the girl-friend behind. I, a ground down survivor of an earlier bust-out, took his place.

An advert for a French roulette croupier was all ready to go into the Evening Standard. Luckily the very good friend mentioned above knew the back story, and was a drinking buddy of the man who needed to know all about me. He listed my skills, legal and other, and promised that, in return for a modest share of the loot, I would look away when the game was afoot, or, for a less modest share, get stuck in full time. Anything rather than stay at the Knightsbridge, where my hands and feet were tied and my once golden future was about as bleak as golden futures can get if you take your eye off the ball, for reasons I would rather keep to myself. On my friend's recommendation, and skilful use of a pre-arranged password, I sneaked in front of all the tossers who might have answered the advert and got the job.

The Playboy's best manager (now deceased, sadly) used the French roulette table to raise the money he needed to play blackjack at the appropriately named Cromwell Mint, in Cromwell Road, a stone's throw from some of London's finest museums. He often popped over for a chat with the inspector at the top of the French table, ostensibly to find out how the table was doing. As their conversation sparkled on the inspector passed some of the bigger chips, kept in deep metal containers safely under his guard, to the manager. Once the chips were out of their box the inspector hid them behind the clipboard listing the names and numbers relating to the game in progress, and mimed an earnest discussion with the manager about how much the table was winning or, by now, probably losing. As they spoke, quietly, the chips were passed to the manager and then taken to the cash desk (when the right cashier was there), to be changed into cash. The French crew got their share at the end of the night. The boss of the French game was not in on the money, but that was no real problem. He was a very ambitious man who spent as much time as he could in the restaurant, socialising with big players in preparation for the promotion to management that he felt was long overdue, a sentiment he was sure the existing management would share once their eyes fixed on the sophisticated way he handled the big gamblers. While the cat was away, for a couple of hours on a good night, the mice came out to play.

The French roulette scams were the usual stuff, honed to perfection over the years. Chips were kept in front of the croupier and placed on the number the ball fell into, still the best way to win at roulette if you can get away with it. Viva the barons, of whom there was no shortage, at the Playboy or anywhere else. And there was another road to riches, back in the seventies. In most places, when you went to the cash desk and signed a cheque, or handed over your possibly hard-earned cash, you were given oval shaped chips in exchange. The oval chips were the same colour and had the same values as the rectangular ones you could place on the table for a bet, but they could only be used to buy table chips from a croupier, and were then dropped by the croupier into a locked metal box, along with any cash changed at the table. The system worked well, and even kept the thieving down a little bit, but the Playboy (and some other unrelated casinos) foolishly broke with tradition and gave the customers a small piece of paper with its monetary value written on it by

160

the cashier, instead of a proper oval chip. The system was so easy to bend that I always assumed that it was invented in the early days by a bent cashier with impressive credentials (an accountant perhaps) and gratefully adopted by a gullible casino owner, dazzled by his cashier's professional qualifications and attracted by the low cost of bits of paper compared to the high cost of oval chips. The piece of paper handed out by the cashier was then offered by the player to the croupier on the table of his choice. The only person a bent croupier had to show it to, after making sure that no inquisitive player could see what was written on the paper, was his inspector, who was of course in on the game. Keeping things to ourselves wasn't difficult. The amount was handwritten in small writing, and small writing is hard to read from a distance. Even the most zealous nark would draw the line at peering through a pair of opera glasses. One cashier's handwriting was sometimes so small that it was hard to read even when it was right there in front of one's eyes. I strongly suspected, but never pursued the matter, on a didn't need to know basis, that the really small writing was done by the cashier who worked closely with the special manager (may his soul rest in peace) when he was dealing with a customer who he knew had a business relationship with the fertile French roulette table. A fine man selflessly extending a helping hand to transactions from which he himself drew no profit. Say what you will about common thieves in other walks of life, and for all I know your harsh words may carry the stamp of truth, but among casino thieves there was not only an endless supply of honour, there were shed-loads of chivalry too.

If the useful bit of paper had £100 written on it, and the coast was clear, the croupier gave the baron £500 and got the financial horse up and running at a champion's pace. It had to be done very quickly, to get the written evidence out of the way before an unsympathetic co-worker suddenly appeared from nowhere, as they often did, the tricky devils, but the prospect of a couple of weeks' worth of cash for less than a minute's work was a powerful incentive. And it was reasonably safe. If you were caught giving a very high exchange rate you could reasonably claim that it was all a terrible mistake. Just not myself at the moment. Awful pressure from her indoors. Getting worse by the day. I only said yes because she was wearing a posh white dress and the future mother-in-law had that look on her dial. You know what they're like. Concentration very difficult in the circumstances. Couldn't be sorrier if you paid me. Good stuff, all that, if you were up against a married man, legally speaking. Nobody would believe you of course, and instant dismissal would follow as sure as night follows day, but being stupid or hen-pecked wasn't against the law, even in the old days. There was still a very good chance of staying on the outside and looking into the nick rather than sitting on the inside looking out, a very important difference you'll be bound to agree if your thought processes run along anything like the same lines as mine.

Late one night an Arab man was playing blackjack for high stakes, alone at his table. Big gamblers don't share tables. They are all control freaks who rant and rave if another player draws a card when they wouldn't, even if, as is often the case, it's exactly the right thing to do. It happened to me once, in Malta. I thought the locals were going to throw me in the sea when we all lost, thanks to my scientifically immaculate decision to draw on a sixteen when the dealer had an ace.

The man playing at the Playboy was a terrible show-off, another trait that often distinguishes the very rich from the rest of us. He always kept loads of chips in front of him, even if he was losing, to show how rich he was and what a fearless gambler the riff-raff were sneakily admiring from their humbler tables. He hit a runner, won a packet, and decided to cash out. He told the friendly manager, who couldn't spend all his time robbing the French table, much as he would have liked to, to bring a tray and take his winnings to the cash desk and come back with loads of cash packets that he could spread all over the table and flaunt in front of the disciples. A perfectly normal way, in his particular case, of rounding off a successful evening at a blackjack table. What he didn't know was that the chip tray used by the manager to carry his chips was known, to a very select few, as the Irish tray. The cheap plastic trays used to store and transport chips in casinos normally hold two hundred chips, in ten rows of twenty chips. The Irish tray was a faulty specimen that held twenty-one chips in each compartment, a design fault spotted by a quick-witted cashier who immediately put the faulty tray to one side, rightly confident that its poor standard of manufacture would come in handy one day. You will have worked by now that the Irish tray, when filled to the brim, held ten more chips than a normal tray and would conjure up, for example, a spare thousand pounds if filled with hundred pound chips.

The manager picked up the chips and stuffed them into the Irish tray. Strictly speaking he should have counted out the chips in stacks of twenty, in front of the player, before putting them in the tray. And, according to another house rule, he should have brought a whole lot of trays from the cash desk and taken all the gambler's chips in one go. But the other trays only held two hundred chips. His razor-like brain was well ahead of the game. The multitude of trips between the table and the cash desk, with chips going one way and cash packets coming back for everyone to marvel at when they were piled up on the table, was just the way the show-off liked it. A good manager has to be flexible when there's a public relations advantage to be plucked from the air. Not to mention a

162

couple of thousand quid. Everybody had a good day (night). The show-off got his show, at a price, the friendly manager and the sharp-eyed cashier got their money, the then owner of the Cromwell Mint copped a chunk next time the friendly manager dropped in for a spot of blackjack, and the secret wine provider at the Cavendish served a whole lot more cheap red wine (cheap to him, I mean. The rest of us paid through the nose). Even the Playboy shareholders had nothing to moan about. The money would have gone anyway. It was stolen from the punter, not from the casino. Everybody dance! When the ceremony was over the special tray went back to its special place. A note of caution: you mustn't try this sort of thing in a modern casino. Things have changed. Put that tray down. And the file. This is a history book, not the nine o'clock news. It's all over now, baby blue. They'll get you through the CCTV cameras and haul you off to the nick. Not even a sneaky game of blackjack on the way. Casino fraud is done on paper now and requires the full participation of the most senior management. It's like banks. The cowboys have all gone home, or to a pub to cry in their beer, if they can still afford beer.

The French roulette boys (all right, some of them) and the friendly manager and the clever cashier weren't the only people making money within the four walls of 45 Park Lane, where strictly speaking only the Playboy organisation should have been coining the stuff. A very attractive young woman came to London from the Middle East to work in a legitimate but short-term job in the glamour business. When her contract ran out she decided to stay in London. She wasn't from a privileged background, or a peaceful one. Think 1948 at the wrong end of the Mediterranean. Staying in London had to be better than going back to a refugee camp. She quickly made friends with some of the Playboy bunny-girls, and with rather more of the male gamblers, and established what could only be described as a floating brothel. Floating because there were no fixed premises, a wise decision when you study the finer details of British law, not because there was water sloshing about below where the action took place. Don't go hanging round the Serpentine and asking which boats the girls are on.

The lady from the Middle East was on to a better thing than she knew. A man who wins money in a casino often becomes sexually aroused, sometimes to a quite alarming degree. It's better than Viagra. And free, if you win. (Women don't, apparently; I can't tell you why not; it's just one more of life's mysteries. And it doesn't happen when you're a bent male player working a bent game with a bent croupier. No mystery there: it's strictly business and you're constantly worried about getting rumbled. The resulting tension makes it impossible to concentrate on sex, commercial or otherwise). If you're right there on the premises, with the right sort of girls waiting for the phone to ring, business booms as soon as the lucky winner trousers his cash. And boom it did. Word soon got round that a pretty girl could earn good money by having sex with certain players. Conditions of employment were exemplary. A girl could refuse any client she didn't like the look of, choose how many hours she wanted to spend sounding like Meg Ryan (in that film I mean. She may be as quiet as a mouse in the privacy of her own home), and walk away whenever she felt like it. The organiser only took a very modest commission. A far cry from the lion's share grabbed by the greedy pimps on the streets outside. No drugs were involved. One of the girls married her first, very wealthy client, so dazzled by the quality of the merchandise that he decided to buy rather than rent. The sex trade had no input from the company, I hasten to add. It was an independent operation, like the thirst-quenching and very popular red wine supplying business at the Cavendish. The vast majority of the girls were not involved. Most of them didn't even know what was going on, or kept well away if they did. Don't worry if your mother was a Playboy bunny during the swinging sixties. She probably didn't even know about the whoring. You can still talk to her. Just don't ask where all the jewellery came from.

The special all ladies floating whorehouse was very different from the activities of a young Arab man who hung around the Playboy at roughly the same time, offering girls to winners and losers alike. A Playboy bunny girl was found in her flat with her throat cut. There were no signs of a struggle. She appeared to have had consensual sex before she died in pain, almost certainly with the bastard who killed her. The crime was never solved. Nowadays DNA from his sperm or from the spit dribbling from his mouth, would have nailed the culprit right away, but DNA forensics hadn't been invented then. The young Arab man was questioned and released, and died young, to not many peoples' sorrow, helped along the way by a large and regular intake of drugs. A lot of people are still convinced that he was the killer.

Sexual fantasies about the bunnies were not confined to the players. Right through the seventies, at least once a week, there was a croupier's party in somebody's rented flat. Starting time was about midnight, after the pubs had shut and the curries had been eaten, for those on a day-shift or a day off, with a second wave pouring in at about 4 am when the casinos shut down. Really desperate souls could hang on from then till breakfast time. Every party had four things in common: there were at least five men for every girl, the music was too quiet because the neighbours kept banging on the wall, there was nothing to drink if you were part of the second wave, apart from the meagre offering you took along yourself and were very careful not to let go of, and a rumour went round that any minute now half a dozen Playboy bunnies would arrive, stark naked under their fur coats.

Needless to say it never happened, even in warm weather. The nearest I ever got to the dream scene was turning up at the usual no-hope party with a friend whose name I've changed to protect the guilty, and finding to my surprise that there were two Playboy girls already in the room. Neither of them was wearing a fur coat, or naked, but my friend rose to the occasion anyway. He walked up to the girls and said, right out loud: 'George is my name and sex is my game,' the first and last line of poetry that ever emerged from his mouth, in my presence at least. The response was a silence you could hear ten miles away.

The only casino parties really worth going to were the Christmas staff parties laid on by the Playboy itself, in its very own Playboy discotheque. A room bursting with crumpet, music loud enough to make a dead man dance, and booze flowing like water under a bridge, soon after a storm. There was a downside though, for some of the chaps. Every year several divorce proceedings were launched by female members of staff who had stumbled upon someone more interesting than their lawfully wedded husbands (not always a difficult task, then or now) and slipped off somewhere quiet to grab a taste of the forbidden fruit. One previously docile wife didn't come home for a week. That sort of thing has always been common among men, but up till then had been comparatively rare among girls. Almost unheard of in some of the quieter counties. In its own special way the Playboy was a real force in the womens' liberation movement, even if the women in question had to pretend to be rabbits.

The Playboy's staff entrance was at the back of the building, in a short street that runs between Park Lane and South Audley Street, the sort of street you never remember the name of even if something exciting happens there. A small door led into a long corridor. At the deep end a security man sat alone in a dark cubicle, looking as menacing as the concierge in a block of flats in Paris. To his left there was a lift that took you up to the staff rooms on one the upper floors. One night I walked into the lift with a girl I recognised as a punto-banco dealer from the table next to the French roulette. She was drop dead gorgeous, from head to toe. We all used to stare at her, wantonly, when the French game was quiet and she wasn't looking. It was impossible not to, unless you were dead. Especially at what would have been her rump steaks if she'd been born into the bovine family, rather than the human one. But sugar and spice and all things nice were in short supply on the day she was born. She stood in the middle of the lift with a pay slip in her hand. Her lips pursed to breaking point. Her eyes narrowed to slits. Her forehead wrinkled in rage. She spoke out loud about a mistake in her pay. Another fucking mistake! Fucking hell! He's fucked me up again! The fucking wanker! And lots more in that vein. I assumed that she was talking to me. We were alone, after all. Nobody else in sight. I didn't like to ignore her. That's rude. I mumbled some words of sympathy, in an attempt to lighten the mood. Her perfect blue eyes poured contempt all over me, like very cold water with something nasty mixed in, and left me feeling about six inches tall. For several hours. I watched her later, behind the punto-banco table, smiling the sweetest of smiles at a big gambler (who later turned out to have been robbing the joint, but not with her help) and marveled at her range, as well as at her rump steaks.

An Englishman came down in the lift one night, carrying on his person a number of high value Playboy chips. By rights they should have been handed over to a special customer in a dark corner of the casino, but the customer had been delayed and couldn't get to the casino before closing time. His wife had died, or something like that. He managed to send a message that he would be in the all-night restaurant of a nearby hotel (no, not the Cavendish) at about half past four in the morning, just after the casino closed. If the chips could be brought there he would take them home, cash them in the next night, and distribute the money later. The Englishman drew the short straw and got the job of carrying the chips past the dreaded security man.

He didn't like it. All casinos have a right to search their staff at any time, subject to certain legal conditions which do nothing to protect the genuinely guilty, and it was often difficult to convince a security man that some casino chips had fallen into your pocket by accident. Sometimes an offer to split the proceeds avoided further embarrassment, but the Englishman knew that the security man on duty was as straight as a die. A clever idea came to him. Instead of changing out of his dinner suit and into his usual jeans and jumper he kept the suit on and folded his street clothes, along with a couple of old shirts from the bottom of his locker, around the chips, which were wrapped tightly in a plastic bag to prevent them from falling on to the floor at just the wrong moment. So far so good. Surely no security man would want to stick his hands in a bunch of old clothes and find himself rummaging through another chap's used underpants. Clever or what?

The Englishman was a quarter of the way up the long corridor when the security man first yelled out 'oi,' loudly. Luckily he didn't know the Englishman's name. The street door suddenly seemed much further away.

At times like this the human brain slips a gear and a reflex mechanism takes over. You do what you have to do without thinking about it first, and much faster than you ever thought you could. Soldiers with memories of active service will confirm this. You don't have to take a croupier's word for it. The Englishman carried on walking as fast as he could, trying hard not to give the impression that he was speeding up, and didn't look back. There were more calls of 'oi.' He heard the security man's cubicle door open and fast footsteps coming up the corridor. He made it through the street door and stood behind a parked pick-up truck. He dropped the bag of chips on to the road, hidden (he hoped) by the truck's big back wheel. He heard the security man's footsteps change in tone as he came out on to the street. He pretended to notice him for the first time. He stepped back on to the pavement, smiling nicely, and walked back towards the staff entrance. 'Sorry, were you calling me?' 'Yes mate. Thought you'd gone deaf.' 'So sorry. Always in a dream at this time of the morning.' The security man explained that seeing someone walk out with a bundle of clothes in his arms meant that he had to carry out a spot check, standing orders and all that, just like in the Army of which he had once been a valuable part. The used underpants theory died in the cold night air. Friendly apologies from the security man for having to do the search. Friendly apologies from the Englishman for forcing him to come out in the cold. Shake him warmly by the hand and bugger off, counting lucky stars.

The security man was no match for Sherlock Homes (very few of them were) and failed to walk round the back of the pick-up truck in search of clues. He wouldn't have needed a magnifying glass. Anxious not to give him any ideas, post-mortem as you might say, the Englishman strolled off at a leisurely pace, as cool as a cucumber, kept well away from the back of the pick-up truck, got into his sports car, drove round the block before coming back to the scene of the crime, stopped where he had dropped the loot, opened the driver's door, scooped up the very expensive bag of chips and drove off at speed, very pleased and slightly surprised that they were still there. Some awful people hang around Mayfair late at night. He parked again and walked to the all-night restaurant. Five minutes after sitting down his whole body began to shake uncontrollably. His contact arrived, saw the shaking, and asked if he was feeling all right. 'No. I damn near got nicked. Is your wife really dead? A joke? Oh good. Glad to hear it. Say hello from me. Here's the chips.' It was a kind of post-traumatic stress. Your brain borrows something to get you through a crisis and then your body shakes like a leaf when your brain pays back, with interest.

A year after I started there, almost to the day, the Playboy closed the French roulette table. The golden goose died without a whisper. The French crew were transferred to American roulette and blackjack. I found myself on a string of low-life tables, aptly nick-named Death Row. It wasn't easy to cling on to the will to live when you were watching a low-life American roulette game to your left and a low-life blackjack game to your right, on Death Row. Stakes rarely exceeded the minimum, some of the players could have done with a wash, and a substantial minority tried to cheat, especially on roulette, but lacked the good manners to offer a share to the staff. As soon as I could I left for a proper French roulette job at Ladbroke's new Hill Street casino.

The Playboy managed fine without my help. Shortly after I'd left the bunnies behind me the oil dollars generated by the 1973 Arab-Israeli war (which came close to turning into WW3 and doing for us all) flooded into London. The wily manager who had done so much to restore my fortunes, and my flagging faith in human nature, went from strength to strength and became one of the few casino managers who could fill a casino purely by the force of his personality rather than by making payments to well-connected middlemen. His charm, combined with the bright smiles of the bunny-girls, filled the Playboy to bursting point with the newly super-rich Arabs and led to the establishment of the Playboy VIP Room, in its heyday the most profitable casino square footage in London. Sometimes the cash boxes on the tables were so full by the middle of the afternoon that the managers had to take them off the tables and put new ones in their place, a level of prosperity never before seen in London casinos. But it was not enough for the management. Victor Lownes, Playboy's man at the top, loved making pep-talks in which he never failed to mention the possibility of one bad apple--aka one bent croupier--spoiling the whole barrel. It's always the poor wot gets the blame. But when the plod shut the joint down in 1981 it turned out that bad apples at much higher levels had been rotting the barrel from the top down.

Not long after the cops had left the premises (after a brief interval during which a new company tried and failed to get a casino going again) the Sultan of Brunei bought the old Playboy building and turned it into his London pied-a-terre, only a minute's glide in a gold-plated Rolls-Royce from the Dorchester hotel, which he also owned, and where a gambler known as the Fat Man bitterly disappointed three young men I once knew. But that's another story.

Dancing in the Dark.

The next two chapters (one less than a page long) hang in space like ghosts. The people and the casinos don't have names. They passed me in the night, in no particular order, in the early seventies, the period I'm at in the main narrative. They knew nothing about each others' activities. I've lumped them together, dancing in the dark but loosely defined by time. The girl in the first chapter was the second most beautiful girl I had ever seen. She had an honest, open face that made you feel that even if everything wasn't all right with the world yet, it soon would be. The man in the second chapter was one of the nicest guys I've ever shared a drink with. I feel unable to move on without introducing you to them both. When their stories are told I'll pick up the thread again and describe what went on at Ladbroke's Hill Street casino, one of the leading combatants in the fight to poach big gamblers from their competitors, arrogantly played out in public, that led to the closure of so many London casinos in 1980 and 1981. I just wanted to slip in the stories of two unknown people I really liked.

The Country Girl.

She came to London from deep in the country. She was nineteen. She learned to deal blackjack. She got a job in a West End casino. She was the best looking girl in the place and the nicest. She had none of the vanity that often spoils a girl blessed with such beauty. She wanted to go out in the world and live, not stand still and be looked at. She had dark blue eyes, dark, dark hair, pale skin and a smile that lit up the room.

She liked to go dancing after a night shift, to the Candy Box, a discotheque near Carnaby Street, specially licensed until seven or eight in the morning for the benefit of night workers, legal or otherwise. She met a tall dark handsome man from the Carribean. She fell in love. She looked terrific dancing with him, the beautiful white princess and the handsome black prince. She thought he loved her.

She tried the heroin he gave her as a gift. She paid him for it when he told her it wasn't free any more. She sold her perfect body when he said it was the only way to earn enough to pay what she owed. She stopped working at the casino. She gave him all her money. She was his girl.

She lurched up to a Greek friend of mine, in the afternoon, in busy Queensway, years later, on a stretch of pavement she called her own. He recognised her immediately. She asked him if he wanted a girl. He said no thank you. He tried to say hello, I know you. She only heard the no and moved on to the next man in the street, trying to focus her pin-prick pupils, trying to make the most of her fading beauty, desperate for the money that would buy her next shot of heroin.

She had the saddest story of any girl I ever knew.

She didn't deserve it.

I loved her, from a distance, long, long ago.

Bernie the Waistcoat.

I once worked with a blackjack pit-boss who always wore a natty waistcoat under his suit. At that time many casinos didn't provide a uniform. You bought your own dinner suit and your own bow tie, and so long as they were both black and of conventional cut the details didn't matter. If you wanted to spend your money on a waistcoat it was up to you. Very few of us did. We thought they'd gone out with the buckled shoe. Boring old men wore waistcoats stretched tight across their middle-aged spread, not cool young dudes like us. So Bernie stood out in the crowd. (Bernie isn't his real name. I've forgotten his real name. Not that I'd tell you anyway. He just looked like a Bernie. Maybe it was the waistcoat). I liked him, in spite of his bad dress sense. I treated the waistcoat as an unfortunate personal failing, like bad breath, and kept my fashion thoughts to myself.

Bernie was popular with the blackjack dealers and inspectors who worked under him. He was most at ease with a raven-haired beauty whose husband robbed banks when he wasn't in prison. Not to be outdone, as feminism got a firmer grip on the half of the adult population that used to stay at home and do the cooking, she robbed casinos. Rather more successfully than he robbed banks, actually. He got caught at least once, she never even saw the inside of a police station, never mind the inside of a woman's nick. There was no funny business going on between her and Bernie, I hasten to add. In a small community everybody knows who's doing who, however hard they try to hide it. In fact the harder they try the more the rest of us nod our heads in silent agreement every time their studied indifference makes it even more obvious that they're at it like rabbits. Bernie and the girl just got on very well. It does happen. Not everybody wants to shag everybody else silly just because they rob the same casino. Anyway, even if Bernie had wanted to upgrade to a hotter relationship, he would have had more sense than to pick a girl whose husband wore a gun as often as he wore underpants, except when he was in prison uniform. Bernie was a very level-headed young man.

The casino we worked in had just opened its doors at two o'clock in the afternoon. There were no customers. I was on the roulette table closest to the one blackjack table that was ready for business. A man I didn't know well was sitting in the inspector's chair, the raven haired beauty was standing behind the table in the dealer's position, and Bernie was leaning against the player's side of the table, looking very important in his waistcoat. The cards were neatly spread in numerical order, arranged in what we call a fan. I couldn't help noticing that Bernie and the others looked unusually alert. Night people usually look a bit lost at two o'clock in the afternoon, after a short night's sleep. Their alertness had to be bad news for the owner of the casino. Something funny was going on.

A short, fat, sweaty man came into the room and headed for Bernie's blackjack table. He walked slowly, squeezing one enormous thigh past the other with obvious difficulty. He finally made it to the table and sat down, breathing hard. His huge arse dwarfed the chair. He pulled over a second chair--blackjack chairs are rather like bar-stools-- and rearranged himself so that each buttock had its own individual support. The relief brought a smile to his face. I tried hard not to imagine him naked. In a strong American accent and a surprisingly deep voice he waved a thick arm over the neatly displayed cards and said 'shuffle up.' The girl shuffled the cards very correctly, and offered the four packs and the cutting card to the American. When he'd made the cut she took the cards that were now in front of the cutting card and put them behind the cards behind the cutting card. The red cutting card was now at the front. Then she put the cutting card into its usual position, about a quarter of the way in from the back of the four decks. (I know this is very boring. It's even more boring when you do it for eight hours a night, especially when all you get is a salary. But you only have to read about it once, or maybe twice if I've explained it badly). So far everything was strictly by the book. I waited patiently for Bernie and the team to throw the book away. It didn't take long. When the dealer has arranged the cards correctly, the next step is to put them in the shoe, the plastic box from which they are dealt. The dealer usually pats the side of the four decks—that's a lot of cards, two hundred and nine if you include the cutting card—against the side of the shoe, to get them neatly lined up before putting them in. The straightening pat ensures that the cards come out of the shoe smoothly when they're dealt and avoids the embarrassing delays that would occur if they got stuck during the game. So far so legal. Then it got real. Bernie produced two sets of carefully prepared cards from the pockets of the waistcoat I had always sneered at, in my ignorance, and placed them against the side of the shoe, behind the cards which the dealer had shuffled and prepared in strict accordance with the rules. At what seemed like the same time, but must have been a split second later, the dealer took the new cards in her left hand and slid them forwards. The substitute cards took the place of the casino's cards that she had just got ready. Her right hand passed the original cards backwards to Bernie, whose hands were now empty. He divided the four legitimate packs into two parts and slipped them into the waistcoat pockets that the carefully prepared cards had been kept in. The special cards that were about to give the crooked American gambler the biggest win he had ever had at blackjack, and the casino its biggest loss. If I'd blinked I would have missed the whole operation. (You might be wondering how I knew that the new cards were fixed. I didn't know for sure, of course. But ask yourself a question: would anyone risk imprisonment to put straight cards into a blackjack game? Exactly).

I was looking sideways on at Bernie the Waistcoat, at an angle that gave me a perfect view of the perfectly executed switch. During the lightning fast changeover Bernie's upper arms stayed remarkably still, as if his hands and lower arms weren't moving at all. The illusion of calm was very important. The day manager was standing only a few yards directly behind Bernie, with his elbows on the cash desk and his eyes on Bernie and the team. Just to be friendly I coughed lightly, caught the eye of the manager, and smiled, in an attempt to keep his eyes off the dangerous game, if only for a moment or two. It was the least a chap could do. Bernie's body was ideally situated between the manager's line of vision and the very illegal switch that had just taken place, but if Bernie's arms

173

had twitched a bit the manager's suspicions could have been aroused, with disastrous consequences for Bernie and friends, probably including a spell in prison, a particularly upsetting experience for the girl. Her husband was due to come out of prison at about the time she would have been going in, and that puts an awful strain on anyone's marriage. My cough just might have kept the show on the road. But if the cards had been dropped during the switch.....

I was filled with admiration. After forty years in casinos that switch remains the most skilled operation I ever saw. Including the sleight of hand of the Frenchmen I first worked with, the crooked ones that is, who were like magicians when they were robbing casinos. It probably sounds quite easy when you read about it. Just fiddling around with a few cards. Anyone can do that. Oh no they can't. Not when they are being watched, and one false move can put you behind bars. Or in casualty. It was a class act, and must have involved many patient hours of hard practice.

My heart was in my throat when the game ended and the American cashed out. Bernie the Waistcoat hadn't left the table during the game. Pit-bosses don't get many breaks at the best of times, and that early in the day there was no-one to take his place. The original casino cards were still in the pockets of the natty little waistcoat I used to sneer at. More incriminating evidence would be hard to find.

The American left the casino as slowly as he had entered it, with a happy smile on his face. The day manager came over to the blackjack table, looking like a man on the edge of a nervous breakdown. He was the only manager in the casino at the time and he was going to get hell when the top brass came in later. He knew how much the casino was losing. He had to bring extra chips to the table several times, as the American's lucky streak went on and on. The casino's loss was clearly visible every time he looked at the number of chips left on the table. Not realising that luck had nothing to do with the day's events, he never stopped hoping that the luck would change and the casino would get the money back. He hoped in vain. The cards had been very well prepared and the American never once drew a card he shouldn't have drawn.

Logic goes out of the window when a casino has a big loss. Superstition takes over, even among the professionals. Especially among the professionals. It's every man (or woman) for himself. Everyone remotely senior looks for someone junior to heap the blame on. The day manager was going to have to telephone the general manager immediately, to tell him about the disaster. And the cards were still in Bernie's pockets. It was possible the general manager might smell a rat, even over the telephone, and order a search of everyone connected with the game, if only to show his own superiors that he was on the case. That would have been the end. They might even have been able to trace the American, unless he moved a lot quicker when he was outside a casino. Or left a fat suit in a phone box and melted slimly into the crowd. I wasn't worried about him, to be honest, I have a quite unreasonable bias against fat men, but I liked Bernie and the girl. I felt very tense.

While Bernie was talking to the manager he remained as cool as the proverbial cucumber. Solemn of course. You're not supposed to laugh when the casino loses a packet and a half. There was no trace of the shakes, no nervousness in his voice, and not once did his hands go anywhere near the waistcoat that held the damning evidence. I did notice that the jacket he normally left open was done up, to hide the slight bulge in the waistcoat pockets where the cards were kept, but I didn't think the manager was sharp enough to spot the difference. The dealer and the inspector acted like silent mourners at a close friend's funeral. You might wonder why I was so tense. There was no profit in it for me when the share-out was made, and no penalty for me if the crime was discovered. That's true, but both points miss the point. I liked Bernie and I liked the girl, and I would probably have liked the inspector if I had known him. And I was a professional, lost in admiration of someone who left me standing. I had just witnessed the equivalent of the impossible passing shot that wins the men's singles at Wimbledon, and raises suspicions that Roger Federer really has sold his soul to the Devil, for a stiff price, or of the goal from an angle no-one has ever scored from before that wins the World Cup, if you're more into football, followed by a performance that would have won Bernie an Oscar if he had been acting for a living rather than supervising a bent blackjack game. To have seen all that talent go to waste for the benefit of a casino owner, a criminal one as it happens, would have broken my heart.

My heart remained unbroken. A while later Bernie got his break and did whatever was necessary to get rid of the dangerous cards. He met the American after work and the American paid up, and that doesn't always happen, as you know.

I never found out how Bernie got hold of the cards. Playing cards in a casino are guarded more fanatically than the gold in Fort Knox. He may have got them from a security man. Perhaps the security man in the same casino who was once caught removing a box full of whisky bottles from the alcohol storeroom, and explained that he was just checking whether somebody could get their hands on the key and nick a load of booze. Now that he had proved it could be done he would recommend an immediate change in the arrangements leading to the issue of the key. He was an Irishman who was well known to be very fond of the whisky, but, much to his surprise, the story was believed and he kept his job. Maybe the lucky escape gave him the confidence to move on to cards. Or Bernie might have got them through a friendly manager, for a share of the loot. But certainly not from the manager who was on that day. He was as straight as a die and as square as Prince Charles. One thing remains sure though. However the cards were acquired the difficulty would have been nothing compared to what Bernie and the girl had just done on the table.

As Bernie and I left the building at the end of the day shift I shook him warmly by the hand and told him that it was the finest operation I had ever seen. He accepted the praise gracefully, and said very modestly that it was nothing really. It just took a bit of practise at home. He was sure I must have done something just as clever at some stage in my career as a French roulette croupier. I never had. I knew when to accept second place. He even offered me a small share of the money. For the cough I suppose. I refused it, politely. I'd done nothing to earn it. Any fool can cough and smile at a creep. Then Bernie went his way and I went mine, walking on air, as you do when the good guys win. He was a very cool dude, the quiet, small man from the North East. I was even able to admire the waistcoat, now that I knew what it was for. I wish I could remember his real name. Not that I'd tell you if I could.

Hill Street.

In 1974 I started work at Hill Street casino, Ladbrokes' answer to the Curzon House. Corals the bookmakers bought all Bob Barnett's casinos in 1972, in a share raid that added a second shaft to their horse-betting goldmine. Ladbrokes the bookmakers went digging for casino gold at about the same time. The brace of bookies turned casino owners acted like synchronised swimmers while they were open for business, and sank in unison when they lost their licenses in the 1980/81 blitz because they couldn't resist breaking the laws. I was right with them there. In casinos breaking laws always made more money than obeying them. It was the way forward. Only the good die skint. Anyway as a career casino robber who was I to lob moral lectures at my fellow casino crims on the other side of the hill? But you have to learn to keep the details to yourself.

"Il faut jamais parler" were the first words the very intimidating French assistant head of the Curzon chemmy room spoke to me when, as a raw beginner stepping nervously into a life of crime, I asked him in a whisper for help with the illegal act one of his croupiers had asked me to perform. The less disciplined rogues at the top of Corals, Ladbrokes (and the Playboy) got into a row about poaching punters, and other matters that should have remained private, and shouted the evidence against themselves so loudly from the roof-tops that even the Gaming Board had to sit up and take notice. It was an enormously stupid act of mass self-harm, but think I understand now why the ex-bookies and the men from Chicago were so silly: the phenomenal profits made on the back of the oil price rise that followed the 1973 Arab-Israeli war made the new casino owners so much money in such a short time that they felt immune from prosecution. Laws, like taxes, were for little people. At the other end of the food chain, always wary of the feeling of the collars, we kept quiet and got on with the job of robbing those at the top, unaware that their arrogance was about to lead to the sudden death of the golden goose. World War One all over again. Lions led by donkeys.

The man who table-tested me told me later that Ladbrokes' first year as casino owners was a bit of a flop, probably because they elected to start from the ground up rather than buy existing casinos, a move that gave rival bookies Corals a head-start. At a board meeting twelve months in someone unkindly pointed out that more money would have been earned if the starting capital had been put in a building society account rather than spent on fitting out casinos and paying croupiers to sit around doing nothing. Luckily for me, eager to get back into the world of the living after a few weeks on the Playboy's dreaded Death Row, things rapidly improved. Sometimes it pays to put your money on the tortoise.

One of the big players to welcome me in to my new spot was a member of a well-known shop-keeping family. He played 32 and the splits in £100 chips, which cost him £500 a go and paid out £10,300 when it came up. That's actually a good way to play roulette. If 32 himself (numbers come alive when you play roulette) arrives early, or if the four numbers covered by the split bets come up more often than the law of averages (the law of law numbers actually, if you want to get technical) suggests, you get ahead, and you could even go home winning. Not often enough to give up the day job, don't get carried away, but sometimes often enough to give you twelve months of free roulette and the satisfaction of pissing off a casino owner. Sadly, like most people, Mr shop-keeper didn't go home when he was winning. He stayed in the casino until he had lost all the money he could sign cheques for and went home looking just as miserable as he did when he came in. The stillness of his features was remarkable. Looking back I think he was what we now call a manic depressive, poor devil, who thought that playing roulette would cheer him up. He was very superstitious. In between placing his bets on 32 and staring stoney-faced at the wheel as the ball's fast spin began to falter, he ran on to the landing behind him and rubbed hard on a short section of the banister. For luck. Staff, especially managers, got out of his way when he was heading towards his lucky piece of banister. If he hadn't got there in time and 32 still hadn't come up he would have suspected the casino staff of purposely spoiling his luck and gone somewhere else to lose his money. Casino rule number one: never upset a loony big player unless his looniness upsets other big players, in which case you do the arithmetic and decide whose departure will cost less. Then one day he stopped coming. I never found out if he gave up gambling, ran out of money, died, went mad, or discovered a luckier banister.

Probably the biggest regular player, before the oil-men left him standing, was the now notorious Robert Maxwell. I'll rephrase that: Captain Robert Maxwell MC. I'm glad he wasn't in charge of my pension (not that I would have noticed; I ruined my own pension without any help from outsiders), but I have always felt uncomfortable about the press he gets. He was the kind of war hero Britain needed plenty of during the dark days of 1939 to 1945. And a volunteer. He asked to stay in England and join the army, in spite of an offer to send him to America to study and sit out the war. At the age of sixteen he had already escaped from the Nazis who would soon murder every member of his family bar one female cousin and gone to fight with partisans all the way from Eastern Europe to the Middle East, and was probably still in his teens when he joined our army. What more do you want? Blood? We nearly got it, many a time. The do-gooding didn't stop in 1945. Out of uniform and well into the Cold War he published boring hagiographies of Soviet leaders, at his own expense, and convinced the old fossils in the Kremlin that they sold like hot cakes in the West, in return for permission for Soviet Jews (in constant danger of being murdered by the leaders of the other side of the Nazi coin) to leave behind them the benefits of living in the Soviet Union. All in all not a bad man to have on your side. But you rarely see much about his war record or his humanitarianism in the popular press, slipped between references to the fat crook who stole the pension pie. A casual reader might think he was a man who spent his business career preparing a big robbery before bunking off to Brazil, rather than a desperate man who tried to rescue his company from a recession-hit take-over that overstretched even his available funds. It was wrong of course, not to mention immoral and illegal, but I remain convinced that if the involuntary loan had got him out of the mess he was in he would have quietly slipped the cash back into the pension pot and nobody would have been the wiser. You may beg to differ. But if you must continue to refer to the late Captain Bob, in writing, as a fat crook please add in brackets 'and former war hero.'

There were other big players on French roulette. Brown-skinned Indian businessmen with interests in oil-rich Nigeria, corrupt black-skinned Nigerian politicians and businessmen, sometimes in the same suit, a few big-shots from the Gulf, already very rich before the oil price rise made them masters of the universe, and the occasional anonymous high-roller from no-one really knew where, a familiar and welcome sight in all high-stake casinos. All the above were impressive enough, and very profitable for my new employers, but they faded into the wallpaper when the oil price shot up and Adnan Khashoggi and the Saudi princes crowded round the private table that was installed for them in a room on the second floor, with its own private restaurant in the room next door.

The princes' billions came courtesy of the millions of years of geological activity that had created a sea of oil under the sea of sand that makes up most of Saudi Arabia, and of the happy fact that their country (named after the ruling family that set it up, amid much brutality, in the early part of the 20th Century) was, and still is, more like a family firm than what most of us think of as a country. Khashoggi's non-royal billions came courtesy of his father's position as court doctor which from childhood brought him into contact with the future senior members of the family firm, and from his own commercial acumen that made him the gatekeeper to whom American and European arms companies bunged large sums of money in the hope that the appropriate prince would sign multi-zeroed contracts for their latest fighters, missiles etc. The polite word for such transactions, which our own Prince Andrew seems to think are perfectly acceptable in day to day commerce, is commission. The breath-taking numbers involved turned Khashoggi into one of the most durable super gamblers in the history of London's top casinos. If you have an unhealthy interest in dodgy billionaires, or plan to become one yourself, or need a spiel to impress the Dragons with, you can google Khashogggi and get some of the details of his very successful deals from a variety of sites. Of more interest, if you're into politics rather than commerce (but best ignored if you're heading for Afghanistan in a military uniform) are the strange combinations of friends and enemies that crop up in the background to Mr K's massively profitable arms deals, which soon went far beyond the frontiers of his native country. Any remaining doubts about money making the world go round will disappear from your conscious mind, along with the urge to fight and die for a bunch of liars.

As the big money came in through the door any lingering respect for the gambling laws went out of the window. For example: the 1968 Gaming Act was very strict about credit. If a player paid by cheque the cheque had to be written out and signed and in the possession of the casino before the player was given any chips. All very long-winded. We didn't bother Khashoggi with all that nonsense. He sat at the table, waved an arm, and called out "ten thousand." One of the croupiers gave him ten thousand pounds worth of chips, under direct instructions from the nearest manager, and put a marker on the rim of the wheel to mark the illegal debt. When the markers hit a hundred thousand Khashoggi signed a cheque, the marker came down, and the illegal process started all over again. All pretty trivial, you're probably thinking, but if such a transaction had been proved in court the casino would have been closed down and the participating staff, including me on many an occasion, would have lost their gaming licences and been forced to work for a living. The horror.

Like most big players Khashoggi always came in with an entourage of hangers-on (sometimes including the horizontal dancing girls who brighten up the next chapter), and often with representatives of the Western arms manufacturers for whom he was a very expensive but value for money guide into the magic cash-filled land of the Saudi royal family. Many of the entrepreneurs liked a drink or two to while the hours away, or to help them recover from the impact made by the astonishing beauty of the horizontal dancing girls. Serving alcohol in casinos (except in the bar and restaurant) was banned by the 1968 Gaming Act, but revived in the rarefied atmosphere of Ladbroke Hill Street's second floor. Ice buckets chilling bottles of the finest champagne were a regular part of the scene. It was all very safe. The private room where laws didn't apply was on the second floor, a long way from the reception desk where Gaming Board inspectors had to sign in before they took a look around the new, clean, non-criminally owned casinos that replaced the bad old places of yore, and filled the air with probity and integrity, milady. There was plenty of time to get a message up the stairs. Plenty of time for a manager to get a cheque signed and the markers down and plenty of time for a waiter to take the ice buckets and their illegal contents back into the legal sanctuary of the private restaurant.

Seen through the eyes of a moral philosopher, the top casino scene was thieving all the way up and thieving all the way down. At the bottom highly skilled low-life thieves stole small amounts of money from casino owners by exploiting the early owners' lack of savvy where security was concerned. At the top, casino owners stole large amounts of money by exploiting the gambling addiction of high-life thieves who trousered billions of dollars in massive bribes from exporters of weapons of mass destruction, or from Western construction companies buying a slice of the action in countries with lots of oil but not so many civil engineers, or from the super-thieves who made bundles from selling drugs to eager addicts from all social strata (leaving a dense trail of bodies along the complicated routes of supply), or by selling girls from poor countries to pimps in rich countries at an age when their heads should be bent over a school desk, not the groin of a middle-aged man. Or from that old stand-by pornography. Deep Throat made over a billion dollars for the American Mafia without wasting a penny on expensive special effects. Greed is good, said the man in the film. Hear, hear, say the politicians and their business friends. A Conservative member of parliament made a very clever arrangement with a casino I once worked in (not Ladbrokes), and successfully combined politics and business in the same safe pair of hands. I won't mention his name. He's vain enough already. He brought a number of mid-range Saudi princes into the casino. Their presence brought about a massive increase in profitability. In return the casino agreed to throw the royal schmoozer's cheques away un-cashed when he lost, but to cough up his winnings when he won. The obvious loss to the casino was offset ten to one by the collective loss suffered by their royal highnesses, mostly from the layer just below the super-princes who came into Hill Street. The simple arrangement brought the elected representative of the people of Great Britain a huge tax-free commission at a time when taxes were a lot higher than they are now, and allowed a future member of Her Britannic Majesty's Government to play with the same value chips as the royal Saudis. The apparent equality removed any suspicion on their part that he might be acting as a kind of commission agent for the casino, the cad. The deception was important because the majority of the main man's taxable income came from business deals with the Saudi princes (which was how he came to meet them in the first place) and it's bad for business to let your associates know that you're picking their pockets. The arrangement was conceived and supervised by a very handsome manager of Polish extraction (now dead) who was once seen standing in front of a mirror at the Clermont casino watching himself slowly transfer a large wad of bank-notes from one hand to the other, in a financial (and less messy) version of watching one's self jack off.

Allow me to digress for a moment from the technicalities of casino life, and introduce a bit of philosophy, politics and economics. It won't hurt, I promise. Everybody in the parallel universe described above is corrupt, and everybody in the straight universe agrees that they are the villains. In the world of fiction they cop it big-time when 007 gets on their case, but make massive fortunes and live on huge yachts and die in bed after years of expensive health care, in the real world. The same immunity spills over into politics. George W Bush ran away from the Vietnam war, fearful that some skinny gook from North Vietnam would take him out with an AK47 supplied by Mother Russia, flew old jet fighters across Texas (when he bothered to turn up), and kept the act going until a couple of million gooks and fifty thousand Americans had died, a few generations of deformed births had been laid down by Agent Orange, both sides had claimed victory, and the danger of death by military service had gone away. That's history. Years later he hired a fat little fucker to spread lies (with the help of sympathetic media-owners) about his rival and rather braver presidential candidate John Kerry, who actually went to Vietnam and put his life on the line. George won the election of course. That's history too. In real life the bad guys nearly always win. Make the most of Obama while you can. And don't take that pill. You're not paranoid. You were right first time. They are all out to get you. So why don't we make sleaze work for us good guys? Sleaze could play a vital part in making the world a happy place for our children and grandchildren. Global warming is here and now. Death by drowning is just round the corner, if you haven't starved already, or run out of water that doesn't have salt in it. Politicians promise us the earth, but they don't know the first thing about the earth they promise us. Scientists do. Scientists are real. They know stuff that economists and politicians can only dream of. Economists use long words to hide the fact that they're only guessing, most politicians are lawyers, their friends the bankers are con-men (and we've got the figures to prove it) but scientists put satellites in space, make moon-shots hit the moon, keep the internet safe for suppliers of porn, and make sure we don't feel a thing when a surgeon waves his sharp little knife around our insides. Einstein's equation lit up the skies and put the lid on WW2. Scientists are the business. What they do works and keeps on working. But we pay them peanuts. The solution is so simple that I can't believe I'm the first person to see it. Re-direct the sleaze. Show the arms dealers and all the other con-men the door. Bung environmental scientists with bribes they've never dreamt of. Give them enough money to play roulette and still go home rich, or shack up in a ten-star hotel with the best-looking whores on the planet. Three at a time if they're man enough. Turn a blind eye when a million a month environmental scientist sends in a tax return with a fiver on it. Don't worry about the hair-cuts. Fill state-owned casinos with scientific bribe takers grown rich on handouts from manufacturers of solar panels and special mirrors. Stand back and marvel as the boffins deliver the goods. See massive arrays of mirrors spring up in useless deserts and reflect back the sunlight that has kept us alive for millions of years but now threatens to heat us to death. David Attenborough won't miss the odd dung-beetle. See massive arrays of solar panels spring up in other useless deserts and supply the electricity

182

we need to keep the world humming without choking the air with carbon. One level down, but still scientific, pay huge bungs to Afghan poppy farmers and tell them to grow genetically improved vegetables designed by rich scientists, with free seeds supplied by rich governments. Build a super-casino in Kabul and get most of the money back and use it to bribe more of the good guys. Machine-gun the cows munching grass in the chopped down rain forest and filling the upper atmosphere with heat-retaining farts, all for the sake of a few billion beefburgers that taste like cardboard. It can be an all American show. American citizen Rachel Carson blew the whistle first, way back in the sixties. Remember Silent Spring? American citizen Al Gore is the man to finish the job. He knows everybody. I'm right behind you Al. Greed is good. Green is good. Change one letter and you change the world. But watch your back.

The late Boris Shapiro, the well-known bridge player, if bridge is your bag, was the public relations man at Hill Street. He was very good at talking to the gamblers. But I didn't like the way he talked to his wife. I hate bridge. I learnt the rules when I was ten and played the game, under pressure, when I was eleven and twelve, and still cringe at the memory of adult comments on how clever I was and how grown-up I looked in my three piece suit. I managed not to play again until I was eighteen, on a Norwegian tramp steamer chugging along from Beirut to Gravesend, a muddy place on the Thames where cargo ships dumped their loads in the days before containers took over the trade. The other passengers were a Scandinavian diplomat and his wife, their infant son, a couple of elderly relatives, and a hot au-pair. Three of the adults played bridge. They needed a fourth. They asked me if I would like to join in. The real me wanted to say no I don't want to play bridge, I hate bloody boring bridge even more that I hate bloody boring golf, I only played both silly games years ago because I had to, and I never want to play either of them again. I'd much rather spend my evenings having sex with your au-pair, in the privacy of my cabin. Or hers. But the words I wanted to say stayed where they were. The smarmy, privately educated, polite person who had taken over my body said yes, of course, I'd be delighted to make up the four. I talk tough on paper but in real life I'm putty in the hands of bossy people who take advantage of my good nature.

Everything went as badly as it possibly could. I thought bridge would only ruin the occasional night, leaving me plenty of time to impress the hot au-pair. These things matter when you're eighteen. But bridge was every bloody night, starting minutes after the last mouthful of dinner had gone down and dragging on and on till midnight or beyond. Sometimes well beyond. Next morning's breakfast was spent talking about last night's game. Anticipating the next night's game saw us through lunch. That's what bridge players do. Three weeks of hell. I wished I'd gone by plane. And no luck with the au-pair. She only wanted to be friends. Big deal. I had plenty of those. Thank God I'd packed a few bottles of arak in my suitcase. At least I had something to do in the privacy of my cabin, during the short length of time I spent there. None of this can be blamed on Boris, I admit, although my heart sank when I found out he was a bridge player. These things can haunt you all your life.

Boris's wife was very attractive, about twenty years younger than he was, at a guess, and very pleasant to talk to. What more could a man want? But when he spoke to her he often ended the sentence with what is politely known as the "c" word. But he didn't say it politely, and he didn't just say "c," he put in the other three letters as well. In the right order. Out loud if there were only staff present. Very quietly if a customer might overhear. I found it really offensive. Call me old-fashioned if you must, but I think the "c" word is the most humiliating word a man can throw at a woman, even if they are married, or even if it's meant as a joke, which I didn't think it was. In all other ways Boris was a very good choice as public relations man, at least until the panic set in. The small-stake British players were thrilled to have a world class bridge player on the premises. A real celebrity. You could touch him! And he was friendly with Omar Sharif, the Egyptian actor who became a Hollywood heart-throb, and another world class bridge player to boot. A sex-symbol and a bridge champion in the same pair of underpants. Oh my God. Omar popped in once in a while and brought many of our middle-aged female bridge enthusiast casino groupies very close to death by over-excitement.

Boris's big X factor was that he was a friend of one of the Saudi-Arabian royals. I think he'd flogged him a race horse. Or bought one from him. That friendship really raised his game. Having one of the new Saudi gambling super stars as a chum was money in the bank for a seventies casino PR. But in spite of his royal connections Boris was thrown off balance by the sheer size of the bets that became commonplace when the Saudis took up serious gambling in London after the five fold rise in the price of oil that followed the1973 Arab-Israeli war, the punishment for the West after America and the Nato countries helped the Israelis with money and military equipment in a war which Israel can fairly be said to have been losing, under attack by a newly re-organised Egyptian army, properly trained, properly equipped, cleansed of corruption in the higher ranks and led by a commander who really didn't care how many Egyptian soldiers were killed in his pursuit of victory. He had plenty of spares.

You could argue forever about the rights and wrongs of Western support for Israel, and even longer about the creation of the state of Israel itself, on land that everyone except one God regarded as
184

belonging at least in part to somebody else. (The old ones will die off said the first leader, the young will forget; there was nobody here said the first female prime minister). But in 1973 you couldn't argue with the Israelis when they said they were in fear of being wiped out. Again. Memories were alive and well on both sides. Jews young and old couldn't forget the naked victims waiting for death in frozen woods on the edge of a camp where the incinerators couldn't keep up with the gas chambers. Arabs young and old couldn't forget the ancestors and relatives who ran from their houses and their land, owned and lived in by the same families for many generations, and were sometimes murdered to make room for Europeans who had been persecuted by other Europeans.

Both sides deserve sympathy and real political help from any reasonable human being. And both sides command empathy. Without a word spoken. If I had been a Jew in 1948, looking back at the horrors of the nineteen forties, I'm sure I would have been as Zionist as the next man, and perhaps none too squeamish about the inevitable collateral damage. If I were Palestinian now, looking back over the last sixty odd years, I'm sure I would like my country and my house back. And perhaps none too squeamish about the inevitable collateral damage.

The Greek tragedies don't even come close.

When the war was over the Saudis joined hands with the other oil-rich Arab countries (and the skint ones) and took the straightforward view that if we wanted to support Israel, fine, be our guests, but you can start paying five times as much for the oil you've been getting on the cheap. If you don't like our price, try the Russians. They might have some to spare, ha ha. World financial markets went into a spin as a tornado of dollars swirled out of Saudi Arabia and Kuwait and any other country with sand on top and oil down below. But not London casinos. They couldn't believe their luck. They caught the blast of money in both hands and enjoyed a bonanza that has still not come to an end. Never has so much been grabbed by so few. That is the relevant point, in a casino book, of the foregoing political rant.

One hot Hill Street night, probably early in 1975, a very senior Saudi prince was having a winning streak, playing at maximums that had never been seen before. The new limits of up to five hundred pounds on a number had been nervously agreed to by the management, under heavy pressure from the Saudis, who now had more than their fair share of all the money in the world and easily put all the other London gamblers in the shade. They played roulette at the same table as their good friend Adnan Khashoggi, the Saudi-Arabian arms dealer who made a fortune slicing large commissions (to use the polite word) off the price of the military aircraft that America, Israel's most generous financial backer, was more than happy to sell to Saudi-Arabia, the country that had put up the oil price to give moral backing to Egypt, the country that had very recently tried to wipe Israel off the map. And you thought drug-dealing was a devious business.

The prince was winning the best part of half a million pounds, a fortune in 1975, and far more money than any London casino had ever lost before. The senior management slipped into a collective panic. The new maximums were a gas when the Saudis were losing, but no fun at all when the bastards had the cheek to win. I was spinning the ball when the prince's luck really took off. Boris gave me the evil eye. He would have liked to see me taken off the table (and thrown out of the second floor window vigorously enough for me to clear the pavement and land in the traffic, if he could really have his way), but he couldn't do either without upsetting the prince. He did try (to get me off the table), but the prince shot him down. No, no, leave him there. I like him, I like him. My friend. Very nice man. Very nice numbers. Thank you, habibi. Boris seethed in silence. Casino managers and public relations men are ultra polite to mega players. It's a major part of their job. In fact it is their job. The level of arse-creeping has to be seen to be believed. If you can still see the soles of his shoes your man isn't trying anything like hard enough.

The panic level rose and rose. Boris lost it first. He stood at the French roulette table, rigid and tense, looking like a man about to deliver an important speech. Which he was. The prince studiously ignored him and continued to pile up his big chips, ready to take to the desk and exchange for a cheque with many zeros on the end. Boris's jowls started to wobble, dangerously. I thought he might have a heart attack, and quietly resolved not to try any of that kiss of life nonsense. Then he embarked on his important, extraordinary speech. He told the prince that it was outrageous of him to win so much money, wobble wobble. It simply couldn't be allowed, wobble wobble, THE SHARE PRICE COULD EVEN GO DOWN!!!!! wobble wobble wobble, the last grim warning shrieked out at a volume only hinted at by the capital letters. The prince took it all with great aplomb, no doubt wondering why the hell Boris thought he should give a flying fuck if Ladbrokes' share price tanked. Did Boris expect him to hand the money back with a royal apology and only keep enough for the taxi home, just because he once flogged him a race horse?

At the cash desk the prince counted the zeros, just in case, trousered his cheque, and headed for the door. The managers stood in a silent row, like condemned men in front of a wall. The prince waved a royal wave at the roulette table where all the money had come from, especially when I was spinning the ball, and paused briefly to pat Boris on the shoulder, a friendly gesture that visibly made Boris feel even worse. There was a curious expression on the prince's face. Perhaps, like me, he was a tiny bit disappointed by the absence of a heart attack. I sat very still at the roulette table, trying to look like a mourner at a funeral, waiting for the torrent of abuse that would come blasting out of Boris's mouth as soon as the door closed behind the prince. I wondered how many "c" words I would qualify for. Even though we weren't married. Behind my mask I felt a moment's warmth towards the Saudi royal family. Between us we'd given awfully-rude-to-his-wife Boris a hard time. Till next time your Highness. Ready when you are.

In 1977 I was offered a job in a newly legalised casino in Holland (a low-stake provincial casino by British standards) that paid me twice as much as I was paid in Hill Street to skin the biggest gamblers in the world. This strange situation came about because the Dutch pay was based on tips, which had been abolished in London in 1968 so that the casino owners could grab all the punters' money rather than see it wasted on the staff. Realistic dreams filled my head, of paying off my mortgage in a couple of years and fully owning a house (sold long ago to pay long-forgotten debts) that must be worth about half a million now, the same sum that pushed Boris Shapiro to the edge of cardiac arrest. The dreams died, for personal reasons, and I was soon back in Hill Street for another year, until I left in 1978 to work for John Aspinall, the London casino world's most stylish crook. A short chapter will explain all about Holland, in veiled terms to avoid domestic discord, but only after I introduce you (thirty odd years too late and probably well beyond your price range back then) to the largest collection of beautiful girls I have ever seen gathered together in one room.

Bring On the Horizontal Dancing Girls.

As the international arms dealers got stuck into their massive deals, after the oil price rise doubled the number of zeros on the cheques, those of us who worked in casinos where merchants of death and their government contacts spent their down-time feasted our eyes on the most gorgeous girls that money could buy. Girls to die for. A very good-looking young Lebanese man supplied the girls who lit up our lives in

Ladbroke's Hill Street second floor super-room. Not any old girls dragged off the pavements of Mayfair. Please. This was crumpet for billionaires. Even the hangers-on were millionaire American and British arms sellers grabbing their share of the dollars the Saudi-Arabian royal family had in eye-watering abundance after the price of the oil sloshing about beneath the desert was suddenly multiplied by five. We're talking top-drawer tarts here. Not girls who could pass on an embarrassing rash the wife might notice (or share) when the men got home, or girls who spent their nights (and days, if they could afford both) as high as kites on heroin. Spaced out freaky people need not apply. A girl could sniff or swallow anything she liked when the night's work was over, in the privacy of her own soon to be paid for home, but if just one needle mark showed up when she stripped down to her working gear she was out on her ear. With no appeal.

Many of the girls were first-timers. First time prostitutes I mean. I don't think any virgins ever graced our enormously profitable roulette table. All were very, very beautiful. One incredibly gorgeous girl sat dangerously close to a co-worker of mine, a wannabe sex addict whose ambitions always outstripped his achievements by at least a hundred to one, and caused him to drop a whole load of high value chips in his excitement. I felt his pain. Before she changed jobs and became a top tart she won every beauty contest she crawled out of bed early enough to enter, and was one of those vanishingly rare girls who still look naked in a thick overcoat. In the dark. My highly skilled co-worker's unusual clumsiness was a side effect of a spontaneous but mercifully hidden orgasm, brought on by the lurid images of himself and the outrageously beautiful girl in very rude naked contact that were racing through his brain. He told me all about it later, half boastfully, half in embarrassment. He needn't have bothered. I knew straight away. His eyes went all funny. I know that look. Not quite Merlin when the magic comes on strong, but a very close relation, and impossible to miss when you know what you're looking for. When you've seen one spontaneous but mercifully concealed orgasm you've seen them all. Trust me.

We men are so weak. Whoever came out with that sentence about chaps being tethered to a maniac should have all his books in the National Curriculum. Close to the top. An invaluable guide for the next generation.

The goddess sitting next to my friend even made one of the Saudi princes lose his cool. Not easy, that. Saudi princes, the most thoroughly spoiled men on Earth, are very hard to shake. But the prince's confident voice collapsed into a George VI stammer when she spoke to him, and faded away completely when she leaned across the roulette table the better to hear his words of wisdom and, with value for money firmly in her mind, to provide him with a perfect view of her perfect chest. I tried hard not to join in the stare from roughly the same angle as the prince, who was sitting right next to me, and got through the night without dropping a single chip. Some of us are made of sterner stuff. My boarding-school headmaster would have been proud of me.

I noticed that in spite of being the centre of attraction, except when the little white ball was dropping out of its narrow wooden groove and into a little rectangular slot in the shining brass wheel, the girls were very much in awe of the young Lebanese. They talked among themselves like real-life Charlie's Angels talking about a real-life Charlie, a name I'll borrow to disguise his real identity. It wasn't just because he opened up vistas of fortunes far beyond their wildest dreams, provided they kept on opening their legs. He was, by any standard, even Hollywood's, an exceptionally charismatic and good-looking man. George Clooney is a natural to play him in the movie. But one night Charlie pushed his luck an inch too far. As an honoured guest of Adnan Khashoggi, arms dealer to the rich and famous, Charlie was allowed to run up illegal markers on the wheel (just like the boss) but usually called it a day at a thousand pounds, stopped playing roulette, chatted with the ladies, and waited discreetly for AK to clear the debt. On the night he got carried away, perhaps because the girls he had brought in that night were even more jaw-droppingly gorgeous than ever, Charlie went straight into a losing streak and hit the thousand pound ceiling without getting a single pay-out. A quick look at Khashoggi drew no response. Charlie took the lack of a no as a yes and asked me for another thousand. There was no objection from the man. The casino manager nodded nervously. I put another illegal marker on the wheel and gave Charlie the chips. The marker finally hit five grand as Charlie tried to blast his way out of the losing streak with bigger and bigger bets. The failed sex-addict and I kept on spinning losing numbers. Charlie woke up to reality. A year or two later he wouldn't have missed five grand if it fell into the gutter when he stepped out of the enormous Rolls-Royce that became his trade-mark, but in those early days he was just starting out on what turned into a spectacularly successful rise to riches. He stopped playing roulette and looked as nervous as the manager who had nodded through all the extra markers I put on the rim of the wheel, in flagrant disregard of the laws of the land. As one did in Ladbroke's Hill Street casino. Khashoggi (who never actually missed anything) pretended to notice the super-sized marker for the first time. He asked Charlie, in a dangerously quiet tone, just how he was planning to pay it off. Panic. The game stopped. The no longer nodding manager tried to think of a way of blaming the markers on me. I could hear the wheels of his devious brain grinding out an obsequious excuse. That's why I hated straight casino men, with very few exceptions. They always saved their own skins and left you drowning in shit. 'Sorry Boris, I tried to stop him but he didn't take any notice and I couldn't embarrass our biggest players with a domestic dispute. Suppose they'd walked out and gone to the Curzon House? Exactly. I had to let it go and hope for the best. Please don't call me a c**t again Boris'. It might have worked. Boris never liked me very much, even before the prince won all that money.

The girls felt the freeze that came into the room. They shot sympathetic glances at their hero, then remembered that although Charlie physically handed over, in cash, the exorbitant rent that their best-in-class front bottoms commanded on the open market (not least the freshly shaved and silky-smooth one that a gorgeous dark-haired girl described in very matter of fact shop-talk language to one of her co-workers, in a whisper that reached my tender young ears but luckily didn't quite creep into the more distant ears of my if only God would let me be a sex addict I'd happily go to church every day co-worker, who would surely have blown a fuse if he'd heard the smoothie's owner's firmly held opinion that whenever you scratch a man a paedophile pops out so it pays to look like as much as possible like a little girl if you want to cop even more of their cash), the casino gig depended entirely on Adnan Khashoggi of Saudi Arabia. A.K was the man. Charlie was the hired help. Sympathy for the underdog was bad for business. The girls switched off their smiles, looked at the floor, and waited for the boys to re-establish who held the lead and who wore the collar. A long minute later Mr K threw five thousand's worth of chips over to me, and a wintry smile at Charlie. The girls switched their million dollar smiles back on. I sent the little white ball flying round the wheel again and tried to stop thinking about shaving cream.

Recent research on the internet tells me that lower body shaving is now the norm rather than the exception among ladies who share their assets out fairly among the billion or so users of the world wide web. But this is a history book. Seventies ladies whose private parts were public property, for a small fee if you bought the sort of magazines once published by the late Paul Raymond and the still current Richard Desmond, or for a very large fee if the lady in question had access to phenomenally wealthy gamblers looking for something to do when the casinos closed, often trimmed their pubic bushes, especially if Mother Nature had been over generous with the curls. But a smoothie was, if you'll pardon the expression, cutting edge back in the hairier mid seventies. A modern version of my failed sex-addict friend would be in no danger of blowing a fuse. The original was a racing certainty. On a bad day he could even have popped his hand-made clogs.

I knew it had to be a lot, but I never found out exactly how much the girls earned for a night's work. Nice girls don't talk about money, but I think a minimum of a thousand pounds a night is a realistic figure. Big wedge in 1975. I don't think Charlie took much of it. Or possibly any. I came to understand that he moved in on the Saudis to get in with the in-crowd, rather than to make money in the short term. If I'm right, and I have very good reason to believe that I am, it certainly worked. He became a business associate of one of the main men and made much more money from that than he would have got from shaking down his bitches like the common pimp he never was, and slipped later into a very profitable side-line that owed everything to his very visible membership of the in-crowd.

In addition to their already impressive tax-free earnings the girls were often given the odd extra thousand or two by the gamblers. It was usually in chips rather than sordid paper money, so I got a clear view of the amounts the boys gave to the girls. It was supposed to be fun money for the girls to gamble with, but that didn't often happen. The majority put on a few small bets, squirrelled the rest away in voluminous handbags, and cashed in discreetly when the princes and Khashoggi and the arms salesmen were looking the other way. No air-heads, those horizontal dancers whose luminous beauty lit up our nights. They may not all have read Jane Austen's sensible advice about latching on to a single man's fortune, but the job in hand gave them a fair slice of the fortunes of a variety of already married men without having to wash their underpants for forty years and listen to their pathetic lies when they crept home late from the office. Serious investors with a limited working life, they saw no sense in throwing any extra cash at a silly little ball spinning round a big brass wheel.

Some of the hard-faced men who came to power with George W Bush made a good living from selling arms to countries like the princes' Saudi Arabia and Saddam Hussein's Iraq before they became dedicated public servants and sold democracy instead, with a bit of help from some very big bombs. Did any of them make close contact with Charlie's horizontal dancers, I often wonder? Although I don't remember seeing any of the Bushies in Hill Street—but they would have been much younger and looked quite different then, like me—surely some of them must have gazed on the wondrous beauty of the horizontal dancing girls whose perfect bodies were on sale in the exclusive salle privee on the second floor of Ladbroke's Hill Street casino, or more closely, after the casino closed down for the night, in some of London's finest mansions and luxury hotels. Come on guys. Don't be coy. You won't live forever (that's only been done once, allegedly) and you've got time to spare now that the Republicans are out in the cold and there's a Black Man in the White House. Give us the low down before you shuffle off. It's a hell of a story. Those girls were something else. Once seen never forgotten, even by a simple croupier who only saw them with their clothes on. Some of you boys must have had a closer look. You can't all be born again Christians. I'm not asking you to do it for fun, or literary acclaim. That doesn't pay the bills. Get a ghost writer and cash in. (I might be available, for a stiff fee). Publishers pay good money for stories like that, even if you make them up. No need to feel left out if you weren't really there, or you were there but the champagne got to you first and it was all a blur, even with your glasses on. It could be like the sixties. If you remember it you weren't there. But don't worry. Nothing wrong with a bit of poetic licence. Never did Shakespeare any harm. Use your imagination. You must still know what goes where. Even Alzheimer sufferers remember that (it by-passes the brain). If you're still lost for words, expand on the stuff I've written. Don't waste valuable time hawking it round all the literary agents. Rupert does rude books. One of his wives wrote one. There was a passage, a sure winner of the bad sex award if ever I saw one, that brought together a popular form of oral sex and a caterpillar. (Don't ask, and if you're a girl, don't read. You'll never look a blow-job in the eye again. Or a caterpillar). If Rupert bites you've got a best-seller. Sex sells. Dollars pouring through the door. But don't forget the Special Relationship. Try me with an offer I promise not to refuse.

Mister Ten Percent.

Like the Fat Man, Mr 10% is a man with no name who operated in a casino with no name and once again a few survivors will know him and, if they have any sense, follow my example of courteous discretion. He was a seriously ambitious young Arab man who latched on to some of the Saudi Arabian gamblers I described a couple of chapters ago. He demanded a commission from the owners of the casino currently favoured by the new, very big players who had all of a sudden become his new, very best friends. His asking price was ten percent of their losses. Gross. No fancy expenses laid off against. If Mr Big lost a million Mr Ten Percent got a hundred grand. Knock off a zero and hand over the cash. No calculator necessary and don't talk to the taxman, fool. The other side of the deal was equally simple. If the casino owners didn't show him the money the young Arab man would take the mega gamblers to another joint. The casino owners weren't quite sure what to do. Was it a bluff, or was their newly swollen bottom line in serious danger? The young Arab had been looked on as a cross between a court jester and a pimp, and now here he was claiming to be Mr Fixit. Jimmy Savile with a moustache. Well maybe. The big players might hang on anyway. He might not have the powers of persuasion he claimed. But if he did......

Thanks to the knock on effect of the 1973 Arab Israeli war the casino's profits were many times higher than the owners had even dreamt of when they first opened their doors. Those Israeli and Egyptian and Syrian soldiers didn't die in vain. The casino owners really didn't want to see the Saudis go. Games like theirs had never been seen before. Nor had the profits. The money already in the bank made the casino men feel like they were flying high above the law. There was no hesitation among them about breaking yet another law. But they didn't want to give away ten percent of the gross if the enterprising young Arab was bluffing, or overplaying a weak hand. On the other hand they didn't want to give away a hundred percent if Mr Fixit really could fix it and the towel-heads walked (their words, not mine). Decisions, decisions. They took the plunge. Shake him warmly by the hand, keep 90%, and be grateful not to lose the whole bleeding lot. Foolishly, very foolishly, the casino kept accurate records of the amount paid to the young man from the Middle East. The young Arab himself was never stupid enough to write anything down, even though he was earning at least a hundred times more than he had ever earned before.

Once a month a huge Rolls Royce with a sinister number plate swept into a little mews not far from the casino and stopped outside the office where all the casino paperwork was done, legal or otherwise. The very handsome young man jumped out and strode in to the office. On chilly days he wore a beautiful dark overcoat with a mink collar, but still managed to look mean and magnificent. Real men do wear mink. Omar Sharif would have been hard pressed to keep up. The girls in the office really looked forward to his visits. They wore their best clothes when they knew he was coming to collect. They bought make-up they couldn't really afford. They put on their sexiest voices, carefully practised in suburban bedrooms the night before. It's amazing what you can do with words like hello sir, awfully nice to see you again sir, here's the money sir, that's a lovely coat sir. They looked deep into his eyes and dreamt of jumping into the enormous car and driving off to a life of luxury and never ending shopping trips and hot Arabian nights, far from the paunchy middle aged men who ran the office and talked about football and leered at their cleavages when they dressed up to catch the eye of Mr Ten Percent.

His financial arrangement went on for several years and made the young Arab rich beyond his wildest dreams. When it all ended, when the casino licences went into the bin during one of Lady Penelope's long blinks, he still had a big house in one of the best parts of London, which must be worth several tens of millions of pounds today and, unless he ever does something really rash, enough money to live in luxury for the rest of his life. He still plays roulette every now and then, but he never gets carried away. He plays the sensible way. Heavy bets on just a few numbers. If they come up so does he. That's the way to do it. He leaves as soon as he gets ahead, which happens more often than you might think. I rather like him in a strange sort of way, much more than I liked the people he made his money from.

The mews office was raided in the big blitz of 1980/81. The loyal staff, all about to find themselves out of work, shredded furiously and managed to destroy all the evidence of Mr Ten Percent's illicit dealings before the cops came pounding through the door. Their dedication to duty allowed him to live happily ever after and never have to answer any awkward questions about his sudden wealth or, even worse, hand over any of it to the taxman. I'm just jealous. A measly half million would have done me, in today's money. Even a quarter of a million would do nicely. Discharged bankrupts come cheap. Your house is probably worth a quarter of a million, or a lot more if you live anywhere near central London, like I once did. In Chelsea no less. Enough to allow an old geezer to live quietly on a sunlit Spanish mountain and watch the eagles soar and picnic under the cool trees on daily bread and real olives that don't taste of sea water and fresh tomatoes and red wine of uncertain vintage, speaking sometimes in a foreign language. It wasn't that much to ask. Why couldn't I be like Mr Ten Percent? Or even ten percent of Mr Ten Percent. Or ten percent of ten per cent. I'd have used the money much better than he ever did, the flash git. And I'd have been quite happy to feed him caviar and champagne if ever he dropped by for lunch, and ride round the mountains in his very big Rolls Royce, for old time's sake.

About half way through the young Arab's golden years I heard that John Aspinall was going to open a new casino in London, and applied for a job. Time for a change. But first the story of another card so high and wild and all that, followed by a brief history of a tragically short trip to the land of the legal smoke.

The Fat Man.

The Fat Man, the super-baron, must remain anonymous, forever. Like Bernie the Waistcoat and the Country Girl. I won't bore you with the reasons for my discretion. Lists are for geeks. But I'm nervous, like a literary agent who turned down the chance to flog this book because he felt that he was too young to die. The Fat Man is very well connected. I can give you the approximate date of the main event described, 1977 to 1979, and the name of the nice hotel where disappointment set in, but that's all. A very small number of survivors will see through the veil. The Fat Man himself might turn a blind eye. He bloody well should. He owes me money.

He wasn't blobby fat. He was tall, wide shouldered and solid looking. But there was an awful lot of him. He was born in an Arab country that doesn't have any oil. He didn't go home very often, probably for the best of reasons, like staying alive. His head was enormous and very nearly square. He had very little hair. If you could imagine his head separated from his body, which in spite of the bad feelings between us I'm pleased to say has never happened, when you'd cleaned the blood away you would have been left with something that looked just like the marble bust of a Roman emperor at the height of his powers. He had enormous and enormously expressive eyes. If he could live with a drastic drop in income he could still have a great career in Hollywood. I never knew for sure where his bank-roll came from, but it was generally assumed that he dealt in arms. He was said to have made a fortune during the first war in the Gulf, the one where George Bush senior had the sense to cut and run once the oil was safe.

It's often assumed by heterosexual men who spend a lot of time at the gym that women only look for sexual partners with corrugated stomachs and bulging biceps. It's not true. Sorry chaps. You've been wasting your money. The fat man had plenty of admirers among young women who worked in casinos, and not just because of his bulging wallet. I was discussing this once with a very attractive girl in her twenties. She said she rather fancied the Fat Man. I said, to her surprise I think, that I thought I could see why. But wasn't she afraid of being crushed to death if he forgot she was underneath when things turned really personal? She agreed, with a dirty grin, that it could be a problem but was nothing a modern girl couldn't handle.

In the late seventies a Corsican made a deal with the Fat Man to hit the casino where the Corsican was working. He recruited a Frenchman to help with his cunning plan. Actually he was another Corsican. I'd better put that in. I don't want to upset him. Corsicans can be very touchy about being called French, whatever it says on their passports. Try asking a Scotsman what it's like being English, multiply by ten, and don't hang around for the answer. He also recruited an Englishman who had been straight for so long that it was beginning to weigh him down, and suppress his normally high spirits. The team was complete.

The first night was a trial run, but with real money. The Fat Man came in around midnight, walked straight over to the busy French roulette table, loomed over the junior Corsican, gave him a couple of cash packets, and talked gibberish in a low voice and a very good French accent. The senior Corsican sat at the top of the table and inspected the game. Modern closed circuit television had not yet been introduced. Junior Corsican changed the cash into fifty pound chips, kept five of the chips in front of him, and lost the plot. He was new to this sort of thing. A nervous look clouded his handsome face. He spun the ball round the wheel and looked even more nervous. The Englishman took over just before the ball dropped into a number. Fearing an embarrassing and expensive failure he reached across with his wooden rake and pulled the Fat Man's chips over to his side of the table, muttering something meaningless in a fine French accent. Junior Corsican looked relieved and slightly ashamed. The ball dropped into a low number, conveniently close to the Englishman's left hand. He muttered more French-accented rubbish and placed the chips by hand around the winning number, slipping in a Mon Dieu! and a Sacre Bleu! to show how surprised he was that the Fat Man had struck gold with his first bet (five thousand odd pounds if you prefer English money to gold). A big Indian player gave the Englishman a meaningful look. Always keen to make a new friend, the senior Corsican realised that the Indian knew what was going on, perhaps from previous experience, and might be interested in a good run of luck himself. Sadly, when a proposition was put to him a day or two later, the Indian's nerve went.

So far so good. But it was important that the Fat Man continued playing for a decent length of time. A very quick win and an early cash-out raises eyebrows. The first, crooked pay-out allowed the Fat Man to play honestly for a while and build up some cred with passing managers, whose job description includes keeping an eye on big games. When the Fat Man's pile of chips got a bit low the Englishman, or the junior Corsican, who was learning fast after a shaky start, slipped on another phoney bet. It was done with great skill. Even someone watching on TV (mercifully absent then) would have had a problem distinguishing the crooked bets from the honest ones. Time passed and a sense of normality settled over the game. The fat man's stash went up and down. He stopped playing when was winning ten thousand pounds, after only a few illegal transactions among many legal ones. That was the way to do it. If you made the baron win every time things always went wrong. Too damned obvious. But the odd crooked bet meant that he never actually ran out of money, and at one time must have a few genuine winners that put him ahead. Anyone seeing a crooked bet that's done properly, without the luxury of playing it back over and over again when it's been recorded by one of those bloody cameras, is never quite sure of what he's seen. Did he or didn't he is the question that Shakespeare never asked. If the next ten bets are all straight the watcher decides that he didn't. Works every time. I believe the year was 1977. Ten thousand pounds bought a lot more pints then than it does now. The Fat Man cashed out his winnings and left the casino floor, flashing his Roman Emperor smile as he went. Downstairs in the bar he spent some time chatting to one of the managers. He didn't want to act like a thief who slips away into the night. He was very good at his job. The trial run was deemed a success by all three members of the team. Any differences in skill levels were forgotten.

Next day the senior Corsican went to the Sultan of Brunei's Dorchester hotel, the Fat Man's bed and breakfast when he was in London; at the reception desk a suite number was mentioned, a passport was shown and a packet with a French name on it was handed over. It would not have been sensible for the team leader and the Fat Man to actually meet, or for the Corsican's real name to be on the envelope and on the passport. These details are important. Somewhere in private the Corsican checked the contents, carefully. There were six packets of one thousand pounds, each marked with the name of a bank that the Corsican knew had no connection with the casino the money had come from. The use of an unconnected bank was a sensible precaution, and one which many casino bad boys ignored at their peril. The Fat Man had walked out of the casino with cash packets bearing the company name. If any of these had been found on one of the team the game would have been over before it began. The numbers of the notes might even have been recorded. Money spent on defence lawyers would have been wasted. The Fat Man did things properly. He put the casino packets into one bank and took fresh ones from another bank (or from under his mattress for all anyone cared). There were no footprints leading back to the casino. The Fat Man kept four thousand for himself, leaving six thousand for the team. The standard (verbal) contract, back in the good old days.

The Englishman and the Corsicans were impressed, not only by the high professional standards of the Fat Man when he was at the table, but also by the fact that they had actually been paid. It was not uncommon for the main man to scarper with all the cash, leaving his benefactors with no money and no chance of recovering it. And, sometimes, a nasty cloud of suspicion hanging over them at their place of work, with no carefully concealed cash pile to compensate. It's not like you can sue. He nicked the money I nicked from the casino doesn't cut the ice in an English courtroom. In one instance, the day after a particularly exciting dice game at a nearby casino, a young Australian who had planned to marry the Country Girl's very pretty and awfully talkative best friend but jumped ship at the very last minute when he realised that a life spent listening to the never ending flow of words from her mouth might not be a life well spent, however potent the attractions of some of the less frequently seen parts of her body, collected a bulky packet from a receptionist at the Park Lane Hilton. In a cubicle in the gents' lavatory on the first floor he ripped the packet open in a fever of anticipation and uncovered a thick wad of carefully cut newspapers. Along with a note saying so long suckers, have a nice day. It was the last the Australian or the rest of the dice crew ever saw or heard of the handsome American who told such entertaining stories while he played crooked dice, accompanied by such gorgeous girls. With rare exceptions there was honour among the thieves who worked in the casinos, but it was often lacking among the thieves on the other side of the table.

A few nights after the first hit the Fat Man came back for the big one. Roughly the same things happened as described above, but more often and for higher stakes. Hundred pound chips this time. It has to be said that the junior Corsican's nerve sometimes faltered again, probably because of the increase in the size of the bets and the payouts, and at first the Englishman had to do most of the work. This was not surprising, nor resented. He had a lot more experience, which does rather settle the nerves (until they let you down completely when you go on too long). The Fat Man won a hundred thousand pounds, say half a million today, or a million and a half in house buying money. Next afternoon the Corsican paid another visit to the Dorchester hotel. There was a spring in his step. The sun shone down on Park Lane. Hyde Park glowed lovely and green. All was well with the world. Once again he showed his identification to the receptionist, the same one as before, and asked if there was a packet for him. Probably rather a bulky one. The receptionist informed the smiling young man that the gentleman in suite *** had left the hotel shortly after breakfast, in a hurry to catch a flight. He had left nothing at reception, apart from a surprisingly large tip. Was there anything he could do to help? No, said the disappointed young man, resisting the urge to say 'unless you happen to have the odd sixty grand you don't need' in a sour and sarcastic tone of voice. He walked out of the hotel empty handed and unsmiling. The sun didn't look half as bright, nor the sky so blue. Hyde Park had gone brown. An urge to kick somebody, anybody, very hard flooded his brain and took his normal bright sense of humour clean away.

The Englishman was asked more than once if he was sure that it was only the Fat Man who ran off with the cash. Maybe the Corsican did a fifty-fifty with the Fat Man and left his fellow robbers in the lurch? Or included the other Corsican and cut out the Englishman, on national lines? But the Englishman always stuck to his view that the Corsican was as solid as ever for his partners in crime. They were blood brothers, courtesy of a short ceremony involving a sharp knife, some pain, and a large amount of red wine. Corsicans take that sort of thing seriously. You don't steal money from your brother. To this day the Englishman won't entertain the idea that the money went anywhere but into the Fat Man's pocket. At least he paid up the first time.

To Holland.

In 1977 word spread round London staff rooms that legal casinos were about to open in Holland, in country towns and by the seaside, but not in Amsterdam itself. Most Continental countries prohibit casinos in their capitals, to avoid bankruptcies caused by addicted businessmen (and women) sloping off from the office, wasting the day in a casino, neglecting their businesses and going skint, a rake's progress that is none too rare in London. The casinos were to be owned by the state. The wages, based on tips, would be about double what we were earning in London. And for the first year one's rent would be paid by the employer, aka the Dutch government. I was one of the first to sign on, for a job in the windy seaside town of Zandvoort. It seemed like a good idea at the time.

There were illegal casinos already operating in Amsterdam, and maybe in Rotterdam or the Hague, but not in the small touristy places along the coast, or in the dull country towns. An Italian friend of mine, out of work when Tony Mancini sold his White Elephant casino to London Clubs, turned down several offers in London because everywhere else would seem dull (and not very well paid, and overtaxed) after working at Tony's place, and went off to work in a criminal's casino in Amsterdam. He got a very good wage, cash straight in to his hot little hand, and no silly nonsense about tax. He stayed in Amsterdam for two or three weeks at a go, followed by a break of two or three days at home in England. His absence wasn't very popular with his British wife, who had a pretty good idea of how he spent his spare time in a city famous for its liberal attitude to sex. Bunga bunga and all that (copyright Silvio Berlusconi). But she was very much consoled by the briefcase stuffed with banknotes, less than half of it wages, that came back with him.

Shortly after my Italian friend left London I heard on the grapevine that the owner of an illegal Amsterdam joint had been shot in the head by a rival gangster. The killer planned to take over the casino, and felt that it would be much easier to do so if the original owner was dead. You can't fault his logic. But he picked the wrong joint. The former owner's widow took over the running of the casino, told her husband's murderer to fuck off—with a gun in her hand—and made a lot of money for a long time before retiring into well-fed obscurity. Don't believe the adverts. Not all Dutch girls dance around in clogs, smile at the camera, and wave bunches of tulips in the air. I never found out if the place where the killing took place was where my Italian friend dazzled the owner with his fast fingered thieving and never got caught (which was probably just as well in such a deadly environment), but it might well have been. There were a good few illegals in Amsterdam at that time, but fewer than a handful boasted stakes high enough to allow a skilled operator to fill a briefcase every couple of weeks without the owner noticing a shrinkage in the bottom line. To soften the blow my highly skilled Italian friend cheated inexperienced or drunk players by paying them short on roulette. Selectively of course. His arithmetic improved no end when he dealt to hard-eyed men who looked like they might have a gun down their trousers. The variable odds didn't quite compensate the owner for the money stuffed into the briefcase and taken across the North Sea every two or three weeks, but it did help a bit, and it was a nice gesture.

My own stay in Holland, on the windy North Sea coast, about fifteen miles from Amsterdam, was much shorter and much less profitable. Zandvoort, which is to Amsterdam a bit like Brighton is to London (but only a bit) was the site of one of the first state-run legal joints. Sadly my wife and Holland didn't get on together, and in less than a month we were back in England and I was back at Hill Street. I still got my old not bad wage, but it was only about half what I had been getting during my brief Dutch bonanza. The dream of paying off my mortgage in two years died. It was the first of a series of disappointments, most of them self-inflicted in a teamwork sort of way. After another year at Hill Street, sulkily wishing that we were still in Holland (and surviving a massive disappointment which must remain confidential) I got a job at John Aspinall's new casino. It was in Hans Street, just off Sloane Street, not far from Harrods and, more importantly, very close to Chelsea, a part of London where I have always felt much more at home than I ever do in the West End. Or anywhere else, come to that.

Joe's Place.

Interviews for jobs at Aspinall's were held at Joe Dwek's tall, elegant house on the south side of Belgrave Square, not far from John Aspinall's London house in a short street leading into the north side of Belgrave Square. Angelo, John Aspinall's Italian casino manager, who did tend to go on a bit after the first bottle of brandy, once gave me a breakdown of Joe's international background. Part Lebanese, part Egyptian, part Iraqi, part Jewish, part French, and several more parts I can no longer remember. A true twentieth century man. And a terrific raconteur. A fountain of disreputable information about the regulars at Aspinall's. Much more accurate than Poisonous Pete, whom you haven't yet met, and, unlike Pete, never guilty of inventing a story to plug a gap in a conversation. Very sparing with the stories, in fact, and always putting quality above quantity. The reason for the contrast was economic. Joe was never short of the price of a pint and told his rare but true stories for free, whereas Poisonous Pete never downed a pint that somebody else hadn't paid for and had to work much harder to maintain a steady flow of invitations involving free food and drink. Fear of failure often led to embellishment.

Joe's most disreputable story, which I overheard while he was sitting at a blackjack table, gazing wistfully at the cards and talking to the actual players, was all about a very wealthy businessman who went for an annual week's holiday in Las Vegas (on his own but with his wife's possibly reluctant approval) to get down to seven hard days of serious blackjack. What he didn't mention to her indoors was that while he spent the evenings in the casinos playing cards, as agreed, he spent the afternoons lying on his back, naked, on the floor of his hotel room, watching very expensive call-girls wearing stiletto heels and no underpants take well paid turns to walk all over his fairly small body. More conventional activities may have followed, unless a badly placed stiletto heel temporarily damaged a temporarily prominent body part. But I doubt that such a thing ever happened. The girls were professionals, not Mr. Bean's sisters, and would have been very careful not to damage a cash customer who turned up every year, regular as clockwork, and quite possibly gave them as much pleasure as they gave him. Sadly, I never found out whether any missionary or canine position type stuff followed the ritual stabbing. A punter in another room kicked up about something or other. I had to go and pour oil on troubled waters, damn it. As I crossed the landing, past the cash desk and out of earshot of individual words, to conduct another regular ritual with a small player who always put his mouth where his money should have been, in the vain hope of making himself look more important, I heard a roar of laughter from the room I'd just left. Must remember to ask Joe if he can remember that punch line, if I ever see him again, possibly in court if and when he sues me for libel.

Joe was born in Cairo, studied at Manchester University and Harvard Business School, worked on Wall Street for six years, and in 1971 became one of the world's best professional backgammon players and the author of the most entertaining and useful book ever written about the game sometimes described as Ludo for posh people. Less well-known is that the fantastic memory and intense powers of concentration that are de rigueur for anyone who hopes to make a living as a professional player of backgammon (or bridge or poker) have for a long time made Joe Dwek one of the world's best card-counters at blackjack. You can't sue me now Joe, after all that sucking up. Card-counter means exactly what it says. You count the cards as they're dealt, silently in your head, and play for low stakes while a mental picture of the remaining cards builds up in your brain. When (and only when) your calculations tell you that the odds are in your favour you switch to much higher stakes. If you do it properly you'll win more often than you lose, just like a casino. The make-up of the cards remaining in the shoe will, at times easily recognised by the skilled counter, make the player more likely to win and the house more likely to lose. If you want to really study how and why this happens you'll have to look on the internet, and/or read some books. Or see a film called Twenty-One. I've just sketched in the background. I don't want to bore the mildly curious with a long exposition on the background mathematics, or numb their brains with the rules of blackjack. So now you know how to get rich. Go to a casino, sit at a blackjack table, count the cards, and increase your stakes ten-fold when the God of mathematics smiles down on you. The fly in the ointment is that your sudden raising of the stakes will give you away and you'll be banned from the casino, or at least from the blackjack tables. Everyone classed as a card-counter has his photograph taken, discreetly through the closed circuit TV, not by a wannabe paparazzo sticking a camera in your face, and the mugshot and the name are circulated among the world's casinos. Giving a sucker an even break is not popular among casino owners. Giving him an edge is totally out.

I'm not sure I should write this. Someone not paying proper attention could easily lose his house and his wife and kids and all his money. Or commit suicide if he takes it really badly. But what the hell, you're all adults, so here goes: if you can learn to count cards from one of the books, including an excellent one by an American academic who made a small fortune before he was banned from every casino on planet Earth, you too can be a card-counter and get rich. As a bonus you'll have something to talk about if you make enough cash to hang around somewhere expensive and bump into Joe. Once you're sure you really know what you're doing (and you'll be slaughtered if you don't), choose a friend you can trust with your life and go to a casino where the maximum bets on the blackjack games are reasonably high. Don't sweat your bollocks off to win a fiver. Become members if membership is obligatory.

But don't go together to sign up, and don't go as your friend's guest. Or vice versa. Act like you never have met. It's very important that nobody in the casino sees any connection between you and your co-conspirator. Thanks to the lingering and distressing presence of racial discrimination in many parts of the world (however well hidden or downright illegal) your chances of escaping detection are increased if one of you is black and the other is white. A lot of the casino staff will be less likely to think that you are together if you do make a tiny slip. You can help to integrate the races, like all good people should and, with any luck, make a few quid at the same time. Visit the casino on the same day or night, leaving an interval of half an hour between your arrivals and departures. Before you go to the casino arrange a time with your friend when you're going to start playing blackjack, and pick a phrase that you will say to the inspector who is watching the table you're playing on. Something boring like "what time do you close tonight?" will do fine. You don't have to be Noel Coward. The mundane phrase is the signal to your friend that his part in the drama is about to begin. While you are playing, and doing the maths, he can walk around the casino watching blackjack or roulette games, but not playing. He can take a decent sized roll of money out of his pocket and put it back again, as if he's about to play roulette but changes his mind. That move establishes him as a potential big player, not just someone who feels big because he's hanging round a casino. But don't let him play roulette for small stakes to pass the time. That's a bad idea, because later on he has to turn into a big blackjack player. Gamblers usually play for the same sort of stakes whatever game they play. Itsy bitsy roulette players don't suddenly turn into giant blackjack heroes. When your friend hears the code words he sits down at the blackjack table, changes some serious money, and plays for higher stakes than you've been playing for. If you've started playing for five pound stakes your friend should play for fifty or a hundred pounds. But don't talk to each other. Not even the sort of remarks friendly strangers sometimes make when they take a seat at a card table, like "how are the cards running tonight?" And make sure that the cash you both play with comes from a float that you have shared out before you set foot in the casino. The absolute worst thing you can do is pass money between yourselves.

Now comes the bad news. Your counting has told you that it's time to play big. But you can still lose, even when you've done it right. You're much more likely to win than you were when the cards weren't friendly. I haven't been lying. But there's no written guarantee. Casinos have losing nights at blackjack even when no-one's counting. The obscure mathematical rules governing randomness of card sequences can still get you, even when the overall picture is good. Think of the bullet that ricochets off one rock and hits a man well hidden behind another rock. Like in the old cowboy films. Make sure you've got enough money to play two or three times, in case you luck out first time. And don't come over all spiritual if you do win big. Don't think you're one of the chosen few who can't lose. It's not you, it's the maths. If you're well ahead when the shoe ends cash out and get out. You've done what you set out to do. Be scientific. Like most of us you're still only known to tens of people, and you still live in a suburb. You want money, not fame. You're not Henry Gondorf.

You should get away with it a few times before anyone is clever enough to connect you with your friend. Go to a crowded popular casino. Actually you've got no choice if you decide to operate in London. The posh places won't let you in unless you've got enough money not to need to know how to count cards. Head for the middle ground. Don't dress exotically. Do nothing to stand out from the crowd. Don't shout at the dealer or flirt with the waitress. Be a grey man, even if you're really colourful in your private life. Don't use the same password twice. Actually, don't use one at all if your friend can see you clearly when the maths comes right, especially if you have a distinctive voice. Stay grey. Ignore what I said about talking to the inspector. Use a mannerism to tell your friend to get stuck in. A pull on an earlobe or a wipe across your forehead with a handkerchief. Pick something you don't do normally, or you and your friend could lose a lot of money by mistake. It happened in the Greek casino and it could happen to you. Disaster is never far away. But that's half the fun.

Don't play on a table where the cards are shuffled in a shuffling machine. That's a noisy black box where the card shoe ought to be. I have a strong feeling that shuffling machines are death to free enterprise. You could research this on the internet. I'm old school, I went out of the business just as shuffling machines came in, so I'm no expert, but I'm pretty sure the bloody machines have buried the past. (You could ask Joe. He knows everything). Continue to play small while your friend plays big. If you stop as soon as he starts an alert inspector might notice the handover and tell the manager. Don't blame me if you lose and you can't pay the mortgage and your old lady goes off with your best friend. I've done my best. And before you even think about becoming card-counters both of you must learn to play blackjack properly. That is very important. I should have mentioned it a bit earlier, in case you rushed out at the end of the last paragraph and did your bollocks (the trade name for losing heavily). Come back you fool. You must know when to stand and when to draw, when to double and when to split. Do some research on the internet, or find a good book. Ignore hunches and pretty cards and gut feelings. Your gut evolved to process food, not to play cards. Most importantly of all, don't rely on God. If He really is up there He won't have any time for gamblers. And be careful where you play: In Las Vegas the casinos have leaned on the local government (actually they are the local government) and made it illegal for a card player to use any kind of mechanical method of counting cards. That can be rubber bands on your fingers, hidden under the table of course, or a calculator in your pocket. If you're caught you end up in prison. I'm not sure what rules apply if you're counting in your head and someone hears the wheels going around, but it's best not to find out the hard way. You meet some horrible people in a Las Vegas prison. It can be even worse. Not that many years ago, in a casino owned by an avuncular old gangster sometimes known as grandad, in the lawless void that followed the departure of Gorbachev, in St.Petersburg, the most beautiful town in Western Russia, an English couple each got two bullets in the head and a public funeral on the pavement behind the casino (not in front, where it would put the gamblers off) to discourage any other staff from robbing the joint, as the boss suspected they were doing. I understand that he may have been right about the man (I don't mean right to shoot him), but that he was wrong about the girl. She was innocent of any tea-leafery. But her innocence wouldn't have kept him awake at night. Two stiffs are better than one when you're really trying to make a point. The display was not only a warning to other staff, it was a way of showing that the owner didn't give a toss about the police. He'd bought them years ago. If you're ever in St.Petersburg keep well away from grandad's joint, if it's still open. He might have the same rules for card counters.

I'm sorry, I got carried away. I've always been fascinated by card-counters, and bitterly disappointed by my own lack of concentration. I've got a fantastic memory, he said modestly, but I find it hard to focus on the same thing for any length of time, especially when it's only about making money. My mind shoots off to more interesting places. I was telling you about my new job. At Joe's house there was a roulette table in the interviewing room, aka the dining room in normal times. Each applicant for a job at the new Aspinall's casino had to undergo a table test. A table test weeds out the bluffers and gives the really gifted a chance to show off, and possibly negotiate a higher rate of pay. I was exempted from this because I could only deal French roulette and the casino was only going to have American games. After the table test there was an interview with John Aspinall, at his nearby house that seemed to take up most of the short street it was located in. Aspers had the final say as to who was hired and who was fired. Like Alan Sugar, but in private. I had only got as far as Joe Dwek's house because one night John Aspinall was playing French roulette at Hill Street and I so impressed him with my skill and general savoir-faire that he told me to come for an interview. Or recruiting was going so badly that he was desperate to grab anyone he could. The year was 1978, long before the big close-down, and it was difficult to prise well-established staff away from well-paid jobs. At Hill Street he didn't ask if I knew any other games and I didn't feel the urge to burden him with unsolicited information. So when I got to Joe Dwek's house the two managers doing the interviewing assumed that I was a no-hoper when I told them that I couldn't deal any American games, but they went through the motions anyway because the boss had told me to come along. After not being tested I was sent along to see John Aspinall and be told that I wasn't going to get a job. In his office I came clean straight away and told him that I had no experience of American games, but I would graciously accept a trainee position if it didn't involve a pay cut. My generous offer wasn't snapped up. He said he rather liked French roulette himself, but his little club in Hans Street didn't have enough room—a French roulette table is very big—so, much as he would have liked to offer the game to his players, he simply couldn't fit it in. And he wanted experienced staff. There was no room for trainees, and no-one to train them. But if ever I learned the American games I would be welcome to come back and try again. I thanked him and said goodbye, still talking about casinos while I was putting on my coat. I have a tendency not to shut up when most people think I should. For once it worked to my advantage. Something banal I said about joking with winners but keeping out of the way of losers made him change his mind. Suddenly I was a public relations genius. I took my coat off again and got the job. At full pay.

I'm worrying again about suggesting earlier on that you should go out counting cards and come home rich. Here's a cautionary tale. Not long after Aspinall's opened, with me trying nervously to bluff my way through the American games, a young Lebanese called Robert came in to play blackjack. I'm not going to tell you his surname. He played very well, and didn't suddenly raise the stakes, but somebody recognised him as a counter. Possibly Joe Dwek, who was often in the club. The newcomer was told, politely, that he couldn't play blackjack any more, but he was a very welcome guest on any of the other tables. Put more directly, we don't want winners, thank you, but you can play anywhere you're likely to lose. He and Joe became friends (or maybe they already were). Robert continued to pop in now and then and stare wistfully at the blackjack tables. One night, possibly after a drink too many, John Aspinall went against everything I've just said about casino owners and card-counters. He invited Joe and his new friend Robert to come in next day at two o'clock in the afternoon and play blackjack any which way they liked, for an agreed length of time. I think it was five hours. They could count cards as much as they liked, and raise the stakes as much as they liked, subject to the normal table limits. They could even correct each other's play, in the infinitely unlikely event of one of them making a mistake. The table limits were to be from a minimum of five pounds to a maximum of two hundred, low enough to keep the risk down on Aspinall's side if the boys had a really good day, but high enough to make possible a loss to the casino of about ten or twenty thousand pounds. Aspinall liked this kind of gesture. It was in his nature, and if he didn't do it too often it was good for business. Not necessarily on the day, but word soon got around town that John Aspinall was a bit of a sport, not a money-grubbing bean-counter like all the other casino owners. Gamblers appreciate that sort of thing. It's a good way to make a mark again when you've been out of the business for a few years, like he had, and you need to attract a new generation of mugs. Here's the scary bit. Two of the best card-counters in the world were playing with none of the usual restraints, like not being allowed to play or being hauled off to the nick or getting shot in the head, and at the end of their five hours they broke even. At times they were winning a little, at other times they were losing a little, but never enough either way to cash in or give up. So if you've really made your mind up to have a go at counting cards make bloody sure that you read my instructions again and again, and all the necessary books. Make sure that you really know what you're doing before you actually play winner's blackjack in an actual casino. If you lose a bit and your wife hops off it's not the end of the world, and might even save you a bob or two in the long run, but if you lose a lot and your house has to go, it's a bastard getting back on the property ladder. I know. I've been there. Good luck in your new life. I hope you make a packet.

Robert Z and Joe Dwek were two of the liveliest men who ever came into Aspinall's. I'd guess, from what I saw of them, that they were a barrel of fun at a party or in a bar, unlike nearly all the other people I have ever known who dedicate a large part of their lives to playing games of chance. Most gamblers spend their down time dwelling on last night's game, especially if it went badly, or the game they're going to play tonight, the one they're going to win. Yeah, right. Really addicted gamblers are always a pain in the arse, and hate wasting good gambling money on alcohol, the boring bastards. But if ever you do meet Robert Z and Joe D, and are bowled over by their genuine charm, don't play cards with them unless you're playing for matchsticks. Which probably won't happen. I don't think matchsticks are a currency they recognise. And don't even think about backgammon.

Aspers and his Mum.

There have been several books about John Aspinall and what was once known as the Clermont Set. I have never read any of them. It always seemed pointless to plod through attempts by outsiders to penetrate a world where they weren't welcome and write about people I saw in person almost every day. He even wrote one himself, rather badly, but focusing on the excellent work he did as a breeder of endangered species rather than the sort of things I'm going to tell you about. I've got a signed copy on my bookshelf. Yours for a fiver, plus carriage. I did read, long after I had left Aspinall's payroll, an article by Taki (whom you'll meet in the chapter called Background Music), the very literate author of the Spectator High Life column. Taki tells you all you need to know about John Aspinall, rather sharply in my view, given that the author was a man who made Aspinall's casinos his second home. If Boris Johnson has clung on to his day job as editor of the Spectator he might dig you up a copy, if you can spare another fiver.

I don't recall Taki mentioning that, behind the tough ultra right-wing posture, Aspers was something of a mummy's boy. One day he came to work with a streaming cold, taking it like a man and determined not to be beaten. He got his head down over his desk and began to plough through the paperwork, several handkerchieves at the ready. There were a few of us in his office, including a German economist appointed by Sir James Goldsmith to keep an eye on the suspicious people employed by the casino, like me. We all sympathised with Aspers' illness, and advised him to go home and stay there till he felt better. We could cope without him. His money was safe. We were wasting our breath. The stiff upper lip stayed stiff. He refused to move from his desk. His mother, the late Lady Osborne, mother also of James Osborne, half brother of Aspers and uncle of Slasher George, our current chancellor (December 2010), and future head of a later Aspinall's casino after big brother died, came in to the office, took one look at her ill son and said go home John, you can't stay here with a cold like that. He stood up immediately, called for a car and went, not wasting a word in argument with the one person in the world he knew he couldn't beat. I was well aware that Lady O had played a very active part in Aspinall's private games, paying off the police and restraining her son from allowing chancers to sign cheques that would bounce high over Belgravia, but I had always thought that she was working under his direction. Surely the alpha male was in charge. Don't mess with him. But now I knew that the boot was on the other foot.

The snot-stained incident probably sheds some light on the mystery of why he really hated women, with an intensity that I once witnessed when he tore in to an upper class woman late one afternoon, for no particular reason. It was just one of those days. He stood by the cash desk, his face full of rage, and let fly a torrent of misogynist venom at his unfortunate victim. The atmosphere in the room was actually quite frightening, all of a sudden and out of nowhere. Everybody looked the other way, including me. Only his rather nice daughter Amanda pleaded with him to stop, to no avail. I found the sudden outburst of hatred as depressing as it was frightening, the more so because it had no commercial basis. The woman in question either didn't gamble at all, or perhaps scattered a few pounds around every now and then, which to us was pretty much the same thing. Money didn't come into it. What we were watching and listening to with very little enthusiasm was an outward manifestation of an internal obsession.

I liked working for him, and in spite of the above I quite liked him personally, as far as I got to know him, which wasn't actually very far outside working hours, but I had (and still have) very little time John Aspinall's politics. I never seem to take to people who think that killing three quarters of the human race is a wizard plan. However well argued. But because he was a casino sharpie rather than a politician, except for a short time when Jimmy Goldsmith's answer to the Monster Raving Loony Party had its brief fling, I didn't worry too much about the massacre that would probably never be. On balance I much preferred him to Jimmy Goldsmith, the man who put up the money for the new casino. You'll soon see why. He's coming next.

Jimmy.

James Goldsmith, Jimmy to those who chose to believe that he was their friend, was the son of a Major Goldsmith, a man who made his pile from luxury hotels in England and France, presumably after he left the Army. His mother was French and reputedly rather beautiful. He went to Eton to learn the ways of the world. He left a little early, quite voluntarily, saying that a man of his standing should not be a schoolboy. He was right. He became a very successful businessman and accumulated far more wealth than his father ever dreamt of. His first wife was Maria Isabel Patino, the daughter of a South American mining tycoon who made a fortune ripping tin out of the South American earth and gave his name to the grubby appearance that tin takes on if you leave it out in the rain. Miss Patino's father strongly opposed the marriage, on grounds of openly expressed anti-Semitism. His future father in law told Jimmy, right out loud, that in his family they were not in the habit of marrying Jews, rather ignoring the fact that Jimmy's mother was a French Catholic. Jimmy replied that in his family they were not in the habit of marrying Red Indians. After this very frank exchange of views it will come as no surprise to you that the marriage took place in the absence of the bride's immediate family. An elopement opened the door to marital bliss. The new Mrs Goldsmith soon gave birth to a daughter, Isabel. Sadly, the mother died in the process. The child survived.

Jimmy next married Ginette Lery, from France, who produced a son and a daughter, Manes and Alix. During his second marriage he started an extra-marital affair with Lady Annabel Vane-Tempest-Stuart, from a family so posh that they added a third barrel to their name, the better to look down on the double-barrelled riff-raff below. Lady Annabel's father was the eighth Lord Londonderry, one of Adolf Hitler's most enthusiastic English admirers and the man widely believed to be the inspiration for the aristocrat portrayed in Ishiguro's excellent book (and film) The Remains of the Day. Ian Kershaw, author of a book definitely about Lord Londonderry, with the accurate title Making Friends with Hitler, tells us that his Lordship kept a statuette of an SS storm trooper on the mantelpiece of one of the several hundred rooms in the family pile. The statuette was a gift from von Ribbentrop, the Nazi foreign minister and avid recruiting agent for collaborators in all the European countries his boss planned to occupy.

When she first got close to Jimmy Lady Annabel was married to Mark Birley, the owner of Annabel's night club, still going strong on the West side of Berkeley Square and recently sold to a restaurant entrepreneur, whatever that is. Annabel's is directly below the Clermont casino, owned first by John Aspinall, then by the Playboy organisation, after whose loss of licences it became for a long time a branch of the Rank organisation, once famous for making black and white films about the second world war. All the Rank films opened with a dramatic shot of a sweaty body builder bashing a gong. You sometimes see them on the telly during the insomniac hours, or on rainy afternoons. The Rank organisation was named after its founder, J Arthur Rank, a devout believer in one of the many branches of Christianity, who always insisted that his films, however entertaining, should guide cinema-goers along the path of righteousness and must be spinning in his grave at the thought that his once fine upstanding film company now owns casinos and not much else. Most of the films slipped into the dustbin of cultural history, but not all is lost. J Arthur's resounding name has passed into Cockney rhyming slang and now describes a popular sex act requiring only one participant. Sadly, many younger people who have a firm grasp of what a J Arthur is have absolutely no idea of who J Arthur was. Sic transit gloria mundi, even among the faithful.

Mark Birley named the night club after his wife, rather romantically, and kept the name going long after she'd pushed off with Jimmy. That may not have been pure sentiment. Losing a wife with three surnames was bad enough, but there was no point in losing customers by confusing them with a change of name. A chap has to make a living. You can't have a place that's Annabel's on Thursday and Lulu's on Friday. The punters think there's something wrong with the finances and you become a suspected loser and who wants to be seen dead in a loser's night club? Exactly. Anyway, for a lot of men who have been married for a while it's not always the end of the world when her indoors takes a hike, unless a large inheritance goes out of the door with her. I had a friend whose wife suddenly left him after almost two decades of sitting sour-faced on a sofa flicking through dozens of television channels, carefully avoiding anything good-natured. She was part of a middle-class small business family whose daily mood shifted from semi-contented but grumpy to ecstatic when Margaret Thatcher won her first election, shifted sharply downwards when the man with his underpants outside his trousers took over, and fell into despair when Labourite Tony Blair started waving his tea-mug outside Number 10, not realising that now the good times would really start to roll. My unwisely tolerant and gentle friend wasn't crazy about the new (to him) social world he found himself in, but managed to convince himself, against all odds, that he was going into an old country church to marry a pretty girl in a white dress, not open a 20th Century update of Pandora's Box. He wised up fast. In no time at all he realised that almost everybody picks the wrong partner the first time round, and sometimes the second, third, fourth time round, but hung on doggedly for the sake of the children who rapidly joined the cast. When his release came, out of the blue, the good news was slow to sink in. Especially first thing in the morning. But when it finally did sink in, at the beginning of what would have been yet another ghastly day, his joy was unbounded. Then he felt guilty, and tried to remember the good times they had shared, but the best his memory could offer was the occasional silent few hours of sun-bathing, usually during holidays, or the odd hour or so when she gazed reverently round a department store and temporarily lost interest in telling him how inferior he was to almost everybody else she had ever met. He once told me, still whispering out of long habit, that the day she left was the best day he'd had since the day before the day they first met, and that on every anniversary of the happy day he downed a secret celebratory drink or three, the festive atmosphere spoilt only by the thought of the hell the other poor bugger was going through.

Annabel's started off in the fifties or sixties as a haven for young (or young at heart) members of the English aristocracy, but for a long time now would have been hard-pressed to make a decent profit without the money brought in by rich Arabs and rich Indians, mostly at least middle-aged, who out-number the modern day Bertie Woosters by quite a margin. Someone trying to be witty once described the club as being where middle age meets the Middle East (no, I didn't think it was very funny either). The atmosphere is very glamorous. Even David Blunkett was impressed, and he's blind. Most of the women whose expensive beauty gives the place that certain je ne sais quoi are a lot younger than their men. Membership is very expensive. A rare nice man who was part of the Aspinall set in its heyday told me during a game of blackjack that Mark Birley never gave honorary membership to anybody, with the possible exception of a fringe member of the royal family, name and address not supplied. His very sensible stinginess ensured that membership fees alone brought in a good million a year even before anyone spent a hundred or so on a round of drinks.

Lady Annabel gave birth to three children, with Jimmy's help. Jemima was the first. For a while she was the darling of the gossip columnists and, as I'm sure you know, married Imran Khan, the cricketer turned politician who seems to be a lot better at winning cricket matches than he is at winning elections, although as the elections are usually held in Pakistan the final results may not always be as accurate as the cricket scores. Imran may well be the Al Gore of Pakistan (but better looking). Zacharias was next, now better known as Zac, the prominent environmentalist, and was followed by Benjamin, of whom I know nothing at all. On the 24th of September 2006 Zac was pictured in one of the low-class Sunday papers, accused of getting a leg over the wife of a friend, a girl closely related to the Rothschild family. Actually it was in The News of the World, one of Mr Murdoch's titles, so it must be true. For a moment I thought he might be going down the same road as his dear old

Dad, or at least taking a first tentative step. Nostalgia flooded over me. But Zac backed off and made friends with David Cameron instead.

Jemima and Zacharias were born while Lady Annabel was still Jimmy's mistress, which made them illegitimate, strictly speaking. But they were legitimised by a subsequent marriage. Benjamin was respectable from birth, quite possibly from conception. Never awfully good at keeping his trousers on, as you must have noticed if you've been paying attention, during his third marriage Jimmy conducted an extramarital affair with Laure Boulay de la Merthe, who it's safe to assume comes from France. She contributed two more children to Jimmy's final score of eight, and would no doubt have become Jimmy's fourth wife if he hadn't died of pancreatic cancer at the age of sixty two. I think it was during his last marriage that Jimmy uttered his most famous quote (nicked from a famous French actor): "when a man marries his mistress he creates a job vacancy," a sentence which no doubt inspires annual celebrations among militant feminists on the anniversary of his death. A less well known quote from the late Sir James is "I do what I want and everybody has to go along with it," or words to that effect. From what I saw of him in my three years at Aspinall's that pithy sentence showed a very high level of self-knowledge. Even less well known, but very informative when you do know it, was his statement that it was all right living in a democracy for most of the time, but every now and then he felt the need to spend some time in a Fascist country. Perhaps Jimmy and the eighth Lord Londonderry would have got on better than might have been expected.

An economist named Harold Wilson was Labour prime minister in the sixties, and again in the seventies. He was a thoroughly decent man as politicians go (if you ignore his complicity in the rape of Diego Garcia) and laid most of the foundations for the current laws governing race relations, sexual equality, religious discrimination and equality of opportunity in education etc etc. Civil liberties, in other words, which many of us will miss when the current generation of politicians succeeds in taking them away. He also had the sense to keep Britain out of the Vietnam War, in spite of strong pressure from the then American president Lyndon Johnson, who was always in search of someone else to share the blame and bag up the bodies. Harold's only real failing was to fall under the spell of a bossy woman with buck teeth (and much stronger powers of persuasion than the American president) who started life as Marcia Williams but soon moved up in the world, became a very influential member of Wilson's kitchen cabinet, and, in a resignation honours list often attributed (rightly or wrongly) to her own fair hand, Lady Falkender. You can check on the internet if you must, but I think she managed her rise to considerable power without ever suffering the indignity of touting for votes in a vulgar election. At the same time as she was bullying Harold Wilson Marcia Williams enjoyed a friendly relationship with James Goldsmith, the main man of this chapter. I have no idea if there was ever a sexual side to their spiritual union, and no real interest in either person's private life. Or in anybody else's, come to that. My own private life has always been quite enough for me. But personally, and with no scientific back-up or inside information, I doubt it. That may be a result of my strong antipathy to bossy women with buck teeth, an irrational bias I take no pride in, but her friendships with the rich and powerful seem to have been sustained by sheer unadulterated bossiness, not by the more familiar forces that lead so many of us astray.

According to Peter West, to whom I'll introduce you shortly, it was Marcia who turned plain old James Goldsmith into Sir James, as well as turning herself into Lady F, allegedly, in what has been known ever since as the Lavender List. Not literally of course. Even Marcia couldn't tell the Queen who should get a title. Not yet anyway. It had to be done through her influence on Harold Wilson. The first plan, Westy claimed, was to make Jimmy a Lord, several degrees better than a Sir, but a twist of fate put paid to plan A when the satirical magazine Private Eye revealed that the father of Marcia's children (a closely guarded secret at the time) was a Daily Mail journalist called Walter Terry. Marcia had always been very unwilling to share this knowledge with the rest of us. One always got the impression of a low opinion of the public at large. Although she was more than happy to be an important figure in the Labour party, the traditional representatives of what used to be called the working class, and see her name more and more frequently in the political columns of newspapers, she didn't seem all that keen on actual physical contact with the great unwashed. Mixing it with a Labour prime minister was one thing (and gave her powers that bossy people should not be allowed to get their hands on) but mixing with the riff-raff who voted for him may not have been her cup of tea. In her private life she seemed to favour clubbing with Jimmy and other rich friends at places like Annabel's, see above. A knees-up with the coal-miners at Barnsley Working Men's Club would probably have gone down like a lead balloon. I should explain to younger readers that we once had people known as coal-miners, right here in Britain. They had dirty faces and wore helmets with lights on and dug out the old-fashioned black stuff that used to power the electricity generating stations, and could even heat your home if you were clever enough to get it to light. Then Margaret Thatcher, our first ever female prime minister (another bossy lady, but with more even teeth) decided to close the coal mines and abolish the coal-miners, in what was either a reaction to the way their union leader Arthur Scargill blatantly copied her hair style or the first shot in a campaign to get rid of all the old-fashioned industries staffed by oiky members of the brick-throwing classes who thought they were just it because they had a union behind them, and let those clever bankers make Britain rich again. Oops. Peter West told me that the good Lady Falkender was mightily pissed off with Private Eye for daring to poke its nose into the private life of someone as important and influential as she perceived herself to be, but that to her great regret the intrusion couldn't be used in a lawsuit against the magazine. Then, with timing so good that the paranoid must have been tempted to search for a mole, Private Eye ran a story about her good friend James Goldsmith.

According to Peter, Marcia worked flat out to convince her Jimmy that the motivation behind the story was pure anti-Semitism and that he should sue the arses off everyone connected with Private Eye, at the very least bankrupting the magazine and everybody in it, but preferably going for the death penalty for all concerned (I made up the last bit, I think). Revenge was hers, with the help of an expensive lawyer whose exorbitant fees Jimmy could easily afford even before he owned a casino. I would guess that nice-guy Harold Wilson was unhappy about her vindictiveness, but remained powerless in the face of those teeth. If Peter was right, she sure did a good job on Jimmy. In 1976 James Goldsmith issued sixty writs against Private Eye and finally got them with the law of criminal libel, a forgotten law which hadn't been used for a couple of centuries but was still on the statute books, probably because it had never been tested in court. Even all those years ago it must have been recognised as a manifestly unfair and piss-poor example of law-making. I'll bet you've never even heard of it. I certainly hadn't until Westy bent my ear. The crucial difference between libel and criminal libel was that ordinary common or garden libel costs you a shed-load of money if you lose in court, as I'm probably about to find out if Lady F still enjoys a good read and she and I both live long enough, but being judged guilty of criminal libel could put you in prison as well as relieving you of your cash. Hence the name. The nastiness of the law made it very attractive to Sir James. When he stamped on your head he always wore his biggest boots.

The downside of Jimmy's court victory, again according to my man West, the main informant in all the scandals I failed to witness myself, was a reluctance on Harold Wilson's part to recommend to the Queen that a suddenly unpopular figure be made a lord. A lot of ordinary people, not just foaming at the mouth lefties, took the side of the magazine rather than the bossy rich man who had suddenly become a pantomime villain. A lot of other people, alerted by newspaper coverage of the court case, wondered why a slightly left-wing government with liberal tendencies even thought about giving any kind of title to a right-wing asset stripper who ate liberals for breakfast. A compromise was found. Lord Jim went out of the window and Sir Jim crept in through the back door, closely followed by those teeth.

The man who handed Jimmy the lethal weapon of criminal libel was the above-mentioned Peter West, a penniless hanger on to the Aspinall set, and himself a one-time lawyer. Or so he claimed. Peter's advice on the use of the law may not be public knowledge. The lawyer who represented Goldsmith probably grabbed the credit. But Peter West bragged to me endlessly about his part, and other slightly less poisonous people confirmed the truth of his account. The freely offered legal advice brought a very good return. Peter West got carte blanche at Aspinall's when Jimmy put up the cash to open the casino in 1978. Free food, free drink, free cigars, and free use of the club's enormous Rolls Royce (as black as the Queen's, but a bit longer) whenever he needed to move more than a hundred yards, or less it was raining.

Sometime in the nineties, not that long before the end of his life in 1997, Sir James built an extraordinary house on the Pacific coast of Mexico, one of several in what was probably the world's most expensive and exclusive gated community. Security arrangements verged on the paranoid, before going well beyond. He employed a huge number of domestic staff who had to assemble in front of the house and welcome the master home whenever Jimmy popped in for a visit, rather as the rich and powerful did in England during the eighteenth and early nineteenth centuries. You may have seen similar scenes in films where actors like Helena Bonham-Carter and Colin Firth dress up in old-fashioned clothes and talk very slowly in posh voices.

What with all the shagging and all the showing off, not to mention the law suits and the gambling, I never understood how Jimmy found enough hours in the day to make all his money. But he did, big time. More than a billion pounds worth. Not bad for a boy who left school early.

In the next chapter I'll introduce you properly to Peter West, or Poisonous Pete as I like to call him (affectionately). He was awful but I liked him.

Poisonous Pete.

In the beginning John Aspinall was the front man, the gambler's friend, James Goldsmith was the man who put up the money, and Peter West, the man James Goldsmith kept as a pet, was the man most likely to be seen by someone popping in for a quiet spot of roulette at the freshly opened Aspinall's casino. Peter was born into an upper class family with high moral standards. His father was an outstanding hero in the First World War, a war in which you had to be a hero just to turn up; his mother was a saintly woman with a social conscience. Sadly any feats of arms to match his father's have gone unrecorded and all his mother's attempts to pass on her high moral standards failed to take root. Later in life his mother may have come to regret the brief moment of passion that preceded his birth by nine months, even as she held tight to her dream that his good side would one day come shining through. But she probably didn't. Mothers are good people, generally.

Young Peter went to a good public school, either one of the top ones like Eton or Harrow, or perhaps the more intellectual Winchester. He was a clever little chap. When he grew up he qualified as a lawyer, but I don't think he ever did an honest day's work in his life (one thing we always had in common). He survived by scrounging all his daily needs with thick-skinned determination and great skill. None of his contemporaries among the Aspinall set could recall his ever doing anything different. When I say thick-skinned I mean bull elephant thick-skinned, not your average double-glazing salesman or estate agent thick skinned. They don't even come close. But a scrounger can only avoid being a beggar, a very close relation, by offering something in return. Peter repaid the people he scrounged off with witty repartee and malicious gossip, rapidly inventing good stories if there was a lull in the flow of real ones. Like the Devil, whose acquaintance he must have made if the more vengeful of the Holy Joes are right about our future beyond the grave, Peter had all the best tunes. As a drinking companion he was what a good friend of mine calls value for money (always somebody else's money in Peter's case, only sometimes in mine). In a way (excluding the sexual services on offer for a reluctantly modest fee) he was a much posher version of Tongue First Bill, the Chelsea gigolo I got to know during my very brief career as a failed art dealer. Just as I once looked forward to T.F.B's daily visits to the art gallery/lock-up shop, now I looked forward to Poisonous Pete's daily visit to the casino.

On bad days, when he'd run out of what little cash he had to waste on the roulette table, or it was raining outside, or both, he entertained the lowly staff with scandalous stories about the Royal family and/or the aristocrats who cling to their coat-tails. At one time I knew every detail about who was legitimate and who was not in the line of one of those Dukes who own Scotland. The last time we discussed the matter, in the summer of 1981, the score was close to even. I suppose you have to do something to keep warm when it's minus twenty five outside and you live in a draughty old stately home. I assumed that the then current Duke was once silly enough to invite Peter to dinner, and even sillier enough to trust him with family secrets that his Grace was sure would never be repeated outside the dining room. Some hope. Or perhaps one of the ladies present dished the dirt. Peter did have a way with the girls. Peter also explained, frequently, how and why the late Princess Diana was chosen to breed with our future King, as Prince Charles confidently expected to become before he honed to perfection his now legendary ability to shoot himself in the foot. If you make a regular pilgrimage to Kensington Palace on the anniversary of the Princess's death (and it doesn't make you a bad person if you do) you may prefer to skip the next five paragraphs.

Peter explained, frequently, that the powers that be could only accept a virgin as first prize in their search for a future Queen. No easy task in England among girls over the age of fourteen, and not any easier if the search was extended to Scotland and Wales (Northern Ireland was out right from the start. No sense in asking for trouble). Finding a good-looking maiden in her late teens or early twenties was as close as you can get to mission impossible. Even Tom Cruise would have struggled. Young ladies who preferred the company of other young ladies were obviously out, however technically virginal. A middle-aged woman was never on the cards, whatever the personal preferences of the once and future King. And another door was closed: they couldn't play safe by picking a young but really ugly girl who had found no takers in her quest to wave good-bye to her virtue. In the television age one can't have a young Queen who looks like the back of a bus. Anyway Charles would have kicked up. Or thrown up.

Poisonous Pete explained to us that the virgin thing was really, really important. Of course we knew that already. Croupiers of the old school had all sorts of faults, I know that, but naivete was never one of them. We were a captive audience anyway, you can't just wander away from a casino table because no-body is playing and still expect to get paid at the end of the month, so we listened attentively to all of Peter's stories, however often we had heard them before. And Peter always told a story well. He had to. When he wasn't digging up vicious old laws spreading vicious gossip was how he made his living. Anyway it beat listening to him ranting about roulette. I heard the Diana story many times and couldn't help but notice that like most middle-aged men Peter really enjoyed talking about young girls. Especially virgins. I also noticed that, like any gifted raconteur, he allowed himself a certain degree of poetic licence. His fertile brain often came up with new twists that gave the story more colour, but he always kept the basic truth alive with an accuracy that would be admired in a historian.

He explained to his faux naïf audience that the search for a virgin wasn't based on morality and Christian ethics and all that Sunday school stuff. There have always been plenty of serial shaggers among our Royals, and no doubt there always will be. It was all down to the old firm's fear of the power of the tabloids. Foreigners with no respect for our first family (like Australian/American Rupert Murdoch) were taking over the British press. The deference that once maintained radio silence when Princess Margaret got real at Bob Barnett's old night club was long gone. The problem facing the virgin-hunters bore a strong resemblance to a mathematical equation. If a girl wasn't a virgin, then by definition some bounder had got there first. Q.E.D. Suppose he was a cad who would sell to the News of the World (for a handsome fee) the story of how he once upon a time got a leg over the future Queen of England, not knowing (or caring, in the heat of the moment) that she would one day become a fairy princess and the Queen of all our hearts, before being buried under a mountain of teddy-bears. Even worse, more than just the two of them might have taken part, at a drink and drug fuelled orgy in a country mansion with a drive a mile long, the sort of place where the parents don't go out for the night when the young people have a few friends round, they move into the East Wing, by car. A story like that would have blown a Royal wedding right off the front page.

At the time of the search for the elusive virgin no-one anticipated that the papers would soon be full of stories about hot young men who got a leg over the future Queen after the fairy-tale marriage had brightened our television screens. But that's another story. There must be dozens of books to choose from, if you missed them first time round. I read part of one of them when I was sheltering from the rain in an Oxfam book shop. You do that when your main transport is a bicycle and you can't quite raise enough money to go into the pub. The book was written by a woman, very badly, in a sensible attempt to cash in quick while the story was still hot. I can't remember the author's name. It had its moments, but it wasn't a patch on the stuff you can buy in Soho. It was a relief to put it back on the shelf when the rain stopped. There's even a new one now, a bit late in the day, by Tina Brown, explaining that anyway the former virgin was actually a right bitch once you got to know her. A triumph for biographical balance.

We know now that the virgin was found, and had her day as the most celebrated woman on planet Earth. She even caught the eye of

Jacques Chirac, the randy old goat, or Francois Mitterand, ditto. Or both, on different days. But at the time of the search the royal family was just looking for a queen. Not a world super star who would sell millions of newspapers and books and make one photographer enough money to keep him in gravy for life, unless he takes up gambling with the same enthusiasm as his old man.

Princess Diana fans can come out from behind the sofa now and get stuck into Poisonous Pete's own private life, on which I'm something of an expert. As previously explained, Peter's part in helping Jimmy Goldsmith sue Private Eye prompted Jimmy to allow him to use Aspinall's as his second home. Peter being Peter he pushed hard at the open door and made Aspinall's much more like his first home. He had a free lunch and/or dinner every day, unless he managed to scrounge a better one somewhere else, drank as much as he liked, went through very expensive cigars like shit through a goose, and used the club's Rolls Royce as a free taxi, not giving a toss if it was urgently needed to transport the odd billionaire gambler around town. There was even a girl friend, very much in the background. (but he had to provide her himself. Not quite everything was on the house). The kind lady gave him a roof over his head and a bed to sleep in, whenever he could spare a few minutes away from the roulette table, in her nice little house in very posh Walton Street, a stone's throw from the club and very handy for Harrods if he needed her to buy him something the casino couldn't provide. She seemed like a very pleasant woman on the two occasions she spoke to me, guardedly. I was forced to assume that she either had a saintly character and was able to forgive any sin against her, or a wide streak of masochism. I never found out which. Or maybe she saw something in Peter that the rest of the world somehow missed. We never discussed the matter. I'm very polite (or professionally smarmy if you prefer), but sadly she never really took to me or to anybody else associated with the casino. We were the bad guys who took money away from nice people like her Peter.

One afternoon Poisonous Pete came in looking seriously dishevelled and genuinely unhappy. He told everybody in the room that his girl friend had chucked him out (but not why) and that he had spent the early hours of the morning walking the streets and waiting for Aspinall's to open for lunch. Nobody asked why he hadn't spent the night in a hotel, where at least he could have had a wash and a shave. Obviously there wasn't a hotel in walking distance that would let him scrounge a free night's stay. The club's Rolls had been put away for the night, so there was no free transport to a friendly place beyond walking distance, or a comfortable back seat to sleep in. Taxis cost money, so they were out. Heroically we all resisted the urge to applaud. There was the odd malicious grin, but Peter was too lost in self-pity to notice. And then, to our deep disappointment, the girl friend's saintly (or masochistic) streak prevailed. Next day Peter was back home and back to his usual cocky self. Mr Toad after a particularly close shave.

As a gamber Peter West was right at the bottom of the ladder. A wanker if ever there was one. He played American roulette with one pound chips, the lowest denomination we offered and hoped no-one would use. He laid out twenty chips every spin, asking us to advance him the chips and mark up twenty pounds on the wheel. That was and is quite illegal, and may have played a part in Ladbroke's fall from grace when the shit hit the fan at Hill Street, but was tolerated at Aspinall's because Peter was Jimmy's special friend. If we were lucky he paid it off with winning chips when he got ahead. That also was and is illegal. His game was as silly as it was illegal. He tried to follow what he thought was the natural sequence of numbers, which doesn't exist in real life, and insulted the croupier in the nastiest possible way when the predicted numbers failed to come up. He got particularly shirty when six or nine appeared, numbers into which he claimed, quite wrongly, the little white ball fell much more often than it did into any of the others. He refused ever to play six or nine, on something like religious grounds. I said to him surely he should play nothing else if these were the two most frequent numbers. He'd clean up in no time. He said don't be silly, if he played those numbers we'd stop spinning them and he'd lose a packet. I gave up. I knew there was no point in going on. Most gamblers are at least a bit mad, if only when they are actually gambling. You don't have to ask a silly question to get a silly answer.

That was the pattern for the first two years. Quite often Peter left the club with twenty or forty pounds still marked up on the wheel. Some of the croupiers were angry about being pushed into breaking the law, even though they knew I was just carrying out club policy, and were unwilling to get me off the hook by taking the marker down. I sympathised. Not everyone in casinos was like me, only most of them in the good old days. On those awkward occasions I took cash out of my own pocket and paid off the debt myself, with a contemptuous flourish. I can be quite aristocratic where money is involved. For a while. Later on I lifted some chips from an unmanned table when no-one was looking and changed them for cash with a friendly cashier. I didn't mind being helpful but I drew the line at paying for the privilege.

During the last year I was at Aspinall's, Poisonous Pete's luck inexplicably changed. All of a sudden he became a five pound player and a winner, instead of a one pound player and a loser, albeit of not very much. The radical change raised intense and probably justifiable suspicion that

224

something fishy was going on. John Aspinall asked me to investigate. He knew by now that I was an expert on fishiness, having done all sorts of illegal things at Angelo's request. (Not to mention all the stuff the French Connection had blabbed about, and which Angelo had no doubt passed on to the boss in an attempt to burn me off as competition. See a later chapter for details). For a couple of weeks I watched old Pete like a hawk, but I had no intention of sneaking on him or anyone else if I had found out what was actually happening. Fellow former public schoolboys will understand. Only weeds sneak. I formed my own agenda. If I could have got to the bottom of it I would have told the staff involved that the heat was on. So cut me in for a couple of weeks, and then pack it up. Peter's game would go back to normal. The winning streak would be accepted as just that, or forgotten when a real gambler from an oil country lost a million, we would all have a bit of extra spending cash, and everyone would be happy. But I was unable to spot any funny business taking place. I worked all sorts of different shifts and even came in on my day off once or twice, something I really hate doing. If bad apples among the staff really were up to something they were making a bloody good job of it. They sure fooled me. Congratulations all round if you were Pete's friends.

Peter West may have been a penniless scrounger of no fixed address, but he was not a man to cross. He loved a fight. He thoroughly enjoyed injecting as much poison as he could into the Private Eye libel case, and would probably have done it for fun if Jimmy had asked nicely. He had some fun on his own account when he went to a casino in Kensington, played small because he didn't have any money (or a close relationship with the staff), behaved badly because that's what he did best, and got himself thrown out. As his feet hit the pavement the management of the casino in question were confident that a rude English upper crust wanker was no loss. How very wrong they were.

The casino had been bought, not long before Pete's visit, by a Gulf Arab who found himself without a regular casino to go to when the Ladbroke company's Hill Street casino was shut down by the judge, and decided to become a casino owner instead of a casino loser. He contacted the senior Hill Street managers, now unemployed, and asked them to run a small casino with small stakes that he was buying in Kensington, and planning to turn into a small casino with big stakes. He said that they had been very good at relieving him of his money at Hill Street. He was confident that they could help him recreate something just like Hill Street in Kensington W8, and help him relieve large numbers of his fellow Arabs of a lot of their money. Were they interested? Were they? I should cocoa. The ex-managers were over the moon. With most of the crooked West End casinos shut down, or about to be shut down, they were looking at a longish spell on low wages in the provinces if they wanted to stay in casinos, or a spell driving mini-cabs if they insisted on staying in London to be first on the scene when a rare job advert appeared.

When the Gulf man's casino picked a fight with Poisonous Pete, Pete looked into the background of the casino owner and struck gold, literally. On the surface the man from the Gulf (Persian if you're Iranian, Arabian if you're Arab, just plain Gulf if you're invading) was a respectable and very wealthy businessman. But he had started his commercial career by smuggling gold across the Gulf at vast profit, carrying the heavy stuff in small dark boats at night and in constant danger of being machine-gunned by an unfriendly navy. He survived the bullets and set up straight businesses with the money he had risked his life for. Banks and insurance companies and all that. But he kept the gold smuggling going because it was just too profitable to shut down. The only difference was that now he paid other people to duck when the machine guns opened up. The Gaming Board for Great Britain gave the man from the Gulf a casino licence, on the grounds that he was a fit and proper person to hold one, and added the gold smuggling to the very long list of things that they know nothing about. They can't have spent very long looking. Poisonous Pete soon found out about the gold. No-one threw PP out of a casino without getting a long hard look at his private life. He wrote to the Home Secretary to protest about the granting of a London casino licence to an unsavoury foreign smuggler who threw decent Englishmen on to the street. Peter showed me the letter several times. He told me that the Home Secretary was someone he'd known at school, which was probably true. The writing was impressively vicious and very accurate in detail. You could tell he was still a lawyer at heart. I expressed a polite interest but expected nothing to happen, greatly under-estimating the fire-power of a Peter West attack. At the time I hadn't researched in depth what had happened to the excellent Richard Ingrams in 1976.

Within less than a year the Gulf Arab was given a short time to sell his casino to a respectable owner, if he could find one, or be shut down. It happened a year or so after the big blitz of 1980/1981. The authorities seemed less keen to close casinos and put people out of work and add to the already embarrassingly high unemployment figures that were such a noticeable part of Mrs Thatcher's early reign. The new policy was to force a sale, in the often vain hope that someone more reputable would come along with a sack-full of cash. The man from the Gulf had to admit defeat at the hands of Peter West, the wanker with attitude who had so annoyed his staff, and sold the casino to a now defunct casino company originally founded by a Welshman who was once caught on camera stealing chips at a West End casino from a player sitting next to him, another incident on the long list of things the Gaming Board knew nothing about. They happily handed out a shiny new licence.

We just can't get away from gold: in the early eighties Sir James Goldsmith bought a gold mine in a Central American country where a civil war had raged for as long as anyone still alive could remember. The rich were very rich and getting richer and the poor were very poor and getting poorer, or dead. The government ran death squads with the active help of secretive American special forces, the professional killers' presence sanctioned (illegally under American law) by their "Aw Shucks, I'm Just A Straight Shooting Old Cowpoke" commander in chief, the late president Ronald Reagan, a man greatly admired by both Jimmy and Poisonous Pete. Death squads killed tens of thousands of poor people, along with some of the rebel combatants. Most of the casualties were native Indians, the poorest of the poor, sometimes wiped out a whole village at a time. In return the rebels killed as many people as they possibly could who had any connection with the government, but never came close to evening the score. Jimmy knew that buying a local gold mine and taking even more money out of an already poor country would make him a prime target for the rebel guns. But when you've just bought a hole full of gold you really really want to go and have a look. Sir James went to see his new mine, bravely ignoring the possibility of assassination. Well almost. He took Peter West with him as a human shield, without burdening Peter with too much information about his new job. Jimmy had been told that the airport where they would touch down was uncomfortably close to the dense jungle that was a feature of the tragic country, but that the leaves on the trees couldn't be removed by chemical means, like in Vietnam. Too sensitive, so soon after Vietnam had been shut down. Everyone would know where the chemicals came from, even if the locals had the technological means to do their own spraying. Naturally enough the thick green jungle was the favourite hiding place of the rebel fighters. If information had leaked to the rebels that Jimmy was flying in, and it quite probably had, there was a strong possibility that a burst of well-aimed machine gun fire would cut him down as soon as he stepped out of the plane.

That's where Poisonous Pete came in. Sir James insisted that Peter wore his finest clothes and generally did his best to look like a fellow billionaire, as they were going to meet some jolly important people. Jimmy knew that Peter would enjoy that. When the plane landed Sir James suggested that Peter should go out first, playfully joking that the locals might mistake him for Jimmy. Peter could fool the silly foreigners and have a bit of real fun. Not a mutter did he utter about rebel machine guns and dense jungles.

Peter strode out of the plane, beautifully dressed, head held high, chest puffed out, revelling in every second of his short moment of fame, which could have been very short indeed. Sir James kept well back from the door. When no shots came he walked out too and hurried down the steps, keeping his head down and hoping there wasn't a well-informed rebel commander in the nearby jungle who could spot the difference between a penniless gringo scrounger and a cautious gringo billionaire. I wasn't present at the airport on what could have been a fateful day for Jimmy and/or Pete, depending on how much ammunition the rebels had and how long they were willing to hang around before the gringos and their local friends made with the napalm. If I had been there it's most unlikely I would be sitting here now and passing on information supplied by a very close relative of the late John Aspinall. With my luck the rebels would have made it to work on time and blown up the whole damned aeroplane. Sometimes it's not where you are that counts, it's where you're not. I was probably at Aspinall's, helping to pay for the bloody gold mine. They don't come cheap, even in Central American failed states. Be very careful if you're ever foolish enough to make friends with the very rich. They're not like us. Buy a bullet-proof vest, with their money if you can. You'll need it.

Sir James and Peter West survived the rest of their visit to Central America, and the journey home, and died much later of different forms of cancer in their home country. Call me a sentimental old fool if you must, but I'm glad Poisonous Pete didn't catch a chest full of machine gun bullets in his brief role as a human shield. Although I can't say I greatly admired his human qualities (but who am I to judge?) he never actually killed anybody, as far as I know, and he did make me laugh more times than I can remember. I'm glad Sir James didn't cop it either. He paid half of my wages for three years, and never noticed when I paid myself a bit more. I appreciate people like that, even if I don't personally like them.

In the next chapter we'll have a look at how the boys got a new casino licence, at a time when new casino licences were not that easy to get. You needed a good story, and a story-teller of the calibre of Poisonous Pete. Aspers and Jimmy found a good story, but they decided that a whole gang of story-tellers was better than one, however talented. They were dead right. It worked first time.

Background Music.

When Mr John Aspinall and Sir James Goldsmith applied for a new casino licence, after the period of commercial abstinence that Aspers had to agree with Playboy when he sold them the Clermont, their big pitch to the gaming authorities was that the upper class and aristocratic gentlemen of England urgently needed a casino of their own. Like the Clermont had once been, but minus the vulgar people who went there now. A place where they could hang out with gamblers from a similar background. And a place where, if they really felt they had to, upper class and aristocratic ladies could hang out too.

The boys had done their homework. They found a house, rather a lovely one if ever you're passing that way and like looking at pleasing architecture combined with a bit of casino history, on the corner of Hans Street and Sloane Street, which had once been filled with the subdued murmurs and the occasional yelp of old dears playing bridge. A minimal (legal) flashing of cards had to be part of the history of a house if a casino licence was to be granted in those days, but the old dears' bridge games were not, on their own, a guarantee of success. The other important part of a licence application was proving demand. You had to convince the beak that another casino was an absolute necessity. It was still a couple of years before nearly all the other London casino owners were to have their collars felt and their joints shut down, so in court the boys had to prove that there really was a demand for the fun and games they were so eager to provide. Without special pleading on behalf of the poor down-trodden aristocracy the numbers were stacked against the two hopefuls. A good turnout was called for, and duly reported for duty. A succession of lords and ladies paraded in front of the magistrates. Attendance at the House of Lords must have been even thinner than usual. All were intensively supportive of John Aspinall's plan to get back to robbing the rich. Many of the lords (and some of the livelier ladies) had lost considerable sums of money in Aspinall's earlier casino operations, but they wouldn't have a bad word said about their boy. He took one's money so nicely. They all sang the same song: we need a posh gambling joint to hang out in. The unspoken message was that they didn't want to mix with the Jews and the foreign riff-raff who threw their cash around in all the other casinos, adding the crime of having lots of money to the sin of vulgarity. Would you want a rogue like Robert Maxwell, or some Arab in a dressing gown and a towel round his head, to marry your daughter? Of course not. The aristocrats really didn't like people like that. And they didn't like the faceless businessmen who owned the other casinos, or the jumped-up council school boys who posed as managers. So smarmy and so creepy. Some of them even put their arms round your shoulders when they were talking to you. Next thing you know they'll be picking your pockets. And half of them were foreign. Or Jewish. Or both. And prone to talking in clichés. Awful. Bring back our John. He's one of us. Look here, his mother's a Lady (Osborne) and his wife's a Lady (Curzon). What more do you want? Hurry up with that licence you silly little man. I've got to get to the Savoy in time for lunch.

You can't say that sort of thing out loud of course. But the message got across. Some of the magistrates may have come from an upper class background themselves, or wished they had even if they hadn't. Either way they got the drift. A licence was granted and faithfully renewed every year, long after the joint had filled up with the uncouth foreign billionaires whose money was John Aspinall's real target, and whom we allowed to behave as badly as they liked for as long as they kept on handing over shed-loads of cash. Shortly after starting work at Aspinall's I took a sneaky look through the members' address book. Most of the early members had titles and lived in castles and were living proof of the need for the elusive posh casino. But once the joint was open very few of the aristos came springing through the door waving cheque books. Or were particularly welcome if they did. It was the aristocrats' failing performance as gamblers that had forced John Aspinall to sell the Clermont in 1972. His elegant small casino had relied too heavily on Debrett and was no longer providing enough cash to pay for Aspinall's efforts to breed endangered animals in the wilds of Kent, something he did extremely well but at great personal expense, hitherto subsidised by what he always called the gambler's gold. In 1972 the aristocrats were no longer pushing enough gold across the tables of the Clermont to keep the Aspinall animals alive and well and living in Kent. Selling his casino (for two and half million pounds, a handsome sum in '72) was the only way out.

At the time he probably expected never to need to run a casino again. He intended to invest the two and a half million wisely enough to keep himself and the animals and his mother in clover, but he wasn't to know that the worst recession in living memory (until now) was just around the corner. Share prices fell further and faster than ever before. So fast and so far that many left-wing people gleefully forecast the end of capitalism as we know it. Like many others John Aspinall looked on helplessly as his money disappeared into a black hole. After the six lean years were up he knew that his only chance of getting his bum back in the butter (as they used to say in pre-independence Zimbabwe) was to tap into the oil-fired gambling boom that was making fortunes for Corals, Ladbrokes, the Playboy organisation and London Clubs. But he couldn't say that in court. The magistrates would have told him that there were already enough casinos to bleed the Saudis and the Nigerians dry. So tough luck chum. Nice try but no cigar. He had to fall back on the aristos and keep his fingers crossed that the magistrates would buy his pitch. Luckily for him, and for the animals, and for his mother, they did. When the new Aspinall's casino opened one still had to make the toffs feel important of course. It was good manners, and they really had been very helpful. The odd one dropped in now and then for a free dinner, and one hard drinker occasionally lost consciousness in the bar, at our expense. A modest reward for the (unpaid) support for a nobs' casino licence that was so easily (and quickly) converted into a licence to soak up Arab and Nigerian oil money.

Lord Cholmondley, pronounced Chumley if ever you bump into the current title-holder and want to get off to a good start by pronouncing his name properly, was one of the few nobs who actually came in to spend some money. I recognised him as a man I thought I knew as Lord Rocksavage (inevitably nick-named Lord Rock-Salmon by us Curzon House riff-raff). Rocksavage/Salmon was a regular player at the Curzon, the casino where I first learnt how to steal money professionally, with a bit of help from the general manager and a lot of help from members of the French casinos' black-list of croupiers they wouldn't touch with a barge-pole. I was a bit confused when somebody at Aspinall's greeted the man I knew as Lord Rocksavage as Lord Cholmondley, but somebody else gave me the low-down and saved me from committing a social gaffe. Lord Cholmondleys get two titles. While his dad is still alive the designated (male) heir to the title is Baron Rocksavage. In practice this means that the first male offspring is Lord Rocksavage until he hits middle age and his dad snuffs it, and then Lord Cholmondley until he snuffs it himself. And so on and so on, down the generations. (I don't know what happens if ever it's all girls and no boys. Perhaps the oldest girl has to change sex if she really, really wants the title).

Rocky's family pile was somewhere in East Anglia, handy for Sandringham if ever a royal invite fluttered on to the door mat. But being a lord isn't all roses. Even an English king could have his head sliced off if things went seriously agley. It wasn't just the French. Family finances got a bit shaky back in the days of men in tights. Down-sizing was a real and present danger. Then, in a scene straight from Barbara Cartland, love saved the day. A handsome Rocky, or a Chummy in tight trousers, fell for a beautiful Jewish girl from the business savvy Sassoon family. A marriage was arranged and everyone lived happily ever after. A marriage made in Heaven. The girl's parents had built up a massive fortune by trading with India (when it was still part of England), probably bringing back the spices that livened up the food of English people who could afford to eat, and the boy had two titles, one in hand and one still to come. Beat that for a win double. The rich upstarts could pose as aristocrats and the real aristocrats could pay their bills. Everybody dance.

Cholmondley was a reasonable roulette player at Aspinall's, just as he had been at the Curzon in my earlier life. The name had changed but the money hadn't. He could easily blow the odd ten or twenty grand, very handy if the wage cheques were due to be signed and there were no rich Arabs in our part of town. When I saw his lordship again, nearly ten years after I had last seen him at the Curzon, I recalled an incident at the old place, in 1968 or thereabouts. An English croupier, whom I'll call John to preserve his anonymity (like John Doe if you die and no-one knows who the hell you are) had made the jump from nervous goody-goody to casino robber. I knew why, although he tried to keep the details to himself. He'd married a girl who turned into her mother even earlier than most of them do and only felt truly alive when she was buying something high-priced in a shop, or sneering from an expensive car at poor people waiting for a bus, preferably in the rain. Her addictions made her much better at spending money than John was at earning it (even in a sixties casino) and he was always seriously strapped for cash. A baron with a small 'b' was expected. The game was almost afoot. As he was still a fluttering debutante John hadn't been told who the baron was. Need to know basis and all that. Like secret agents. John didn't take kindly to being left out in the cold. He wanted to be one of the in-crowd. Because I was the best friend he had on the table he asked me when the baron was coming in, and was he a regular customer? Did he know him? Right at that moment in walked Baron Rocksavage, with a capital 'B' and a father still alive. Rashly assuming that the John who wasn't a John would be clever enough to see that it was a joke, I nodded meaningfully at the Baron who wasn't a baron. A large denomination chip appeared. Before I had time to explain what a joke was John had very skilfully changed the big chip into small chips worth twice as much as the big chip and passed them quickly to his Lordship, along with a conspiratorial smile that made me feel ill. Good stuff if you're dealing with the right man; it was a traditional way of getting a bent game off to a flying start. A thousand pounds becomes two thousand pounds before a single bet has been laid. 'John' might have been a beginner, but he knew the rules. The trouble was that he didn't know the barons. It dawned on me that John had taken me seriously. The horror. I tried to make him understand, by telepathy if need be, that IT WAS A BLOODY JOKE. Get the extra money back pronto. Say sorry for your mistake, buy a book on humour when you get up tomorrow, and stop fucking smiling. My message didn't get through. Maybe John was brooding about his wife's next shopping trip.

Baron Rocky looked carefully at the money he had been given, and briefly at the chip he had handed over before it disappeared in to the locked metal box at the top of the table. I murmured a silent prayer just in case there really was somebody up there, and made plans for a new career just in case there wasn't. Rocky divided his doubled money into two piles of chips. I thought, hoped even, that he would give one pile back straight away. We could apologise for our silly mistake and keep the matter hidden from the manager and the owner. John would finally get the point, we could all have a laugh, and later on we could do the business with the real baron. But the chips stayed put. John's eyes met mine, in the nick of time. I was able to inform him that it was all a joke that had just gone seriously wrong. Hadn't he heard of jokes? I begged him not to put on any dodgy bets, not to pay the Baron large amounts of money he wasn't entitled to, and never to smile that fucking smile again. The Baron isn't a baron. He's a proper nob. I was having a laugh. I thought you'd understand, you moron. The crucial information crossed the table in Nicois, the Italianate dialect we'd both picked up from the Southern French croupiers before they were sent packing, which we and the Frenchmen used in the same way as Cockney criminals once used rhyming slang to confuse the early coppers and keep their rough hands off their collars. The Baron obviously didn't understand a word of what I was saying. I had counted on that, quite confidently. Lots of posh people speak French, sometimes really well, but very few of them have much of a grasp of Nicois. Actually even other Frenchmen find it hard to understand. It's like a member of Margaret Thatcher's first cabinet trying to understand someone from Liverpool. When Rocky had blown one of the piles of chips, after nearly an hour of silent career planning, he quietly handed the extra chips back to John. He said, very politely, that we had given him too much money, by mistake obviously, and he would now like to give it back. He hadn't done so before because he hadn't wanted to make a fuss or cause us any embarrassment. What a gent! Thank God there was one honest person in the room.

Although not actually a title-holder, although many people can no doubt think of one or two that would fit like a glove, Nicholas Soames MP was another impressively aristocratic player at the new Aspinall's. He came in every now and then to play roulette and to bray, not always in that order, and not for very large sums of money. But Nicholas is a close relation of Winston Churchill, one of my few heroes, and a descendant of the Duke of Marlborough no less. Very posh, even if he didn't have an actual title. So I tried really hard to admire him. An uphill job. Nicholas has never done anything particularly memorable in political terms, although he had even then achieved some fame in the House of

Commons by constantly taking the piss out of dear old John Prescott, a sad waste of talent given that John Prescott has always been so skilled at taking the piss out of himself. Ride 'em cowboy, as his secretary may well have said in a private moment, over her shoulder. Are you pleased to see me, or is that a croquet ball in your pocket? We could go on all night. Nick's favourite parliamentary catch phrase was: "Bring me another gin and tonic Giovanni!" making the point that not only did John Prescott have a working-class job as a steward on a North Sea ferry before becoming a Member of Parliament and minister of everything Tony Blair didn't really give a toss about, it was a working-class job which in those days was usually done by Italians (Giovanni is Italian for John. Get it?). And we all knew what Italians were like. Tanks with six gears, five of them reverse, all that old stuff. Cutting edge in 1945, but wearing a bit thin by 1978 and totally passe now, if you'll pardon my French. Good old Nick. Such a reliable conduit to times past. A true upholder of tradition. And still going strong. Apparently, on learning that old Etonian David Cameron had made it into Downing Street, with a bit of help from another Nick, he expressed the view that at long last England was getting back to the natural order of things.

It has nothing to do with casinos, but I feel compelled to tell you (in case you didn't already know, but probably did) that Nick's dad Fatty Soames, more correctly known as Christopher, was the minister in Margaret Thatcher's first government who, soon after the 1979 election that first brought the good lady to power, got the short straw and had to hand the country formerly known as Rhodesia to a black government after one time Spitfire ace Ian Smith's attempt to run the country as an independent white ex-colony, like New Zealand but with a much higher proportion of natives, many of them recently deceased, had run out of steam. The transfer of sovereignty had been agreed before the election and couldn't be wriggled out of so soon afterwards. Throughout the proceedings our Margaret, an outspoken supporter of the South African apartheid government and a firm holder of the view that Nelson Mandela was just another terrorist who should stay locked up for at least another twenty seven years, and be damned grateful not to feel a noose around his neck, looked quite horrified at the idea of giving anything away for free, especially to a bunch of darkies. Or maybe she had a psychic dream about a man with dodgy specs called Robert Mugabe.

Others provided a gentle chorus of aristocratic background music, but none of them deserve more than a couple of lines. Charles Benson springs to mind, untitled again, but big and fat and rather jolly and the owner of the fruitiest and poshest voice in the joint. He was probably the Charles whom Alan Clark mentions, in one of his interminable diaries, as the man he kept losing money to when they played backgammon at Aspinall's. Charles Benson, if it really was he, always seemed to be strapped for cash in those days so Clark's losses were probably a very important source of revenue. In his day job Charles was the racing tipster for a popular newspaper, very skilled at telling you how to lose your money on a horse in a properly scientific manner.

A youngish man with an almost equally posh voice (and a vile temper) was a regular blackjack player at Aspinall's. As an even younger man he played chemmy at the Clermont until his very wealthy father got fed up with signing large cheques payable to John Aspinall and suggested that if John was so keen to have his idiot son hanging round his bloody casino, and vice versa, he could bloody well give him a job. And this was the last cheque he was going to sign, ever. The boy was on his own. The job offer was made, and quickly accepted. The suddenly penniless player became the manager of the Clermont. I think it was the only real job he had ever had, if you're kind enough to consider a casino manager as a man with a real job. It nearly became a career for life. Six years after the Clermont was sold the errant boy was lined up for a management job at the new Aspinall's, until an unpaid debt to the Playboy Club got in the way. The Gaming Board regularly gave casino owners' licences to all kinds of riff raff, including foreign gold smugglers, but wouldn't give a casino manager's licence to a man of good family who happened to owe a few quid (fifty thousand if you're a stickler for details) to a casino that would soon lose its operator's licence. So the would be manager became a player, and a very obnoxious one it has to be said, in a reversal of his previous reversal.

Last, but definitely not least, there was Taki. He's not an English aristocrat. He's not even English, being Greek (Taki is a very much shortened version of one of those long Greek surnames made up mainly of 'o's and 'i's and 'u's and 's's). But as a young man, and well into middle age (and into the living present for all I know) he boffed his way through a long and beautiful queue of aristocratic English girls, effortlessly brushing aside competition from upper class young Englishmen who had never quite recovered from boarding school. So I take the liberty of awarding Taki the title of honorary English toff, first class, in recognition of his long history of close encounters of the rude kind with female members of the English upper classes. Something must have rubbed off.

Taki was never just a gambler. In between boffing London's top totty (and the odd country member) and snorting coke, for possession of which he spent a short time in prison, long after I had left Aspinall's, he wrote a column for the Spectator magazine, an old copy of which you might find in your dentist's waiting room. Actually I think he still does. If

235

I'm right, and if you enjoy a very well written racist rant (in English, you don't have to brush up on your Greek) go straight to the High Life column. You'll be in Seventh Heaven.

Such was the background music. There were other nobs in the chorus line, but none quite interesting enough for me to waste ink on. I refuse outright to bore you with descriptions of the lower ranks. In the next few chapters I'll try to paint you an honest picture of my life as (eventually) a manager at Aspinall's, Hans Street, arguably the most elegant casino ever to open in London but not, in my time at least, the one most rigorously determined to obey the laws of the land. I hope you enjoy it at least half as much as I did.

Laws Are For Little People.

I quickly discovered that John Aspinall and I saw eye to eye on how a casino should be run. His new joint opened. He called all the staff into a room for a talk. I feared the worst. Bad apples spoiling the barrel, integrity (in a casino?) and a sickly appeal for togetherness. All one happy family. The usual stuff droning on for at least half an hour. How wrong could I be? John Aspinall came into the room, told us that we wouldn't make any money if we obeyed all the silly laws, and left the room after less than a minute. Angelo lit another cigarette, looked completely unsurprised, unlike the rest of us, and wandered off. The other managers present, John Aspinall's half-brother James Osborne, Jim, hereafter referred to as the nice manager, and Joseph, Sir James's watchdog, looked slightly embarrassed by the boss's unusual candour but kept their thoughts, if any, to themselves. The rest of us tried to look busy. There's a blackjack table in the corner. I'll stand there. You get behind the roulette. Try to smile if anyone wanders in. It's two in the afternoon. It's legal now. I think we obey that law (we did, most of the time).

Because John Aspinall was skint, the casino was opened with Jimmy Goldsmith's money. He paid for the house, the decoration, the wages, and the bank deposit that the law insists must be in place to pay anyone cheeky enough to win big before a new casino has had a few days to build up a pile of cash. He also lent John Aspinall his nominal half of the starting capital. To the outside world it looked like a partnership, but in the beginning it was all Jimmy's money. Aspinall's should really have been called Goldsmith's.

One afternoon, shortly after we'd opened, I was in the main gaming room on the first floor. Angelo was standing at the cash desk on the little landing outside, deep in conversation with the cashier, a keen cricket player. I couldn't hear any of their words, but their body language spelt illegal, not cricket. Angelo left. I walked over to the cash desk to find out what was going on. Angelo came back, saw me talking to the cashier, hesitated, then led me into a small room that looked down on to Sloane Street. Speaking quietly, with a serious look on his still handsome face, he explained that an emergency operation was under way, and that my help would be greatly appreciated. He knew how to make you feel important. It was like this: a company delivered the food for Aspinall's animals at regular intervals. When a certain amount of money was owed they sent a bill and he sent a cheque. But the last bill hadn't been paid because Aspinall didn't have any money. The company wanted ten thousand pounds, now. No cheque no food. No food meant dead animals. That was serious. John Aspinall was, as everyone knew and many, including yours truly, applauded, a dedicated and accomplished breeder of endangered species, for love, not money, but was also a man with the usual less than warm affection for his own species that is almost de rigueur among dedicated lovers of nature. Common anyway, if not actually de rigueur. If three quarters of the human race had been declared in danger of dying of starvation my help would not have been needed. That would not have been serious. The meeting of minds at the cash desk was about how best to raise ten thousand from club funds without it coming up wrong in the paperwork, where Goldsmith's watchdog, off that day, not by coincidence, was bound to spot the deliberate error.

Angelo acted like a man wearing gloves to protect his hands from contamination. The dangerous words were laid out carefully, as if on a table that had sprung up between us. I could pick them up, study them carefully and, if I didn't like what I saw, put them back and walk off. Angelo would pack them away again and look for a more willing accomplice. He didn't have to. I hadn't done anything illegal for ages. You get withdrawal symptoms. There is only one cure. I understood the reasons for tact and secrecy and imaginary gloves. Theft, fraud, and breaches of several gaming laws jostled for space on the table, plus the need to avoid personal embarrassment. You don't want your business partner (and friend) to know that you've nicked his cash, even if he has plenty to spare and you're skint, even if you have every intention of slipping it back later. I didn't have to be told that if I talked out of turn everything would be denied and I would be labelled as a crazy. I was worlds away from the honour among thieves that I was used to among ordinary people who robbed casinos. We stuck together like glue when things got hot. One for all and all for one. Just like those old guys in France. But I was quite happy to join in the robbery, the first I had committed for some time. It made me a partner in the (nominal) casino owner's crime, a handy insurance policy if ever I needed to do a bit of fund raising on my own account. You never know who's looking through a crack in the door. The downside was no mention of a fee. But I was very happy to help keep the animals alive and well and living in Kent for free. John Aspinall was the good guy (if you ignored the dreams of mass euthanasia) and Jimmy Goldsmith was the ruthless asset stripper with a pocketful of cash. I'm in.

I won't bore you with the technical details. It was easy then. Too easy, if you knew enough people who would sign anything you put in front of them. You picked a big cash player whose profile fitted the necessary win, adjusted the paperwork to look like he'd been in, and signed papers to replace the chips that had been paid out when he "won". But you didn't actually put the chips on the table. The phantom win became the swag. Ten thousand at the drop of a hat. The crucial thing was to have a cashier on side. It was very similar (on a much smaller scale and

238

for a much nobler cause) to the way the three million pound man earned a crust, until a virus gummed up the works. Two more signatures were urgently needed: one from an inspector and one from a croupier. I provided the first and promised a gullible croupier that Angelo would be extra nice to him if he'd provide the other one. It was a good day, apart from the lack of payment. I tried to convince myself, without any real success, that virtue is its own reward.

Another more serious crisis came along. The club was badly run. Not intentionally. It was the natural result of a culture clash. John Aspinall's Clermont had been staffed by well-educated and enthusiastic amateurs who worked skillfully with minimal direction. Angelo was used to that. The staff recruited for the new place came from Ladbrokes, Corals, Playboy and London Clubs, big companies run on quasi-military lines, with a sharp dividing line between officers and men. Their staff were well trained and competent, but regimented. Initiative was looked on as a disease and stamped out on sight. Angelo and the other managers acted like they were still at the Clermont. The new croupiers waited to be told when to breathe. The result was chaos. One night Angelo told me that Jimmy Goldsmith had described the club, quite accurately, as the worst run casino he had ever seen. He was coming in the next night to play all the games. If we hadn't pulled our socks up he would take his money out, the casino would close, and we would all be out on the street. I must explain at this point that anyone employed by a casino cannot play there. For example John Aspinall held a manager's licence from the Gaming Board and therefore wasn't allowed to play in his own casino (not that it stopped him), but Sir James just owned the place, or more probably he owned a company that owned the place (I get a bit lost in the jungle of high finance) without holding a specific job. That technical distance allowed him to be a member of the club as well as owning it. Just the man to carry out a school inspection. He was also well known for his extreme ruthlessness in business and for his complete indifference to the welfare of the lower classes, a category which included all his staff and (in case you're feeling left out) most of the rest of the human race.

Next night I came in early, after a stiff drink and what could have been my last sneaky look at the girls in a posh Belgravia bar, and rearranged the way the croupiers were deployed. Up till then everybody worked on every game, regardless of whether or not they were any good, and we all kept smiling and waited patiently for the weak to get strong. Very liberal, I'm sure you agree, but not how Jimmy Goldsmith turned a modest family prosperity into a billion pound fortune. Something more modern was needed. I put all the best roulette croupiers on roulette, all the best blackjack dealers on blackjack, and just about scraped up enough decent staff for punto-banco, the dumbed down version of the elegant old French game of Baccarat and very much our weak spot. Then I crossed my fingers and wished I'd stayed in the bar. Sir James came in, played all the games, and pronounced himself satisfied (but only just where punto banco was concerned). Phew. The club stayed open. As usual I received no fee, and Angelo didn't even say thank you. In fact he treated me with intense suspicion for the remaining three years I stayed at Aspinall's, convinced (wrongly) that my taste of power had turned me into a rival for his job. The rescue operation was not difficult. Angelo should have done it himself, or made a plan and delegated it. But the two or three bottles of brandy he inhaled every day made a mess of his attention to detail. So he dumped it all in my lap and left me to sink or swim. He did pick the right person, I'll give him that. He recognised that I liked the freedom at Aspinall's and that I was more than willing to defend it. Some of the other staff, better qualified than me in technical terms, seemed to miss being told how to breathe.

This is only a back of the envelope calculation, and almost certainly a gross underestimate, but I reckon that between my keeping his gambling club open that night and his death twenty odd years later, John Aspinall made at least three hundred million pounds from his casinos. I'll give you a bit of perspective, courtesy of an old friend who worked in Aspinall's next casino, long after I had found work elsewhere: a Kuwaiti gambler inherited a hundred or a hundred and fifty million pounds from an uncle, and decided to become what John Aspinall called a hero, his flattering term for very big gamblers like Kerry Packer, Hassan Enany, Adnan Khashoggi, etc. Much more elegant than whale, the word they use in Las Vegas for the ultra big players, and much more flattering. If he ever does a Vegas show, Paul Simon should slip a new line into one of his old songs: I'd rather be a hammer than a nail, I'd rather be a hero than a whale. Copyright after the comma. Four or five members of the audience might get the joke. The Kuwaiti saw the windfall as a handy stake for a hero, and lost it all at Aspinall's (then known as the Aspinall Curzon and located in the old Curzon House) in less than a year. And that was just one player. But in all the time that passed since I saved his skin when his friend Jimmy threatened to pull the plug John Aspinall never formally recognised my vital role in his rescue and never paid me the odd million (preferably in cash) which I think would have been a fair commission. And I never liked to ask, trapped by middle class politeness. Jimmy Goldsmith must have made a similar amount from a business he would have closed down if it hadn't been for my hard work, helped along by a stiff drink and what I feared would be a last mingle with the Belgravia girls. I never heard a peep from him either. Of course it's possible, if not highly probable, that neither he nor John Aspinall knew anything of my heroic part in the action, and that Angelo claimed all the credit. He was jolly good at that. But now the truth is out here's one last wave before I go down for the third time: if any of the very wealthy Aspinall, Packer and Goldsmith descendants would like to hand over a large donation, to make what's left of my old age more comfortable and help kill the hangover that hits every bankrupt when the ball is over, I'm all ears. Damian Aspinall is the new John Aspinall (in terms of casino ownership), Zac Goldsmith recently bought a fifteen million pound house (partly with my money, in my view), and Kerry Packer wouldn't have bought into the Aspinall Curzon and left even more tens of millions to his descendants if I hadn't kept the Aspinall's Hans Street casino open. Put bluntly, none of the younger generation are short of the price of a pint. So come on chaps. Keep a straight bat. We're all public school. One percent of my underestimate will do fine, discreetly passed under a table at the Cavendish hotel, for old time's sake, surrounded by the ghosts of the Playboy's best manager and the Italian who never paid, and a host of Frenchmen whose names I've long forgotten. In cash. I'll send the suitcase back, first class. And no Greyfriars nonsense about postal orders in the post.

Business began to boom once the culture clash was sorted out. It usually does when you tap into one of mankind's earliest and most compelling addictions. Sex pays too, but the punter doesn't hand over all his cash to the first whore he gets a leg over. A gambler does, once he gets hooked on to his favourite game. Our first famous gambler was the late Francis Albert Sinatra, better known as Frank. He was singing at the nearby Albert Hall and popped in afterwards for a spot of blackjack at his Limey friend's new joint. He had played at the Clermont casino in the sixties when it belonged to Aspinall and was famous for an incident that took place shortly after he was introduced, VIP style, to the tall, broad man who was hoping to relieve him of some of his fabulous wealth. After a warm handshake, Frank—who always liked big men, possibly because he'd been turned down for military service during World War Two on account of his general weediness—took a handful of tickets for the next night's concert from his pocket and offered them to his host. The normal reaction to a personal offer of tickets from the super-star for a concert that always sold out within minutes was gratitude and, if the recipient was part of the English upper crust, a discreet bit of groveling. Ever the elegant rebel John Aspinall handed the tickets back and said that he didn't really like pop music. But thanks awfully Frank, all the same. No, don't put them away. I'm sure somebody else would love to go. Frank Sinatra's first reactions were intense surprise and a brief flash of hostility, then laughter and the unsurprising information that no-one had ever done that to him before. It could have been very different. A friend who was there told me, years later, that one of Frank Sinatra's heavyweight entourage asked the singer, in a close to the ear whisper that echoed off the big windows of the Rolls Royce show room on the other side of Berkeley Square, "hey boss, you want I should rub out the goddam Limey son of a bitch?" The answer was obviously no, and from then on Frankie and Johnny were the best of friends. In 1979 (or thereabouts) Frank Sinatra was back at the Albert Hall. He appeared on a television chat show (probably Michael Parkinson's, a big fan of Ol' Blue Eyes) and said that when his concert was over he was going to gamble at Aspinall's, the best casino in the world. News to us, the second bit. We were doing well, but not that well.

The singer duly arrived with his latest wife, the widow of one of the Marx brothers, my all time favourite funny men, sat down at a blackjack table, and started to play blackjack for five pound chips. The minimum stake. Angelo asked me to watch the game very carefully, and keep an accurate record of exactly how many fivers Mr Frank Sinatra won or lost. The new Mrs Sinatra began to stroke my arm, insisting to her husband that the stroking would bring him luck. I had a lucky face. I hoped Ol' Blue Eyes wouldn't let fly with a fist if I looked like I was enjoying it too much. I'm a company man if there's half a chance of robbing the company, but I deplore violence. I needn't have worried. Frank even smiled at me when he got an ace on a ten and the dealer drew a six on his own ace and the famous super-star won seven and a half quid, allegedly. If I'd played my cards right, and been a few inches taller (and wider) I could have been the mouse that hung out with the Rat Pack. I kept looking at the five pound chips and thinking hard. There had to be something interesting going on. I had a pretty good idea what it was but I was keen to get it in writing, so to speak. When the game finished I asked Angelo why Frank Sinatra, then the world's most famous crooner, and a very big film star in his spare time, and close friend of and occasional bag-carrier for the incredibly rich American Mafia (however hotly denied) was playing blackjack for the sort of stakes I used to play. Angelo, who was very proud of their shared Italian roots, and could be a bit of a Mafia poser himself at times, actually told me what was going on instead of fobbing me off with the usual lie.

The five pound chips were not really five pound chips, he explained quietly, they were five thousand pound chips. A much more suitable figure for a world super-star. The details had all been agreed long before the cards were dealt. Both parties stood to gain. The outcome would be settled in Switzerland in a bank that didn't answer silly questions from foreign tax collectors. If Aspers won he trousered the whole lot tax-free. Whichever way it went for Frank the American gambling commission looking into his latest application for an American casino licence would not be disturbed by stories of the humble applicant getting involved in huge money card games in London, England. The American authorities liked their casino owners fine and upright and free of vices. Lady Penelope would understand. Probity and integrity, that's the way she likes it. But fivers were fine. As usual I got no extra payment for my part in the conspiracy. Maybe Sinatra won a packet and there was no cash to spare. I can't remember now. It was a long time ago, I can't check it out, and I'm the only one left alive. The secret dies with me.

Our next very big player was a Saudi-Arabian called Hassan Enany. He had played American roulette at Ladbroke's soon to be shut down Hill Street casino when I worked there, but he liked the newly opened Aspinall's because in the early days he was almost always the only super-star on the premises. At Hill Street he had to compete with the Saudi royals and Adnan Khashoggi, the famous merchant of death. Enany played for the same high stakes as the royals and the arms dealer, at least twice the maximums allowed for normal mortals, and laid out anything up to twenty thousand pounds per spin. Then. In the first year at Aspinall's he lost two and a half million pounds—more than enough to allow John Aspinall to clear his official marker with James Goldsmith, not to mention the unofficial ten grand I helped him nick. In its first year the casino made about two million six hundred thousand pounds (not counting the Sinatra contribution, if there was one). The closeness of the impressive figures made Mr Hassan Enany very welcome every time he came to his London house in South Audley Street, to spend his days conducting business and his evenings playing roulette in our private room upstairs. Back home in Saudi Mr Enany was said to operate in the same way as Mr Khashoggi, but in the construction business rather than the arms trade. When an American or European construction company agreed to build something huge for hundreds of millions of pounds (or dollars), the final price always included a commission, as bribes are called in polite company, or when Prince Andrew is listening. Half went to the super gambler and half to whichever prince was connected with whatever was being built. In seventies Saudi-Arabia no big money got very far before a prince caught his fair share, like a skilled fielder in a game of cricket. The fail-safe arrangement was the same that Mr Khashoggi had to accept. If the shit hits the fan the prince isn't there. In the nineties (or the early days of the 21st Century), the shit and Mr Enany's fan got awfully close. The kingdom decided to build the King Fahd stadium, an Olympic style sports palace good enough to host international football and tennis games (perhaps even the Olympics themselves one day), and show the world that Saudi-Arabia was not just a place where dubiously convicted foreign criminals had their heads chopped off in front of an enthusiastic crowd (with God's blessing) and a princess who did what comes naturally with the wrong chap at the wrong time stood in a sand-pit waiting to be shot dead by laughing policemen. It was a very big job. A British construction company got half the stadium contract. A German company whose name escapes me got the other half. The British company was used to Saudi commissions. The German company was not. They said nein, nein, ve don't do ze bribes, ve do ze job und ve go home ven ze cheque has cleared. Still no sense of humour. The flexible Brits were horrified. No doubt Mr Enany and a prince felt the same way.

Somebody talked. There's always one. News of the Anglo-German squabble leaked out to the excellent Observer newspaper. Reporters door-stepped Enany at his South Audley Street house/office. But the paper got no further than it did a few years later when they tried to get to the bottom of the weapons bribes that just might have passed between British Aerospace and a Saudi prince. Don't upset the Saudis was the British government's attitude. Too much pressure could lead to a lack of co-operation between our spooks and theirs, with dire effects on the everlasting War on Terror. The Saudis might stop passing on the vital information they extract from the usual suspects, along with the odd handful of fingernails.

Whether the Enany story was silenced by threats of legal action from the gate-keeper and the royals, or by pressure from the British government, keen as ever to suck up to our best ever customer for weapons of mass destruction, I cannot say. You'll have to ask the Observer. Whose lips may be well and truly sealed, for sound legal reasons. They're going skint already and don't need any help from a bunch of overpaid libel lawyers. Or I might find out the hard way when my book goes viral. Watch this space.

At Aspinall's the other croupiers and I took no interest in the morality of billion dollar deals between governments, with or without bribes. We got our own bribe every time Mr Hassan Enany walked through the door. With the guvnor's permission, in the Aspinall spirit of laws are for little people, an attitude which, unlike all the other casino owners, he shared with his grateful staff, Angelo arranged for Enany to become our first tipper. The tips weren't chucked across the table every time the big man had a win, like they were in the good old days when the London casino owners (with the honourable exception of Honest John) nicked the tips. Discretion was called for. When Enany won two or three hundred grand, big bucks when you could buy a nice little house in

244

Chelsea for 30k, he slipped us two or three grand before he cashed out. Angelo gave the money to me and I passed it on to the croupiers, split fairly into equal shares. Like when other croupiers and I robbed other casinos. Old habits die hard. In a week with one Enany win and one Enany tip we doubled our wages, with a bit to spare.

Our next tips came from Australia, courtesy of a man with long experience of the power of a well-placed bung. John Aspinall informed us that Kerry Packer was coming, talking Australian. I knew a bit about the big man from down-under. Son of a wealthy media magnate. Australian version of English public school. Got cricket players out of boring old whites and into garish colours (better on TV). Made them get the game over in a day instead of wasting a whole long, pleasantly alcoholic weekend. Didn't believe in land rights for Australian aboriginals, the people who were there long before Captain Cook "discovered" the big island at the West End of the Pacific (the abos knew it was there all along). Uncanny knack of making people from the opposite end of the social scale believe he was one of them. Nick-name Goanna, thanks to a remarkable resemblance to an antipodean lizard. Once suspected (still is by some) of paying for the murder of a bank manager slow to come across with an important loan. Fervent admirer of Genghis Khan. The last was no surprise. If, like me, you've spent a lifetime in the company of the very rich, at work in my case, perhaps in an exotic private life in yours, you must have noticed that an awful lot of very rich chaps are avid fans of the mass-murderers who take up most of the space in history books. Blackie loves Nappy, Bernie loves Adolf (with reservations), and Aspers was keen to wipe out three quarters of the human race. Etc etc. Perhaps they'd all like to get stuck in themselves, secretly, but making lots of dosh keeps them too busy and doesn't leave enough time to kill lots of people. In which case long live capitalism. I also knew, but only because John Aspinall told me, that Kerry Packer was a big, rough bugger who broke dealers' fingers when he didn't like the cards they gave him. I resolved to inspect in safety rather than deal, and then realised that it was an Aspinall joke. He had a thing about big boys' jokes. In my personal experience the only violent thing about Kerry Packer, occasionally, was his language. But I did hear that he once threw a blackjack shoe through a casino window and into Curzon Street, after a long and very expensive losing streak, luckily without braining a single pedestrian hurrying back from work or looking for a whore. Always look up when you walk past a casino with more than one floor. A flying blackjack shoe is a very deadly weapon. Duck if you see one coming.

Packer's heyday was funded by Australian Labour Prime Minister Bob Hawke, aka the Silver Bodgie. Hawke was a drunken, lecherous, foul-mouthed, corrupt politician, typical of his time, before standards declined. The Bodgie allowed the Goanna to shift his money all over the globe, a privilege denied to his fellow Aussies, in search of the highest rates of interest and the lowest rates of tax, or no tax at all in carefree places like the Bahamas. See John Pilger for details. He's a proper Australian journalist, not some roving Pommie hack bad-mouthing the backward colonials. He even wrote a book about it: "A Secret Country." His books aren't a barrel of fun, but they're very well written and they give you the stories that politicians would much rather keep to themselves. Just don't read them if you're in two minds about committing suicide.

In came Packer, raring to go, and looking exactly like a man with a nylon stocking (size large) pulled over his head. You may have seen that description in the popular press, when he was alive, but you had to be there to get the full effect. (Some vulgar people substituted condom for stocking. Funnier, but less accurate). For a moment I thought I was back in Skip's first joint, the night the tax collectors came in with sawn-offs. Then I calmed down. Packer signed a massive (tax-free) cheque and got stuck into a great game of blackjack, slapping five one thousand pound chips on each of the seven boxes where the bets go. That's thirty five grand gone if they all lose. Or thirty five in the hand if they all win. Or more, either way. If your first two cards add up to nine, ten or eleven you can double your stake. If your first two cards are identical you can split them, subject to certain exemptions, and if the new hands make nine ten or eleven when the second card shows its face you get another chance to double. Goanna pursued all options aggressively. Thirty five grand often turned into fifty or sixty.

During the game a series of pithy statements slipped through the stocking, invariably about himself. I sensed a total lack of interest in anyone who wasn't buying, selling cheap, or getting in his way. A couple of gems linger on: 'People with big arses need big chairs,' said while pulling over a second chair and supporting half an arse on each, after flopping uncomfortably over the sides of one inadequate piece of furniture (a manoeuvre I last saw in the early seventies when Bernie the Waistcoat and his fat American friend made a serious dent in the profits of a casino I still cannot name). "I'm greedy. I've always been greedy,' after piling on another ten grand to double a split hand that turned out well. What? I thought you gave all that tax you saved to charity. But I always looked forward to Packer's blackjack sessions, in spite of the information overload. The amounts of money that changed hands during Goanna's super-size games were so outrageous. Dramatic even. Left Shakespeare a mile behind. And that's when you're watching. Sucked right in, even though it isn't your own tax-free millions at stake. Using your own takes you right off the scale. That's why gambling is so addictive.

Drama is fine, but money is finer. Parker was the second donor to be recruited, hot on the heels of Hassan Enany, Saudi's answer to Bob the Builder, when Angelo got the nod from Aspers that it was OK to take tips from the mega-players. The tipping was done in the same way. If Packer won a hundred thousand or so, which he quite often did (though not nearly as often as he didn't), we got the small change. Usually about three grand, once again easily enough to double our weekly wages. Tipping was limited to the ultra big spenders, for two very good reasons: they had vastly more money than the small players we privately referred to as wankers (not always without affection) and they played alone in a private room on the second floor, far from the madding crowd. We couldn't have tipping where the wankers spent their money. Too many undisciplined eyes. Too much risk of loose talk drifting in to the ears of the Gaming Board, leading to the closure of the casino and the end of the world as we knew it. The end of the world never came, but a dastardly bit of work by a popular newspaper sent our new gravy train flying off the tracks. One night Kerry Packer was at the cash desk, in the semi-public area just outside the main (wankers') gaming floor. He had lost track of his money. Only very slightly mind. He was very good at money. He asked the cashier to check his numbers, and tell him exactly how much he had won or lost. The cashier did a quick calculation and quietly gave him the figure. We try hard to be discreet. Packer repeated the figure back to the cashier, in his usual booming voice. He couldn't whisper if you paid him double. Standing near the cash desk, apparently minding his own business, a well-bred but skint young man, the type that John Aspinall used to call a penniless fortune hunter, was paying close attention to every word. I thought I recognised him as an even younger man I'd seen at the long closed Apron Strings casino (accurately described in the last chapter but one), where many a callow youth made the transition from well-bred and wealthy to well-bred and poor. At least until a close relative died and did the decent thing in a will. His inherited wedge had obviously gone into the gamblers' valley of no return, but not all was lost. The young man's standing in society was still good. He was just a bit slower at paying his bills and travelled from Chelsea to Belgravia on a bus (the Aston Martin long gone and the funds received handed over to Nick the Pole, if my identification was correct). His aristocratic demeanour made it easy for him to become a member of Aspinall's, even though he couldn't afford to do much once he was inside.

The popular newspaper, one of the middle class ones, took him on as a high-society nark, at quite a decent wage. Very Evelyn Waugh. His job was to deliver big name casino stories for the paper's gossip column. He quickly grasped that pay-dirt often bubbled up to the surface when a big player was cashing out, and struck gold courtesy of the (one-way) loud conversation between the billionaire media tycoon and the humble cashier. Packer's gambling numbers were hot news. A nark's dream come true. The figure that appeared in next day's paper was spot on. To the penny. We waited nervously for the ape-shit bollocking. But not for long. Goanna strode into Aspinall's like only Australians know how, blasted Angelo and me with every known variation of the "f" and "c" words (plus a few Australian specialities that went over our heads) and demanded back every penny of a recent two thousand pound tip. He assumed, naturally enough, that one of us had sold the story to the sort of newspaper he would have been proud to own and reckoned that it was a poor way of thanking him for the illegal tip. I didn't blame him. Not cricket at all, in clothes of any colour. Luckily I hadn't yet fed the money to the multitude. Some of them may have been none too keen to hand it back. Especially the less skilled staff room poker players. When Packer paused for breath the nark story was offered to the irate Australian. Profuse apologies and more "f" and "c" words flowed from the appropriate mouths, but Packer bought it, eventually. The penniless fortune hunter was nailed and vigorously encouraged to surrender his membership (the age of broken legs having long slipped into history; not that Aspers was ever part of that scene, to give credit where it's due). A happy ending, you may be thinking. Well no, not really. Collateral damage had come in through the door and tipping flew out of the window. Packer may have given that particular tip back, after we were all friends again, or he may not. I can't remember. I had so much money then. Oh happy days. But John Aspinall realised that Packer might have mentioned the tip to the cashier in case it affected the calculations, not knowing that a newspaper nark was hanging on to his every word. The nark, angry about being rumbled so soon after his best story yet, might shop us to the Gaming Board. So all illegal tipping, including Enany's, was stopped, and never started again, and all breath was held until the shit didn't hit the fan. Thanks, nark. Hope you got the sack. There was another tipper, a very rich Iranian, one of London's biggest ever roulette players in his day, whose name I'm going to pretend I've forgotten. Sadly he only came into Aspinall's twice, on my days off, so I never saw any of his money. The bastard who handed out the bungs when I wasn't there lacked my sense of fair play. Wrong sort of school.

I'll slip in a number or two, to keep things in perspective. The trouble with history books is that figures that would once have impressed now sound like nothing at all. Ten thousand dollars at the drop of a hat. Are you having a laugh Bob? Let's get up to date: If Kerry Packer were still alive and still playing blackjack, as it's safe to assume he would be, each of his bets would be for twenty-five or fifty thousand pounds. That's per box, all seven of them, not the total money on the table. But don't feel too sorry for him, now we're getting real. He had plenty of cash to gamble with. The corrupt deals between "mates" in Australia, in which he was a very active player before (and after) he got Pilgered saved him a billion or two that would have gone to the taxman in a country with an honest government and helped no end when he felt the urge to play a bit of blackjack.

I don't like to be totally negative, even about a gambler I wasn't personally very keen on, and not just because he lost his rag on a bad day and called me an effing c at least twice. So here's a Kerry Packer story with a happy ending: once upon a time, in a desert town called Las Vegas, in a country called America, a big Australian man won a huge amount of money at a very high stake blackjack table. When he stopped playing, astronomically ahead, he struck up a conversation with the pretty girl who had dealt the magic cards. He was in a good mood. No blackjack shoes flying out of the window and crashing down in the sand. He asked how much money she owed on her house. When she told him, slightly surprised at the question but excitedly anticipating his next move--or hoping she was--he offered a tip that would pay off the whole mortgage in one go. She thanked him profusely but, surrounded by witnesses, had to explain that all tips were shared with all the other staff. Personal tips were not allowed. The management were very strict on that point. Her eyes misted over and and her lower lip trembled. So near and yet so far away. Packer called for a manager. One rushed over, tongue at the ready, like a new British prime minister on a first date with Rupert Murdoch. Packer ordered the manager to fire the girl. On the spot. Now. Her face fell. She wondered how a man who had seemed so nice could turn so nasty. The manager carefully balanced the need to show human decency towards the girl against the need not to upset a big winner and fired her immediately. Packer handed over the money and told the manager, loudly enough for anyone within a hundred yards to hear, that as she no longer worked for the casino she could keep it all for herself. The manager, anxious to keep alive the casino's chances of getting its money back, and not wanting the casino next door to cop the cash, agreed almost as quickly as he had agreed to fire her less than a minute before. He agreed again when the order came that as soon as the girl had found a safe place to store the money her old job was hers for the asking, with no loss of wages. The friendly manager had turned into the most agreeable man in Las Vegas.

Kerry Packer smiled a very broad smile. The girl burst into tears of joy and jumped up and down in excitement and clapped her hands together, just like a young actress she'd seen in a teen movie on the TV in the house she now owned outright.

Isn't that a lovely story? All together now: aaah.....

We had other big players, by which I mean players who could lose a million pounds in a fairly short time and not even think about jumping off a cliff. The seventies were a good time to be a Nigerian politician, if your gang was in power, and a bad time to run a business in down-town Beirut. Those two unrelated accidents of history came together in far away London. A Lebanese man who, before breakfast, still owned a viable bank, went to work one morning, looking forward to another profitable day, and found himself standing with his hands in the air while one of the many Beirut militias (Moslem or Christian, I can't remember which) walked in and took over his sturdily built office block. Unfortunately for the banker his building was perfectly placed to rain down fire on a rival militia's nearby headquarters, and sufficiently robust to absorb a lot of the inevitable return fire. Position, position and position, as the shopkeepers say. Sand bags and ammunition boxes replaced boring old office furniture, a nervous looking sniper assumed the position by a window, the staff were escorted on to the street (without being killed, slightly to their surprise) and all banking was cancelled with immediate effect. The owner--let's call him Robert, a lot of Lebanese men are called Robert--was suddenly out of a job. But still alive, not always the case in similar circumstances in seventies down-town Beirut. Or now even, in a country whose two immediate neighbours feel free to shoot the place up whenever there's something in it for them. Luckily Robert had some money under a mattress, not necessarily in Lebanon, and flew to London to take up residence in the many-starred Mayfair hotel. The Mayfair, a very nice hotel just to the South of Berkeley Square, had (still has) a big casino on the first floor. At the time the casino, known as the Palm Beach, was one of the best in London, attracting so many big players that a rival casino group bribed a civilian police clerk to provide the names and addresses of the owners of luxury cars whose number plates were seen outside the Palm Beach, allowing the other casino company to get in contact with some very valuable punters. It seemed like a good idea at the time, but led to the loss of its licences in the coming blitz that closed down half the West End casinos, in 1980 and 1981.

Robert went into the casino during the afternoons, when it was comparatively empty. A big roulette player stood out like a figure in a painting. A discreet inspection, from a distance, told him whether the man was winning or losing. No rocket science needed: if the target was

250

winning he got lots of pay-outs; if he was losing he had to keep buying chips with his own money. You'd be an expert in five minutes. Robert walked away from the winners (why would a winner want to go to another casino?) and always sat down next to a loser, first asking politely if the seat was taken. After a decent interval, spent playing roulette like a man who expected to lose, he tried to strike up a conversation. Sometimes he got a look that would have stripped paint, if he'd been wearing any, but more often than not his natural charm set the words flowing. The spiel never varied. Doing badly too? Thought so. I never win here. I only come in because I live upstairs (establishing himself as a man of some substance) but if my luck doesn't change soon I'll be living on the street--pause for a quick laugh at such a ridiculous idea. I've started going to a little place that's opened up near Harrods. I always seem to win there. And they send a car to pick me up. Such nice people. Within minutes the big player, in almost every case a tall Nigerian wearing a handsome robe and the finely decorated hat that tells the world that he is a good man who has done the pilgrimage to Mecca, asked if he could come too, to the magic place where everybody wins. Never one to bogart a joint, Robert cashed in immediately and selflessly brought his new friend to our new casino. No-one ever told me how Robert and Aspinall's first came together, but it didn't take me long to realise that he was, to put it coarsely, pimping for us. Financially, I hasten to add. Nigerian after Nigerian came in, fresh from the Palm Beach, chatting animatedly with his good friend Robert, lately of Lebanon, and lost a million or two that he'd sliced off his own country's fabulous oil wealth. Once inside the casino Robert played a dual role of court jester and disciplinarian of croupiers when the big man complained about the unprofitable numbers. After a few days the latest Nigerian would disappear from the scene and make room for the next mug to be seduced by Robert's spiel.

Robert always gambled with money slung at him by the big Nigerian players, grateful for the introduction to the magic casino where everybody wins. I instinctively played my part. John Aspinall's sensible instructions about ignoring silly gaming laws (but not writing things down like the casino owners who lost their licences all did, but we didn't) were still ringing in my ears. I went to ludicrous lengths to make sure that Robert got the benefit of any doubt whenever there was a dispute about where his chips were supposed to be, a policy that always ensured that he went home winning. The nice manager was right behind me. He was our main contact with Robert. One day, after a very profitable game (for us) I passed by the bar and saw him attempting to discreetly hand over to Robert five one thousand pound cash packets. Doing it discreetly was a good idea in case the big gambler to whom the money had recently belonged also passed by and smelt a rat. But being discreet is not so easy when you've made an early start on the gin. The packets flew all over the floor, greatly to the amusement of all the other drinkers. I knew for a fact that the big gambler was nowhere near and picked up the scattered packets, making a show of not trying to hide what I was doing. I gave them to Robert, smiling broadly, and told him to be more careful with his money. You won't win every time you come in, I lied. The amount of cash scattered was about double what Robert had won that day, partly with my help. But who's counting? Maybe the gin doubled the money. Or he'd left some on deposit the last time he dropped in. Mine not to reason why.

Not long after the tips went down the pan, luckily with no long-term damage done except to one's future annual income, and the flow of Nigerian oil money was running dry, another two dramas came along in quick succession, followed by the accidental death of a dream. Angelo had an Italian friend who owned a restaurant in a smart part of town, not far from a flat I once lived in. He wasn't a major casino player, private poker games were more his bag, but he liked to drop in about once a week for a bit of low-stake roulette and a chat with his old mate Angelo. My co-workers and I always looked forward to his visits because he almost always brought in a bit of high-stake crumpet. He soon became friendly with most of the staff. So friendly that some of them took to visiting his restaurant late on a Saturday night. That wasn't strictly approved of. Even at Aspinall's staff weren't supposed to mix socially with gamblers. But John Aspinall had told us, right out loud, that the casino wouldn't make any money if we obeyed all those tedious gambling laws. I guess the staff decided that if the boss could be a rebel then so could they. News of the restaurant visits got back to Angelo, who tried to put an end to the friendly gatherings. No-one took a blind bit of notice. In any other London joint all those concerned would have got the sack (or a sharp written warning threatening the sack) from the managers of casinos that would soon lose their licences because they were breaking the gambling laws too, but failed to mention the breakages to their less senior staff. But scaring the croupiers with horrid letters was more difficult in a casino whose boss said bollocks to the law. It was also well known that Angelo and, rumour had it, a member of the owning family often risked their hard-earned wages at Maverick's stylish but illegal private poker games (I'll introduce you to Maverick in a moment).

The reason for banning contacts between staff and gamblers was of course to prevent fraudulent co-operation breaking out between the two groups. By the time Aspinall's opened in the late seventies pretty well everyone in a senior job in a London casino knew about the red wine and the money transfers at the Cavendish. Like me, many of them had been there with their hands outstretched when they were young and foolish. But most of the old lags had been bought off with high salaries and generous bonuses and were keen to make sure that none of the new boys got up to the old tricks. And they were well aware of the power of the new-fangled closed circuit TV cameras that took such a lively interest in our day to day affairs. Nothing to do with finding God or becoming addicted to morality, I assure you. Just pure greed. And fear. If someone did manage to keep the old traditions alive the money that disappeared would make a hole in the managers' bonuses and might even bring suspicion crashing down on them, both without the consoling benefits of a pocket full of stolen cash. Live and let die was the motto of the new casino managers, however close one might have been in years gone by.

I was told to keep a close eye on the friendly restaurateur, who was on something of a winning streak and playing for rather higher stakes than we had seen before. Not by Angelo. The man was his friend. An intervention by Angelo would have been embarrassing for both of them. Another manager told me to do what I could to stop the restaurant man winning, or cheating. Which usually amount to the same thing. I got the impression that cutting losses was the order of the day. No clumsy attempts to get any money back. Just stick a finger in the dike. I suppose the outcome could be called a success. I hovered ostentatiously whenever the lucky man played, without ever seeing a bent pay-out. The winning streak came to what may well have been its natural end. I didn't enjoy my time as the sheriff. I don't look right in a white hat. Black is so much more me. But I secretly hoped that something really was going on, and that the restaurant man (or one of his hypothetical accomplices) would approach me with an offer that I wouldn't refuse. We could have a couple of astonishingly lucky nights, then pack the whole thing in and keep our spotless reputations intact. With a bit of spare cash in hand to ease the pain of closure. But it never happened. Sometimes you just can't get the staff.

It all blew over. I was convinced (and severely disappointed) that everyone concerned was innocent. The restaurant man enjoyed a bit of roulette, the boys enjoyed a bit of Italian cuisine, and we all enjoyed looking at the crumpet. How disappointing. But the little outburst of paranoia gave wings to an idea that was taking shape in one of the more devious chambers of my mind.

I was getting more useful by the day. I'd helped Johnny rob Jimmy when the animals were hungry. I'd kept the joint open when Jimmy threatened to pull his cash. I'd done the book-keeping for Frank Sinatra's secret game. I'd oiled the wheels of commerce when Robert and his latest African friend popped in for a punt. Mr Fixit or what? Payment was overdue. Time to bring in some old friends. The French Connection, Hashish, the Cockney Frog, or one of the Gibraltarians who so impressed me with their skills in the good old days. Or Gunga Din (not the name on his birth certificate), if I could track him down, the Indian croupier who amazed us all with the almost supernatural skill with which he could rob a roulette table only a few months after he started in the casino business. A born natural if ever there was one. A magician no less. No racism in his nick-name, by the way. Just sincere praise. He really was a better man than the rest of us put together. Rudyard Kipling would have fingered him straight away. If there had been an immigration policy in place that let in the highly skilled but kept the riff-raff out Gunga Din would have walked straight on to the red carpet. The plan put a spring in my step. I began to feel like the Corsican as he strolled into the Dorchester to collect the Fat Man's monster pay-out. The figure I had in mind was fifty thousand pounds, a tidy sum when I was young. Not that I wouldn't have been flexible if the number had grown naturally. And don't scoff at my modest ambitions. I know it's small beer compared to the three million pound man's haul, or even the Fat Man's hundred grand, but I was never addicted to Rolls Royces and all that bling, like the 3M man, and the croupiers would only have copped 20k each from the Fat Man's haul if he hadn't torn up the contract and done a bunk with the whole bloody lot, the bastard. I just wanted enough to live in the Pyrenees, not have to drive miles to work, sit in the shade of a tree reading books about Albert Einstein, drink red wine when my head started to hurt, and play with my growing gang of sun-tanned children, far from the madding crowd and the irritating sounds of roulette balls whizzing round the rims of roulette wheels. Not an arms dealer or Saudi prince or shop-owner within a hundred miles. A small reward for a man who once kept a few millionaires on the gravy train. Fifty thousand pounds had an iconic quality in my mind, courtesy of two events: in the late sixties a cashier I knew (and thoroughly disliked) was stashing the night's cash into the casino safe, after closing his employer's casino, when he was jumped by two big strong men, tied up, and relieved of almost exactly 50k. Only he wasn't. The police never managed to prove it, but in real life the cashier lobbed the stash out of a small window, last opened when Queen Victoria was on the throne, straight into the welcoming hands of a very charismatic playboy type manager (playboy with a small p; the man in question was never on Hugh Hefner's payroll) waiting patiently in the darkness outside. Here's a clue: no trace of a forced entry by two burly men was ever found, and the cashier was a dab hand at tying himself up, for reasons you don't need to know. The plan worked. Everyone knew what really happened, but there wasn't any solid evidence. The cops went home baffled and the cashier and manager lived happily ever after.

The other fifty went to a man whom any fan of P G Wodehouse (and who worth talking to isn't?) would, like me at the time, have recognised immediately as the reincarnation of the Efficient Baxter, latterly of Blandings Castle. Less the glinting glasses, but with all other qualities intact. Bossy, grabby, ambitious, humourless, randy and in charge. In this case of another casino safe. It happened a bit later than the skilful lob, but at a time when 50k was still well worth having. By then casino safes had a split key, half of it kept by the duty manager and half by the cashier who would close the casino with him as the sun rose slowly over London. No more solo acts. A sensible security measure, designed to stop any pilfering during the hours of business by either key-holder. One Saturday night rather more than 50k was being put into the safe by the two half-key holders, after the opening ceremony of clicking the two half-keys together to make one working key. The Efficient Baxter (second edition), employed by a man with a large share in the casino to keep a close eye on the people employed by his racier partner, removed exactly 50k and distributed it around his jacket pockets. Just like that. Quite casually. In silence. The cashier, not in on the game and genuinely surprised to see Mr Nasty but Clean behaving like the rest of us, asked what was going on. This cash has to go in the bank first thing in the morning, while you're still tucked up in bed, snarled the Efficient Baxter. On a Sunday morning? asked the cashier, smoothly, still hoping for a share, however small. Silence filled the air, but no money changed hands. This time only one partner lived happily ever after. Two good reasons why 50k stayed lodged in my mind, like an icon or a fading dream. Today I would of course add a nought if I found myself assuming the position for one last time, the pace quickening, the heart beating in anticipation, the stern look in the eye telling the super-baron that non-payment was not an option. Sadly such a scenario is vanishingly unlikely to interrupt my peaceful pensioner's life. But when I shuffle off my mortal coil, probably fairly soon, I plan to leave instructions in my will that a Pandora's Box be opened on the internet and the names of the Efficient Baxter and of all the other pseudonym holders whom I didn't like when I was still breathing will flash onto your computer screen.

My old friend the French Connection shot down my very reasonable plan, in the nicest possible way. He'd left the casino business, unwilling to work long hours--or short hours--for straight pay, however high. A principle was at stake. Rumour had it that he was now the front man for a credit card gang, chosen for his good looks and his effortless air of affluence. (His long acquaintance with French career criminals probably didn't do any harm either). The new job followed a strict pattern. One of the gang nicked a card from someone who looked genuinely prosperous. Usually an older man. Posers with lots of front but no actual credit tend to be younger. The Connection practised forging the signature (a new skill he picked up very quickly) and as soon as he could produce a decent copy--in an astonishingly short time--went straight to Harrods to buy something small and valuable and easy to sell. With his confident smile in place he looked just like Omar Sharif as he dashed off his new name. Everything was done in a tearing hurry (without letting it show) to cash in before the victim noticed that the card wasn't where it should be and spoiled the fun by cancelling it. I have to say that I don't really approve of that sort of thing, however well done. You might steal an honest man's card. One of mine even, before the bailiffs moved in. I feel strongly that only casinos, bookmakers, drug-pushers and arms dealers should be robbed (the last two very carefully). But this is a history book. Everything has to go in. My approval is neither here nor there.

Meet Maverick, aka Arvin Desai, from India. Maverick ran an illegal poker game in one of the better parts of London, paid no tax on the proceeds, and was unknown to the authorities until somebody talked, probably after losing more money than he could really afford. Maverick was a skinny little man, pleasant enough to talk to if he wasn't after your money, even more pleasant if he was. His nick-name came from the saloon card-sharp's boot-lace tie he wore at all times, making him look like a thinner version of the actors in the television series and the film. Maverick made his money in much the same way as John Aspinall had made a packet from his private chemmy games, in the fifties, long before he opened the Clermont casino and went sort of straight. The poker players paid rent in the form of a half hourly table charge and bet against one another, not the house. Just like chemmy, but calling for a million times more skill. The rent bought a seat in a well-run poker game, in a nice house, with none of the silly rules that take the edge off a poker night in a casino. Alcohol was served (free) to those who felt the need, long before you could buy a drink in a mainstream joint. Closing time was when all the players felt like going home, to mourn a loss or celebrate a win. The game was dealt by very attractive girl dealers, who earned more in a couple of nights than a licensed casino would have paid them for a five night week and as a result were much friendlier than normal casino staff. Angelo was a regular at Maverick's games.

Late one night Angelo was coming out of the house just as a policeman was coming in, with a camera and several more policemen. He was unlucky. Other players got out quickly enough to remain anonymous, but Angelo got the full mug-shot treatment. The financial effect was severe. He had recently sold his share in a family business and bought a thirteen acre building plot in a posh part of Surrey, on which he planned to erect a very large bungalow. I know the area well. I lived just a few miles away at the time, in a smaller house with a half acre, sold years ago when another sure-fire plan went belly up. The land cost a hundred thousand pounds, Angelo told me proudly, a lot of money at the time, and left him with no money to pay the builder if for some reason his salary stopped coming in. Which it very soon did. After the raid on Maverick's stylish game John Aspinall had to suspend Angelo on no pay when the Gaming Board relieved him of his manager's licence, delighted to land a direct hit on Aspinall's after a couple of years of trying to get to the bottom of all the illegal stuff they were convinced we were up to, most of the snooping done by a small man, said to be a retired spook from MI something or other, who had swopped spying on the Soviets for the much less dangerous task of spying on casino owners. John Aspinall called our public enemy number one the human toothpick, sometimes rather nervously.

Every toothpick has his day. But the affair blew over rather more quickly than most of us expected. Having an Old Etonian co-owner may have helped, at a time when the government was full of them. Angelo got his licence and his job back, after a short but nail-biting time, made a full financial recovery, and got on with building his luxury house. Maverick got a bit of flak on account of the raid, but died of natural causes soon afterwards, a well-timed end which saved him a packet in fines and back taxes. I was sad when he went. I didn't know him well, but I liked what little I did know. I liked Angelo too, and greatly admired him as one con-man admires another (the Saudi jaunt, coming soon, was a cracker), and I wanted him to like me. I'm soppy like that. But Angelo never got over the suspicion that I was intriguing behind his back. The nicer I was to him the more he distrusted me. I guess he thought I was keeping my friends close but my enemies closer, as they say in Sicily. The years of watching his back during the Aspinall private games, wondering whether Lady Osborne had slipped the usual copper enough cash, may have damaged his faith in human nature beyond repair, and may even have been what pushed him into a heavy reliance on alcohol, often the lonely man's best friend. I was very sad when he died, many years after I last saw him, at the comparatively young age of 67 (I think). Another illegal poker game burst into life within days of Maverick's death, in a different house, run by someone close to him when he was alive, dealt by the same highly skilled girls, and played by the same players. Gamblers and the people who feed off them are admirably unsentimental about death. It's just a bad hand of cards.

Back to the master plan: Angelo bumped into the French Connection totally by accident, in the very nice house mentioned above.

Minus the uniformed paparazzo. At one of Maverick's games. Before he died. They got to talking. My name came up. Frenchy assumed that Angelo was one of us, as Margaret Thatcher used to say. They were both playing for big money, leading Frenchy to make the very reasonable assumption that a modern casino manager could only play high-stake poker if he was robbing the joint he was working in. There was some truth in his assumption. A colleague (who now lives in Heaven) told me in confidence that John Aspinall once sent Angelo to the Middle East to collect a hundred thousand pounds, exactly half the money a big Saudi player owed to the casino. The player went home, the cheque bounced, the Saudi had no plans to come back to London in any hurry, and no assets in London. He couldn't be sued in a British court and legally obliged to stump up the cash (no assets and no punter on the scene added up to no case), and Saudi Arabia's religious law forbids the operation of casinos (they all gamble over here where God can't see them), so he couldn't be sued there either. Chances of getting the money owed looked pretty dismal, as chances go.

A quick explanation is called for: unlike pretty well all other businesses in our green and pleasant land, British casinos are not allowed to accept part payment of a debt. A vital part of the 1968 Gaming Act, slipped in for a good reason. There is no residue left over that a casino owner might be tempted to beat out of the unfortunate gambler. A perhaps unnecessary law in these quieter times, but very important when some of the best casinos in London were owned by some of the most eminent criminals in the world. (It's still all or nothing now, even though the bad guys have gone home, allegedly). But a part payment done informally is awfully hard to police. Off went Angelo, to Cairo I believe, after John Aspinall's eloquence had convinced the Saudi gambler that his reputation would be higher if word of his earlier refusal to pay up didn't go flying around town. His friends wouldn't despise him as a tight-wad, or suspect that he didn't really have quite as much money as the size of his palace suggested. But social death hovered if bad words slipped out on to the gamblers' grapevine. Let's split the difference, habibi. Pay half and enjoy the silence. An Englishman's word is his bond. Angelo came home, very quickly, and handed over eighty thousand pounds in cash. He explained that the gambler had pleaded poverty at the last minute. Maybe his palace was hocked up to the eyeballs. Maybe his apparent prosperity was like one of the mirages that were a common feature of his sun-scorched native land. Who knows? Either way it was eighty or nothing, and bollocks to a bad reputation. Angelo took the eighty and narrowed his smile. John Aspinall, a hard man to fool, knew exactly where the other

258

twenty was, but decided not to fight a very good manager over an obscure point of principle. You could play a lot of poker with twenty grand.

During a pause in Maverick's poker game the French Connection, when Angelo casually mentioned my name, said I know Dave, and embarked on a glowing, unsolicited and, from my narrow viewpoint, highly unfortunate description of my hidden casino skills and of my ice cold nerve when the game was afoot. He meant well, bless him, and hoped that his excellent references would help me make a packet and get out of the fading casino game. Like he had. No reasonable man could find fault with such a noble sentiment. If one can't expect a kind word from a chap one once robbed casinos with, then from whom can one expect a kind word is the question that springs to mind. A friend in need and all that. Next night, in the casino, Angelo came sidling up to me, looking just like a real live Mafia man. He put his right arm across my shoulders and his mouth unnecessarily close to my left ear. Although totally lacking in homophobia, like all good liberals, I'm not actually very keen on close contact with persons of my own sex. Even when both of us are fully clothed. But, filled with the optimism of (comparative) youth I thought great it's my turn to trouser a quick twenty, and tried not to act like a man keen to escape an unwanted embrace. I shouldn't have bothered. I bumped into an old friend of yours last night, Angelo said, smoothly. Silkily even. We had an interesting chat. A very interesting chat. A really very interesting and very long and very informative chat. He held back the old friend's name, to intensify the dramatic effect. After a short but pregnant pause very accurate details of past misdemeanours whispered into the air. Nothing wrong with Frenchy's memory. Or attention to detail. It was clear that what Frenchy didn't know about me wouldn't have covered the back of a small postage stamp. His encyclopaedic knowledge had a disturbing edge. I began to understand how a famous person feels when he discovers that a stalker is taking a close interest in his daily life. Even the Fat Man got a brief mention, and Frenchy wasn't in on that one. The Corsican must have talked. Very rare. My dream of a quick twenty faded fast. Angelo studied my face, looking for signs of panic. Time to get a grip. I switched on my ice-cold nerve and waited patiently for the next chapter. The lack of panic got to him. I'd let him down again. He blurted out Frenchy's real name and glared his disappointment. I was supposed to look like a squealer who sees a black car full of men with hands under their jackets creeping slowly up the street, not like an Englishman feigning interest in a dull game of cricket. He gave up and walked off in a huff. His lack of stamina left me depressed. I was all psyched up for a long (verbal) fight. Desperate to keep things going for a bit longer, I called out that of course I knew old Frenchy. Nice chap, as foreigners go. Glad you got on

259

so well. But he's a bit of a fantasist, don't you know. Angelo kept on walking.

It was a hollow victory. Pyrrhic might be the word I'm looking for. Thanks to Frenchy's well meant hymn of praise there was more chance now of my sipping tea and munching cucumber sandwiches with the Queen than there was of getting the good guys into Aspinall's. If they had stormed through the door clutching signed references from the Pope, the Chief Rabbi and the Archbishop of Canterbury, assuming that I could have talked Frenchy into forging all those signatures, they wouldn't have got a single job between them. A dream died. Bloody Maverick. Lazy bastard. If he'd spent twenty three out of every twenty four hours running a corner shop, like proper Indians do, instead of sitting on his skinny arse for a few hours a night at an illegal poker game Frenchy and Angelo would never have met and I'd be rich.

A Day in the Life of a Gnome.

Mr X was a small man, from Pakistan. Not much over five feet tall when he took off his shoes, not much more than three inches taller when he put them back on again. His short stature and the cast of his features made him look remarkably like a garden gnome. I'm sorry about the cryptic name, by the way. I'm not trying to shield a fellow low-life, I'm trying not to give the bastard a chance to sue me. You'll see why later. He was a businessman who sold forged bank drafts for a living, successfully enough to lose a quarter of a million pounds, in cash, during one year alone, playing punto banco at Aspinall's casino in Hans Street. It's safe to assume that his customers didn't know that the drafts that he sold were forged, and that they thought the prices were low because the drafts were stolen. It's equally safe to assume that had they known that Mr X's forged drafts were only really worth the scrap value of a few grams of nicely coloured paper, not the large number of pounds printed on the front, and that they had never been anywhere near the well-known banks whose names appeared next to the sums of money that his buyers thought they were getting on the cheap, they would not have parted with even the comparatively meagre sums that they did hand over. But they knew nothing. One shady but dim customer was so foolish that he paid good money, which Mr X blew on the same day in yet another failed attempt to beat Lady Luck at her own game, for a draft with Barclays DCO on one side and the totally fictitious Mr X Bank on the other. There really is one born every minute. Or in that case, two. I have to admit that Mr X never talked to me in fine detail about his daily life in the banking business. However I am confident that I have described his business plan with some accuracy.

At the beginning of his banking career Mr X conducted business from a public telephone box in Kensington, on the corner of Palace Gate and Kensington Gore. If visiting public buildings with an interesting history is what lights up your weekends—you won't be far from Kensington Palace, of Princess Diana fame, if you prefer these things on a bigger scale—I'll give you directions. The phone box is not hard to find. Unlike Dr Who's more famous blue one this old red box always stays in the same place and in the same century. Take the tube to Gloucester Road station, and hope that the lift is working when you get there. The stairs go on forever. Turn left when you step outside and walk up Gloucester Road until it becomes Palace Gate, with no real warning and, as far as I can see, for no good reason. Turn right at the top of Palace Gate, open the door of the phone box you see in front of you, holding your nose in case someone has recently popped in for a piss, step inside and you are in what was once the international headquarters of X Inc, purveyors of dodgy bank drafts to the criminal classes and the terminally gullible. There is absolutely no charge for this visit unless you feel the urge to make an old-fashioned phone call.

If Mr X were still in business today, and if he's alive he probably is (unless he's in prison again) he would notice that one wall of his old office is covered with photographs of beautiful women with no clothes on, often crouching on all fours. They smile seductively at the men who take a leak in the darker corners of the box, and at the small minority who make a phone call. Telephone numbers are provided. Immediate arrangements can be made to meet the lady of one's choice, for a small amount of time and a large amount of money. But all is not quite as it seems. The two businesses once conducted from that particular phone box (which I think should from now on be pointed out to the passengers of the open-topped sightseeing buses that pass right by) have one striking feature in common: what you see is not what you get. Buy a bank draft from Mr X and receive a piece of scrap paper looking remarkably like a valuable bank draft, but worth nothing at all. Telephone one of the women whose lurid photos it's hard to ignore, hoping to meet a beautiful young girl taking time out from a career in Hollywood to get a leg over yours truly and meet a middle-aged woman from the suburbs, plastered in make-up. At the same price. Life in the big city is not easy for the unwary. Greed and lies are all around. Even in Royal Kensington.

The owners of Aspinall's casino were rather fond of Mr X. And why not? Quarter of a million a year cash punters are not that thick on the ground even now. But the staff really disliked him for several very good reasons, none of them connected with race. He always came in at about seven in the evening, just as the day shift staff were looking forward to a nice relaxed dinner after making a packet for their employer from people who had come in earlier, at a time when they should have been at the office. He was always rude and offensive, and he always picked a (verbal) fight with one of us. Or all of us. The rudeness came through the door with him and had nothing to do with anything we ever said. Worst of all he always played punto banco, which forced us to put on three extra staff. We couldn't shut down the blackjack and roulette tables in case other players came in, and we only had five or six croupiers to spread around the place. So it was goodbye breaks and hello cold dinner. He wasn't big enough to be a tipper, and anyway the Kerry Packer incident had shut down the illegal tipping. So all in all he was about as welcome as tooth ache to the staff, who were not on commission or on bonus and had no direct interest in the amount of money he lost. If he came in you had a cold dinner and you didn't earn any extra cash. But if he stayed away you got your dinner hot and you had time to lose money playing poker in the staff room with my close friend from Southend, whose rota I carefully arranged in a way that gave him access to all the least skilled poker players.

One night Angelo warned me that Mr X was coming in early next day and was planning to make use of a little known gaming law that is very unpopular with casino owners. The law states that if a player can prove that a casino is breaking the gaming laws in any way he can demand back all the money he has lost that year, or, even worse, all the money he has lost since the casino first opened. Angelo wasn't quite sure which, and I couldn't even remember reading the law when I was swotting for a manager's licence. Perhaps two pages got stuck together. But either way it would have meant handing back a minimum of a quarter of a million pounds, and that was something John Aspinall really wasn't keen on doing. So I was told to make sure that everything on my day shift was done strictly by the book. If I let the side down the rude little bugger would get back most of the money he had been clever enough to make from his dodgy drafts and stupid enough to throw away on the punto banco table.

You might think that obeying laws is easy, and it shows what a fine person you are if you do (although perhaps a touch boring). But in the early days at Aspinall's breaking the gaming laws was the default position. John Aspinall's mercifully brief pep talk had been our operating instructions. A company man to the fingertips, I told all the staff that we had to operate strictly ballroom for once, and even explained why we had to behave in that odd way. They all promised to do their best. Some of the more timid ones looked relieved. By a stroke of good luck all the nicest guys were on that day. There were one or two who could have been there who didn't like me all that much, and who might have dropped me in it just for fun, the swine, too callous to care if John Aspinall found himself short of quarter of a million quid and I found myself short of a job. It was the Gunfight at the OK Corral all over again. Him or me. Mr X or Dave the Rave. One of us had to bite the dust. I was nervous, but not because I was scared. It was the idea of being law-abiding for several hours that was really shredding my nerves. But I had to see it through. It was one of those times when a man has to do what a man has to do.

X came in, looking more like a garden gnome than ever. That's not a racist remark, by the way. I don't do racist remarks. I'm one of the good guys. Some of my best friends are foreigners. Actually most of my best friends are foreigners if you include the Scotsmen. If X had come from Scunthorpe he would still have looked exactly like a garden gnome, only a little paler. Make that a lot paler. But that's neither here nor there. The similarity to a gnome was down to the shape of his features, particularly his nose and his very close together eyes, and the evil look that was permanently etched on to his face. Personally I would never have bought a second hand box of matches from the man, let alone a forged bank draft. But perhaps he put on a quite different expression for his victims, like those people who put on a different voice when they speak on the telephone.

He sat down at the punto banco table, glared aggressively at everybody in the room, got out a thick wad of cash not printed by himself and told us to hurry up and shuffle the cards. All in his normal I came bottom in the exams at charm school and I'm proud of it kind of way. In those days we used six packs of cards on punto banco. (Now it's usually eight, for technical reasons I won't bore you with). Six packs is a lot of cards. Three hundred and twelve to be precise. When a dealer shuffles such a thick wedge of cards he can't just divide them in two and shuffle away, unless he has hands larger than the average shovel, a description that didn't fit any of my co-workers on that day, he has to break them down into at least four little piles and then shuffle pairs of the little piles in a logical order. Sometimes he loses the plot a bit and finishes up with more little piles of cards than he had originally planned, which looks a little scruffy and can lead to comments from superiors, but it doesn't really matter so long as all the cards end up safely in the shoe. The dealer shuffled. Mr X cut the cards. The dealer put them in the shoe. The game started. Mr X played a few hands. The only croupier still on a break came into the room to give a last break to the croupier who had just shuffled the cards. The new dealer quietly pointed to a little pile of cards that the shuffling dealer had accidentally left on the table, the wanker. I hadn't noticed them either in spite of, or perhaps because of my frantic efforts to get everything just right. What was that word again? The new dealer asked me, still very quietly, what the fuck was going on. I had a horrible vision of a quarter of a million pounds flying out of the window and landing on top of Mr X's shiny new car. The only straw to clutch at was that the cards were to the dealer's left and Mr X was over to the dealer's right where he couldn't see them. But when the dealer stood up to let the new dealer sit down Mr X would have a clear view of the cards, start a rumpus, thank God for making his dream of getting his money back come true barely three minutes into the first shoe, and leave me to explain to John Aspinall that he was about to be a quarter of a million short. Immediate action was called for. I rested my right hand firmly on the sitting dealer's shoulder, so he couldn't stand up and reveal the potentially very expensive cards, and used my left hand to quickly put the spare cards in my jacket pocket. Ambidextrous or what? Then the dealers changed over and the garden gnome was none the wiser, yet.

There was still a problem. Casinos provide punto banco players with an elaborate score card on which they can keep track of whether punto wins or banco wins, or there's a fairly rare draw. Writing all this stuff down allows a player to feel that he's playing scientifically, the poor fool. Mr X always filled in his score card. Most punto banco players do, and then study them as carefully as fortune-tellers study leaves at the bottom of a cup of tea, with roughly the same rate of success. Mr X went a bit further and counted the number of times the bank won and the number of times the punto won. Plus the odd draw. You could say that he was just a touch obsessive. Then he added the two together and got the total number of hands that had been played. The final number is never exactly the same, sometimes the rules make you draw an extra card, sometimes they don't, but the number of hands in a shoe always falls within a fairly small range. As at least a deck of cards would have spent the whole shoe in my pocket, the total number of hands was going to be a long way short of what it should be. I needed a plan. One came to me, just in time. It wasn't great, but it just might have been worth a quarter of a million.

I would come over all outraged as soon as the gnome added up the numbers on his score card and started to shout. Then lean across the table and grab the shoe with my right hand and look inside it for the missing cards. The big wooden shoe and the left side of my open suit jacket would hide my left hand as it dropped the cards formerly in my pocket into the discard slot, a long thin hole in the middle of the table where the cards are dumped at the end of every hand. The noise made by my rattling of the shoe would mask the sound of the cards falling into the big tin below the discard slot. Then I would accuse Mr X of counting the hands wrongly. In my best Oxford accent. It's not my bloody fault if you're no good at arithmetic, Mr X. How dare you suggest that anything crooked could happen at Aspinall's, that shining beacon of honesty in a dishonest world? Never been so insulted in my life. It might work, I thought, without much conviction. I began to wish it was my day off.

For the first half of the shoe Mr X hardly won a hand. Finally he got a very good hand, but the dealer beat him with a lucky draw and took the last of his cash. Mr X threw the shoe across the table in a rage, scattering cards everywhere, and stormed out of the casino, minus the five thousand pounds he had come in with. I couldn't believe my luck. The number of hands played, or not, would never be known. The storm was over. The sky was blue. The sun was shining down on Belgravia. John and Jimmy's quarter of a million was safe. My promotion prospects were back on track. Even better, when the shift finished I was off for a couple of days. If Mr X came back tomorrow and had another go at getting back his quarter of a million (plus five grand) it was somebody else's turn to shred his nerves trying to remember all the silly rules. I slipped the missing cards into the tin where they belonged, shook the sharp-eyed croupier warmly by the hand, and decided that my guardian angel really was on top of her job.

Allow me to slip in one last tale about the foul-tempered Mr X. It might be of interest to people of either sex who have a passionate interest in English literature, or to men with an unhealthy and potentially illegal but equally passionate interest in little girls, or to dealers in second-hand cars. Or to all three wrapped into one complex character of ill repute. Mr X came in early one afternoon. I asked him if he would like me to open the punto table. He said no, very brusquely, and got into conversation with a Greek billionaire. The Greek's proper name was Nic(k) Marcou, but I always called him Nick the Greek when he was far enough away not to hear. I had never seen Mr X and Nick the Greek in conversation before, but they were both regular afternoon players and they usually nodded a minimal but polite greeting in one another's direction. You could stretch a point to breaking point and say that they knew each other. It was a day when we had a poker game in the evening. Nick the Greek was a very keen poker player who never missed a game unless he was seriously ill. He sometimes came in early on poker nights and sat around agonising over whether or not to invest fifty thousand pounds in playing blackjack during what was left of the afternoon. The trouble was that if he lost at blackjack he would have no money for his beloved poker game. Hence the agonising. He could easily afford to lose fifty thousand at both games, but he recognised the strength of his own addiction and gave us strict instructions not to listen if he begged to go over his daily limit. Not a penny over fifty grand. Even if he started to foam at the mouth or threaten physical harm. The agreement was written on the card that every top casino has for every player and had the force of a contract, backed up by signatures all over the place.

Mr X said to Nick the Greek that business was rather slow, not mentioning that he sold forged bank documents for a living. Times were tight and money was thin on the ground. It wasn't long after Margaret Thatcher won her first election. Matron had taken over the

266

school and Matron did like a good recession. Stiffens the backbone. Just what the boys need. Especially the wets. As a result Mr X was selling an almost new Jaguar at a bargain price. Was Nick interested, at about eighty percent of its true worth? It was a very nice car, he said, positively sagging under the weight of all its extras. That was true. I'd seen the Jaguar outside the casino on several occasions, radiating wealth from its spot beside the kerb. Mr X always used it to bring his ill-gotten gains to the casino and transfer them, via the punto banco table, to the well-stuffed pockets of Mr John Aspinall and Sir James Goldsmith. And, in the form of food, to the gorillas and snow tigers down at the zoo. The car seemed very big for such a small driver, but many wealthy men who only just break the five foot barrier (with or without shoes) really love fast cars. You often see them peering maliciously through the spokes of the steering wheel, looking for someone to run over.

Nick the Greek was a skilled negotiator. He didn't get to be a billionaire by paying the asking price for anything, ever, or at least not since he was about eight years old. He quickly knocked the cost of the Jaguar down to about sixty percent of what it was worth. When the new low price was agreed, grudgingly, he paid in cash. Mr X handed over the keys and the documents and took the money straight to the punto banco table, which I had started to open the minute I saw his hot little fingers curling round the notes. Within an hour he had lost it all and was taken home, in his normal foul mood, in a chauffeur driven car generously provided by the casino. After Mr X had gone home, skint, Nick the Greek couldn't stop talking to us about the couple of thousand pounds that he had saved through his shrewd negotiating skills. It really made his day. He was still talking about it, to us gambling sharks and to his fellow poker players, at four o'clock in the morning, long after he had lost his daily ration of fifty thousand pounds.

Neither of the addicted gamblers ever saw anything strange in their actions that day, or in the imbalances that stood out like two sore thumbs. That's how addiction takes over your life and turns your brain upside down, whether you're addicted to gambling, alcohol, pornography, methylated spirits, glue, nicotine, drug taking, or sniffing girls' bicycle seats. Addiction makes you lose the plot. It's as simple as that. Everybody else sees it but you don't. It's very sad, and it leads me straight to the literary connection I mentioned earlier: my theory is that Lewis Carroll was sitting in an illegal Victorian casino, penniless among the ruins of yet another failed roulette system, too miserable even to conjure up a vision of a ten year old front bottom, when all of a sudden the story of Alice came crashing into his head. There is sound backing for my theory. Under his real name, which I can't remember, Lewis Carroll was a respected academic mathematician as well as a shy teller of stories to little girls who he hoped might take their clothes off before he ran out of words. He could well have been trying out a roulette system that would have made his fortune, but got the formula wrong. Lots of mathematicians do that, and not just the professionals. I tried it once, based rather flimsily on a modest pass at O Level Maths in 1957, at Berkhamsted School, where Graham Greene first learnt how to do his sums. Ex-croupier Steve, the then new and very proud owner of the Cromwell Mint casino, got the money, right up to the moment when I spotted the glaring error. Also known as the moment my cash ran out. Happily, in my case, the long-term damage was minimal. The cash wasn't really mine in the first place and when my failed attempt to smash down the mathematical wall put up by Blaise Pascal with the inadequate weapon of my O Level came to an abrupt end I quickly realised that robbing casinos was a much better bet than taking on one of France's greatest mathematicians and sprang from my seat at the Cromwell Mint roulette table in the best of spirits. Maybe Lewis carried on feeling as sick as a parrot. Perhaps he'd been planning a simple story about a little girl going for a walk in the country, admiring the beauties of Nature and keeping well away from mirrors or rabbit holes, as soon as he'd cleaned up at roulette, but the financial loss and the addiction fried his brain. He couldn't concentrate properly any more and out of the mad stew boiling around inside his head came the psychedelic and frightening stories of Alice that we all know and love.

Before you scoff, remember this: most great music and most great works of art and literature come from people you would quickly edge away from if they sat next to you on a bench in Hyde Park and struck up a conversation. Like me, walking round Chelsea talking to a girl who wasn't there. Or Wagner, Mozart, Ezra Pound, Thelonious Monk, Ernest Hemingway, Virginia Woolf. Bat-shit crazy, every last one of us. Sad to say sensible, honest, decent, good people generally vanish without trace, leaving nothing but the odd fading photograph in a family album. Only the nutters and the a-holes make a splash. As Orson Welles didn't quite say in The Third Man, but you'll get the drift, Switzerland had five hundred years of democracy and peace and love and out of all that came the cuckoo clock. And at the end of the film (a serious contender for the best film ending ever made) when the bad man he is playing is dead the beautiful woman who loved him walks straight past the good man who loves her without so much as a glance to her right. That's how it is in the real world. The Devil doesn't just get the best tunes. He gets the whole fucking lot.

268

Lily the Pimp.

One afternoon Lily the Pimp came into Aspinall's and stepped straight into one of those hot-as-hell winning streaks that all gamblers dream of. He's finally lost it, you might be thinking. Lily is a woman's name. A woman who provides girls for chaps to rent is a madam. A man who does the same is a pimp. You're right and I'm wrong. Any dictionary will back you up. Let me explain. It's a personal thing. I met several madams of the old school when they came to gamble in the casinos where I worked. They were all nasty, manipulative and greedy women and I never took to any of them. Their only virtue (compared to most of their male rivals) was that they wouldn't pick up a razor and slash a tart's face open as a punishment for some real or imagined offence. But don't get sentimental about the bitches. They often knew a man who did. Lily was different. She was kind to her girls. They respected her and she respected them, and they really liked her as a friend. Her only rival in the vanishingly small world of righteous pimps was "Charlie," the Lebanese man who provided the horizontal dancing girls for the Saudi royals and their hangers-on, who flung more money on to the French roulette and punto banco tables in the second floor lawless salle privee in Ladbrokes' Hill Street casino in an hour than many of us see in a lifetime. I remembered a phrase common among those of us who spent our formative years at boarding school, and found myself thinking of Lily as one of the boys. Not because there was anything butch about her. Oh no. She was very pretty, and stayed that way for much longer than most women do. It was her confident, friendly manner and her honestly emotional smile that made me class her as one of the boys. I never told Lily about her new name. I don't like being swiped across the face with a handbag, even by a friend. I never told anybody else either. You're the first to know. Don't spread it around. Show respect to a lady. Anyway the name is long past its sell by date. By the late seventies she'd put her ill-gotten gains into an honest business and left her racy past behind. But I still thought of her as

Lily the Pimp, in an affectionate sort of way, until long after the music died.

In the early seventies Lily sometimes worked a roulette table with the French Connection and Hashish and the Cockney Frog, and me. Baroness Lil. Nothing serious. Just a hundred or two here and there to help us all through the day. Female barons were quite rare, which didn't harm the cause because nobody believed that women could do that sort of thing, it was a man's world then, and Lily was a regular punter and above suspicion so long as we didn't get silly. It wasn't always plain sailing. On one occasion the French Connection decided (wrongly as it turned out, not to my surprise) that Lil was trying to pay us short during an otherwise amicable share-out, and called her a dirty c**t, in French, which she spoke as fluently as he did. Curiously enough the expression doesn't sound half as bad in French as it does in English, but it's still no way to talk to a lady, or a friend, or someone you're robbing a casino with. Or in this case all three. Happily the bad feeling faded fast. The truth is that when you were robbing casinos there was always the faint possibility that it could all go terribly wrong. If the casino owner was respectable (by the very low standards of casino owners) you could find yourself out of work and skint, or, in extremis, behind bars. If he was a proper criminal you could find yourself hobbling along on a broken leg. Or two. Or lying very still and not breathing. The tension sometimes exploded into ill feelings and bad language. Nowadays we call it stress and take pills to make it go away.

Lily and I became friends. We danced one night at the Candy Box, the Soho disco licensed till dawn to sell drinks and play loud music to those of us who earned our livings at night. I didn't like going there. It could be a violent and nasty place. But there was nowhere else for friendly young people to go to in those days, very late at night, apart from casinos where you would be tempted to waste the money you had gone to all that trouble to steal. Some horrid people were regulars at the Candy Box. The country girl's bright young life was stolen from her by a man she danced with at the Candy Box, and turned into a living hell on pavements and back alleys in less and less classy parts of town as the drugs and the beatings and the sexual diseases took her remarkable beauty away. Not long after Lily and I danced our only dance, after she escaped from my two left feet and clung to the French Connection for the rest of the early morning, a man was stabbed to death in a fight over a small amount of money. He fought so hard to add a few extra minutes to the end of his life that his blood was smeared along the whole length of the bar before he died. On another night a disgruntled young criminal pulled a gun and burned a scar along the side of the shaven head of the brick-shit-house-built bouncer who denied him entry and showed him up in front of his companions. Respect may be a modern word, but it's not a modern concept. There was no way the shot could have been sufficiently well aimed to graze a moving head in an effort to make a point. It was either a warning shot in the air that went wrong or a failed attempt to blow the bouncer's brains out.

Not that Lily was a stranger to violence. When she was a little girl in 1948, in what was then called Palestine and is now called Israel, she lost all her family to the fighting between men we then called Jewish terrorists and men we still refer to as Arab terrorists, during a prolonged burst of what we now call ethnic cleansing. Lily's relatives took no active part. The dead members of her family were unarmed civilians, not terrorists, or men in uniform, if you insist that there's a difference. In today's strangled phrase they suffered collateral damage.

Occasionally, when she wasn't talking or laughing, the light that usually shone in Lily's eyes went dim and a sadness came over her like a second skin. I saw that fading of the light in the eyes of other survivors of military murder (including European Jews who escaped to London before the Holocaust took so many other Jewish lives away) but not so often in the eyes of men and women who had been armed and able to fight back. A Polish croupier I once worked with who knew Lily and, like me, took to her straight away, carried both burdens in different chambers of his brain. Jerry the Pole was a low-ranking soldier in the Polish Army when Nazi troops crashed across his border and, after a hard struggle, wiped out most of the suicidally brave Polish defenders. He fought like fury, survived the massacres, joined the Russian Red Army and continued the fight against the Nazis he now had good reasons to hate. But like most old soldiers he rarely spoke of the war, apart from once telling me of the cold night he and two Russian soldiers walked twenty miles across a frozen landscape to kill a stray dog and bring some fresh meat to the wounded men they had left behind. That incident, and the heavy fighting that came before and after, left him psychologically unharmed. But a story he heard from a Russian soldier he fought with had the same effect on Jerry the Pole as the murder of her family had on Lily.

Before the start of the war he was to fight and die in the Russian soldier had a friend in Moscow whose pretty twelve or thirteen year old daughter caught the eye of the paedophile and mass-murderer Lavrentin Beria, one of the darkest and dirtiest stains on the sad history of the human race. Beria, you probably know, was the boss-man of the KGB (NKVD then), the organiser-in-chief of the murder of millions of innocents, a man always eager to obey every order that sprang from Josef Stalin's twisted mind. One sunny afternoon in pre-war Moscow Beria's big

271

black car kerb-crawled a line of girls coming out of a school. A window opened and a finger pointed at the girl of his choice. She was told to get into the car. Fully aware of who he was, and what he was (children grew up fast in pre-war Moscow) the girl ran away. The big black car came back next day. The window opened again. A bunch of flowers was thrust into the air. The girl refused the flowers and got ready to run. Beria called out that the flowers were not for her, they were for her father's funeral. She got into the car and was never seen again. Jerry didn't know for sure what happened to her father, or the rest of the family, but it's safe to assume that they were murdered too. That filthy incident bore down heavier on Jerry the Pole than all the years of savage fighting he endured as a soldier in the Polish Army, the Red Army and, finally, the British Army, which he joined in the confused last months of the war as the Red Army rolled Westwards and what was left of Hitler's Eastern army crawled back home to die in hopeless defence of the rubble that was once Berlin. Jerry fought well in his last uniform and was rewarded with British citizenship when the war ended. He became a French roulette croupier in a London casino and, I'm proud to say, one of my best friends.

One night in nineteen seventy something, Jerry and Lily and I were sitting together at a French roulette table. Just the three of us. Nobody else in the room. The gamblers had gone home, the waiter was asleep in his little kitchen, the man in charge of the table was taking a leak, and the married manager was getting a leg over a young girl croupier in the privacy of his locked office. Lily had no money in her bag. I couldn't put on any funny bets to make up for her lack of currency because Jerry was as straight as a die, the only straight croupier I ever respected rather than pitied. I guess he'd seen enough real corruption long before he ever set foot in a casino. He wouldn't have turned me in, but I liked him too much to embarass him and I didn't want to see the sad look that would have appeared on the face of a man who had never faltered during six years of war. We were all tired at the end of a long night. No-one spoke. Outside, in the darkness, Swinging London missed a beat. Inside the room, in the gloom beyond the lights that glared down on the roulette table where not long ago gamblers had crowded round like moths round a flame, bad memories of the bad things my two friends had seen leaked from their heads. A silent queue of some of the twentieth century's saddest victims shuffled along the wall and stole the light from their eyes.

When we were business partners Lily often brought into the casino a stupendously beautiful and very expensive Asian call girl, whose English husband was one of only two men in London who didn't know what his wife did for a living (her father was the other one). I knew her husband, but I never had the heart to break his heart and, for a long time, nor did anyone else. I do know that they divorced later on, because I once met his second wife and in England you're only allowed one at a time. But I never knew who jumped first. He may have found out about his first wife's exotic private life and felt left out, or she may have decided that as her earnings far exceeded his it was time to shack up with a man who could keep up. Or live alone and keep all her money to herself. I never met her dad.

On the day of her hotter than hot game at Aspinall's, Lily came in carrying a big handbag overflowing with plastic one thousand pound cash packets. She usually risked a few hundred pounds on the low stake open-to-all table downstairs, but on this day she asked to play on the big boys' table in the private room upstairs. The big table was normally reserved for the likes of Hassan Enany, the man Western construction companies bunged when they wanted to build something expensive in Saudi Arabia, or Adnan Khashoggi, the man the armaments companies bunged if they wanted to off-load a few squadrons of shiny new jet fighters, or Kerry Packer flashing his tax-free cash. But none of them were there that day, and we were nothing if not flexible. Angelo's expert eye, undimmed by the bottle of brandy he had inhaled on the way to work, quickly calculated that there was about fifty thousand in the bag. A very accurate reading, confirmed a few minutes later when our cashier saw a casino name on a packet and phoned a friend who told him that the good lady had just cashed out fifty grand, most of it winnings. Angelo quickly said yes to Lily's request. He didn't want to see the well-stuffed handbag flouncing out of the door and heading for another joint. I was asked to stand and watch the game. Angelo went downstairs to top up on the brandy. There was no-one in the office watching the television. Lily changed one of her cash packets and started to play roulette with five pound chips. She bet on a small group of numbers, rather than spreading chips all over the table like the born losers do. She hit winners right from the off and put all her winnings back on the table, still on a small group of numbers. The way to go. She hit more winners, then switched to playing in hundred pound chips (the maximum allowed at that time unless you were born in Saudi-Arabia). Soon she was winning fifty thousand pounds. Then sixty, then seventy by the time I got word to Angelo. He wasn't pleased. Luckily she'd dropped back to fifty up before she cashed out and left the premises. Good for you Lil, I thought. I've always liked you. A hundred grand in two days sure beats the few quid we once squabbled over. Angelo looked pale. He told me Aspinall would be furious and gave me a meaningful look. It didn't worry me much. Unlike Honest John I didn't have an inbuilt hatred of women (quite the contrary on a good day) and I knew that mega gamblers like the Saudi super-stars and the scar-faced

Nigerians in robes were losing millions at Aspinall's while my old friend Lil was only winning tens of thousands. We were in no danger of going broke.

Lily came back next day with her winnings intact. The good news. She stormed straight in with hundred pound chips. Her luck was still in. The bad news. Soon she was winning another fifty thousand. When you're hot you're hot. Angelo told me to watch her like a hawk, direct instructions from the boss, and make sure that no funny business went down. In big games a fair amount of discretion is allowed when a chip is badly placed. The benefit of the doubt usually goes to the gambler, so long as it doesn't happen too often. But in Lily's case my instructions were that all the benefit of all the doubt was to go to the casino. Panic, misogyny and greed were setting in. Any decisions about paying badly placed chips were to be based on the exact position of the chip when the ball fell into the little slot on the wheel. I didn't like it. Unfortunately it was not long after the French Connection had spilled the beans to Angelo, thinking he was doing me a favour, bless him. If Lily's name had come up during their conversation (which was quite likely: the world of crooked casinos was a small one and almost everybody knew almost everybody else), Angelo was probably convinced that I had arranged the previous day's winning streak. I would have done of course, if she'd asked. But she didn't. Lily had probably gone as straight in her gambling life as she had in her business life. It's a common failing.

Angelo told me, with another meaningful look, that John Aspinall would be glued to the television screen in his office and watching my every move. Things changed. Lily began to lose. She kept piling on the big chips in the hope that her bad luck would turn good again, but it didn't. When you're hot you're hot but when you're not you're not. Lady Luck lost interest and left the room. Soon Lily had spent all the money she'd won that day and was biting into the money she'd won the day before. Early signs of bad temper increased the tension. Then it happened. I had had no reason yet to intervene in the smooth running of the game. I just stood there looking serious, like a judge, and smiled cautiously when our eyes met. But a chip Lily put on at the last minute was badly placed, slightly overlapping the line between the winning number and the number next door. If you're familiar with a roulette table the chip was almost entirely on number eleven, the winning number, but very slightly overlapping number eight. Lily immediately said that it was supposed to be fully on number eleven. On a normal day we would have accepted the lady's claim that the chip was supposed to be on number eleven, moved it to where she said it should be, and paid her three thousand five hundred pounds. All her other chips were properly placed.

She only played what we call splits on a few numbers, and eleven was not one of them. Her claim was quite in order. There was a big difference in the pay-out. A split covers two numbers, in this case eight and eleven, and gets paid seventeen to one. A straight up bet covers only one number, and pays thirty five to one. Times a hundred. You could buy a nice Jaguar with that in those days, before circumstances forced you to sell it to a Greek at a knock-down price. I told the dealer to treat the disputed chip as a split and pay the lady one thousand seven hundred pounds. I avoided Lily's eye. Lily demanded three thousand five hundred. When I screwed up the courage to face her and say no, sorry, I can only pay you one thousand seven hundred she looked like an old friend betrayed. But not for long. The very reasonable question 'are you a fucking boy scout now?' spat into the air. I suppressed the urge to say something about girl guides (lack of in the room) and put on the sort of smile that really hurts your face if you leave it there for too long. Angelo came in and backed me up, reluctantly. He usually got somebody else to do the dirty work when a fight broke out, but Lily had demanded to speak to someone more senior than me. Quite sharply. The smaller pay-out was made and very grudgingly accepted.

In the end the money was gone, Lily the Pimp was gone, and the friendship we once enjoyed had gone with her. John Aspinall switched off his private television, happy that a woman with too little money and too much luck wasn't going to walk away with any more of his cash. Angelo went back to his brandy, happily convinced that he'd put me in my place. I switched off the painful smile, shut the table down, checked how much we were winning, helped myself to a couple of hundred to calm my nerves, and walked away too, happy not to have to let an old friend down any longer. I saw Lily a few years later, in a different casino, and then quite regularly until I retired at the beginning of 2006. We got on fine again, I'm pleased to say. Her suspicion that I had joined the boy scouts, grown-up section, had obviously faded. (A likely story). She never was one to bear a grudge. The incident at Aspinall's was never mentioned.

Lily told me later, when we were talking again, that the Fat Man took against her, for no apparent reason, and demanded that she be excluded from a very smart casino they both went to. If Lily wasn't banned they would never see him again. As he was a very big player (one of the biggest in the world) and she was normally a small player, the dirty deed was done and hastily wrapped in a flurry of insincere apologies. Another good reason for me to drop him off my Christmas card list. But what the Fat Man wanted the Fat Man got. Shame it didn't work in other ways. I would love to be able to say that what the Fat Man owed the Fat Man paid.

I still feel bad about that day, Lily the (ex) Pimp. You were right. You should have been paid. But John Aspinall's hard eyes were boring down through the television camera and Angelo's suspicious mind's eye was flicking through Frenchy's version of my curriculum vitae. I might as well have been handcuffed to a ring on the wall, like Beria when it was his turn to take a bullet. I can send you a cheque if you like. I've got a cheque book I forgot to hand in when I went bankrupt. The bank will laugh if you try to cash it, but you can hang it up in a nice frame and look at it once in a while and remember an old friend who feels bad about a day that dawned in hope and died in despair, a long time ago.

I'm right out of packets.

Last Words.

When a casino manager meets a very big gambler the unwritten agreement is that the big gambler provides the arse and the casino manager provides the kisses. Everyone knows his place in the drama. Just occasionally the manager gets the upper hand, psychologically speaking. The manager always gets the last laugh in private of course because the players always lose in the end, courtesy of the odds, but that's not the point I'm struggling to get over.

I last saw Kerry Packer in the summer of 1981, at the beginning of my final afternoon at the old Aspinall's in Hans Street, before I went to work, for twice the money and half the job, in a casino next to a motorway that runs from Madrid to a town in Northern Spain. Packer came into Aspinall's with David Frost, a man I'd only seen once before at Aspinall's. He'd just been introduced to someone new and was treating her to the most effusive display of new friendship I've ever witnessed. I felt like a man drowning in a tidal wave of honey, and I was only an innocent bystander. I'm sure he was sober. On that day in 1981 he and Packer were involved in a business deal, judging from their conversation, and dropped in to Aspinall's for a very well cooked lunch. After lunch David Frost insisted on playing roulette. Kerry Packer sat nearby and nagged at Frost to pack up the silly game and come with him to wherever they were supposed to be going. At that time Kerry Packer was no longer a gambler at Aspinall's, highly disgruntled since we had slashed his maximum stake on blackjack. Angelo told me that word of Packer's illegal tipping, referred to in an earlier chapter, had leaked out of our four walls. He told me as little as he could, of course, because he never really trusted me. But he hinted that a bit of high level smoothing had gone on and that the smoothing had kept the tipping story under wraps and the casino open. That may or may not have been true. Like most people who get through a couple of bottles of brandy a day Angelo often had difficulty in distinguishing between what was really happening and what the brandy was telling him was happening. On good days he spoke perfect, cynical casino sense, on bad days he could have stood in for George Bush. But the tipping story had the ring of truth. Either way, whatever the truth was, Angelo felt obliged to give me some background. He was worried that I might give in to pressure from Packer, a very persuasive man, and allow him to up his new stakes and get back in the game. Angelo made it very clear that if that happened Pandora's Box would re-open and all the old troubles would come crashing back down on the casino. Packer could no longer play blackjack at five thousand pounds a box. His new limit was two thousand. And that was final.

Packer didn't want to know. Whoever broke the news to him was probably not allowed to reveal the real reason for the demotion, or handled it badly. Or both. He never softened his stance. He stopped playing blackjack and said that he would never start again if he could only put on a measly couple of grand per box. It was a real blow, commercially speaking. World class multi-million pound blackjack players didn't grow on trees, even in 1980s Australia. We persuaded him to play punto banco at his old high blackjack limits. Punto banco obviously hadn't figured in the smoothing process. But he soon got bored and stopped playing the silly game. I can't say I blame him. Punto banco is the most boring card game ever invented. Its only virtue is that it's the game with the lowest edge against the player. The narrow margin makes it very popular with big players, particularly from South East Asia, who hope to win by playing big and running away the minute they get ahead. They're trying to earn a living and don't worry about dying of boredom. You can see their point. Most jobs are boring.

When you play punto banco for the same stake every hand, the maximum in Packer's case, the only decision you ever have to make is whether to back the player or the bank. Don't worry about what that means. Just think of it like this: you can put your money here or you can put it there. Here pays evens, there pays very close to evens. How's that for excitement? It gets worse. The cards are drawn or not drawn according to fixed rules. There are no options. You can't split, you can't double, you can't decide to break the self-imposed card drawing rules that shrewd blackjack players abide by (and still lose, but not so quickly), because you're feeling lucky or God just had a word in your ear. You can't do anything except put your money down and hope you put it in the right place. If you did you win. If you didn't you lose. And that's it. I didn't make up the bit about God, by the way. A female blackjack player, a lady of many years, once told me that sometimes she knew, really definitely knew what the next card was going to be. The word came 'from God's mouth to my ear.' The sad thing was that God's powers of prediction turned out to be no better than Mystic Meg's, and the good lady lost all the money her late husband had thoughtfully left behind. Kerry Packer could easily have played punto banco from home by yelling "punto" or "banco" down the phone when the croupier's disembodied voice told him it was time to bet. Or hung up, found a brush, and opened a tin of paint.

So there we all were, on my last day at Aspinall's, sitting close together in a small room. David Frost was playing a mind-numbingly boring roulette system that involved laying out ten chips to win one. What we in the trade refer to, cruelly but accurately, as a wanker's game. Kerry Packer was sitting next to the roulette table, with his arse overflowing a chair and a pissed off look on his face. I was wracking my brains for a way to turn him into a roulette player and make him lose money at Aspinall's again. I'd never seen him so close to a roulette table before. There must be a way. He had always derided roulette as a sheila's game, the worst insult a macho Ozzie can hit you with. Both John Aspinall and James Goldsmith had tried and failed to get him to play roulette and they were his friends, as far as very rich people have friends. So what chance did I have? I tried anyway, mainly out of malice. I was leaving the job very soon, there was no money in it for me, but I just didn't like Packer. I wanted him to lose some money again, some of the millions he had avoided paying in Australian taxes thanks to his close friendship with a variety of corrupt, over-sexed political friends. I can be a bit of a puritan on bad days. A small part of the attraction, heavily outweighed by the malice, was that some of the money he lost would go towards the upkeep of Aspinall's animals. The beginnings of a plan began to form in my mind. I sat next to Packer. He didn't like that much. I said smarmily, trying to sound confident: you don't like this game, do you Mr Packer? Nah, flamin' sheila's game. So far so bad. Then I explained that although my favourite game was blackjack, which is actually true, there was a way of playing roulette that made it worthwhile. I ignored the unspoken suggestion, clearly visible behind the stocking, that I should shut the fuck up and fuck off, and came out with what turned out to be the killer line: you have to have a lot of nerve and you have to have a lot of money. His face changed. He was back at his expensive Australian version of an English public school, aged about fifteen. Another boy had said come on then Packer, bring it on. Or whatever they say at the poshest levels of young Australian society before fists fly. He couldn't say no to a fight. It was in his genes. Through clenched teeth he asked me what this magic fucking system was. He knew that I was suggesting that maybe he didn't have enough nerve, and that maybe he didn't really have as much money as he liked to make out. And he knew that I knew that he knew.

But it made no difference. He had to respond. Wimping out was not an option. For a brief moment I almost liked him. David Frost ignored our exchange and concentrated on his deadly boring roulette game, determined to win a fiver even if it took all day.

I explained to Packer exactly how he had to play, if he had the nerve and the money (unspoken). The following figures applied to big players in 1981. Today you multiply by ten and still find plenty of takers. He had to place the maximum bet of forty chips, valued at two hundred pounds each, on a number in the middle of the table. Number twenty nine will do nicely. (Don't worry about where the chips go, and don't try to find out the hard way. It's very expensive and you'll end up living on the street). That's eight thousand pounds, so far. Then he had to place the maximum of four thousand on each of the even chances, black, odd and the high numbers in this case. That's another twelve thousand. They pay evens if you win, which is why they are called the even chances. You probably worked that out for yourself. Finally, two thousand each go on the two to one bets. The column and the dozen bets, to be boringly technical. That makes a stake of twenty four thousand (two hundred and forty thousand today). I told him he would be paid about a hundred thousand if he hit the bull's-eye. Actually it's £98,400, but quoting precise figures makes you sound like a geek. I was the other tough kid, not some nerd who knew all about numbers. I said the big stake is why you need a lot of money, and you need the nerve because if some numbers on the wheel come up you lose everything, or nearly everything, and a lot of people can't handle that.

I hadn't given in my notice yet because the Madrid job still had to be confirmed, but I was starting a two week holiday the next day. The written job offer came in the post about a week after the Packer and Frost show. I phoned in my resignation. Before I left England I phoned Aspinall's again, to say goodbye to a friend. Get this, he told me excitedly, Kerry Packer had suddenly become a wild roulette player, spending twenty four thousand a spin and winning or losing hundreds of thousands of pounds a night. He was occasionally heard to mutter I'll show that Pommy bastard who's got nerve, the meaning of the pithy phrase totally lost on the very few people who ever heard it. My friend wondered what had happened. Did I know anything he didn't? Everyone in London knew that Kerry Packer hated roulette.

The two staff who were working on conversion day must have missed my spiel, perhaps traumatised by the deadly dull nature of the game they were dealing, or because I was speaking quietly while slipping Packer the oil, tinged with acid. For some reason I kept the story to

280

myself and told my friend that I knew nothing. Just a twist of fate. You're the first to hear what really happened.

With the perfect vision that hindsight always brings, I can see clearly now that my last day at Aspinall's was the peak of my career as a casino bad boy, first class. With consummate skill I talked one of the biggest gamblers in the world, whose cheques never bounced, thanks to all those honest Australians who paid their taxes, into losing millions of pounds in a game he had always refused to play, ever, before I got up close and personal. Beat that if you can. Even Lord Sugar might have put me on the short list.

Packer stuck with roulette for quite a while after his conversion, and then went back to blackjack for the last years of his life, often taking Joe Dwek along for the ride. I never saw him again after the day we became friends. He died before he had a chance to thank me for bringing a new game into his life.

In the Shade of a Jacaranda Tree.

In 1981 a casino the size of an aircraft hangar opened in a lay-by off a motorway a few miles North of Madrid. No licence was available for a casino actually in the city. That was the usual policy on the Continent, as we used to call all the countries nearest to us on the map. Most of our immediate neighbours ban all legal casinos in their capital cities. They don't give a toss how much money tourists chuck away (they're only foreigners after all) but they don't want their own nationals going bankrupt in casinos that are uncomfortably close to their offices and shops. In Britain we're made of sterner stuff. All our top casinos are slap bang in the middle of London.

Some of my fellow Brits had already gone to Spain, to casinos that were up and running in holiday resorts on the various costas. It was a bit like a working holiday: much warmer than England, a beach or two, booze at half the price, and plenty of sex for the singles and the more agile married men (and women). All good stuff I'm sure you'll agree, but the wages were often lower than in London. I was looking for big money, money that would get me out of casinos before I got too old and died young, like so many of the Frenchmen I worked with in the sixties. Fringe benefits were of no interest. The casino outside Madrid was more my thing. The big money was waiting to be flung on to the tables by the legitimate businessmen and the big time crooks of the proud Spanish capital. Both classes of citizen would swarm in every night for the first five years or so, like they did in London when casinos first took off in the early sixties. In a very few years I would make enough money to pay off my mortgage in England, stick what was left under the mattress, and live happily ever after. As a bonus, the old skills might get a new airing. That was plan B, after the French Connection unwittingly put the skids under my plan to enjoy a larger share of the profits I was helping to generate at Aspinall's.

The pay in Spanish casinos was based on tips; real tips, regulated and recorded by the gambling police and given straight to the staff, unlike in London in the early days where they went straight into the boss's pockets (less whatever the managers managed to nick) and then were abolished outright by the 1968 Gaming Act. I knew that Madrid based tycoons and villains alike would play bigger and tip bigger than the tourists and the hotel and restaurant owners and souvenir sellers in the casinos in the holiday towns. It was a long way from the beach, but there were plenty of swimming pools. Close your eyes and lick some salt and you couldn't really tell the difference. My wife and I and three young children squashed into an old but reliable Land Rover, in between the many black dustbin bags that held our worldly goods and the one decent suitcase I slung in to impress the owners of the hotels we would have to stay in on the long drive to Madrid. The casino wasn't open when we arrived, so we had plenty of time to settle in to our new life. We found a flat a short way from the village centre, at the end of a dusty path that led across a sandy wasteland dotted with tropical looking trees. One sunny afternoon we had a picnic in the shade of one of the trees. As the children played in the sand I saw a shining vision of their future. They would grow up speaking fluent Spanish. We would roam the heights of the Pyrenees in winter, and in the summer swim in the Mediterranean and marvel at the miracles under the water. After paying off the mortgage on our nice house with a big garden in England we would buy a little house with a garden on the roof in Cadaques and spend the summer holidays in the magic village where it all began. Life just couldn't get any better. The tree the children were playing under became a jacaranda tree, in a new legend of my mind. It almost certainly wasn't really a jacaranda. I don't know (or care) what a jacaranda tree actually looks like; it was a throwback to the wild happiness that came over me when I read about one standing alone in the wilderness, somewhere in Africa if I remember rightly, and wanted to fly there on the next plane. Travel books can do that to you. Even now, in old age, the picnic we all shared under that tree floats back into my mind's eye, usually after too much red wine. I see the children, young again in the blue shade of the green leaves, tucking into their simple food and drawing figures in the sand and me, almost young, dreaming in the sunshine beyond the shade.

Hashish drove in to the village one day, a nice surprise in more ways than one. We weren't getting paid, thanks to the delay in opening the casino, my funds were running low (there wasn't a cash machine on every corner in those days) and Hashish had a few hundred dollars in his pocket that he could lend me to pay the rent. Other Frenchmen appeared, all of whom I'd last seen in London during the French heyday in the sixties, before native trainees like me drove them out. Another old friend, from the Greek part of Cyprus, turned up one bright and sunny afternoon, with his nervous English wife and their lively young daughter. His wife had very good reasons to be nervous. Life with her likeable but volatile man may never have been dull, but nor was it easy. His plans rarely went according to plan, however good they looked on paper. Her nervous tension first got a grip when my Cypriot friend left a London casino and opened a Greek taverna in a posh part of town. He was a natural host and a hard worker and the business prospered right from the start, unlike many croupier-founded enterprises. Then he lost all the money he made from the restaurant by playing poker with much more enthusiasm than skill. Throwing bank-notes on a blazing fire may well the world's fastest way of getting rid of surplus cash, but playing poker badly comes in very close behind. The restaurant was sold to pay off the gambling debts. To get back in the black the ex-restaurateur and his growing family went to Lebanon to manage a small but high stake casino in the mountains, not far from the ancient temple of Baalbek where, in times of peace, world-renowned classical orchestras play beautiful music under the stars. The Syrian army was roaming freely over the Lebanese countryside. One night, after the casino had been open long enough to accumulate a decent hoard of cash, a Syrian major parked an elderly tank in front of the casino and pointed its long gun barrel at the front door. He ordered some of his men to surround the building and shoot dead anyone stupid enough to climb out of a window, and ordered the Lebanese owner of the casino to tell his staff and his customers not to do anything rash. He gave the owner ten minutes to come up with a sum of money equivalent to at least fifty years of the major's current salary, plus a bit extra to keep the enlisted men quiet. If the cash didn't appear in the allotted time the first of several shells would come crashing through the front door. In the ninth minute the owner came out with a bag. The major accepted his pension, in dollars, ordered the tank driver to point the big gun at some rocks instead of at the casino (but keep a machine gun trained on the door), and led the rest of his men indoors to celebrate their win and help themselves to more money. During the celebrations a drunken soldier pushed his automatic rifle hard against my friend's wife's stomach. Inside, inches away from the hole from which the bullets would fly if the soldier's finger squeezed the trigger, by accident or for fun, a six month old embryo was getting on with the usual preparations for life in the world outside. The mother's nervous tension rose to a new, much higher level, and stayed there for a long, long time. Several years later, in peaceful, newly democratic Spain, she was still knocking back tranquilisers in quantities that would have worried her London doctor to death.

Visions of drinking red wine and passing the cash round at the Cavendish all-night restaurant floated into my mind, like a modern version of one of those interiors that Rembrandt did so well. The past rushed up into the present. In quiet corners of local bars (the most popular being The Yellow, in Spanish 'El Amarillo,' which you will remember fondly if you were there too) plans were made to rob the new casino, just like in the old days. Laissez les bons temps rouler, as they say in French. For sound reasons (but not from any kind of nationalistic bias) Spaniards were not included in the plans. Nearly all the Spanish croupiers were trainees and barely able to do their jobs properly, never mind rob the joint, but while most of the expatriate staff were in supervisory jobs, a hard core of French and English croupiers were working on the tables. It was agreed that some of the few would be open to persuasion and that the nervous Spanish beginners could be relied on not to have a clue about what was going on around them. But the first casino crookedness didn't involve the croupiers at all. An English pit boss on the American roulette and his French counterpart on the French roulette got together with an Italian gambler who owned a couple of very high tech roulette balls that could be controlled electronically by a man standing close to the wheel and operating a device safely hidden in his pocket. Every night the enterprising pit bosses slipped one of the special balls on to one of the tables they were in charge of, picking a different table every night so that the big pay-outs would be evenly spread out and making sure that the techno crooks knew which table to play on. It was way beyond anything I'd ever seen before. In London we relied on bluff and dazzling speed and sleight of hand, not advanced technology. I suddenly felt very old-fashioned.

The gang operated without detection for about a week. Then an English pit boss who had become a good friend of mine noticed that a roulette ball was behaving very strangely in the wheel of one of the eight American roulette tables. The ball hovered and zig-zagged in a way that he had never seen before and then fell into number 28, the number on the green baize table with the most chips on it. A man he had seen playing the night before was paid out. Another man stood staring at the wheel, both hands pushed deep into his big bulky jacket. The pit-boss watched the same thing happen again at the end of the next spin. Once again the ball hovered strangely and then fell into number 28. It was the beginning of the end of what could have been a long and profitable partnership. The boys should have picked another number and made the trajectory of the ball a bit less erratic, but they were getting greedy and careless and didn't know that they were being watched by someone who knew a thing or two about the law of gravity. The straight pit-boss went to tell one of the directors what he had seen. Soon he was talking to three of the most senior staff, none of whom wanted to know about the dancing roulette ball. They even suggested that he was imagining it all. You haven't been drinking again have you? He persisted. Meanwhile a few more 28s came up and the money rolled in. Or out, from the casino's point of view. The directors, watching on camera, began to take the pit-boss seriously. The two visible members of the gang were approached by casino security men. Guns were drawn (but luckily not by the security men, whose training was rudimentary) and a couple of bullets were fired into the ceiling.

Throughout the drama my friend the straight pit boss showed no signs of fear. I was as impressed as everybody else, but not really surprised. His pretty young wife was the former female junior javelin throwing champion of a then Communist East European country. A woman who could turn her husband into a kebab at a hundred paces. With her eyes shut. In the dark. She also had a fiery temper. A man who takes on a woman like that doesn't come over all faint every time some Mafia ponce starts waving a pistol about.

After the shooting stopped and the gangsters made their getaway all the balls on the French and American roulette tables were checked with a magnet, on the advice of someone who must have paid close attention during science lessons when he was at school. Two of the balls, one from each game, stuck like glue to the ends of the magnet. A Frenchman and an Englishman were accused of the crime, as I suppose you have to call it, and were arrested. One of them, new to the game of robbing casinos, hadn't had enough time to build up his resistance to interrogation and confessed. Patriotism tempts me to blame the Frenchman, but my new status as a historian forces me to finger the Englishman as the weakest link.

Just as the two bad guys were getting used to life in a prison cell rather than a Spanish luxury flat, they were called in to see the prison governor. He told them to get out of their prison uniforms and change in to their normal clothes, neatly laid out on his desk. He gave them their passports and explained that they were now on a form of bail. He pointed to a large wall map that showed clearly where the Spanish/French frontier wandered erratically through the Pyrenees. He told them that they were being given their passports on trust but that this didn't mean that they could just roll up at a rural frontier post high in the mountains, like the one with an easily remembered name that he was pointing at with his pencil, and slip unnoticed into France. The casino crooks' eyes lit up as the subliminal message crept home. They knew that at such a sleepy place there was often no-one on duty, or if there was someone there he would be sitting half-pissed in a wooden hut and looking forward to going home, or to the nearest bar, or to sleep, and very unlikely to take the slightest interest in two foreigners moving quietly from Spain into France. Perhaps confusing his captives with common criminals of low intelligence the prisoner governor went on to say that border controls were slack at these remote crossings now that France and Spain were fellow members of the European Union, unless ETA terrorists had just murdered someone nearby, which they hadn't for a while. But would the newly paroled prisoners like a pen and a small piece of paper? Not all foreigners are good at remembering Spanish names.

They borrowed some money from friends (or collected it from a stash built up before their electronic balls became the property of the Spanish police) and headed straight for the frontier, as keen as the prison governor to relieve the Spanish taxpayer of the burden of feeding and housing two foreign prisoners who had only robbed a casino rather than committed a real crime.

Then, from my selfish point of view, everything went pear-shaped, for entirely personal reasons which would be of no interest to you, and had no connection with the events described above. My wife and children went home first; shortly afterwards I gave in my notice at the Madrid casino, converted my first and last very large pay cheque into a banker's draft (a real one, not one bought from a man in a phone box) and started out on the long drive back to England. It was the beginning of the end.

Friends.

During the more than twenty years between my return from Madrid and my retirement on January 2006 I worked in a quiet casino in Kensington and lost all interest in the gambling business. It was just a job that paid the mortgage and later on paid the rent. I gave up my dream of financial independence, unethically acquired, and my dream of living half way up a mountain. That was the bad news. The good news was that I read all the good books I had always wanted to read, in the breaks that interrupted my undemanding job as an inspector of games I knew backwards, listened to every note that Miles Davis ever played through a pair of domestic hi-fi speakers on the back seat of the car that took me to London and back from a series of houses I no longer found it easy to pay for, made friends with straight croupiers for the first time in my life, and took an interest in the real lives of the gamblers rather than seeing them only as mugs to make money out of for my employers or money for myself if there was a corrupt and profitable relationship to be had. It wasn't a moral conversion I hasten to add. Things had changed deep down inside. A build-up of psychological blows affects you like a build-up of certain poisons. Each small dose is not enough to kill, but one day they reach a critical mass and something dies. When imagined myself helping to run the Kensington casino, like I had helped run Aspinall's, panic set in. That part of me was no longer there.

I saw my other self every hour of every day. Plainly visible, but unable or unwilling to move back in and make me whole again. It's a strange feeling. Imagine looking at yourself in a mirror and reaching out a hand. Your reflection's hand moves away, instead of joining up at the surface of the glass. When you walk forwards he walks backwards. I shouldn't have been so horrid about Lewis Carroll. He and Alice had come back to haunt me. It took twenty-seven years for the two of us to fit back under the same skin. A tremendous relief when it finally happened. Call me over sensitive if you like, but the thought of only half of me being put in a box and done to a turn when Jesus decided that it was my turn to be a sunbeam really preyed on my mind. I suppose I was mad, in a small and silly sort of way. But not dangerous, even to myself.

Sociology and politics took over my life. I saw things clearly now. Things like: modern British casinos have always displayed an admirable lack of racial bias. All customers are welcome, whatever their nationality or religion. It's the colour of their money that counts. Not the colour of their skin or the country on their passports or which of the many gods they talk to before they go to sleep. This fine liberal policy ensured that you often saw people playing together on London casino tables whose respective countrymen back home were killing one another in a proper war, with armies and air forces, navies even, or in a guerrilla war with whatever weapons they could lay their hands on or strap to their bodies. It happened during the long war between Iran and Iraq, when the late Saddam Hussein was still our good friend. Most of the Iranians gambling in London casinos had fled their home country. They were seen as enemies by the fundamentalist government that had replaced the Shah and would have had their property confiscated and their lives put in danger if they had stayed at home. If they were gay they might well have been dangled off the end of a crane. But they were still Iranian. Some of the Iraqi gamblers were Saddam supporters, some were exiles trying to stay alive by keeping well away from home, just like the Iranians. The Saddam supporters were here on business, perhaps buying more chemicals to turn into poison gas, or conducting honest businesses, or on holiday. They could go home any time they liked. It was the exiles who had to watch their backs. Even in London Saddam's murderers managed to take a few lives. But both groups still thought of themselves as Iraqis. Yet men and women of both countries often shared a blackjack or roulette table without raising their voices or engaging in hand to hand combat or letting fly a burst of automatic fire. They partied on while their countrymen killed one another in huge numbers, four or five hours flying time from London. Standing behind the tables we treated them as equals. I couldn't help thinking of Basil Fawlty telling his staff not to mention the war.

Once in a while the echoes from these distant conflicts livened up the gamblers' talk. I was watching a card game one night, the new, dumbed down form of poker, trying really hard to stay awake. The players were two Iraqis and a Syrian. Both Iraqis were exiles and no fans of

Saddam Hussein, but both were horrified by the lack of precision that was such a prominent feature of Donald Rumsfeld's precision bombing, if you happened to be living in a Baghdad street at the time rather than in Washington DC or London, England. One of the Iraquis was a lawyer, the other was a doctor, and the Syrian was a very talented film maker. All three men knew that the war in Iraq had nothing to do with democracy and everything to do with a failed attempt to get hold of Iraq's oil, and that the war in Afghanistan had nothing to with democracy but everything to do with building and guarding a lucrative oil pipeline from Central Asia to the Indian Ocean. Foreigners aren't as stupid as our political leaders would have us believe. Particularly the ones who take the trouble to qualify as lawyers and doctors and very talented film directors and have a firm grasp of the history of countries that many Americans, from their then president down, would be hard-pressed to find on a map. The card dealer was a very small and very beautiful Vietnamese girl. There wasn't much of her, but what there was reached the highest standards ever dreamed of by man. She was born in Vietnam into a family not long migrated from Mongolia, and raised in England, where her internationally mobile family brought her when she was a baby. She had the bud-like mouth and the high, wide cheekbones common among young women from the steppes, and perfect slanting eyes of uncommon beauty which gazed confidently and intelligently at the three men. Out of nowhere a great panorama of blood-stained history swept past my mind's eye and kept me from nodding off. Eight centuries before the card game took place the cruel military genius Genghis Khan conquered most of the known world when his army burst out from the same part of Central Asia as the girl's more recent ancestors, followed a century and a half later by the even crueller Tamerlane, another mass murderer who trashed the Arab countries and left behind nothing but the smouldering remains of great cities that had once been the intellectual centre of the world, and enormous mountains of skulls. Now, in the twentieth century a small girl with a rare beauty and a gentle soul had come to London to deal cards to the descendants of the Arabs once terrorised by her ancestors of long ago. Sometimes things do get better.

All three players had very good cards and expected to win. The girl with the beautiful eyes turned over her cards and beat them all. The Syrian laughed out loud. He said to the Iraqis: 'We might as well give up now. We'll never beat her. She's from Vietnam. They even beat the Americans.' The bitter joke went down a storm with the Iraqis, acutely aware that it was mostly American soldiers rampaging round their country in pursuit of what had seemed like such a good idea at the time, if you were big in oil.

Other conflicts took their seats at the card tables. Two young women were playing blackjack. I had never seen either of them before. A Palestinian man, a regular small player, came to the table and politely asked if he could join in. He spoke very good English, with a recognisably Arab accent. They said yes, of course, equally politely. Nervous looks flashed across their faces. He chatted to the girls as the game went on. He was a very friendly man with a very sad history. I knew from an earlier conversation that he had been taken to Jordan as a child when his family, along with three quarters of a million other Palestinians, fled from their home during the ethnic cleansing that accompanied the founding of the state of Israel, an episode not often mentioned in polite company, usually drowned out by shrill talk of the inhumanity of Palestinian terrorists when loose talk does veer in that direction. He asked the girls where they were from, telling them, with no particular emphasis, that he was from Palestine. They looked embarrassed. They said that they were on holiday in London, and avoided any mention of their nationality. I quickly guessed what the answer would be if ever there was one. Finally one of them said that they were from Israel but she hadn't wanted to tell him that because now he would hate them. He smiled the genuinely warm smile of a genuinely nice man, put a hand on her arm and said I don't hate you. I don't even know you. But I would give anything to live in my old house again. Last time I saw it I was five years old.

I thought I saw a flash of sympathy in her eyes, or perhaps a flash of guilt. There was clearly a spark of empathy between these three visibly decent people, all of them victims of historical injustices too powerful for an individual human being to resist. Left to themselves, far from the hard-eyed politicians, they might even have brought about something approaching a just peace between their two countries. Human history is written in blood. Cruel invasions are two a penny. But sometimes people once at each others' throats manage to live together. It doesn't bring back the dead but it does help the living. English people of German or Gaelic descent don't slit the throats of their countrymen whose ancestors came over with William the Conqueror. The girls had almost certainly lost family members in the Holocaust, like almost all European Jews had, and found in Israel a sense of safety and belonging that their ancestors had never known, but at the expense of a little boy forced out of the house he was growing up in. Armed men (and women) of the Irgun or the Stern Gang, who didn't hesitate to kill civilians, were getting closer and closer and already firing at the village. Before he left the home he never went back to the little boy saw neighbours die of shrapnel wounds or gunshot wounds, ordinary people who treated him kindly in his first few years of life. By sheer good luck, and with help from some deeply unselfish people, he and his extended family escaped death, he got a good education, he had reasonable success in business, and he had enough money forty odd years later to play blackjack with a couple of very nice and very polite Israeli girls who weren't even born when he fled from his house. As I watched the poker table the two card games came together in my head, like partners in a dance of death. The Vietnamese girl with beautiful eyes and I joined hands with the young women from Israel and the men from Baghdad and Damascus and a hill village in old Palestine. We walked on to the killing fields of Iraq and Gaza and Southern Lebanon and the parts of what could once have been the new Palestine, the blobs like smudges of camouflage splashing over the low ground between the Israeli settlements high on the hills. We were dressed in bright clothing and carrying gifts of peace and love, like hippies from long ago. People crowded round and threw sweets and smiled and waved flowers in the air. A handsome Israeli machine gunner with a bored face opened fire, from a distance. An Arab man with a chest too big for his body came close to us, squeezed something he held in his hand, and exploded in a sheet of flame. The blast blew his head off his shoulders, as often happens when a suicide bomber's clock strikes zero. His sad and angry eyes stared down as his head flew upwards into the sky. We all fell dead, killed by both sides. Our blood spun round and round like a dervish dancer and disappeared into the sand. Genghis Khan laughed as he watched us die. Ariel Sharon's pudgy hands beat out a round of applause. Arms dealers counted their cash into two piles, one to take to the casino and one to leave in the grey safety of a Zurich bank, none to waste on tax. Holy men gave thanks. Prime ministers and presidents looked away. It was all crazy, like in a dream. It was a dream. I woke up. The girl from Vietnam smiled her lovely smile, as if to say don't worry, I didn't made any mistakes while you were sleeping. You know I never do. Have another nap if you're really tired. I'll take care of everything. You know you can depend on me. The grey-haired man from Syria leaned across and patted my knee and said don't worry I'm getting old too. And the world went on its merry way.

Little Mother.

In 2004 a stomach ulcer turned nasty and damaged a nearby blood vessel. Blood gushed into my bowel and into the world outside, via the obvious route. Punishment for drinking too much red wine in cars. A grey-faced stranger stared from the bathroom mirror. In the ambulance I thought about dying. Surely no-one so grey could stay alive for long. The French croupiers I worked with in the sixties all died in their fifties or late forties and I assumed that it my turn now. Only a bit late. I was 63. I lay on a hospital bed. Somebody else's blood poured through a tube and into my left arm. Ulcer-killing medicine poured into my right arm. Calmness crept over me. It was like floating again on the super-salty water of the Dead Sea. If this was dying it really wasn't too bad.

A nurse spoke into a phone. Her voice echoed faintly around the ward, as if from miles away. A young woman with a history of self harm was missing, last seen in the darkness of the hospital grounds. Don't kill yourself, you silly bitch, I found myself thinking. I've come here to save my life. If you take yours you're taking the piss. Then I felt terrible about being so unkind to a girl I didn't even know. But by then I had lost three quarters of the blood you can lose without dying and slipped into the zone where you're not quite yourself. That, I hope, explains the dark shadow across my mind. The nurse's voice echoed again around the big, busy room. Good news. The girl was alive and well and uncut and on her way back into the light. I was really pleased that the unknown girl was OK. The incoming blood was outnumbering the outgoing blood and I was getting back to normal. But I still kept thinking about death. My wife and children wouldn't see me any more and I wouldn't see them. Their faces appeared, but faded back into the dark, as if they knew it was too late to say goodbye. I searched my memory for help, scared of slipping into unconsciousness and not finding a way back out. I tried to focus on the good times when I was a sun-tanned snorkel-diving teenager in Beirut in the fifties, or working in crooked casinos in the sixties and driving round in flashy sports cars with pockets full of somebody else's cash. But all the pictures faded. I tried to conjure up an image of the Dutch girl I knew in 1970 when I lived in Spain, but she refused to come to life. Just a blur where once her beauty lit up the night. I thought maybe she's dead too. Then, unasked and unprompted by any conscious thoughts my mind jumped back to 1950, to the first grown-up friend I ever had.

When I was eight years old my father moved to post-war Germany, to re-establish the British Reuters news agency on what was very recently enemy territory. Just in time for Christmas 1949 the rest of the family moved into an enormous house in an upper middle class area of Frankfurt am Main. A house with rooms for servants. In January, just after my ninth birthday, I was sent to the English School, a short walk from our house. A school just like an English prep school, but close to the centre of what was left of a very old German town.

I often saw a boy hanging around in the street near the school. One day he came to talk to me through the railings that ran round the playground. He was a year or two older than me, at a guess, and his name was Eddie. He was German. Talking to strangers was forbidden, especially German strangers, but I found a place behind a wooden shed where we could chat away unseen. His stories turned my head. Eddie's world of guns and wars and gangsters and whores and pimps sounded much more interesting than English history and Latin grammar, even though I didn't know what all of the words meant.

Eddie's biological father was a German soldier of low rank who disappeared, unnoticed by all but a few close companions, in the mud and the blood of the Eastern Front. He thought he'd be home by Christmas, as the tidal wave of murder spread Eastwards, but he was long dead and sort of buried before it all went horribly wrong and what was left of Hitler's armies crept home, or were sent to freeze to death in Siberia. When the war was over Eddie's mother was a widow, living in poverty in a defeated country and trying hard to feed her infant son. A deserter from the American army moved in and became her live-in lover, taught Eddie how to speak American, and may have taught his mother a new trade. A few years later Eddie became my friend.

I wrote a letter to the English School's headmaster on my father's big typewriter: David Petty was seriously ill and would be unable to attend school for some time. I copied my father's signature from a document in his desk and posted the letter to my school. From the following Monday morning I left home every day at the usual time, school satchel in hand, and met Eddie down town at the office block which housed the administrative headquarters of the American occupying forces. The building was formerly the head office of I G Farben, the chemical company that made Zyklon B, the cyanide gas used to kill millions of Jews and a much smaller and less frequently mentioned number of gypsies and homosexuals and mad men and mad women and anyone else the Nazis felt had no right to stay alive. The office block was set in nice gardens, a stark contrast to the deadly product forever associated with the company name. Not that the gas was made there. The offices were the headquarters and administration centre. Letters to the commandants of the death camps were dictated by men in sober business suits and neatly typed by modestly dressed secretaries. Thank you for the supplies, all of whom arrived safely, and are now dead. Tests on the new gas went even better than expected. But further tests are needed. Payment [not very much] is enclosed. The company looks forward to the next consignment, at the same price. A respectful request: could the commandant please make sure that all the specimens he sends are in reasonable medical condition. The efficiency of the gas could be exaggerated if it is only tested on run down prisoners in poor health.

Eddie had a grown-up friend (maybe a relative) who worked as a handyman in the cellar of the old poison gas building. He made me a very professional looking shoe-shine stand, modelled on the ones you see in hundreds of old black and white American films. The price was two hundred American cigarettes, a highly prized currency in post-war Germany where many people smoked ground up acorns and tried to believe it was tobacco. My father's connections with American news agencies brought him special coupons that allowed him to buy American cigarettes and pipe tobacco very cheaply at the PX (Post Exchange), the American military supermarket. He didn't need all of them for his pipe tobacco and left the spares in his desk and didn't notice when a few went missing. My pocket money was enough to buy the cigarettes I needed, happily handed over by the shop staff to a lying nine year old boy with a fistful of coupons and a small amount of American military cash. Eddie booked a pitch for my shoe-shine box outside the American soldiers' rest and recreation complex, near the main railway station in down town Frankfurt. The weekly rent was the usual two hundred American cigarettes, paid to local gangsters with whom Eddie was on more than nodding terms. Eddie explained, for my protection, not as a threat, that the penalty for non-payment was a bashed in face. I hate to think what Eddie may have turned into when he grew up, but when we were children he was very kind to me. And now I knew what a gangster was: he was a man who bashed your face in if you didn't give him his cigarettes on time. My customers were American sergeants and corporals and privates. I shared the lobby where I polished shoes with a number of young prostitutes. One of them had a baby girl with her at all times, lovingly wrapped up in cheap blankets and lying in a wicker basket.

Business boomed. The soldiers paid me nickels and dimes for their shoe-shines, but soon realised that the girl with the baby was a friend of mine. Her youth and her beauty made her the star of the show. The soldiers gave me big tips to get to her, way beyond the price of a shoe-shine. Suddenly I was a pimp, aged nine (without knowing what was for sale) and my best friend was a teenage tart. The money didn't stop there. The other girls accepted me as a welcome addition to the work force and tipped me for pimping them to the best paying soldiers when the star was busy. Money money money. I didn't know there was so much money in the world. I was as happy as I ever have been, sitting among the soldiers milling around and talking American, watching the hustling German girls circling like sheep-dogs and calling out their eternal invitations in fucked-up American slang, and listening to the jazzy music that spilt out from the doors that led to the bars and dance places where I couldn't go. To a child who had only known school and home and the rare excitement of a trip to the cinema it was like running away to the circus and stowing away on a pirate ship and joining the most glamorous army in the world all on the same day, with the painted girls thrown in for free. When I should have been leaving school I packed up my stand, said goodbye to some of the girls, and set off home with my pockets full of cash. I gave a lot of it to beggars in the streets, often with missing limbs, presumably blown off in the war. Many of them must have been monsters when they were in uniform, but I was a sentimental child and I couldn't walk past them without handing out some cash. Nearer home I stuffed money into charity boxes for British and American servicemen, the men who had fought on my side when the killing was going on. I gave my money away more stealthily on Allied territory. I didn't want adults who knew my parents to see how much money a child of nine was carrying around.

It was on my second day as a shoe-shine boy that I made friends with the girl who brought her baby daughter to work in a basket. I really liked her and she seemed to like me. She was very pretty, with big brown eyes and a lovely smile. I thought she was a princess, until Eddie told me that she was a whore who went with soldiers. Eddie knew everything. I

296

guessed that a whore was lower than a princess, and that made me sad, but at least I knew now that a whore was a girl who talked to soldiers. I still didn't know why the soldiers gave her money. When my princess went off with a man in uniform and volunteered to be raped, for a small amount of cash, she always left her precious basket close to my shoe-shine stand. I kept a close eye on the baby while I was shining shoes and her mother was fucking a soldier. The tiny girl smiled a lot. It must have run in the family. Money was tight and food was scarce in a smashed up country. The girl was young and on her own and, I guessed later, had turned to whoring to provide for her daughter rather than have her flushed away in a dangerous back street abortion. I never blamed her when I grew up and filled in the gaps. She didn't start the war.

When my whore/princess came back from wherever she and the soldiers went she always gave me a hug and a smile and a small part of the small amount of money she got in exchange for access to the normally hidden parts of her body. I hated taking her money. I was rich and she was poor and it was obvious that she and her daughter needed the money much more than I did. But my clumsy attempts to give it back made her angry. It was my payment for looking after her daughter, the only person she really loved in her loveless whore's world, after a war. Her adult life was obviously very different from the childhood dreams that the war swept away. I suppose my looking after her baby brought a little warmth back into her life and made her feel human again. I put her coins in a separate pocket, away from the soldiers' shoes-shine payments, and always made sure it was the first money I gave to the wrecks sprawled out on the pavements. Still two or three years away from the startling events of puberty I wasn't equipped to think of her as a girl friend, and auntie seemed like the wrong word for someone so young. But I felt very close to her, even though I never knew her name. So I gave her a private nickname: little mother. Not as a substitute for the very kind hearted real mother I had at home, but because she was a grown up and her daughter was like a little sister to me, and no other title seemed to fit.

One day there was an armed raid on a lock-up garage near the railway station. An ambitious gang of German counterfeiters were printing scrip, the special dollars issued to American soldiers. American military policemen kicked down the door. Shots were fired. One man was killed, someone said. I tried to run for it in case the shooting spread. I did know what guns were and what guns did, even if I was a bit hazy about whores. I was arrested by an enormous American military policeman. He asked me if I was passing funny money through my shoe-shine business. No sir. I was doing well, but not that well. I panicked. A more senior military policeman called out 'let the Limey kid go'. He was laughing.

Relief. Maybe I'd fixed him up with little mother. Can't remember everyone's face. While I was under arrest I stared at the enormous pistol the enormous military policeman kept in a holster on his hip, dead level with my frightened eyes. He looked just like John Wayne standing there ready to draw. I didn't even try to move. I thought that if I ran away he'd pull out the gun and shoot me and my little head would explode like a melon. He asked me why I wasn't at school, still looking for something to hang on to me, unhappy at being laughed at and ordered to let me go. I said I'm English. That did the trick, but don't ask why. He nodded wisely and walked off to look for the real baddies. I went home early, pleased to escape.

Most of the soldiers using the women were good-natured young men just looking for a moment's comfort in casual sex with an unknown girl, a long way from Philadelphia. It didn't worry them that their brief encounters bore no resemblance to true love (whatever that is). They were generous with their money and not vindictive with the girls because their countrymen had been firing machine-guns at them not so long ago, or trying to burn them to death in tanks with their lethal 88s. All that was over now. No hard feelings. That's what soldiers do. But my heart sank when an older corporal with hard eyes and thin lips paid me for a shoe-shine, without a tip or a thank you or a single word spoken, and headed straight for little mother. Even a nine year old knew a bad man when he saw one. The other girls knew that death had come into in their room. They felt pity for my friend, mixed with joy that it was not their turn to take a beating, or die. I stared and wished that I could push aside a tough soldier twice my size. In my mind I stood between them with my gun pointed straight at him, and he walked away, scared of getting a chest full of bullets from the Limey Kid who shined shoes when he wasn't shooting bad men dead.

In real life little mother looked at the corporal, and then at me. A smile flickered on to her face and quickly died. She knew that bad times were coming. She brought the Moses basket and its precious contents to the usual spot beside my box, crossed herself, walked off with the corporal to the secret place where they did the things I didn't know about, and turned round just once to give me another flickery smile. Then she was gone. I carried on shining shoes, constantly looking around to see if she was coming back to give me the hug I really looked forward to and the handful of money I didn't want. I dreamed dreams of a happy ending, but I knew deep down that a horrible grown-up thing was happening, like when a bomb from an enemy aeroplane blew away a house on the other side of our road when I was three years old and living in England and the war was still going on.

Little mother was away for a long time. Much longer than the usual talk. I got more and more worried and more and more scared. I wanted to go and find her, but I didn't know where to look. I knew I should have stayed at school. My very big adventure didn't seem so big any more. I still loved my new grown-up friend, but I wished I'd never strayed into her scary world. Then I saw her, walking slowly, her eyes red from crying and her throat swollen behind the hand she held up to her neck. She walked straight past me and squatted down beside the Moses basket where her baby lived. I moved across and put my arm round her shoulders. She went stiff and shrugged me off. I felt terrible. She didn't like me any more. Then she put an arm around me and laid her head against my face and started to cry. I cried too, from sheer relief that little mother still loved me, and then stopped immediately and pretended to be tough. In those days only cissies cried.

She never told me what happened that day, but when I was a bit older I sort of understood. Most likely the corporal set out to hurt her, you could tell that from his eyes, and might have been planning to murder her, but couldn't hurt her really badly or kill her because another soldier came in to fuck another girl in the awful place where the girls earned their money. The corporal hesitated and my friend, wise in the ways of the world, kneed him in the groin, wrenched free, and stayed alive.

Little mother wiped her eyes and forced herself back to something like her usual self, and even flashed me a shadow of a smile. She lifted up her baby in a basket and left the improvised whorehouse a couple of hours before her usual knocking off time. She rubbed me gently on the back and said Ich gehe nach Hause, in German, and see you tomorrow in the American accented English she was beginning to pick up from the soldiers.

Next day I met Eddie at the poison gas office. We played in the lifts, which were unlike any lifts I have ever seen since. They moved more slowly than lifts normally do, and had no doors. You got in and out when the floor of the open lift was level with the floor of the lobby. The previous occupants may have had an aversion to small sealed rooms. Our favourite game was to jump in or out of the lifts at the last minute, before we got crushed to death by the door frame (I'm sure there was an automatic cut-out that would have saved our lives, but we were too skilled ever to find out). In a corridor where men in suits and modestly dressed secretaries once went from office to office in pursuit of the perfect poison one of the American military policemen who patrolled the building threw us out, and two little boys headed off to a whorehouse. On the way, in the sunshine, Eddie told me that a pimp was a man who beat up whores who didn't hand over their money, like gangsters beat up shoe-shine boys who

299

didn't hand over their cigarettes. But he still didn't tell me what whores got paid money for. I suppose he thought everybody knew stuff like that.

We got to the whorehouse. The soldiers hadn't arrived yet. The girls were getting ready for another day in their second home. While I was setting up my box and feeling important I looked across and watched little mother adjust her blouse and pull her skirt tight. She saw me looking and gave me her real smile, her friend's smile, the one that lit up her eyes, not the lips only smile that the soldiers got. I felt silly and fiddled with my shoe-shine box. When I glanced over again she looked as beautiful as the princess I thought she was, squatting on her haunches against a wall and talking to the fair haired girl who was her best friend. The girls sometimes sat like that when business was slack. Standing up all day is very tiring, even when a soldier with whisky breath and his trousers round his ankles isn't pressing you against a wall. I was glad they were happy. I still thought they went to talk to the soldiers when they left the big room, but after yesterday I knew that even talking was very dangerous if you were a whore, and that pimps and corporals could beat you up because that was what they were allowed to do. Made brave by my embrace of the day before, I walked over for a chat, to practise my German and let little mother practise her new American English. As I got nearer I saw the fair-haired girl's thumb and index finger meeting in a circle and the index finger of her other hand slipping in and out of the circle. They were both laughing at whatever it meant. Then the fair-haired girl saw me coming and stopped laughing and placed one hand firmly on each knee. Little mother stopped laughing too and looked serious, like a schoolgirl caught doing something she shouldn't. I was standing right in front of them. I felt awkward and shy and I couldn't think of anything to say, a few yards and a million miles from where I should have been. The girls didn't say a word. I thought I must have done something wrong, like kids do without knowing. To try to break the spell I asked little mother, in my simple German, if she was all right today. The old smile spread across her face. She stood up and rubbed the top of my head and everything was fine again. A young soldier with a friendly face was waiting for a shoe-shine. I went back where I belonged and made his shoes glow. He paid me double and grinned sheepishly and asked about the girl with the brown eyes and the cute smile. I sent him over to talk to little mother and proved that we really were friends again.

On the morning of the Monday which would have been the first day of the third week of my career as a shiner of soldiers' shoes, my father received a letter from the English School. Was my illness of a really serious nature? Was my life in danger? Was I actually still alive? He took it very well when I admitted to playing truant and forging his signature. He was a very tolerant man. I didn't mention cigarettes, Eddie, shoe-shining, or my friendship with a teen-age girl who got money for talking to soldiers. Or my arrest on suspicion of handling counterfeit money. Or the thugs who hovered out of sight on the edge of my dark world. Or the man who nearly killed my best friend. I said I spent the days talking to strangers and watching the trains pull in and out of Frankfurt's main railway station, like big versions of the model trains in my play-room up on the third floor of our house. For my own protection from myself I was sent to a liberal German boarding school and learnt to speak fluent German as well as the usual academic stuff.

At the end of the first term my father drove me home to Frankfurt, in a big armour-plated Humber car with marks like spiders' webs on one window, made by well-aimed Italian bullets when it was a military vehicle in Abyssinia (Ethiopia now), a country that Britain and Italy fought over during World War Two. On the first day of the school holiday I told my parents that I was going to a toy shop near the railway station. I promised not to talk to strangers. The first part was a lie. I went looking for little mother and her baby daughter. I'd missed them when I was at boarding school, especially when I was alone at night. My nerve went when I stood outside the old building. I couldn't go in. I wasn't ashamed of little mother because I was a nice middle class private schoolboy again, and I wasn't ashamed of myself for leading that strange life for two weeks. I'd been really happy there (except when I thought my friend was dead). But I felt uneasy outside the place where I once felt at home. The thugs who would have crippled me for a couple of hundred cigarettes seemed more frightening now, and the scary man might come back to finish what he started, and even kill me as well as little mother because I knew too much and I once wanted to kill him. Which I did at the time. Or my friend could be dead and cold and under the ground and my little sister could be all alone in the world. I hated being scared. I thought that if I stared at the old building for long enough I would find the courage to stride in and find little mother and share a hug, just like old times. She might even tell me her name. But I couldn't do it. I started to walk home. Then I imagined that she had seen me through a window and come out to look for me, carrying her baby in the basket. She might still be out there, lost among the crowds in the busy streets. I walked back, looking around me all the time. She was nowhere to be seen. Suddenly bold again, thinking that she might be inside but scared to come out because the pimps would beat her up, like Eddie said, I walked in to the old place. Hostile looks came my way, from the soldiers and the girls. Without my shoe-shine stand I was just a child in a place where children were not welcome. My nerve started to go. I was about to walk out when a soldier recognised me and said to a friend hey look, there's the Limey kid, and hi kid to me. I smiled and waved and felt at home and walked over to the girls. I couldn't see little mother anywhere, or the Moses basket, but I saw the fair-haired girl standing alone. She said hello. I asked if my friend was there today. I told her that I went to boarding school now and that was why I hadn't been around. She smiled and said sie kommt nicht mehr hier. She doesn't come here any more. A soldier came to take her away. She slipped her arm under his and started to walk to the secret place. It was her job, I knew that, and she had no time to tell me more about my old friend. But she turned her head for a last look, beamed a smile in my direction almost as beguiling as little mother's old smile, waved her hand in the air, and called out weg gegangen. Gone away.

I was sad not to see my little mother again, but relieved too. There was no bad news. She couldn't be dead. And I was sure the fair-haired girl would tell her friend, and mine, that I hadn't just walked out and forgotten all about her. I chose to believe that little mother had gone somewhere really nice. She wouldn't have to talk to soldiers any more and she and my little sister would live happily ever after. I walked home feeling on top of the world and never went near the old building again. The dream was over. I was a schoolboy again. No more soldiers. No more whores. No more gangsters. No more guns. No more heads exploding like melons. I could go home and read my Biggles books and play with my model railway and no-one would ever try to kill my best friend again.

Sometimes I wonder what made the long-buried memory spark into life and bring back the whore I thought was a princess, to bring me comfort when I thought I was dying, like I'd thought she was nearly sixty years ago. The girl who loved me when I was nine years old and we both worked in the floating whore-house in the American military building in Bahnhof Platz, Frankfurt-am-Main, Occupied West Germany, in 1950 AD. Sometimes I wonder what really happened to her and her daughter, the little family I became part of for a tiny stretch of time. Not so often though, now that I'm well again. We're all older now and it doesn't seem to matter so much any more. But I wish it did. I know it should.

Chelsea Girls.

The future disappeared after my brush with death by ulcer. The past rushed up and took its place. Memories of Chelsea in the sixties and early seventies crammed my grateful head with comforting dreams of days gone by.

The modern village is very different from the royal borough where I once hung out and later lived. Arrogant bankers blow their tax-funded bonuses on flash houses where once painters and sculptors created works of art. Dodgy Russians look over their shoulders, hang on tight to their share of the old Soviet Union's crown jewels, hope to avoid a polonium lunch, and save old English public schools from bankruptcy. But the ghosts of the artists still haunt the places I once knew, and on a good day the phantom beauty of the girl from Amsterdam still dazzles the passers-by.

When I went back to work in the mid-summer of 2004 I was given nice easy day shifts, in case I collapsed and started shitting blood again. I made the most of my invalid status and sometimes left the casino at about eight in the evening, when the sun was still over the roof-tops and birds with sore throats were still singing in the trees. Once in a while I drove the short distance South to King's Road and took a long soft look at some of my old haunts.

A favourite was the Chelsea Kitchen, for forty odd years the cheapest place to eat in any style along King's Road, until you got past World's End and everything except the road itself went sharply downhill. The menu was cheap and cheerful and never changed for the best part of half a century, but the real attraction was laid on (not always literally) by the waitresses, ex-au-pair girls from the Continent who slipped sideways into real jobs, probably illegally in the days of work permits for even our nearest neighbours. The Chelsea Kitchen ex-au-pairs (oh-what-a-pair-girls in our wittier moments) were like a magnet to us young English chaps, keen as mustard to get a leg over girls who wore far less make-up than their English sisters smeared across their faces. The first of the ex-au-pairs were mostly French—very exotic when Brigitte Bardot was hot—but the French girls were soon outnumbered by young Swedes, at least partly because the Nordic girls were more inclined to shave their armpits. No under-arm road-kill for the girls from Stockholm. In their down time the Swedish girls hung out in a pub in Old Brompton Road, close to where I once lived on a diet of breakfast cereals, cheap wine and Bob Dylan records (the foot-wide black plastic round things with a hole in the middle). The pub was a social centre for the girls already over here and an informal labour exchange for newcomers sniffing out the best jobs, legal or otherwise. The actress Britt Ekland was rumoured to have been a regular there before she turned her back on Chelsea babies' bottoms and married Inspector Clousot. I went there one night, drank too much Pernod, and made absolutely no impact on a bar full of girls with blonde hair and blue eyes and smooth armpits, talking Swedish and smiling out loud. Bliss it was to be alive in 1965, even if you went home alone.

The Casserole, the best Chelsea restaurant ever (but now an ethnic restaurant that wouldn't look out of place in Basingstoke) was a bit further down King's Road. The owner was the aggressively gay and very talented Ned Sherrin, the king (or queen) of the sixties satire boom that first brought David Frost's narrow face and nasal accent to our television screens. All the waiters were pretty gay boys, ruled with a rod of iron by an older gay man called Queenie, who lashed the regulars with an acid tongue long before being horrid to your customers was de rigueur for successful restaurateurs. It was a fashionable spot, justifiably expensive in the evening, but at lunch time you could stuff your face and mingle with the beautiful people for the price of a gin and tonic at the top-floor bar of the newly opened Park Lane Hilton.

Like any successful social centre the Casserole was a coat of many colours. Girls went to look for husbands and already captured husbands went to look for girls. Chelsea maidens guided their male escorts to lunch at the Casserole, confident—or hopeful at least—that they wouldn't ogle the pretty young waiters. It was posher and safer than the Chelsea Kitchen. In that common place, where anything up to half the lunchers didn't even live in Chelsea, a future husband might flash a sneaky look at the fresh faces and neat bottoms of the girls from across the water and have second thoughts about restricting his freely given genes to the English upper classes. The Cass also served as a useful filter. A girl could never quite be sure about some of us boarding-school boys, but if her new chap took no notice of the Casserole waiters she knew she was barking up the right tree. If he could resist them he could resist anything in trousers.

Real gay men sat in discreet pairs, or alone. One of them was a well known lord who starred in a very public scandal. The gays weren't necessarily hungry for food, but came in anyway to admire the boys and dream rude dreams without fear of arrest. Undercover policemen looking to boost the crime figures lurked in public lavatories, not fashionable Chelsea restaurants. Let me explain. Life was different then. Queen Victoria died in 1901, I know that, but her spirit hung on and on among the old fogies of all classes who sprawled across the benches of the House of Commons when they had nothing better to do, and among the public schoolboys who weren't clever enough to become nuclear physicists and had to make do with a career in law. Ye who live in liberal times may not know that being an actively gay man was illegal right up till the mid sixties. Not all love was free. Camping around was fine, or wearing make-up (at a pinch), but botty-bashing or shirt-lifting or wrist-jobs could land you in the nick, for quite a while if you lacked the kind of cash a decent lawyer would expect to wrap his sweaty hands round. It doesn't get a mention in the National Curriculum (not much interesting does) but Queen Victoria's selective puritanism was behind the harsh laws that punished the boys who liked other boys rather more than they liked other boys' sisters. She issued firm instructions that unnatural goings-on between chaps were to be stamped out with the utmost vigour. It wasn't just attitude, like when our Prince Charles goes on about things. Victoria never really accepted the demise of divine right and the rise of Parliament. As far as she was concerned prime ministers answered to her, not to the riff-raff who voted them in every few years. Her stern words put backbone into the men. (Margaret Thatcher probably kept her portrait next to the flying ducks). Chaps who strayed paid a stiff price, as Oscar Wilde found out the hard way. But the ladies got off lightly. The government men were ordered not to mention what girls who liked girls got up to when no-one was looking. The Queen would never believe that her fellow women could do such dreadful things. Not even lower-class women. Or servant girls. Or suffragettes. Men foolish enough to question the royal wisdom could wave goodbye to a career in politics. Their silence ensured that the Sapphic delights remained legal and never, as far as I know, attracted feminine equivalents of the coarse euphemisms I listed earlier. (There was an upside. Many of the political men were no doubt relieved that the girls could carry on regardless. Even the most heartily hetero fellows secretly rather liked that sort of thing, as a spectator sport of course, you can't be a lesbian boy, but would not have wanted to be caught staring saucer-eyed at an illegal activity. A bit of a scandal was one thing; a stretch in a Victorian nick was something else).

During one unforgettable Casserole lunch I was told that a heart-stoppingly beautiful girl I was gawping at, sneakily and carefully even though I was pissed, was Lady Chelsea, a local resident and a regular luncher. But don't get carried away, or phone a libel lawyer if the cap fits. The perfect girl may not have been Lady Chelsea, or Lady anywhere else, or even a lady at all. My lunchtime companion was a ferocious social climber who flung titles about like confetti at a wedding, in the hope of improving his own social standing. I didn't care. I'm not snobby. I'd just seen the most beautiful girl in all England, thrown in free with a lunch that cost seven and six (thirty seven and a half pence in decimals) and that was good enough for me. I wouldn't have given a toss if she'd come from the worst council estate in town and talked like a geezer from the docks. Julie Christie, Samantha Eggar (she of seven names), Marianne Faithfull, Twiggy, Jane Asher, Jean Shrimpton, et al were all well-known gorgeous sixties girls who must surely have popped into the Casserole every now and then, and at least two of them were hot stuff at acting, but the goddess I saw that day left every one of them choking in her dust. The uncrowned queen of the sixties: long blonde hair, big blue eyes, lipstick that glowed in the dark, legs that went on forever (in brightly coloured thigh length boots), a blouse knocked up between two blinks of a blouse-maker's eye, a very short skirt, and a father who owned most of the borough, according to the fellow piss-artist I was having lunch with, who was trying to imagine her with no clothes on (not difficult if you ignored the boots) and drooling at the thought of all that naked beauty combined with all that money, he told me excitedly as she walked out through the door and disappeared into King's Road without a second glance at her two most ardent fans. Vivat Regina. I don't care where you come from, or what sounds come out when you open your gob, but please come back here tomorrow. I will if you don't. I'm a croupier. I can afford another seven and six.

I'm straying off casinos, my chosen subject. Old people do that, especially when they're thinking about girls who wouldn't even notice them now if they came down the chimney in a Father Christmas suit. I'm sorry about that. There is no cure. Back to work now, still in Chelsea but up North, in Fulham Road.

Of all the casinos I ever visited as a paying customer the one I liked the most, by a mile, was a tiny Chelsea gambling club called the Apron Strings. The old White Elephant was the most exciting London casino ever, super-charged with electricity and all that, but I would have been stripped to the bone in five minutes if I'd sat down at the poker table, and I knew there was no-one to make friends with on the French roulette table. I was never a paying customer there, just an excitable drinker-in of atmosphere (and future historian). At the Apron Strings I could sit down and play, and, as I'm about to explain further, live to tell the tale.

Like sexy Erik's Pair of Shoes in Hertford Street, the Apron Strings was named after an American crap-shooter's prayer (a plea to Lady Luck for money to buy his child a pair of shoes, in the case of the Shoes), using words stolen from a traditional blues once popular with roving street-minstrels in the Mississippi delta. The mythical dice-player's girl-friend was up the duff and couldn't fasten her apron strings any more. The crap-shooter responsible needed all the dollars he could lay his hands on. The obvious place to get them (to a deluded addict, or a man with a pair of loaded dice up his sleeve) was at a dice game. Babies, born or unborn, featured in many a prayer as the crap dice went bouncing down the table and the praying gambler's money came bouncing along behind them.

The Apron Strings was in the middle of a row of small shops, just past what used to be the Queen's Elm, on the corner of Old Church Street and Fulham Road. Laurie Lee drank there in winter when he left the cold, damp English countryside behind, and moved into his Chelsea flat. Sad to say the building that was once an excellent pub is now occupied by an estate agent, and, if you believe in that sort of thing, Laurie Lee's horrified ghost. The Strings, as we sophisticates called it, belonged to Nick, a handsome Pole in early middle age. I never got to know his surname, possibly because it was long and Polish or, more probably, because Nick felt that his surname was nobody's business but his own. Early casino owners were rarely communicative about their private lives, often for very good reasons. Most of his customers were wealthy young men, some of them the offspring of the chemmy players at the Clermont, John Aspinall's first public casino, where wealthy and or aristocratic players handed their fortunes over to Honest John in the carefree days when he was able to operate without a partner (unless the Billy Hill story really is true). Many of the young men at the Strings inherited large sums of money in their early twenties and quickly gambled away as much of it as their trustees would let them get their hands on. I liked them. Lots of children of my generation wanted to be train drivers, or fighter pilots, but I always wanted to be Bertie Wooster when I put aside childish things. The wealthy young men (some younger than me; I was pushing twenty-five when I first hit the Strings) were lively and sociable, had very pretty girl friends, and gave the club an upper crust Bohemian atmosphere that was difficult to find anywhere else in London, except (without the gambling) in the famous drinking club in Soho, whose name I've forgotten, where thirsty actors and poets and writers of prose went to get bossed about by a lady called Muriel, a right old battle-axe who could have given acid-tongue Queenie a run for his money. And then some. Evelyn Waugh would have felt at home at the Strings. We may have just missed a book called Vile Gamblers.

The club was tiny. There was a small reception area at street level, and a short flight of stairs down to a single basement room where a chemmy table took up most of the space. A French roulette table took up the rest. The card table was where the real money changed hands. The roulette table was a side show for the entertainment of card players who came over during the shuffle, anxious not to interrupt the flow of money from their trustees to Nick's bank (or wherever he kept his money). When the chemmy game was in full swing there was usually only one lonely croupier at the roulette table. The Strings was always sparsely staffed. Nick never was one to throw his money around. He took for granted that the sort of gamblers he allowed in would never even think of robbing him, however enthusiastically he robbed them with his gambling games. Why waste money on an inspector when there's nothing to inspect? His misplaced confidence made it easy for me to slip in under the radar. I didn't burden him with the information that I worked in a casino, and I looked and sounded just like the mugs he was really looking for.

The lonely roulette croupier was a friend of mine, who gave me the occasional leg-up when I was losing without expecting anything in return, like the friendly trustee I never had. In a small way it made up for my parents' tragic failure to hand over a small fortune when I turned twenty-one. He and I had both trained at the Curzon House, but he left as soon as he had enough grasp of French roulette to get by in a technically undemanding small club, whose Bohemian atmosphere suited him much better than the po-faced stuffiness of the Curzon House. It wasn't real robbery. The money we re-directed was nothing like the money that changed hands during the proper criminal co-operation between the croupiers and the barons at the Curzon House and the other top clubs. Takings at the Strings' roulette table were nowhere near big enough to absorb that kind of hit. It wasn't about winning; it was a friend helping a

308

friend not to go home skint. I won once in a while by playing straight, and occasionally lost when someone else came to the table and my friend had to withdraw his helping hand, but most of the time I broke even after what felt like a pleasant evening back at boarding school, minus the silly rules and plus the pretty girls. All in all the nearest I ever got to being Bertie Wooster, luckily without the aunts.

I never saw her when I was there, but I was told that the actress Shirley MacLaine, Warren Beatty's good-looking sister, sometimes came into the Apron Strings when she was filming in London. Another refugee from stuffiness, but one who came to gamble of course, not to work or to steal money. Movie stars earned more than croupiers even then. All right, most of them did.

The manager of the Strings was called Charles. Charles was about thirty years old and prematurely bald. Bird's egg bald. No doomed attempts at silly comb-overs. He had that seven feet high and six inches wide figure only ever seen on a certain breed of Englishman, and a rare ability to bend from the waist up into a human semi-circle when he curved down to speak to a player at the chemmy table, usually in response to a request for more money to lose. The long, aesthetically pleasing arc, combined with the backward tilt of the bald head and the smiling face made him look like a friendly vulture closely inspecting a still living lunch but too soft-hearted to sink his teeth in. Don't be misled though. Charles was an excellent casino manager, very adept at helping the customers to ride their money into Nick's valley of no return. And very, very discreet. Once, in answer to an aggressive demand for more money from a gambler who was already in deep trouble, I heard him murmur, in impeccable English: 'I'm awfully sorry sir, we simply can't let you have any more. Your last cheque is.......hesitating.' Note the absence of the sordid word money, and the introduction into dry banking terms of the elegant and unexpected 'hesitating'. And the presence of the royal we. He was class, was Charlie.

The club member who introduced me to the Apron Strings was an ex-stockbroker who worked briefly at the Curzon House, in an hour of need. You may remember a brief mention of his existence when I recalled my brief and deeply unsuccessful career as a dealer in fine art. He made a packet chasing the shares of a temporarily successful entrepreneur called John Bloom, the first man to sell washing machines in England at a price the average family could afford, lightening at a stroke the work load of millions of women. His photograph should have hung in every kitchen in the land, smothered in lipstick kisses. His early success was spectacular. The magic machines sold like hot cakes. Money poured in. The company floated on the Stock Exchange. The share price soared. A Conservative

Member of Parliament, with a long history of walking away from other peoples' companies just before the bailiffs moved in, became chairman of the company. (The M.P.'s eldest daughter got engaged to my respectable brother at about the same time. That has nothing to do with the story). Everything came up roses. But not for long. Others got into the washing machine game. It wasn't that difficult. All you needed was a friend with a lorry that could get to Italy, where all mechanical things were made before China took over. And back. Profits fell and then went into reverse, all unbeknown to the agile chairman and the ecstatic investors, including my soon to be co-worker. The desperate Mr Bloom frantically moved money around the company in an effort to hide the depressing truth that the business was going down the pan, and hoped for better days.

The better days didn't come. They rarely do. My friend lost all his money, and his job as a stockbroker. He had been trading on his own account, a technicality which need not trouble us in detail, but which was against Stock Exchange rules—they do have rules there, I was surprised to hear—and became a trainee croupier at the Curzon House (casino) Club. John Bloom had his collar felt, avoided arrest, but was fined. He sensibly gave up on an England that had no respect for an entrepreneur and went to California to start a restaurant with a Henry the Eighth theme (minus the blood-stained executioner's axe), which sold crap food at high prices instead of good washing machines at low prices. He met with modest success, proving yet again that you can't keep a good man down. The Member of Parliament spent more time in the House of Commons on rather less pay than he would have liked to become accustomed to, and, for a reason entirely unconnected with washing machines but which discretion forbids me to discuss, which is a shame because it's very funny if it's true, which it probably is, the M.P's daughter and my respectable brother became disengaged.

The ex-stockbroker started work at the Curzon House, borrowed £500 (a tidy sum in the mid-sixties) from one of the few people in the world who would lend him more than the price of a pint, and invested it all in Australian nickel mining shares. Nickel was jumping out of the ground all over Australia and was much in demand on the world market. If you wanted to kill large numbers of people in proper military fashion you needed lots of nickel, or you did then, they might use a different metal now, and the Vietnam War was raging. My friend made a second packet on the Stock Exchange, gambling fearlessly (but successfully this time) in small Australian mining companies that became large Australian mining companies almost overnight, apart from a few that became empty offices where con-men once coated drill bits with nickel ore and extracted large sums of money from gullible Aussies before going walkabout with no forwarding address. His money grew and grew and grew some more. He even paid back the original £500. Then he cashed in, got married, rather to everyone's surprise, opened a restaurant deep in the country, and fathered five or six children in between the cooking and the washing up.

While the ex-stockbroker was still working at the Curzon House, in between speculating on the stock market and gambling at the Apron Strings, and before the mining money came pouring in, he devised a cunning plan to run a mini casino at the annual ball that some fox-hunting enthusiasts he knew put on every year to raise money for their hunt. It's not cheap getting all togged up in fancy red gear and going out and killing a fox and getting pissed. Or vice versa. He was friendly with all the right people and very close to getting it all fixed up and the money rolling in. Several of us put some of our not very hard earned cash into the business and agreed to share the work load, rather than waste our profits on hiring croupiers who would almost certainly have robbed us, the bastards. The money was kept, in cash, at the ex-stockbroker's flat in Chelsea. There were no plans to involve dull bankers and nosey tax inspectors in our private business affairs.

The ex-stockbroker shared his very large flat with several other young men and young women, including the former colleague who often helped me out when I was losing money at the Apron Strings. One morning, or more probably one early afternoon, it was discovered that the young man in question had gone missing, and that all our cash had gone with him (to East Africa, I heard later).

You can't win 'em all. But I never held a grudge against the chap who did a runner. He was great company when he was around and he certainly gave me more money at the Apron Strings than he relieved me of later. And I'm not really awfully keen on hunting. I said a silent goodbye to the cash and a silent good luck to the friend who trousered it. Some of the others whose money disappeared were less amused. I understood. They had really looked forward to being casino owners and they didn't have special pay-outs at the Apron Strings roulette table to fall back on.

One day the Strings went modern. A blackjack table appeared, upstairs and alone in the reception area. A girl was trained for about five minutes by someone who it's safe to assume didn't know much about the game, or was drunk. Or both. On her first night she edged in behind the blackjack table, like a reincarnation of an early Christian tip-toeing into a sun-scorched Roman arena densely populated by lions who hadn't seen a decent dinner for a week. Nick didn't waste money on an inspector, any more than he wasted any money on in-depth training. She was on her own. We were waiting. Decent chaps to a man, at a level well hidden from a frightened young trainee of the female sex, we felt her pain but didn't let it show. The opportunity of a lifetime was taking shape right before our eyes. We weren't planning to eat her, like those hungry Roman lions would have done in a trice (she was quite small), but we were hoping to take her for every penny that Nick could spare.

A blackjack table has seven boxes where seven different bets can be placed. You probably knew that. When the bets are down the cards are dealt and the stake cannot be altered, in theory. At the Strings the theory collapsed. The stakes were something like fifty pence to five pounds. Times ten today. At least. It was a long time ago. The blackjack players were all very experienced and, in many cases, including mine, a cut below the wealthy young heirs playing chemmy one floor down. The combination of a rookie dealer and a bunch of dodgy geezers (however well-spoken) and no inspector was, as foreseen and actively discussed, a licence to steal.

It was easy peasy: you put a big stake on the first or second box and if your first two cards were disappointing you waited until the dealer was concentrating on the cards at the other end of the table and drastically reduced your bet. She was far too busy trying to stop her hands shaking and add up the value of the players' cards to notice any fast moves on the edge of her peripheral vision. It gets better. If you started with a small bet and got good cards you piled on extra chips while she wasn't looking. The players at the other end of the table changed their bets when the poor girl was concentrating furiously on the first boxes. It was like tennis. One minute the player this end has the ball, next minute it's the other chap's go. The odds for the smart players leapt from mildly in favour of the house to wildly in favour of the punters. Only the players in the middle of the table had it tough. It's the angle. Pythagoras and all that. A successful middle man had to be very brazen, or very skilful, or play by the rules and take his punishment like a man. Needless to say the last option never caught on. To keep the pressure at nervous breakdown level (and help the brave man in the middle, even if it was his own fault for turning up late) we gave the dealer hell every time she made even a trivial mistake, hoping to stamp her confidence even harder into the sand and hold back the moment when she got wise to our little game, Nick slung us all out on to the street, and we had to go back to working for a living.

One of the most skilful cheats stroke professional blackjack players was a youngish actor who appeared in nearly every bad comedy film made in Swinging London during the sixties, and even managed to

312

sneak into a couple of good ones when no-one was looking. In films he was always at the middle or bottom end of the supporting cast, but on the Apron Strings blackjack table he was the star, the only one who could really handle the middle boxes. He succeeded where the rest of us failed by making the dealer laugh. When her shoulders shook and the tears of laughter ran down her cheeks the small amount of skill she had accumulated went straight out of the window and our thespian colleague made his switch undetected. She'd found a friend at last and forgot for a moment that she was dealing blackjack to a bunch of rude bastards with lightning fingers and minds like razors. It was difficult not to applaud the young actor, a reaction he rarely inspired in his day job.

Not surprisingly the table never won. Nick smelt a rat, swallowed his principles and employed an inspector, a good-looking young American who happened to be in London at the time and regularly told anyone willing to listen that he was a world class authority on the game of blackjack. The fun on the table came to an end. But not for everybody. The new American inspector came into the Curzon House with a variety of very pretty girls, one of whom I recognised as the high society girl-friend of a wealthy young gambler at the Apron Strings. Her regular boy-friend must have been so deeply engrossed in the chemmy game that he didn't notice when the crumpet sloped off with one of the staff. Or he thought she was still in the loo, gossiping with the red-head whose dad owned Scotland. The smooth young American played roulette at the Curzon for surprisingly high stakes, suggesting that either he had a private income to draw on or that Nick still wasn't getting all of the profits from his new blackjack table. If you're a gambling man put your money on the second horse, however arse-clenching the odds.

When the 1968 Gaming Act started to bite, licensing and bureaucracy and all that boring stuff, Nick shut the door and turned off the lights. London's only Bohemian casino was no more. But the memories linger on. Whenever I'm in that part of London I turn off King's Road, walk up Old Church Street, pass the Chelsea Arts Club, still open to selected piss-artists with links, however tenuous, to the world of art, pass the dead Queen's Elm, wave at Laurie Lee's ghost leaning into a drink at his usual spot by the door, turn left into Fulham Road and walk along a row of little shops, one of which was known as the Apron Strings when I was young. Once, not that long ago, after sneaking off early from a day shift at Maxim's casino not that far away, I parked my car outside the old place, a la recherche du temps perdu. Thirty something years had passed since the French roulette wheel finally stopped spinning, the chemmy cards were ripped up for the last time, and one of the places where I misspent my youth became yet another bloody antique shop. But nostalgia isn't what it used to be. I suddenly felt very old. The elegant girls with the long legs and the laughing eyes were scary old battle-axes now, walking nervous dogs across the hills and valleys that came down to them in Daddy's will. The reckless young gamblers huddle together in old mens' clubs, dribbling into their port and fervently praying that old tweed-knickers won't start barking orders down the mobile telephone. The fast-fingered and fast-tongued actor is dead. Bad luck on him of course, but good news for the rest of us. No more awful films to sit through. And the kindly, nervous (and very pretty) girl, desperate for a friend when she dealt blackjack to a gang of thieves, probably plays cards with her grandchildren now, in a quiet house in a quiet street in a quiet suburb of a quiet town. I sometimes wonder if she remembers the days when she was young and foolish, like we all are once, with any luck. If she does think about us every now and then, with a tear in her eye, I hope she understands that we didn't really mean to be horrid. I hope she's gracious enough in her declining years to accept my very late apology on behalf of the whole bunch of rude bastards. It was business. Nothing personal. We liked you really. Some of us rather fancied you. But money makes the world go round, so they say, and we were keen to keep it spinning at the proper speed and flicking off our share. Yesterday when we were young. A chance like that doesn't come along every day. You have to grab it when it's there. Greed may not be good, discuss, but it's hard to resist when it's staring you in the face. I can only hope that we never drove you to thoughts of suicide. I didn't think of that at the time.

Dark thoughts of old age crowded into my head. I didn't linger long outside the door of what had once been the Apron Strings, in Fulham Road, in the evening sunlight of that summer's day not so long ago. The thought came again that if the young gamblers and their girls and the blackjack dealer were old now, then so was I. I don't normally waste time thinking about being old, but when I do it hits hard. In a corner. One way out and no way back in. So little time. So many friends gone. No religion to fall back on, like a little boy's comfort blanket or a little girl's cuddly toy. A good day was tumbling into a bad day after such a promising start. Maybe it's best not to go back to the places where you once spent happy times. Panic flared in my brain. Don't stand there said a voice in my head. Get away now. I ran to my car, something I don't do so well any more, and took a couple of swigs from a bottle of cheap red wine, the liquid in car entertainment I often used to blot out the boredom of the long journey home. The red medicine sent a familiar burning sensation across what was left of my stomach, bringing comfort. Hysteria died a natural death. Reality stood up again, proud as a man with a medal pinned to his chest. In vino veritas, as the Romans were wont to say after a well organised piss-up inspired someone to talk too much and get it in the neck as soon as the last slave had cleared the last goblet away. No human voice had shattered the silence of the warm evening air. No devilish hot-spot had opened up in an English pavement. Stephen King was nowhere to be seen. Back where he belonged, in New England. It was all in the mind. Nothing supernatural. Just an old man floating for a moment in that cold and lonely space between life and death, trying not to fall apart outside a shop that was once a casino where he wasted his time and sometimes his money when he was young.

What's that chaps? A quick shoe of chemmy? Why not? Haven't played for years. Shuffle up please dealer. My usual seat Charles. Get that cheque book open. Come along now. Or shall we go upstairs and play blackjack?

Empty Rooms.

An excruciatingly painful haemorrhage invaded my scrotum on or around April Fool's day 2005, almost exactly a year after an exploding ulcer nearly snuffed me out on or around April Fool's day 2004. A very careful operation took away the pain that even maxed-out morphine injections couldn't blot out, along with exactly fifty percent of the testicles I started out with. The right one, if you're a stickler for detail. In search of better days long ago I drove over to Curzon Street at the end of a quiet day shift at Maxim's casino in Kensington and took a long nostalgic look at the Curzon House, the urban mansion in whose elegant rooms I made my entry into the glamorous world of casino gambling in 1964. The house always looked well maintained, presumably by the latest Lord Curzon, or by a female descendant if the wrong sort of sperm hit the egg and the male line petered out. During the first years of the 21st Century I passed the Curzon House many times, but I never saw anyone go in or out of the big front door. Maybe the Curzon family leaves it empty and rising in value by a few million a year, like a magic purse that keeps on filling up with gold coins. Perhaps the huge rooms are free of furniture and only cleaners walk across the deep pile carpets where punters scurried from table to table until their money ran out or the casino shut down for the night. I had a real urge to walk in through the front door and take a last look at the beautifully decorated restaurant on the ground floor, where the gamblers stuffed their faces as quickly as politeness would permit before getting on with the serious business of losing their money to the croupiers waiting upstairs. And then climb the wide curved staircase to the first floor and wander through the old rooms I once knew so well, with only the curtains and the carpets and the ghosts for company.

I had often visited the Curzon House in my memory. Dead people come back to life. The croupiers are there, and the heads of the games, and the waiters, and Julian the manager. And me. And the barons on a business trip. We're all in it for the money. Up to a hundred gamblers think they're in it for the money too, but nearly all go home with less than they came in with. The Barnett family are in it for a lot more money than the rest of us put together. But very sparing with their genes. Each of the brothers had one wife and one son and called it a day. In every room someone is stealing money, or hoping to steal some before work comes to an end in the wee small hours of the morning. Sadness creeps in with the dawn if closing time comes and there's nothing extra in your pocket.

As far as I know the older Barnetts are dead, along with most of the players I saw every night. They were all old when I was young and time, like an ever rolling stream, carries her sons (and daughters) away. Most of the staff from my days are dead, too, especially the Frenchmen and the Belgians whose jobs we trainees were paid to take away. Few of them lived much beyond fifty. Two who beat the odds were Victor, the kindly old Belgian who took me on when I came back to casino work in 1971, after living happily in Spain and Chelsea until the cash ran out, and Maurice, another Belgian once in charge of the French roulette and of the most insanely optimistic comb-over I have ever seen. One solitary strand of hair sprang out just above his left ear, drew a perfect straight line across the shining dome, and petered out an inch away from the small outburst of hair just above his right ear. You could only marvel at the careful way he put it in place every day.

Both the Belgians crept into their seventies, seriously ill but still breathing, if rather raspily at times. A rare achievement among the first wave of gambling staff. Like the first generation of rock and rollers they tended to shuffle off early, for pretty much the same reasons, but often leaving a lot more money for their grieving descendants to squabble over. Too many cigarettes, including the ones in other peoples' mouths, too much booze, too much tension, made even worse by the frequent urge to kill everyone in the room, and too much working at night. Working at

316

night is not good for you. If you really must work at night don't save any money for your sixtieth birthday party. Spend it while you can. And don't panic if you hang on a bit longer than you expected. Enjoy each day as it comes, but go bankrupt and let somebody else worry about the debts.

That's the sad part of growing old. Every time you look over your shoulder somebody else isn't there. I hate it. I think of the things I would like to say to old friends who have gone. But you can't communicate with the mess in a wooden box six feet under the grass in a garden outside a church (or near another of God's many houses, depending on which religion your parents chose for you) or with a pile of ash barely big enough to fill a dark green ash-tray. I not only can't say the things I'd like to say, I can't take back the things I wish I hadn't said. I suppose that's why so many people believe in an afterlife. How nice to get a second chance. I wish I knew how to latch on to an invisible friend. Worst of all, you know it won't be long before somebody looks around and notices that you're not there. Remember old Dave the Rave? With the long hair? When he had hair. He worked at the Curzon. Oh yes, I remember him. No, sorry, I'm thinking of another Dave. He lived in Battersea and worked at Crockfords and nearly got knifed at a blackjack table. What a piss-artist he was.

No wonder old people turn to alcohol and hope they can still keep it down. Or cling to their grandchildren and wish they could look like that again. Or keep a painting in the attic.

On the night in 2005 when I drove into Curzon Street, just for fun, I parked right outside the old Curzon House Club. I didn't expect to see anyone I knew. No second comings. I just wanted to wallow in distant memories of when I was young and travelled everywhere in noisy sports cars and impressed the girls with my long dark hair and smouldering eyes and jingling pockets. I'm easily pleased now that I'm old. Staring out of a car window at an empty house seems like a barrel of fun to me. A few nights later I had a dream. I was standing in the Curzon House's French roulette room, right where I stood on a shiny red ten pound chip back in 1965 and fought off a waiter who sincerely believed that any chip dropped by any gambler was his by divine right. The room was empty. But not for long. Two big French roulette tables loomed out of the darkness in the half light of the darkly furnished room, manned by the ghosts of men I once knew. They weren't all dead, the ghosts I saw. But the ones still alive were the age they were in 1965, living ghosts from another time, like me. I saw Golden Bollocks, young and cocky as he strolled through those empty rooms, pushing his luck with the gamblers, proving again and again that he could say things that would have got anybody else the sack. I liked him. He was the funniest man I ever knew. And kind-hearted with it, though he would be furious with me if I said that to his face. He stopped for a chat. He said let's go back to Portugal and see if the Swedish girl is still there. And the girl from Holland whose father built villas on land bought for sixpence, the gorgeous bikini girl who walked along the beach in the sunshine of the day on the hunt for handsome young men she could take home at night, young men her father threw out of the house just before their dreams came true and then had sex with his own daughter, with her illegal but willing consent.

The man with dark glasses smiled at me. White teeth gleamed in the semi-darkness. France's answer to Terry Thomas, hoping I'd brought some decent crumpet along, dead or alive. Big bald Tony sat next to the married woman who won't leave his side. He still looked like a Roman emperor, handsome and arrogant, only soft with the tiny woman who loves him. Julian walked through from the cash desk, to take charge and look for ways to make extra money. As can only happen in a dream he sat down on the thick carpet and played with his little daughter, many years before she was born and became the only person he truly loved during a lifetime dedicated to making money.

The hard man who once went up drainpipes walked in, carrying a tray full of drinks and hoping for an extravagant tip. He may well still be alive. I hope so. I liked him too. But it makes no difference. In a dream we're all equal, the living and the dead. A young man with my old young face passed by and looked straight through me. He doesn't know who I am. I know him. It's easy for me to remember, impossible for him to see himself in me. Forty years back is like a minute to me, with my photographic memory and my dreams of being young again, but forty years ahead is a black hole to him. Anyway who wants to see forty years ahead?

Dave the Rave is busy, looking for money to spend on sports cars and make him look more like the upper crust young man he never really quite was, but would have liked to be in those days long ago. Don't knock yourself out Dave. You're going to lose it all anyway. Everything goes down hill after you sit under the jacaranda tree. Baby-faced Paul McCartney plays roulette for small stakes. It's obvious that he hasn't played before. He tries to look confident but looks like a teenager sucking hard on his first cigarette.

Middle-aged Jewish matrons look fondly at the handsome young man they would be happy to have as a son. Beautiful Jane Asher stands behind him, holding up a cake that must have taken all day to decorate. She tells him to stop throwing his money away, and smiles for the camera. Julian glares at Macca, annoyed that he's playing for small stakes. He likes people who have lots of money to lose lots of money and give him a chance to steal what he sees as his rightful share. Not nervously slip a few low-value chips on a few low odds bets and go home even.

The actress sits at the roulette table, looking dignified among the dedicated gamblers staring at the little white ball spinning round the wheel. She doesn't play, but quietly studies how to act a gambler. The real players glare at her and hate someone who can resist the temptation they give into every night. She looks at me as I once was and says so this is what you do when you're not living in my house. Johnny the writer stands behind her, thinking hard about how to write a gambler. The roulette players get restless, like monkeys in a cage with humans staring from the other side of the bars, humans who can walk away any time.

Spectral players call out honest bets in bad French. Ghostly barons hand over crooked bets with a whisper, to be placed by the spirits of crooked croupiers. The crooked ghost of the crooked night manager of the Cavendish all-night restaurant pours red wine into Curzon House coffee cups and watches the barons make the money that makes his fortune. Little Leonard Tobin starts to win big. He's beaten the odds again. He smiles his superior smile, still keen to show his mother what a clever boy she's got. The ghost of Alice glares at the croupier she's kicking and hates him for seeing her descent into someone who behaves badly in public places. The ghost of the Italian who gambled away five restaurants dreams of a huge win in the electric atmosphere of the White Elephant, multiplying the money he's stealing at the Curzon. In my dream he dreams of sharing thousands of pounds with the crooked croupiers he has let down so often. Then we can all be friends again and drink red wine by the gallon and shake hands and grin, like only drunks know how. Dream on, dream on, elegant Italian man.

On the landing by the cash desk the country girl dances close up against the handsome black man who steals her life away. Her lost beauty lives again, full blast on her perfect face. Abe sleeps, upright against the wall. He's supposed to be watching us but he only sees his dreams. Christine Keeler stands on one side and Mandy Rice-Davies stands on the other. They giggle and pout professionally at the sleepy old man. Stephen Ward takes a photograph and says well done girls, there's a good one for the family album. The cigarette man covers the table in bright red ten pound chips. Mummy comes in from the blackjack room and tries to look interested when he asks her to admire his big win. A hairdresser hops and skips behind her and at the snap of a finger combs back a hair that has dared to spring out of its proper place.

The Dutch girl comes through the door. First time I've seen her since 1971. She looks straight through me. I'm still not there. Her out of this world beauty and her flame red hair light up the night. All the men in the room stop talking. Julian is schmoozing a big gambler when he sees the vision. He breaks off in mid sentence and switches on his sexiest smile and follows her across the room like a dog. She ignores him and walks into the blackjack room and sits next to John Aspinall. Aspers looks up from his cards and glares at the woman who dares to interrupt him.

Old Victor, the quiet man from Belgium, comes out of the darkness to shake my hand and offer me a job. I tell him I've already got one and point at my younger self selling a ticket and trying to keep the pound. He nods his head and pats me on the back and says yes of course and walks back into the darkness. Lily the Pimp sits down in the wrong casino and sizes up the men, looking for customers for her girls. Prince Abdullah lurches in, drunk or drugged, probably both, and challenges me to a replay of the matches game I beat him at in 1965, the game we both saw in Last Year at Marienbad. I tell him OK, but only after he gives me the twenty I won back then, the twenty he never paid. Show me the money prince. Freddy the bodyguard glares at me and says of course the prince paid. He always pays. He's got all the money in the world. He's from Saudi Arabia. Stop trying to cheat him. He's a prince for Christ's sake. You're only a fucking croupier.

Hashish and the Cockney Frog come up the back stairs from the scruffy staff room in the cellar. They replace Roman emperor Tony and the man with dark glasses in the croupiers' seats next to the big brass roulette wheel. The extravagantly handsome French Connection takes the place of the quiet young Belgian collecting bets at the bottom of the table. Frenchy smiles at Lily the Pimp and apologises for the filthy names he calls her a few years later. Lily smiles a wintry smile and presses her bets, big time. Frenchy gives up on Lil and grins at the middle-aged lady sitting on his other side, clinging hard to what's left of her youthful good looks. She drops her chips and squirms in her chair. The Cockney Frog beckons me to come nearer to the table and play roulette. Suddenly I'm winning a thousand pounds, a tidy sum in nineteen sixty whatever it was. Hashish raises an eyebrow and looks just like Roger Moore. The Fat Man pushes his way through the crowd, scattering Jews and Gentiles alike. He grabs me in a bear-hug and thrusts an old green Harrods bag into my hand. His big face blots out the room. There's the sixty thousand I owe you, he says. Don't spend it all at once. And don't forget your friends. Sorry to keep you waiting. I was late for my plane. No time to go to the bank. God you look old. Don't come to the old country. I'll be on the island if you're passing through.

320

In the opening that leads to the cash desk little mother stands and stares with her big eyes. She holds a small girl by the hand. Standing up now. Last time I saw her she was lying in a shopping basket while her mother was fucking a soldier. They look a bit older than in 1950, but not much. Little mother is well dressed and well groomed and the old beautiful smile still lights up her face. But she's not smiling at me. She doesn't see me and she doesn't hear me when I call. I grab my old self and ask him for help. None comes. Too late anyway. The doorway's empty. Mother and daughter have gone again. Tears prickle my eyes but I don't go looking. She's nowhere I can find her. It doesn't matter. She looked good and so did the kid. It's a sign. They escaped the hell they lived in when we were friends.

Dream turns to nightmare. Other ghosts come into the room, out of the wallpaper, through the silent doorways, from behind the big curtains. I don't know them. They're not real. Their dead eyes glow red in the gloom that filled those old casinos. They claw at my face and drag me down. I'm surrounded by horrors, I'm struggling to breathe, I'm frightened to death. The young man with my old face looks into my eyes and still doesn't know me, even when I shout for help and reach out my hand. The floor starts to sink. Our feet are gone already, into the soft darkness. The darkness creeps up our legs.

I screamed in the night and woke up shaking and soaked with sweat. My wife thought I was dying, for real this time. Not yet. Still breathing. Unlike most of the people in the big dark room, a room just like all the rooms I spent my working life in. Home from home to the people who passed through that life. Rest in peace all those who are gone. See you soon if the Holy Joes are right. Or not if they're not.

Go back to sleep dear. I'm not dying. I'm not drowning. I'm just waving from a dream.

Maybe it was all a dream.

The End.

Printed in Great Britain
by Amazon